# NOT TO THE SWIFT

*Books by Tristram Coffin*

MISSOURI COMPROMISE

YOUR WASHINGTON

NOT TO THE SWIFT

# NOT
# TO THE
# SWIFT

*A Novel by* TRISTRAM COFFIN

W · W · NORTON & COMPANY · INC · *New York*

# NOT TO THE SWIFT

"Things are in the saddle and ride mankind."
—*Ralph Waldo Emerson*

# *Chapter* ONE

By EARLY morning, the long rain had ended, and the Potomac lunged swollen and clumsy through a wide channel. Its roar had changed to a sullen, soft murmuring, and yet to Malcolm Christiansen it carried the undertones of danger. A morning mist steamed over the river, and crows flapped in anxious search of food among the tangled vines and sycamores.

At the top of the bank, a placid canal, so still that its surface was a bright mirror for the overhanging branches and the sky itself, ran parallel to the river. Malcolm Christiansen walked its still-wet towpath, his heels leaving marks in the soft earth. As he walked, he turned his face slightly upward to feel the glow of the early sun and breathe the sweetness of the air after the storm.

He stopped to watch a flock of ducks as they waddled toward him—like a delegation of fat bakers, he decided. They stared at each other; the ducks curious yet greedy—they plainly hoped for crusts of bread; he with pure enjoyment.

He was aware at this moment of the impermanence of his joy. The awareness crossed his mind like a searchlight scanning the dark midnight sky. It was as if only here, in the privacy of early morning on his daily walks, was he inviolate and safe. Elsewhere, the muscles tensed, the heart beat more rapidly, the nostrils smelled the stench of man's dung, the ears heard shrieks and groans and obscene laughter. He pushed aside this truth with sudden passion. Forcing his attention to the ducks, he saw them again as absurd and comic creatures. He smiled happily. "Crazy, dumb ducks," he said aloud.

His three companions, serious young men in dark suits, smiled as one. Malcolm Christiansen knew their thoughts. In their place he would have felt the same. Thank God he's in a good mood, they were thinking. Not like Thank God I didn't miss the bus, or Thank God I put the windows down before the rain. Real Thank God.

Everyone knew that Malcolm Christiansen was as nice a man as you'd want if he was in a sweet humor. But you never knew what he was going to be from one minute to the next. If you worked for him and he went into a black mood, you went into it with him. He could do that to you. He could break down the door of your own private self and overpower you with his feelings. If he was happy, Christ you were gay. But if he was down in the mouth, you were sore at the world and you couldn't fight it.

He was the President of the United States. . . .

There are jobs that give a man or a woman an extra two feet of height. Take a nun. You see her, and you begin to feel the holiness clear to your fingertips, and sometimes you resent the fact that they have it and you don't. Or a Marine color guard. You straighten up and waves of patriotism go up and down your spine. The President, he's just a few steps down the throne from the Big Guy himself. It doesn't make any difference what he is personally or whether you agree with him, he's still Number One. Maybe they don't think that way in England or Italy or Zanzibar, but when we put a fellow in the White House right off he loses the wart on his nose and a little halo starts playing around the bald spot in the back of his head.

The four watched the ducks and then moved on. "Mr. President," one said. "Mickie is pretty far back on the trail. Shall we wait for him?"

A few hundred yards to the rear a fat man struggled to keep up. He was an unlikely figure on the canal towpath at six o'clock in the morning. He had large proportions, a wide grin when he was sure others were watching him. He was dressed in a dark, fashionable summer suit and a black Homburg hat cocked over his left ear. He stepped into a soft pile of duck manure and swore rhythmically.

The sight moved President Christiansen to laughter. He shouted, and there was a faint twang in his deep voice, "You look like a toad climbin' a hill."

Mickie Moonan did not choose to answer. He plowed heavily onward. This was part of the game. The daily ritual of lifting the spirits of the President of the United States. Mr. Christiansen demanded his hours of innocence. Laughter, the birds he loved, a gun under his arm, the fresh smell of out-of-doors. Without them, the air escaped from the handsome balloon and it shriveled. The psychiatrists would probably explain that he had not actually enjoyed life since he left the little town in North Dakota. So he wanted to play the boy. Something like the mother of four pretending she was still a virgin.

When Michael Farrell Moonan, Jr., reached the President, he was panting noisily and perspiring under his hatband. He said with an exaggerated air of injury, "Sir, accept my resignation."

Mr. Christiansen laughed again. He said, "Mickie, you could bring smiles to a Jew funeral."

The President was in high spirits this morning. Moonan sighed.

> A little time to laugh
> A little time to sing . . .

Precious little time it was. "They are not long the days of wine and roses . . ." Just a brief moment. Mickie heard the whirring undertones of the river, and he thought of a simile—Malcolm Christiansen sitting guileless in an oarless boat as it whirled in the bloated stream. It was like a sequence in an old serial movie. The audience knew how close the roaring falls was. It crunched popcorn anxiously and read the title, "Who will save him?" But the passenger smiled sweetly, unaware of danger.

The trouble was this wasn't an old movie, rerun for laughs. Moonan knew that. This was here and now. Listen to the thunder crashing. Watch the lightning flash. Trouble everywhere. Germany and Russia were like two angry drunks in a bar; they might spring at each other any moment. What held them back was a weakening fear of disaster. The peace Malcolm Christiansen talked so much about, as though it was a virtue he brought upon the world, was going, going, gone, kaput, konyets. At this point, there was nothing left but to believe, damn you believe, in Chris' luck, and tell the reporters and the congressmen that the President was hard at work on a miracle, and this was no time to rock the boat.

If any of these thoughts reached Mr. Christiansen, he did not show it. Instead he looked waggishly at his press secretary. He said, grinning, "Men, don't you think we should try Mickie on the obstacle course?"

The Secret Service men nodded smiling.

The victim groaned. Play the game. Begone dull care. Laugh and the world laughs with you, Malcolm Christiansen. But let your lips turn down and the stock market breaks. Old ladies turn over in their beds and die. Children cry in fright. Cabinet meetings are called. Riots occur.

The President enjoyed the game he played. That was plain to see. What a tyrant he was, Moonan thought. Yet, *ora pro nobis*, let him be in a serene mood when the German crisis drops on him gently, gently please.

"Colonel," Moonan said, "this is a violation of my civil rights. I'm going to complain to Senator Tate. He is good for one more bleeding-heart speech, and my cause is just. I'm not going to run any obstacle course."

President Christiansen abandoned his boy-on-a-lark role. He became George Washington at Valley Forge, Lee rallying the Confederates outside Richmond, Davy Crockett and the Alamo.

"Mister Moonan," he said, "there are some duties we must perform whether they appeal to the flesh or not. There's more to life than just good eating and the like. There's setting a good example for your fellow man, and no lagging in the ranks, and hold your head high. Up and at 'em."

With this pronouncement, Mr. Christiansen stepped off the tow path. Below was a wild and tangled area overhung with trees and murky with damp gloom. Honeysuckle matted the ground and crawled up tree trunks. Briars lurked sharp and treacherous. The President climbed down the bank. His shoes made little ledges in the soft dirt. He waved his arms and called out, "Come on, men!"

Moonan teetered on the edge. Then, clutching at saplings and a wild grape vine, he slid down the slope. His hat tilted over one

eye. Deliberately he corrected the angle of his hat. Mr. Christiansen grinned at the sight.

The President led the way down the hill. It was a rough path,
weeds and grasses pressed down by dozens of adventuring feet.
He remembered this was where the phlox bloomed blue on the
hillside in April. When he first saw it, he had felt a pang sharp
and clear. It reminded him of the walks with his father along the
wandering creek. He pointed out each flower, he marveled at
the flight of hawks soaring overhead, he listened in joy to the
meadow lark. A field of phlox was a piece of the sky dropped to
the earth and taken root.

The noisy thrashing of the men through the underbrush startled
a crow roosting on a dead sycamore tree. It uttered a harsh, "Caw,
caw, caw," opened its wings and flapped off angrily.

The crow was his mother's side of the family. Looking for
trouble, expecting it, hungering after doom. Many nights he had
listened to the creakings on the stairs as a boy afraid, mortally
afraid of her God. Even now, he would suddenly come awake in
the hour somewhere between two and three, and wonder what
kind of a doom sat downstairs at his desk. He could visualize it,
a black, shapeless thing.

The trail drew him to the water's edge itself. The river ran
thickened and muddy, eddying over gnarled roots of trees and
drowned patches of grass. He looked at the current. Yesterday
morning, before the storm, the river had been low and moving
slowly. A man's life sometimes seems like a river. Here a mere
trickle in a dry bed. Or a mountain stream falling full of sunlight
and joy. Or smooth and slow-moving as a creek in summer. Or
racing swiftly to empty into the oceans and be lost forever. Any
section of the river could be torn from its course by the storm.
The sky is clear in the morning, and by nightfall the black clouds
have gathered and sit waiting. Suddenly the sky is streaked with
lightning. The air booms with thunder. There is a faint smell of
sulphur. The deluge falls. The stream runs wild.

The weather people claim a storm is an accident. The careless
throwing together of winds, hot and cold air masses, and so forth.
But to his mother's people, that was not the text. The storm and
the flood were God's warning. "And God saw that the wickedness

of man was great in the earth . . . and I will cause it to rain upon the earth . . ."

It was odd how often recently his thoughts had turned inward. There had been whole years before his Philippine campaign when such thoughts never occurred to him. He shut off the speculation uneasily.

Moonan came clumping noisily behind him now, his shoes sucking in the mud. The President said, "You'll never qualify as a scout. The enemy would hear you coming a mile away."

Moonan made a face. "Who wants to be a scout?" he asked. "All I want is my breakfast. I am a civilized man. When I wake in the morning, my first thought is to feed the inner man, so he'll be charitable to me the rest of the day. Colonel, you're a heathen."

They tramped downstream toward the distant roar of Great Falls. The river changed its character because the flow was blocked by boulders. The river flung against them in blind anger or coursed around, always pressing onward in reckless haste. Dead branches drifted in the stream, battered against the stones, broke, and were drawn on.

The hikers paused while the President tossed rocks into the muddy water. Mickie leaned against a tree and panted. A Secret Service man called, "Look!"

He pointed his arm upstream. A heavy pine board, a planking torn off a shed on some upland farm, its rusted nails curved by the violent wrench of departure, rode the current. A gray cat clung to the board with its claws dug into the wood.

It was not a handsome cat. It appeared scrofulous, half wild, the kind of untended cat which won grudging admittance to a hill man's farm by chasing rats. Its wet fur clung to its wretched body. It cried out in panic.

Mr. Christiansen turned and stared. He knew then and there his visit to the Garden of Eden was over. The God-awful world was before him.

"Get that cat," he ordered.

A Secret Service man broke off a low limb from a tree with a violent jerk. He stepped to the soft, crumbling earth at the river's edge, and reached out with the limb to pull in the board.

"You won't get it," Mickie said matter-of-factly.

The current pulled the board into midstream, but not until they saw the cat closely. Its green eyes looked at them, not with hope, as a man or a dog might in such circumstances, but angrily. In its eyes Mr. Christiansen felt he could see its thoughts: You are all in on this dirty joke, this thing you call life that picks up stray cats and throws them in the river for no damn good purpose or reason.

Beyond the reach of the watchers, the board was caught in a new current and drifted into a still pool close to shore. The President and the Secret Service men crashed through the underbrush to the spot. Moonan stood where he was.

The would-be rescuers were too late. The heavy flow of water caught the board again and spun it into the foaming spray and, finally, threw it furiously against a boulder. The cat was tossed off. They had a short sight of him with his feet clawing the air. Then he was pulled under.

Mr. Christiansen said, as though to himself, "That's no way to go."

Mickie sloshed up and overheard the remark. He said, "I don't know, Colonel. Certain gallantry in that cat. He was fighting it all the way, giving the Devil a struggle for his money."

President Christiansen felt himself suddenly filled up, choked with anger. The world had broken in upon him. There was nothing he could about drowning cats or the trials of our elderly citizens or moon rockets or the unexplainable rages of the Russians. So why knock on his door? These things were decided by Our Father Which Art in Heaven. And if He decides that the experiment down here has gone far enough, that's it, brother. But if He thinks I'll give them one more chance and meanwhile scare the daylights out of them, that is the way it will be. So why do Congress and the British Prime Minister and the Soviet Premier rap so insistently on Malcolm Christiansen's door? Don't they know? And why try him with such ominous sights as a dying cat?

The President said hoarsely, "Let's get out of here."

The chauffeur waiting in the parking lot quickly threw away his cigarette. The Commander in Chief would not want to waste time getting the engine started. When the party reached the black limousine with the top down, it was purring softly. The driver asked Mickie in a low voice, "Back to the big house, sir?"

President Christiansen did not give Moonan a chance to reply. He shouted furiously, "Where do you want to go, you boob?"

Everyone was frozen, hardly dared move even a finger. A hot wind blew scraps of paper across the concrete parking lot. They were aware of the sound of the river crashing against the boulders, the smell of bacon cooking in the house on the hill, ducks waddling on the grass near the parking lot.

The President, instantly contrite, took his place in the car. The escort car moved ahead first, then the Presidential limousine followed up a winding road. On either side the road was closed in by woods. Government property, or it would have been swept away years ago by bulldozers. Sunlight wandered gently through the trees.

The deep cool woods reminded Malcolm Christiansen again of his father. This time his face seen through the rain-streaked window of the railroad station. He walked out of his father's life for a uniform and regular pay, and Nils sat on the wooden bench as if turned to stone. The look on his face! The Colonel groaned in memory of it, and Moonan looked at him in alarm.

You cannot imagine that face, you cannot, Mr. Christiansen thought. Unless you have seen, turned your head at the exact moment of the soft thud and the screech of brakes and seen the mother's face as the child is hit by a truck.

The President had long since given up hope of ever explaining this incident. How do you explain to others that your father was a pacifist. Not a nut or a freak. He hated war. It was as much a religion to him as his mother's Pentecostal faith. As soon as the boy could read, his father took him to the family Bible—it was a huge black tome—and turned the pages to Psalm Thirty-Four, and asked him to read aloud. The childish voice said awkwardly, "Seek peace and pursue it." That was to be his creed. But when he grew up he put on a uniform and went to war. His father pleaded with him in the station at Minot to give up the service, and when Malcolm could stand it no longer he walked out, and turned around once outside and saw the face. When he had first taken office and told the chairman of the Senate Foreign Relations Committee that the mission of his Administration was peace, the old man had said, "My friend, you are off on a crazy chase for a virgin who will tease you, but never let you take her into your arms." But the chase had gone on, interrupted by agonizing moments of doubt.

Colonel Christiansen envied Mickie his religion. As he saw it, you sinned; you confessed; you bent your knees; you paid your penance; you listened to words murmured in Latin; you were absolved. You were free.

But not Malcolm Christiansen. His suffering began while he stood under the dripping eaves of the station in North Dakota. He dared not look back twice at his father. On the train all the way to Minneapolis he listened to the wheels as they clicked over the ties and a line repeated itself over and over again. "If I sin, then thou markest me, and thou wilt not acquit me from mine iniquity."

There are some men who enjoy staggering through life under the burden of a cross. Not Malcolm Christiansen. He had searched for ways of escape—cheerful companions, fishing, hiking, stout lieutenants to shoulder his burdens.

He was hungry. He wished they had stopped for coffee and doughnuts. What fun they had sitting around the table while Mickie told stories. Some of the best times he ever had. He turned to Moonan now and asked, "Whatever happened to that hoodlum who stole your pants?"

The storm is over, Mickie thought. Secretary of State Silas King had called him the night before and said for God's sake get Chris in a good humor, all hell is breaking loose and we have to tell him. "It's that bad?" Moonan had asked. "Yes." "The Germans?" "Yes." So it was up to one M. F. Moonan to slide down a muddy hill, ruin his Florsheim shoes in mud puddles and smile, brother, smile. He ought to send Silas a bill for services over and above the call of duty as prescribed in the Civil Service manual.

Mickie told his story, it was about the fifteenth time, and everyone laughed. Even the driver.

The road to the city ran along an avenue high above the river and leaped abruptly into a nest of suburbs. From the first glimpse on the hill, the subdivision with its hundreds of similar roofs gleamed in the early sun. A boy rode a bicycle and tossed newspapers on porches. A group of early commuters waited at the transit stop. Pretty young ladies in gay cotton dresses. Men in light suits. A schoolboy with a summer job and a lunchbox. They heard the burst of sound from the police siren and looked up from their meditations. Mickie looked at them carefully. They were the common soldiers of the Christiansen Crusade, part of his thirty-six million voters. How was their faith holding out?

A woman recognized the President in the open car. She smiled and waved, saying something to the others. Instantly, all their faces turned to the car grateful and smiling. One especially fetching, a young lady with charming legs, waist tugged in snugly, dress low cut but not excessively so, golden hair courtesy of the beauty parlor, the all-American dame.

Mr. Christiansen did not see any of the commuters individually. This was his beloved, worshiping, faithful public, his answer to the critics and the cynics. And how he loved them, too! There was nothing to match the great hungry, affectionate roar from thousands of throats, the applauding hands of the worshipers, the feeling of adoration that reached up from the crowd with a love no woman could give. This was payment to him, and him alone! Was this proof he was blessed? He sat back to enjoy the ride.

On the left now, atop the rocky height, were the spires of Georgetown University. Industrious Jesuits cramming knowledge into thousands of minds like packing apples in a crate. The President would like to have these busy brothers working for him. He would send them to Capitol Hill to use their skill and persuasion on the non-believers. Senator Maze Bledsoe for one. Bledsoe had a worldly smile which seemed to say to Mr. Christiansen, "I know you're only a two-bit Colonel with a queasy gut." And if the Jesuits could silence that priest, Father Werther, who made such trouble for him in Congress by crying out about "appeasing Communist murderers and destroyers of the faith." How could the world ever settle down with people like that always scraping open the old wounds? There was the incident at his press conference last week. A reporter asked him to comment on this "appeasement" blah. He blew up like a powder magazine exploding. Used some of the words Mickie had told him to save for just such a time. "Despicable . . . outrageous . . . misleading." They wouldn't ask him that again for a while.

The official cavalcade—motorcycle police, lead Secret Service car, limousine, police—reached the edge of the old town of

Georgetown. Traffic was officially becalmed around them. Drivers and passengers looked curiously. What greatness was passing by? Or what funeral? Why it was Chris! Hurrah for Chris! Others farther back, unseeing, pressed their horns impatiently.

They crossed the brick pavement of Georgetown with its rows of little shops and drove up on the freeway. There was always a foul stench halfway across the freeway. Smelled like a glue factory. The President intended to talk to someone about it. Stop the stink. But there were always so many other things to talk to officials about, he forgot it and held his breath going by.

There is so much you have to hold your breath about. Also turn the head the other way. A President could not think about all the misery and trouble. That is what he told the Cabinet. You fellows were appointed because I have confidence in you, and you've been successful in your own endeavors, so I expect you to handle the problems in your areas without bringing them all to me. That's your job. This is a team operation. And if you don't feel competent to know exactly what to do, ask your secretary. She'll tell you. Laughter. And we've got a traffic control manager in this Administration. My assistant, Judge Herring. When a matter comes to the White House, he will steer it to the right department, and make sure it's taken care of. Heads nodded gravely.

Mr. Christiansen wondered why Silas King wanted to see him this morning. His Secretary of State didn't come running over for idle chatter. He was far too practical. Time is money.

They were on Washington Circle. The Cancer Clinic on the right. Across the street the hospital. Clean and hopeful-looking buildings. Someone dying, someone being born there this instant no doubt. The feeble death rattle, the lusty cry of the infant. More births than deaths. Important problem, the Science Advisory Council assured him. People living longer, jamming up Social Security rolls, raising taxes. Birth control discreetly pushed was the answer. Queer way the French practiced it. Withdrawal, the pale young scientist said.

Small dowdy shops. Pawnbrokers. One "Generous George." Dirty windows. Shopkeepers were yawning, opening their doors, letting down the awnings, wondering if it would be another hot day. A dog raised his leg on the ginkgo tree. A Negro woman carried an empty milk bottle to the tiny grocery with the faded orange front. No one paid any attention to the cavalcade. They don't count their blessings in this part of town.

The motorcycle policeman turned on the siren. Two cars hovered at the next intersection ready to dart into a left turn in front of them. Make way. Stand back. Learn your place. The cars waited while the President and his escorts whizzed past. Mr. Christiansen looked purposeful. The drivers could tell their secretaries or call home and say, "Guess who I saw. Not more than fifteen feet away. Chris. At Pennsylvania Avenue and Twentieth Street."

They crossed 17th Street. Two old-fashioned buildings standing sentinel, the red brick Court of Claims and the elegant old lady, the Executive Building full of White House assistants, squads of them. Mr. Christiansen had no idea what they did. During the Civil War, Abraham Lincoln studied the war maps there. What a terrible time to be President!

The limousine turned in the White House driveway. The officer at the gate saluted smartly. The President exhaled a long, exasperated breath. Back to budgets, petty feuds, strong-willed men in Moscow and Bonn, arguments, and the low-calorie diet.

Damn!

# Chapter TWO

MALCOLM CHRISTIANSEN stepped reluctantly out of the limousine and up onto the White House portico.

This was always a difficult moment, for as soon as he was in the shadow of the great white columns his mood changed. He might be laughing heartily at a joke of Mickie's, and suddenly the laughter would ring hollow and macabre in his ears. The pillars stood softly shaded in the morning light. He asked himself did they look this serene when Lincoln, returning from a morning ride, heard the cannons had shelled Fort Sumter. Or when the Sunday silence was broken with word of Pearl Harbor?

The President entered the lobby. He was struck by the mildly melancholy aroma of cut roses. This is a gloomy old place. Full of antique furniture and solemn birds staring down from oil paintings to see if you pick your nose, use the wrong fork, or make a mess of the job. Formal state rooms full of heavy silence. Someone always watching you. Even ghosts walking the halls. One of the old Negro servants said he had seen "ole Abe Lincoln a-walkin' that upstairs hall. Yes sir, he was walkin' slow and thoughty, and his eyes were maughty sorrowful."

Mr. Christiansen's predecessor, Matthew Thompson, told him during the inaugural ride up Pennsylvania Avenue, "You will think you hear voices, and you will dismiss them at first as the humming of the electric clock or your imagination. But after a few months in office, you strain to hear the dim murmur of the past, and you wish they wouldn't mumble so, because theirs is the voice of experience. Unhappily, you can never make out their words."

What a hell of a thing to say!

Malcolm Christiansen felt most of all a jarring lack of certainty in this creaking temple of history. Now in the Marine Corps you knew what tomorrow would bring. Reveille, mess call and on through the day to taps. You had your orders and you obeyed them. If you had a problem that sat on you, you could buck it up to the next rung in the ladder. But here—shifting sands. You got so you hated to pick up the newspaper. Little shudders of apprehension went through you before you had even focused your eyes. You were so damn glad when the headline was only a murder or an earthquake.

He recalled the comment of Viktor Radilov, the Soviet Premier, and the wry, half-bitter look on his face.

There had been an argument during their meeting, and Silas King said belligerently, "You people are pretty sure of yourselves."

Radilov replied, "They will tell you in Poland that the optimists are teaching their children Russian, and the pessimists Chinese. No one can be sure of tomorrow, but we Russians are fatalists."

Mr. Christiansen took the elevator up to his quarters and sat in the brown leather chair before the television set. He did not even take off his cap. There was a smiling fellow on at this time of the morning. Wakes up the town with a gleaming set of teeth and a cheerful voice. Buster Brighton, servant of mankind, glad eyes behind shell-rim glasses, a crazy hat and a shelf of medicine and jokes to drive away your aches and cares. How is your liver this morning? Take Korolol. Downhearted? Did you hear that one about the Turk's mother-in-law. Let Buster Brighton brighten up your well-regulated day.

The President turned the set on and sat back with an air of pleasant anticipation.

In her very own room, Ada Mae Christiansen listened to her husband's footsteps in the hall. What was his humor this morning? She strained to catch the sound of his feet on the carpet, hopeful he might be in the mood to approve her little project.

Ada Mae was lonely. She had no one to talk to like her kinfolk and girl friends down home in Pender County, North Carolina. A woman needed to gently flush out her hopes and fears and to paint her dreams before a sympathetic soul. The Washington hostesses frightened her—their hard, bright eyes, their malicious idle chatter, their battles and conquests. They reminded her of the man-eating fish she saw swimming swift and vicious in the river the time they had duty in Brazil.

So, Ada Mae retired to her room with a romantic novel her secretary would bring her. This room had the frilliest lace curtains, a hand-crocheted coverlet on the big four-poster bed, rosebud wallpaper, hooked rugs and a cherry chest of drawers. She had selected every item in the room herself, even the sampler with the motto, *"Esse Quam Videri."* Malcolm asked her why she wanted all that "old-fashioned junk" around. She did not tell him, having learned the wisdom of silence. This was exactly like Nancy's room as she remembered it in the old Vance mansion near Wilmington. Nancy was her chum at the seminary, and the Vances were high-quality folks. Ada Mae visited her one Easter and my, how they looked out on the big old full moon and talked as girls do about their ideal mates and clung to one another. Nancy was going to marry a man who would be governor of the state, and they would live in the mansion at Raleigh, and have the finest parties in the old Southern way. "Hospitality hath no charms as in Dixie." Ada Mae said she would be satisfied if her man was a judge, but most of all he must be truly pure in heart and love her dearly. Nancy told her not to be so romantic, that men didn't love you for your nature, but for the shine in your eyes, the way you walked, the curve of your blouse, in other words, a three-letter word ending in "x."

When Ada Mae met Malcolm at the officers' dance, she knew he was the one for her, although she was almost betrothed to the millowner's son who was at Chapel Hill. Lieutenant Christiansen, she knew intuitively, had ideals. Her family argued with her. Why throw herself away, with all her beauty and fine chances, on a Lieutenant with no family and no money? Ada Mae had her way, and the trail of broken hearts in Burgaw, they said, would turn the Cape Fear River red.

True, marriage had not been exactly according to her dreams. Malcolm was so willing to be shared. Also, he was not interested in Ada Mae's troubles. He always said he had enough of his own. But, after all, here she was in the White House as wife of the President of the United States. And, Pender County had an official "Ada Mae Day" on her birthday in April.

She hoped that Malcolm was in a good mood this morning. She wanted to ask him to appoint Nancy's husband to a good government job. He had not done too well back home, and it would be such fun to have Nancy here in Washington with her. They could talk and confide. There was no use asking the President, though, unless he were smiling.

Listening, Ada Mae could gain no clew from her husband's footfalls. She must wait to see how he seemed at breakfast. If only there was a wishing fairy as they told her when she was a girl.

Downstairs, Moonan walked to his office. His view of the White House was loose and ungirdled. It was the setting for a play, a farce or a low tragedy at times. The framed paintings, the immense cut-glass chandeliers, marble mantels and splendid carpets were the props. He himself was an actor with a walk-on part. God knows, he was not here out of any driving desire. He had told Colonel Christiansen, "My job is describing the crusades from a safe mountain top or wine shop, not getting down there in the battle. I don't have the figure or the guts for it. Let me be the minstrel." And he had recited with feeling for Colonel Christiansen one of the hundreds of poems that populated his memory.

> We are the music-makers
>   And we are the dreamers of dreams,
> Wandering by lone sea-breaker,
>   And sitting by desolate streams;
> World-losers and world-forsakers,
>   On whom the pale moon gleams:
>
> We in the ages lying
>   In the buried past of the earth
> Built Nineveh with our sighing,
>   And Babel itself in our mirth;
> And o'erthrew them with prophesying
>   To the old of the new world's worth;
> For each age is a dream that is dying,
>   Or one that is coming to birth.

The hell of it was, Mickie discovered, he was a part and parcel of Malcolm Christiansen. He could not separate himself from "the hero with a heart." In fashioning this creature, Mickie had poured in his own blood. So here they were together at the White House, host and parasite, Pygmalion and Galatea. Moonan was not long in discovering Mr. Christiansen's secret; he was not a crusader either. He was more like the Wizard of Oz.

Someone, God knows, had to look after him. Brother Moonan, the job is all yours. Sometimes when alone, Mickie laughed at himself, the fat mick, nursemaid to what some of the boys in the pressroom called, privately of course, "the beloved hoax." Well, he would do the best he could. You only have one trip down here.

Rounding a corner, he came on a bronze statue of Mercury. He stopped, for this was the first time he had ever noticed it. A thought that had been forming all morning since the episode of the cat burst into full bloom.

He told himself, not sadly or angrily, but with the thrill of awareness, My friend and companion, we're in the grips of a Greek tragedy. We're moving steadily toward the horrors that fate has decreed for us, and there's nothing anyone can do.

> God hath undone me, and I cannot lift
> One hand, one hand to save my child from death.

That was Andromache, and her son was going to be thrown from the wall of Troy. I am Michael Moonan, and my land and my prince are damned. Well, watch the show.

He bowed to Mercury and, more lighthearted than he had been all day, went on to the West Wing. This was the working quarters, the nests of offices where President and secretaries played at the game of running the affairs of 160 million people. The wing had been tacked on by Teddy Roosevelt. He walked down a narrow, white-painted hall to the office of Judge Herring, the chief of staff. He would have the morning intelligence report.

Moonan had heard last night that the AP was quietly pulling together a staff of war correspondents and flying them to Germany. The word was that a limited war might explode.

Dontcha worry, honey chile,
Dontcha cry no more;
It's jest a li'l ole atom bomb
In a li'l ole limited war.

It's jest a bitsy warhead, chile,
On a li'l ole tactical shell,
And all it'll do is blow us—all
To a li'l ole limited hell.

Judge Herring was in his office. He was hunting a lost paper clip with the zeal of a scavenger combing through a trash heap. It should be in the ink bowl, but it was not. A malefactor had disturbed the ecology of his office, and it was not funny.

The walls advertised the tenant. The space was crowded with autographed photographs in black frames. "To my friend and distinguished colleague, Phil Abbott, Speaker, U. S. House of Representatives" . . . "To a great Governor of Delaware, Charles S. Du Pont" . . . "Herring, you are indestructible, Senator Maze Bledsoe." A picture of the Senate Appropriations Committee at the site of a huge dam. Herring was noticeable on the end—small, spare, hard-used, a sharp nose, eyes shrewd and eager.

He discovered a paper clip and slipped it on a memorandum. Then he went to work on the President's appointment schedule. Moonan looked over his shoulder at the line-up.

8:30 to 9 A.M.—Staff conference. Remember to tell Jim Sypher not to bring up the racial disturbance in Charleston. This wasn't the time to disturb the President. Instead, a quick go around the room, present and accounted for, and everything shipshape, sir. Also, speak to the President's economic adviser and remind him he's not lecturing a seminar. Mr. Christiansen's smile wore pretty thin at the last presentation of the cost-price factor. It bored the hell out of him.

9 A.M.—Dr. Maynard, director of the Outer Space Agency. Remind the good doctor to bring simple charts and enlarged photographs. Thank goodness, he had fine news to put the President in a cheerful mood. The U.S.A. had successfully explored a moon crater.

9:30 A.M.—Conflict. The ladies who wrote the winning essays on "The Christiansen Crusade—What It Means to Me" were arriving for a cherished smile from the Crusader himself. But this was the same hour Secretary of State King was coming over. Put the ladies off, take them on a tour of the White House state rooms. Of course, the President might not want to smile after he saw Silas. Have to play it by ear.

10 A.M.—or as soon thereafter as possible—Mr. Christiansen would take off for a swim in the White House pool and a showing of the television program "Leatherneck." This was his sacred half hour. Dramatized episodes from Colonel Christiansen's biography, *A Hero With A Heart*.

11:30 A.M.—The Judge would like to work in Maze Bledsoe. The Colonel didn't like Maze—that was the rub. Bledsoe treated him as a fellow politician, and this outraged the President. Anger showed in his ears first. A fine crimson. Time to change the conversation. Mr. Christiansen, as every school child knew, was not a politician. He was called, as Moses, to lead his people. Maze did this deliberately; he liked to get under the Commander in Chief's hide. Yet it was as important as sin to get along with him. Maze was chairman of the Appropriations Committee. He decided how much money would flow from the tap.

There went the morning.

Judge Herring reached down and picked an apple from the crate by his desk. He polished it with a handkerchief and bit into it with a loud crunch.

Mickie said, "Eating the fruit of knowledge again. No good can come of that."

"Apples," the Judge replied, "are nature's way of providing virility and longevity to mankind. You can go into the apple country and see robust old squires who are siring at eighty."

"Hiram, you are the constant optimist." He lifted an apple and looked at it reflectively. "Judge, did you ever read Euripides?"

Herring did not look up. He replied, "I don't have the time to read these foreign sex novels."

"All right, I give up. Has the morning report come in yet?"

Judge Herring pointed to his desk. There it was in a blue cover and labeled "Top Secret."

Moonan picked it up, but before turning back the cover said, "What is it we spend a year for intelligence activities? Six billion?"

"Six billion, five hundred and sixteen million, eighty-two thousand."

"I'll save you six billion five hundred million. Give me twenty first-rate reporters, and let me put them in key places, and you can dismantle the whole God-damned Central Intelligence. But, of course, that wouldn't be practical. They would turn up so much mischief that the heads of state would leave for their underground shelters with orders to push the button in two hours."

He sat down on one of Herring's hard wooden chairs and began reading:

Gottfried (the news photographs showed a tall, close-cropped Teuton with wild eyes and a saber scar on his cheek) seems determined to provoke an incident on the border with East Germany. He held a meeting last night near the frontier town of Hof. We estimate 50,000 were present, with 7,500 of that number from East Germany. Gottfried defied the Soviet to "halt this demonstration of affection for the Fatherland." He called on all present to swear an oath to reunite Germany and said, "The sin of partition can be wiped out only by the blood of Germans. This is our das Schicksal (fate)." Wild applause greeted his remarks. His verbal attack on the Slavs was particularly violent. He gave no clew to his next move but said, "The hour is approaching when we must strike, all of us, soldiers, students, captive Germans, workers and peasants."

Our informants say the German Army Command is almost completely behind Gottfried. The exception is General Von Staudt, chief of staff of the Army. He is awaiting the time when he can drive the hardest bargain. Gottfried is thus held back from seizing power until this moment arrives. Chancellor Ehrlich has a façade of authority, but that is all. Gottfried's Freiheitbund is organized throughout West Germany and has underground cadres in the East. The Freiheitbund is well disciplined and equipped with small arms.

Our sources claim knowledge of Gottfried's master plan. This would begin with general strikes in East Germany to tie up communications and transport and render the airfields useless for the large Russian jets. The general strikes would also scatter the Soviet and GDR security forces. Armed volunteers, guerrilla units actually, would cross the border at several points to create diversions. The Army would make a separate thrust. Gottfried would proclaim himself the fuehrer of an "entire German nation."

The Soviet Union is aware of this plan, and has sent a special envoy, V. Poltovsky, an assistant to the Foreign Minister, to negotiate personally with Gottfried. Reportedly, Poltovsky offered to agree to a unified Germany under Gottfried if he would accept disarmament and the present borders. Gottfried refused.

The U.S.S.R. has sent fresh troops west across Poland to the Elbe and into Czechoslovakia. They are motorized and equipped with tactical atomic weapons. The missile bases in Hungary and Czecho-slovakia have been placed on the alert. We estimate that the Soviet has two armies along the border or not far behind it. At the same time, Moscow is concerned lest in the confusion of possible war and uprisings the Chinese may find it timely to move into areas of Asiatic Russia to "protect" the Communist ally.

The British Government proposes that Gottfried be kidnaped and flown to Tasmania . . .

Mickie leaned forward and with a slight grunt of effort put the report on the edge of the Judge's desk. He lit a cigarette, flipping the lighter wheel three times before a spark came. He asked, "How long did it take to make the world, professor?"

"Seven days and seven nights."

"And we can destroy it in seven seconds. The progress of man."

Mickie sat musing. The cigarette was held lightly in his lips, and only his breathing drew in a trace of smoke and exhaled it.

In the beginning, the scientists claim, there were clouds of gases in the universe. They floated together in one flaming ball, and began to cool. The gases on the outside became solids like the skin on a balloon. $H_2O$ combined to make a layer of clouds a hundred miles high. It rained for a million years or so. Huge, crushing tongues of ice rolled across the crust. Somewhere life began two billion years ago. How? Divine intervention or a bolt of lightning striking a puddle of stagnant water full of organic chemicals. I'll leave that to others to decide; it isn't important to me. Millions of years of trial and error for the fragile spark of life. Sacs and gills and lungs; caves and villages and cities. And there was man. He was like the other animals, cunning and fierce with a talent for survival. He cared for his young. He killed his enemies. He hunted for his food. But there was something new. Man was creative. He made spears to throw at his stronger foes. He carved and sketched on the walls of his cave. He created the slingshot, the bow, and the catapult; the raft, the canoe, and the sailing ship. He made a language, and sang songs and told tales. He built forts and magnificent temples and aqueducts. He developed armies and systems of belief and government. He transformed the crust of earth into steel and stone for his cities and his arsenals. From gunpowder to atomic fission in a thousand years. Now supreme over his earth, except for a few raids by

fire ants and locusts and water hyacinths, he can destroy himself
—past, present and future. Accidentally. Into this world we came
by accident. Out we go the same way.

> Dust into Dust and under Dust to lie,
> Sans Wine, sans Song, sans Singer, and—Sans End!

Judge Herring was making notes with a pencil. It made scratching sounds as it moved across the paper.

Moonan threw his cigarette into a small spittoon. He asked, "Do
you know if Silas King has any proposals?"

It took the Judge a few seconds to disconnect himself from
his notes and focus on the question. He replied, "Yes, I believe
he has a plan of persuasion."

"Money talks?"

"I think that is the idea." The Judge was more interested in
finding a way to get Senator Bledsoe to see the President than
in this conversation. He said, "Oh, I think this crisis will go away
like all the others. We get lathered up, and the crisis will begin to
fade away."

"That's an interesting theory. The Herring theory of crisis.
Each crisis dissipates after achieving its goal, which is to tense
the nerves and increase the heartbeat, ruin the nerves and test your
religion. Job brought up to date. Otherwise, men would sink into
such a stinking calm they'd lose their zip, and with it control of
the earth. Probably to starlings and UNIVAC. The machines
can run the Executive, the starlings will take over Congress."

Judge Herring buzzed his secretary and gave her the appointment list to be typed and distributed. He was used to this morning
philosophy and paid little attention to it. He asked Mickie, "How
was the President feeling this morning?"

"Upset. You know how he is. He can be more disturbed by a
broken mirror than riots in Africa. This morning we saw a cat
drown in the river. He expects the worst."

"Too bad." The Judge hastily abandoned his plan of bringing
Maze Bledsoe in to see the President.

Across the lobby from the Judge's office, a colored woman
cleaned the small toilet just off the press room. She sang softly to

herself. No doubts assailed her, made her day anxious. She was safe in the arms of the Lord and protected by Malcolm Christiansen.

The press room existed physically in the West Wing, but owed no deep allegiance to it. Neither by umbilical cord, paycheck or other form of loyalty. This enclave was an abrupt right turn just inside the door to the West Wing. Its guardian spirit was an ancient deer head perched unsteadily atop the bulletin board. An antler was draped by a hideous hand-painted tie bought by a photographer in Japan and removed while he slept on the lumpy leather divan next to the wall. The desks were chipped, scarred and pitted; they were littered with old newspapers, Coke bottles and telephones. On a table were limp cards left from last night's poker game. A typewriter squatted malignly on a desk. It had a sheet of yellow paper in it with a line of obscenity typed on it. This was for the benefit of the cleaning woman who met attacks on Christian faith by painfully typing a verse from the Holy Writ.

The reporters came early this morning. The buses growled by on Pennsylvania Avenue laden with government clerks given a glimpse of the dark birth of crisis in the folded newspapers on their laps. Eyes turned prayerfully to the great pillared mansion standing clean and hopeful in the morning light. Chris, you'll take care of us, won't you?

The newsmen began arriving at the great, barred gate at 8:30, much like crows perching on the tree tops at the smell of death. They showed their passes, were nodded in by the guards, and walked up the shaded drive to the West Wing. They stood in the press room or slumped in chairs in the lobby. Little groups gathered.

"What's the Colonel going to do?"

There were many answers, given in varying degrees of piety.

"Appoint a committee."

"Go deer-hunting."

"Wait for his luck to pull him out."

"Threaten to raise the tariff on Volkswagens unless the Germans act in keeping with the American system of free enterprise."

"Send Mickie to his priest to intercede with the Higher Authority." There was confused discussion on whether Mickie knew any priest that well.

Someone suggested that the President was like the Churubusco turtle. What in the hell is that?

"The monster of the Hoosier highlands. A string correspondent in the remote reaches of Indiana sent to the Indianapolis *Star* a dispatch on lined yellow note paper. It told of a gigantic turtle seen by farmer Ollie Ochs on his back forty near Churubusco. The beast was as big as a dining room table. The *Star* put the story on page one, there being no statehouse scandals that day to amuse the readers. Within three days, curiosity seekers, professors, preachers, photographers, and a team from the Hearst Chicago bureau descended on brother Ochs' farm. He took the searchers to the exact spot where he saw the animal emerge from the farm pond. For three days, the strangers beat around Churubusco. They never found the turtle. He existed only in the eyes of the believer."

Laughter.

Then a reporter who fancied his deep voice and sometimes played in amateur theatricals intoned, "The race is not to the swift, nor the battle to the strong . . . "

The rest of the quotation was drowned out by the cry, "Press conference," and the rushing and scraping of the crowd as it surged into the hall toward Moonan's office. It was only a prank by a photographer. The mob melted back into chairs and groups, and waited with the air of resignation that characterizes a death watch.

*Chapter* THREE

THE CROWD of reporters in the lobby grew sulky from waiting, and restless with constant alarms and starts. Many sat listless in the chairs. Others wandered outdoors and stood staring across the broad lawn at the tourists watching them from the other side of the fence.

Soon after nine fifteen, there was a move in the White House lobby. It was like the sudden swelling of a wave in a serene sea. Many reporters, without knowing what was happening, stood up and began moving with the throng toward the entry.

This time they were rewarded. Silas King, the merchant prince, strode into the White House wearing a look of massive confidence and a $250 suit. Hitting the barricade of journalists, he smiled a hearty $20,000,000 smile.

Voices assaulted him. "Why are you seeing the President, Mr. Secretary?" . . . "Will Gottfried take over the Bonn Government?" . . . "Do you think war will break out between the two Germanies?" . . . "What have you heard from Moscow?" . . . "Do you favor calling an immediate session of the UN?" . . . "Do you have any information on Russian troop movements?"

The Secretary of State put up a well-manicured hand in the manner of a traffic policeman. "You fellows sound like ambulance chasers. There's nothing unusual about my visit. Happens several times a week. Came to give Chris a briefing."

"What are you going to tell him, Mr. Secretary?"

The Secretary said playfully, "Now, Mr. Bowser, you wouldn't stop a young man as he walked down the street with a bouquet and ask him what he was going to tell his sweetheart. That is what the lawyers call privileged. I can guarantee you, though, that I don't take any message of alarm with me."

Someone on the edge of the crowd said, "God's in His Heaven, the stock market is steady, all's right with the world."

Silas King's bland air of amiability suffered a slight relapse. He frowned and looked to see if he could identify the voice. Secretary King did know a considerable number of publishers, and they were always glad to be told about the troublemakers. But there were no guilty looks in sight. The Secretary put his hearty smile back on and made his way past the large center table, gift of a King of Siam when they had kings, marvelously carved by girls who, he heard, became blind at twenty-one from the exacting workmanship. Once past the table, he was safe. He had observed that reporters lost the scent, so to speak, once that table was reached. They slouched back to their lairs.

The press, an institution provided for running timely advertisements in print and sagacious editorial comment, he could understand and appreciate. But not the lack of respect for authority some of the hired hands flaunted. The insolent description of him that appeared in the London *Economist*. (The entire air-mail edition at the news stand near the State Department was sold out an hour after its arrival.)

The British chappie wrote:

One can imagine the Secretary as the Governor of a well-run Roman province so distant from the Eternal City no noble would desire it. He would be a Legionnaire who worked his way up to this autocratic position by his genius in organizing the supply trains that were more important to the Caesars than their swordsmen. This Governor would not be an heroic warrior figure, but rather comic— short, bald, square; saved from laughter by a skill at artificially creating confidence. It is a manner of the voice, like the wireless announcers who sell toothpaste so superbly.

Mr. King is a perfect example of America's gift to the modern world, the manager of those vast and complex institutions known as corporations. He is the graduate of a small mid-country engineering school and has no intellectual or aesthetic pretensions. He has not the slightest interest in Aeschylus or Bach or Corot. He has no host of gods to confuse him. He is simply a fanatic of the sect of the Big Buck.

Mr. King is not the Secretary of State because of an overweening passion to improve the disorderly state of the world. He simply wants to reduce taxes, and Q.E.D., the only way is to cut down the heavy expenditures for arms. Therefore, he has moved with the aggressiveness of a huge lorry on a narrow highway to an understanding with Russia that will make this possible.

Peace in our time, that will-o'-the-wisp deep in the forest, may be captured because a determined capitalist means to cut taxes. Or, again, he may achieve just the opposite.

The Secretary nodded to the white-haired chief usher. The latter bowed low and made obsequious movements of his lips.

King told him, "I think Atlas will go up three points in the next week."

Another bow. Wordless, but eloquent thanks written on the usually haughty face. Only Mr. Silas can give the tips to put you on Easy Street.

Secretary King swept on to the office of the Secretary to the President. He waved an arm and said, "I'm a little early. Going in to see Judge Herring."

Herring was a steady sort of fellow. He might have an idea on how to approach Chris. Silas King thought of the President as "Chris," because, after all, he had made him President. You aren't expected to genuflect before the man you put in as manager of your company. You call him by his first name to remind him of your relationship.

This was a bad business he had to take to Chris today. There was a danger of panic, with some damn fool shooting a gun and putting us in a war that could cost a hundred billion dollars.

But it wasn't wise to let on how bad things were. Play the game as if you were sure you had the winning cards. Bluff, that's the secret.

Foreign policy, now, was a strange operation. Not like running General Motors. Instead, like wandering blindfold in a forest, reaching out with your hands groping for trees, trying to feel the path with your feet, being scratched by briers, wondering if the path would drop off into the river.

The prime ministers, premiers, kings, sheiks, generalissimos, nabobs and chiefs were such prima donnas. The Defense Department was on your back to keep them happy, so we could put bases on their soil to pop the Russians or the Chinese or whoever in hell we were mad at at the moment. The United States didn't feel normal unless it was mad at someone. So to keep the allies happy, toss away a billion here, another there, buy them a navy to play with, send them jet planes to crash, build dams, irrigate deserts while our own corporations are starved for capital. Appropriate, appropriate, appropriate. No consideration of where the money is coming from. From the hides of the preservers of the American free enterprise system.

These sheiks, for example, were never satisfied. If you give Sultan X an armored car, Mohammed would threaten to run off and join the other side unless he got an airplane, gift of Uncle Generous. That nasty little dictator's son that came over a year ago and asked me to provide him with a red-haired movie queen for his bed. Some crazy idea he had picked up from a smutty book, that redheads were the best. End the cold war! Turn the bombs and tanks into tax rebates!

Judge Herring rose respectfully at the presence of Silas King. It is always wise, the Judge had learned, to act deferentially to any man who can amass fifty million dollars. There is a goodness that flows from money, like the taste of expensive Scotch and the aroma of Havana cigars.

"How is Chris feeling today?" Secretary King asked.

"Out of sorts. You know how he gets sometimes, Silas. Jumpy. Thinks the world is coming to an end because he sees his shadow. He saw a cat drown in the river early this morning on his walk."

"I don't understand that kind of thinking," King said in exasperation. "What in the devil difference does it make whether a cat drowns? That is a perfectly normal occurrence. I don't get excited unless A.T.&T. drops five points. Then I pick up the telephone and find out why."

Judge Herring asked with a respectful nod of the head, "What sort of news do you bring the President?"

"Poor."

Silas King looked at him bluntly, not inviting sympathy or aid, just stating a fact.

In his office, President Christiansen fidgeted at his desk. This room annoyed him. When the President of the United States entered his office it should be as a priest entering the inner shrine. When a visitor stepped across the threshold, he should be visited by a sense of awe. In other words, the right stage setting. Not this place. The room was not like any command post Mr. Christiansen had ever seen or imagined. It was small, oval-shaped and soft-colored, a washed-out green. It looked just as though a woman had designed it. He sat with his back to a curving row of French windows and a formal garden. A typical woman's idea! When the President turned his head to the left, there was George Washington on the wall. The old soldier seemed to have a sour stomach. Honestly, how would you like it to have that portrait staring at you? If the President turned to the right, there was Herbert Hoover, and a small amount of inspiration you got from him! Straight ahead was a large globe of the world. A plastic reminder that wherever you went, trouble was brewing.

Mr. Christiansen had tried to impress his personality upon this room. He brought in his regimental flag and a really good color photograph of his headquarters in the Philippine mountains. But they were somehow blurred out. This was like trying to etch your character on the sea. The room resisted him. Or rather it ignored him.

Mr. Christiansen tapped the blade of a gold and intricately designed paper knife on the underside of his desk drawer. It had been given him by the Arabian King. He examined it. On the blade a beautiful maiden—at least according to Arab standards—was losing her virtue with magnificent poise to a bearded sheik. He really admired the young lady. How fine it would be to go through life with such detachment.

The President's visitor was talking so earnestly his high fore-head glistened with perspiration. Dr. Maynard, the director of the Outer Space Agency (lots of space, need agents, ha-ha), was describing the successful exploration of Greater Lambda Crater on the moon.

Mr. Christiansen supposed he should be enthusiastic. Congratulations, scientist, and to those brave explorers who have tested the vastness of space for the glory of God and the U.S.A. But the fact was the Russians got to the moon first. What if we did explore a hole in the moon? They got there first. Who are the explorers they mention in history? The ones who got there first.

Christopher Columbus. Name ten who explored America. De Soto, Hudson, Raleigh, Daniel Boone . . . It does come hard, doesn't it?

Dr. Maynard said, "We have encountered an amazing phenomenon in a huge pocket under the crater. It is a dazzling yellow gas, and has been named Chrion in your honor. This gas has deadly powers of annihilation of life. It literally eats up the oxygen in the air."

The President asked, "What made you think I wanted a poison gas named after me?"

Dr. Maynard blinked at him in mild amazement. He explained earnestly, "Mr. President, we are thinking in terms of the discovery of a new element, and the honor of living through all the ages of knowledge . . ."

Mr. Christiansen spoke with an edge on his voice. "If it hadn't been for you scientists, we wouldn't be in all this trouble, and be blowing each other to smithereens, and that sort of thing. It's too much for me to understand why you want to invent this stuff." He slapped his hand down testily on the desk.

"I can understand, Mr. President, your justified anger at the way the world finds itself. But, sir, as long as man possesses an inquiring mind, knowledge will grow. I can answer you in the words of Dr. Einstein after the first atomic bomb explosions, 'Science has brought forth this danger, but the real danger is in the hearts of men. ' "

Oh damn these clever professors with their quotations. Why can't they own up and admit they are guilty, and they have brought this trouble on the earth? Malcolm Christiansen felt so impotent, so lost and wordless in the presence of these fellows.

He adopted a severe air, as though he were dressing down a junior officer, and said, "Well, all I can say is why with all the high I.Q.s running around and all the money we throw out for research—I saw the figure the other day, several billions—you scientists can't make a start in improving man. You claim you can do anything."

"I don't want to beg the point, Mr. President, but those who control the funds and facilities needed for research never seem interested in the human spirit. Most of the research in the United States, and I presume in Russia, too, is directed to improving the military sciences. Genetics, which may offer valuable clews to human behavior, is starved. So the scientist, like most human beings, must go where the current takes him—into a laboratory working on the dynamics of a new bomb, or a research office trying to bring a new dimension to television or a hormone to restore beauty to aging faces. With your permission, I will draw up a project for a further investigation in genetics."

Mr. Christiansen was by now weary of the subject.

"Oh, all right," he said vacantly. He stood up to indicate the interview was over. Dr. Maynard gathered up his charts hurriedly. Silas King came in the door. He smiled and said, "Well, what do we have here?"

The space director explained his report in brief.

"Damn good work," said the Secretary of State. "Make the world sit up and take notice of the United States. Just what we need. Comes at the right time."

Mr. Christiansen looked on Secretary King fondly. Here was a man he could count on. Lead him through any storm. Storms seemed to mark his life. The thought drove him back through time.

A gray sky hung low over the lonely sweep of prairie. A solid, sullen gray. The air was still, too still. Clothes strung out on a line hung listlessly. This gave a peculiar sense of deadness and of mysterious and imminent peril to the scene. Man seemed so little in evidence, to be unimportant. There was a long, endless line of utility poles following the road, and an occasional farmhouse and barn squatting like ducks on a still pond. A light covering of snow lay on the ground, bare now since the harvesting of the wheat.

A man and his boy—he looked about eleven or twelve—were riding east in a small truck.

A wind whirled up out of the north. They saw it first as it suddenly bent and trembled the branches on a woodlot half a mile away. Then it hit the truck with jarring gusts. The wind was cold and moist.

The man said, "It looks like we're in for snow. Could be a bad one." He watched it approach anxiously, as if trying to gauge the fury of the storm.

The snow came softly, in fact it muffled the sound of the wind.

The flakes were so large as to look like small white flowers found along streams in the woods. The snow was so dense that far objects soon blanked out. The woodlot was there one moment, faded out entirely the next. There was a curtain of snow that moved closer and closer around them until only a small patch of the road ahead was visible. That, too, was lost when the burden of snow became too heavy for the windshield wipers. The man stopped the truck and turned off the motor. The boy was surprised by the silence, a soft, suffocating shshshsh.

His father put his arm around his shoulder.

"Look there, to the right. See the light over the barn door? Look hard." There was a tone of urgency in his voice.

He did not see it at first. When he did find it, it was a naked illuminated light bulb swinging in the wind.

"That's where we're going—the light," his father said. "I'll go first. You hang on to the tail of my mackinaw."

The boy discovered the true character of the snow when they started across the field. It was not benevolent. It slapped and stung and gagged and blinded him. Nothing the boy had ever seen or felt or heard was as violent and antagonistic. He felt in his heart that it was trying to destroy him, and this both bewildered and frightened him. He lost sight of the barn and the light. He could see only his father's back. Once he stumbled and lost his hold on his father's mackinaw. He cried out, "Paw, Paw." The cry was muffled and lost. Snow flung in his open mouth.

There was some connection between father and son that did not need sound to cry the alarm. The man turned back, and wordlessly grabbed the boy's hand, pulled him up and on. They had to climb a fence. This was enormously difficult, because of the driving snow.

The boy was sure they were lost. He remembered stories of men walking round and round in circles in a blizzard just going from house to barn, and when they were tired they fell down and never rose again. He was terribly afraid.

And then, having almost lost hope, he saw the light swinging back and forth on a short arc. It was a glorious sight. He thought now of how Silas King, a tough, competent, wonderful guy was like that light bulb.

The Secretary of State slapped him affectionately on the shoulder and said, "I don't understand it, Chris, but just looking at you gives me a lift."

King talked to him easily for several minutes about fishing, a sport they both enjoyed, both being essentially farm boys despite the titles that lay on them. And so the sense of outrage and fear that surged so strongly over the President this morning receded still farther until it was remote and dammed.

When Secretary King saw the uneasy look in Chris' eyes had left him, he said casually, as though it might be an afterthought, "Colonel, I'd like you to do a little chore for me. It'll help me calm down those emotional Germans. They love you and will do anything you say. They admire military heroes; never saw a people like them unless it was us."

"What is it, Si?" Silas King not only made him feel secure, but also benign, as though he were a Caesar who had only to come to the window and smile and wounds healed and the grain grew.

The Secretary immediately grew businesslike, nailing down the deal, arranging the payments. "I want you to make a television address to the German people. All you do is let them know we respect and support their desire for reunification. We're on their side, and we've got things moving in the right direction. But, all bets are off if they try to shoot their way across the border. We won't help them, and no one else will, and they will suffer for their foolishness. Appeal to their sense of honor and order. We have some German experts in the Department that can write you a jim-dandy speech."

The President was tempted to believe Silas. The smoothly flowing stream of history with Malcolm Christiansen benevolently steering the ship of state. Hardly any effort, merely an occasional dip of the paddle. Yet, he saw once again the swollen, surly stream of the flooded Potomac, its dirty waters drowning clumps of lovely wild flowers, catching an old piece of board and swinging it around like a piece of straw and slamming it against a boulder. The cat, its matted fur close against its scrawny body, its eyes wild and resentful of its fate.

He asked in a dead voice, "We're in trouble, aren't we, Si?"

Secretary King hesitated. How much exposure should he give the President? This man was like a photographic plate. He could not stand much light. King himself had made his way by going boldly out into the sun while others lingered in the shade. He decided to be discreet. He would present the crisis in its broadest form, the sharp corners filed off.

Mr. Christiansen interrupted him to ask, "But how can these Germans think they'll go anywhere, I mean beat anyone in a military action, because our agreement with Radilov was to disarm both sides of Germany, and I guess that's been done, hasn't it?"

"Well," Secretary King replied apologetically, "not exactly. The Pentagon bucked like hell and the Germans have resisted, and instead of dragging you into the argument I've been trying to work it out. I'll admit I didn't think we were this close to the edge. The Germans have quite a few weapons. The British Ambassador called me yesterday in quite a sweat. His intelligence people think the Germans can and will launch a limited attack. The Germans, the Ambassador said, don't seem to give a damn about the consequences."

The President joylessly remembered Premier Radilov, the Russian, as he talked of the Germans. His face grew passionate and dark and wild whenever his mind touched that subject. His English veered off into crazy zees and yas as he said, "German militarism is taking up the sword. The Bonn rulers are conjuring up a new complication, they are on the point of unleashing a new war. There is only one way to safeguard peace for Europe. That is to disarm Germany."

Silas had thought this was merely a propaganda speech, that he was putting up a show for them. Mr. Christiansen had not agreed with his Secretary of State this time. The President recognized the anger and bitterness that comes to frightened men. He felt it, it was intuitive, and he had a stubborn faith in his intuition.

He asked Secretary King now, "Have you said anything to the Russians?"

"Oh my God no. Not until this is straightened out. They might get excited and rush in and occupy West Germany. You know how they feel about the Germans."

Now that he knew what was inside the shadow, Malcolm Christiansen felt in a way relieved. He supposed it was like death. A man gets sharp, cruel glimpses of it all his life. He may see its shining sword over him. But when the blow falls, it is strangely gentle. What Silas showed him was bad, but not too bad. And, thank the stars, here was good old Silas with a prescription. Cure the illness with a speech.

"Do you really think, Silas, that they will listen to my speech?" "Oh sure," he said confidently. "Your words will cool off the main body of German opinion long enough for me to talk to my friends in the German steel and banking community. I can show them they'll lose their shirts in any wild grab for East Germany. And they are practical men. Then I'll talk to the Russians.

"We've a plan some of the boys have worked up in the Department. It's for a joint East and West German council to work out details of removing economic barriers and widening cultural exchanges, and that sort of thing. It will make everyone happy but the Germans. The plan gets both the Russians and ourselves off the hook. Neither of us want to fight over Germany. The other nations will be greatly relieved because the danger of war will be defeated. The Germans, of course, will shout and bang the table, but they'll get used to it. They'll have to. The world is too small and crowded to be able to afford a war."

Silas King sat breathing easily, the buttons on his vest rising and falling gently, his mood mildly contemplative.

"You know, Chris, in this job you learn a hell of a lot about, well, I suppose you call them national traits. Who would ever suppose the Germans would have such a wild streak? Or the Russians would be as suspicious and touchy as an old maid? And I haven't found any people, well, except the Swiss, who honestly understand the value of money."

He shook his gleaming bald head in wonderment.

Malcolm Christiansen had heard enough. The long mouth straightened out primly. He had heard the fearful revelation, his spirit was purged, the solution was held out. Let the Secretary of State keep his problems to himself.

King was quick to detect the change in mood. He was not a skilled salesman for nothing. He said, "Well, now that we've patched up the world, Chris, how about a date for surf fishing?"

The dear ladies of the Christiansen Crusade contest sat in the lobby. They were on the divans and chairs under the portrait of

Abraham Lincoln and his Cabinet. They fluttered with excitement, like humming birds hovering over scarlet sage. Wasn't it
simply wonderful, said Mrs. Adkins, to actually, really see democracy in action, to see how that great and good man, Malcolm
Christiansen, calmed the angry seas of the world. Such spiritual
force! One can see it on his face, don't you agree, dear? You
feel so much more secure, too, to have a man in the White House
who believes in God and the power of prayer. The Lord and
Malcolm Christiansen watch over us.

The dear ladies were dressed in their splendor—bright dresses
not too daring and not too protective; fresh hair-dos, charming earrings, dainty high heels, a touch of perfume. Just because you are
a grandmother is no reason to let your figure go and dress in gray.
There is still life in the old girl yet!

The white-haired usher approached, presented them with a
short, dignified bow and said, "You may come in now, ladies."

They arose, smoothed their dresses, wished to goodness they
had time for one short peek in the compact mirror, but let's hope
for the best, and tripped daintily behind the usher. O heart, I hear
your beating!

Through an outer office where the staff barely glanced up and
there, at last, was the oval room. A hushed silence, a drawing in of
the breaths. The room had a golden glow, sunlight touching the
desk and the walls and the flag. The desk where he made so many
momentous decisions cleared of all but a neat, precise pile of communications and golden paper knife.

Now, here comes the marvelous one himself. A tingling up the
arms and legs and back as if touched by a light feather. An inward
trembling. Here we stand alone in the presence of Malcolm
Christiansen. His face is heavy with thought, shadows of concentration about his eyes. Then he sees us, and his face lights up.
He looks at us deeply and he smiles. He tells us, "I am indeed sorry
to have kept you waiting so long." Little gestures of the hands
which plainly say, Oh, dear sir, it is our privilege to wait. "You
know, we have so many, well, grave problems, I guess you would
call them, in Government these days, they just won't wait for own
desires and pleasures, you might say. We are kept at the grind
stone pretty much of the time, but I guess that's what we were
elected for."

The eyes of the faithful blessed him.

Actually, Mr. Christiansen had not seen them when he entered his office. He was brooding over the unjust and arbitrary way that human affairs were managed. Men were constantly being thrown willy-nilly into turmoil without their wish or say. Some had more and some less trouble, and there was no explanation for the way this whole complex and intricate system operated. There would be a war. He felt the fact heavily, as though his blood and bones had turned to wet sand. He no more doubted it than he doubted that the mangy cat was a warning to him. They were the clews of man's fate. He could not change it. He could only accept as Job. "Man is born unto trouble, as the sparks fly upward."

So his mind was like the fierce stare of resentment of the cat riding on the pine plank. And then he saw the ladies. Not as individuals, warm flesh and blood, but as the public whose love sustained him.

The President spoke to them, and he felt on him the glow that any actor, orator or lover does when his message strikes deep and sure.

"I am, of course, deeply touched by the eloquence of your essays, and it's too bad you didn't have a better subject to write about." Protestations. "Like, for example, Mr. Washington whose painting there inspires me when I feel sad as you're apt to in this job, believe me. I try to do my humble best to serve my country, and I'm always encouraged by these meetings with real flesh-and-blood Americans like you. I'm afraid my business is too often with bureaucrats and politicians and generals.

"I would like to be able to guarantee you people that the world was shipshape and in no danger of trouble. But no man can do that. I have just talked to Silas King, and he has warned me there may be trouble brewing across the waters. But he has a sensible plan that you will hear a lot more about later on . . ."

He broke off as a new stream of thought surged fiercely through him.

"Will you tell me, ladies," he demanded harshly, "why we can't have peace in this world?"

## Chapter FOUR

LATE THAT day, Mickie Moonan sat in his office staring at his typewriter. He took off his shell-rimmed reading glasses, laid them
on the desk and rubbed his forehead. Christ!

His secretary was in the next room reading a paper-back book.
He could see the back of her head set off by two huge blue
earrings.

"Marie," he called, "you can go now. I'm not going to get this
thing finished for a couple of hours. I'll get someone from the
Message Center to type it." He was laboring on his version of the
President's speech on the German crisis. Four others were writing
separate versions. At midnight they would meet in the Cabinet
room and thrash out the finished product over black coffee.

Inspiration, the muse, whatever the hell it was, had left him,
scrammed, skedaddled. What he really needed was a steam bath,
a massage, and a pretty girl to flatter him with her attention. That
would restore his soul. But it takes time to organize these restora-
tions, and time was on the wing.

There should be somewhere in the vast, unexplainable reaches
of government an agency to revive the spirits of the statesmen, he
thought with a spurt of animation. Dancing girls, sparkling wits,
oxygen, masseurs—all supplied in a moment's notice, rushed over
in a golden station wagon. How much more rational governments
would act with this simple, inexpensive reform!

He pushed the typewriter stand away and stood up with the
heavy, awkward movements of a bear rousing itself from hiber-

nation. He heard Marie's high heels tap, tap, tap, tap through the empty lobby. The guard murmured good night to her. The door opened and closed, and there was silence again.

Moonan picked a cigarette out of the pack. He lit it deliberately and walked out into the lobby. The central chandelier was turned off. Two small wall lights and the glow of the passing day illuminated the room. He stood spread-legged before the portrait of Lincoln. Abe, old Abe, what would you say to the fools who want to blow themselves and the world to bits? You tried to reason with them, didn't you, and they wouldn't listen. And so you said, "Human nature will not change. In any future great national trial, compared with the men of this, we shall have as weak and as strong, as silly and as wise, as bad and as good." What a terrible indictment for the future, old Abe!

He turned away, going toward the narrow entry. He smiled wryly at a stray memory. The police reporter, a portable O'Henry, watching the daily violence in the lives of little people. A madman—he must have been—threatened to explode a home-made bomb in a small west-side church. The priest was trying to talk him out of it.

"But why shouldn't I?" the man cried wildly. "I'm damned anyway, ain't I? What difference does it make how I go?"

The priest, softly urgent, asked him to consider the fate of the innocent who would die with him.

"Why should I?" he retorted. "They never done anything for me."

Logic, beautiful logic. But they crept up behind the logician and knocked him out with gas before he had a chance to pull the pin.

The White House guard opened the door for Mickie and followed him outside in the dusk. "Mr. Moonan," he asked, "do you think there'll be a war?"

He answered, "Andrew, I long ago gave up thinking. It's a destructive habit. Besides, it is misleading."

He sat down on the step and was refreshed by a breeze that sprang up and gently waved the leaves on the elms shading the driveway.

"Andrew, I'll tell you what our problem is. Simple. The world is too small. Too many people in it. We're standing cheek to jowl, butt to butt in a boat on a stormy sea. One sudden move, and the whole damn bunch is in the drink. It would be easier to bear if we liked our shipmates, and they liked us. But the Russians just don't believe in human freedom. The Germans are wild men who break out into a sweating rage every generation and try to kill as many as they can before they're stopped and put in a strait jacket. The Chinese have a low opinion of human life. The Jews won't eat pork. The Hindus won't eat beef. The aborigines of New Guinea eat their neighbors. And all the others think we are money-grubbing monsters. Yet none of us can afford to rock the boat. That's the fix we're in.

"So, Andrew, enjoy the simple pleasures. An evening breeze, champagne, a romp in the hay, a fifty-cent cigar. 'A little time for laughter, a little time to sing.' "

A telephone rang erratically in the press room. They ignored it. The shadows deepened and the breeze died.

The guard asked, "Mr. Moonan, you know the President very well. What do you think he will do about this war?"

He did, of course, know Malcolm Christiansen well. The Colonel would be surprised if he realized how much Mickie knew. They had met in an unlikely place, a camp clutching a wide edge of rock on a mountain. The mountain straddled Mindanao, southernmost island of the Philippines.

A war of sorts was going on. There were strong and differing opinions on the war. Only a few facts were available. There was a peasant uprising in the southern Philippine Islands. One of its leaders was the controversial young intellectual, Santiago Virata. The rebels were using guns stolen from government arsenals, surplus American mortars picked up from gun runners who will sell anything for cash, and some Czech rifles. This latter proved, of course, this was a Communist invasion of the Philippines, and was aimed at destroying the American position in the far Pacific, robbing the Standard Oil Company of California of its oil leases, the Dominican Order of its great estates, and overturning the rightful government. This was the seed sown by the Gill newspapers. The New York *Times* described this as a purely native uprising long overdue against a corrupt Administration and supported by the Obispo Maximo of the independent Filipino Catholic Church.

A Marine regiment was strung out along the Diuta Mountains

thanks in good part to Luke Gill. He was the publisher who had been described by President Thompson at a Gridiron Club dinner as "a frustrated Caesar in a checkered vest. His legions are under-paid minions who make up statements for stuttering Congressmen, and his arsenal is a forest full of wood pulp." (Mr. Thompson was too clever for his own good, even his friends admitted that.) Gill thought that wars were good for a people and a tonic to their blood—and, conveniently, wars sold newspapers.

The Philippine revolution stirred Gill's creative instincts. His Washington bureau wrote speeches for any congressman or senator willing to get a headline denouncing "this outrageous Communist invasion of a free country." When the Cardinal in Boston and Father Werther, the priest with such a television following, also demanded U.S. action, Gill knew his crusade was on its way. The Administration in Washington did not want to become entangled in a war, holy or otherwise. But to quiet the critics, it sent a Marine division to the Philippines. After all, the Philippine government had requested military aid; this was not to be a recapture of the islands and return to the days of Aguinaldo 60-odd years ago.

The Gill newspapers broke out a banner headline in red and blue, CRUSADE TO SAVE ASIA SAILS TODAY. Six months later, the war skidded into a minor catastrophe. The Filipino troops kept turning their arms over to the rebels and deserting. Flame-throwers and atomic cannon tore up a good deal of moun-tain landscape without routing the enemy. A popular singer, a Marine reservist, was killed by a sniper's bullet while defecating, and his admirers were outraged by this useless sacrifice. A news-paper photograph of weary troops moving out of battle on Christ-mas Day after a long and dirty siege sent thousands of letters raining down on Congress. Capitol Hill began muttering about calling off the escapade, and an investigation was proposed.

Luke Gill summoned his best reporter, Mickie Moonan, and in his high-pitched voice said, "Find me a hero. That's what we need. Americans never get enthusiastic about a war until they have a hero. Robert E. Lee was worth ten divisions to the South. The Confederacy wouldn't have lasted a year without him."

So Moonan set out as a modern Peter the Hermit, to arouse the populace behind the crusade. He did not go happily. He weighed too much to get around comfortably in bad terrain. He enjoyed steaks, good liquor, and well-dressed women. He distrusted battle-front sanitation. "A good soldier," he grumbled to the publisher, "is one who learns to adjust his bowel movements to primitive conditions. God knows how many Napoleons the world has lost to constipation."

The search for a hero was not easy. There was no St. George at headquarters in Manila. It was engaged in a valiant but hardly epic struggle to keep valuable gear away from thieves and the black market. So Mickie headed south, flying over forests, mountains and expanses of water. The position farthest in the heart of the rebel country was on a ledge of the Diuta Mountains. Here in an old Spanish fort was encamped the "Irish Regiment," so named for its colonel, one Dennis O'Brien. He seemed a natural hero to Moonan; adjectives burst on him even before he left Clark Field.

Mickie's plane glided between two mountains, pulled up, swung hard to the right and landed on a beautiful airport the Seabees had built at a cost of $10,000,000. He loaded his gear into a jeep and rode down a newly constructed highway to the front lines. He arrived at the old fort, a fat man sitting uncomfortably on the narrow seat of a jeep. He had a portable typewriter, a quart of Irish whisky for the hero, and a green flag with a harp on it. But O'Brien was gone, rushed down to Davao with a fever. The replacement was a Colonel Malcolm Christiansen, who had been stationed at the American Embassy in Tokyo.

A few minutes after Moonan came to the fort erected centuries ago ("Old Glory now flies from the ancient stone ramparts where the Spaniards brought their cross and civilization to Asia," he wrote), the brilliant sunshine was rubbed out by black clouds. The rain fell with the howling fury of an insane mob. Water dripped down the walls from the high, narrow windows of the fort. Lightning knocked out the generator, and kerosene lamps were lit.

Even in this gloomy setting, *Macbeth* in modern battle dress, Malcolm Christiansen had the smooth-faced, untroubled look of a man who, by one stratagem or another, has been able to evade the normal travails of life. He had a healthy, clean undergraduate look. Also an appealing frankness. He didn't pretend to be a military hotshot or a great mind. He had no very good idea why he or the Marines were there. It was simply an order, and he accepted orders without inquiry.

His chief of staff was the operator. He was a Jew, very ugly, very quick and perceptive, very smart. He had a plan—drop all the modern weapon gadgetry, train the whole regiment in guerrilla warfare, and attack the main rebel base in the valley below. He said, "The only way we can end this war is to capture or kill the brains running it. This requires surprise, and you can't surprise anyone when you advertise your advance with helicopters, flamethrowers and bombs. They just fade out into the jungle."

"You're putting all your eggs in one basket," Mickie said. "What if it doesn't work?"

The major frowned and cast a knowing glance at Colonel Christiansen. "Not a chance that it won't succeed," he said.

Mickie understood. The Colonel was one of those men who will undertake any danger so long as he does not fully comprehend its perils. That was all right with Moonan. He was not out here to assess character. But he had planted a shoot of worry in Christiansen's mind, and he asked the visitor, "Do you think there is a great risk in this plan?"

"Risk?" Mickie asked. "Colonel, without it you and I would not be here. It's the spirit of creation." And off Moonan went on one of the stories drawn from long hours of waiting in police stations and foreign hotels and press rooms. His stories had to be watched to be appreciated. There was the gradual swelling of merriment in his face and form and a series of light gleeful tremors. All this exploded with such a pantomime of mirth that his audience roared quite unmindful of the time, the place and the occasion. The Colonel was immensely pleased with Mickie. They became friends.

Colonel Christiansen told Moonan a good deal about himself in little spurts of confidence. He came from a small town in North Dakota. The big fellow in his life was his father. He was a blacksmith and a mechanic who repaired farm machinery. He had a strange streak in him. He was a pacifist, one of the same breed as Borah and La Follette and Norris and Lindbergh. That spirit pervaded the Western plains, and the boy grew up thinking that if only wars could stop the orchards of Eden would bloom again on earth.

From what the Colonel told him, Mickie could picture Nils Christiansen as a tall, stooping, gentle man who loved the world that lay outside the walls. The man and boy would drive across the prairie in an old Chevvy truck, and if the man saw a meadow lark or a stream or a woods, he would stop and show the boy.

Perhaps it was his wife that drove the man to the friendship of the out of doors. This was what the Colonel seemed to be saying without exactly spelling it out. She was determined. She had small horizons. She belonged to a small and angry fundamentalist sect. She was jealous of her husband's hold on the boy. The boy, man and wife fretted back and forth as two limbs on an old tree rubbing each other when the wind blows. In the end she shook the boy loose. Her family was active in politics, and she got him an appointment to the United States Naval Academy. So the pacifist's son went off to be a marine, not understanding why or the consequences.

Colonel Christiansen put little faith in his own ability. "I'm not the brightest guy in the Corps," he said apologetically. Then he grinned. "But I'm lucky. The luckiest man alive."

Then he told of the strange role of chance in his life. An amazing path, as the Colonel told it. He was an alternate appointment to the Naval Academy. The principal drowned canoeing in Devils Lake in a sudden storm. He was always at the right place at exactly the right time.

"You do believe in luck?" he asked Mickie with sudden earnestness.

"Why not? Something pushes us around, fits us into our places, and decides the race."

As they talked, Mickie kept wondering if this was the right man. Was he made of the dust from which heroes are created? Wasn't it Gerald Johnson who said, "Heroes are created by popular demand, sometimes out of the scantiest materials . . . such as the apple that William Tell never shot, the ride that Paul Revere never finished, the flag that Barbara Frietchie never waved." Time and chance did it. Plus a few other things—the shape of the face, the color of the skin, the depth of tone. Malcolm Christiansen was open-faced, light-colored and with a bass voice. This was the man who.

Moonan took the rough materials, and began creating the hero. All America remembers that dramatic story, reproduced later in the hit movie, *The High Road to Glory*, of the night of the attack. This was the moment just before the Marines plunged down the mountain trails and spread out in small guerrilla units. This was the dark of the moon, and the immense sky was filled with the million glories of the southern constellations. The Marines stood straight and tall. The flag fluttered in a slight breeze. (In the movie, the background music was heroic Wagner.) The camera followed the eyes of the waiting men of battle to the erect figure of their commander. Colonel Christiansen said, "Men, I have a few words to say to you. You will go shortly into battle. There are few brave men in the world, and there are few cowards. The average man takes his colors from the man next to him. These words were spoken by Teddy Roosevelt at San Antonio, and they are good today. We are all in this together. God bless you, and good luck!"

Mickie had written the script.

Actually there was little to the battle. The Marines surrounded the rebel base, having met no resistance, and opened fire. It made a great racket echoing in the valley an hour before dawn. The answer was a short and incredibly weak volley. The insurrectos were already defeated by the soldier's ancient curse, typhus. They had no strength or will to resist. This was not the way Mickie wrote the story, but then every writer must take his liberties with life, scrub off the dirt, doll her up, give her a song. He wrote of the clash of battle, of valor and victory.

Moonan's story—it won the publishers' annual award—was:

SOMEWHERE IN THE DIUTA MOUNTAINS, PHILIPPINE ISLANDS (delayed) —Two hours before midnight, 5,000 American heroes were born.

They stood at attention listening to the final words of their commander before one of the most daring attacks in all military history. They were farm boys from Iowa, kids who played ball in the crowded streets of New York, young Negroes from the cotton fields of Mississippi. All were members of the famous Irish Regiment of the U.S. Marine Corps.

Few of them, except a tough old master sergeant here and there, had ever heard a shot fired in anger. They were in a strange setting, a rich green upland jungle almost 8,000 miles from home. This is not a land where battles can be won by nuclear might and guided missiles, but a land where men's spirit and the will to fight for a just cause can triumph.

That spirit was given his men by Colonel Malcolm Christiansen, a hero with a heart. He is the son of a mechanic from the windswept prairies of North Dakota . . .

Mickie liked the phrase, "a hero with a heart." He could imagine the five-cent readers nodding their heads over it as they hung on the straps in the subway, munched their toast in Child's, or drank their coffee on Park Avenue. It didn't leave you. You caught yourself thinking about it with your foot up on the bar rail at Terry's two days later.

The remarks delighted and amused Colonel Christiansen. Not because he actually thought he was or would be a national hero, but simply because he was very much concerned with himself. He was not interested in anything that happened outside of himself. To make a fact important to him, it had somehow to be related directly back to him and his own well-being.

Mickie told him, "I'm going to put on the prophet's robe this once, Colonel, and tell you that the public itch for a hero is so great you can't miss. They'll be writing songs about you."

This struck Christiansen as so outrageously comic that he had Moonan repeat it to the officers' mess several times.

When the news reached the states, the Gill newspapers threw a banner headline across the front page—GREAT U.S. VICTORY—REBEL BASE CAPTURED IN DARING ATTACK. A crowd gathered in the crisp autumn night before the moving news signs on Broadway. A special thanksgiving mass was ordered in Boston. The American Legion post in Minot, North Dakota, opened the bar and gave free drinks. An enterprising florist announced a new "Christiansen Rose." A San Francisco bar created a cocktail, "Crusader's Choice." Congress rang with oratory. The Washington *Post-Times-Herald*, sedately pleased, editorialized, "Never Sell America Short."

When this news sifted back to the mountain fort, the Colonel accepted it as a gleeful prank of fate and Michael Moonan. He told Mickie, "Now—there are some people who bring you good luck. It's there all the time, you understand, waiting to be brought out, but it takes this other person to get it working. You bring me good luck, so you're either going to have to join the Marines, or you get me a job working for your newspaper."

The Colonel had no thought of the consequences of being a hero. Mickie did. The roar of the presses, the clatter of the tele-

type, the busy voices of the commentators might destroy this man.
It takes a certain deft agility to live up to the fiction written of
you, and few have the talent. But what is worst of all is when the
public grows bored with its hero, and he is nudged rudely aside,
and no one will listen to his interminable and desperate stories but
a taxi driver or a doorman or a bartender. Moonan had seen them—
the futilely angry Medal of Honor winner defeated for Congress,
the fat king once upon a time thrown out of Monaco because he
couldn't pay his gambling debts, the fabled beauty and mistress of
a dictator who couldn't even pick up a life guard now. Spoiled
eggs, burned toast, sour milk, bad gin.

There was one, only one, revealing incident in the Philippines.
This was the Colonel's interview with the rebel leader, Virata.
Christiansen was surprised to learn of his background, an honor
graduate of the University of California, a dramatist who had had
one play performed on Broadway. The Colonel remarked to a
group of reporters, "Why, this man should be on our team, with
all the advantages and so forth he's had."

The Baltimore *Sun* reporter said with a blandly innocent face,
"Colonel, why don't you try to convert him?"

So Virata was brought over to the clean and tidy Quonset hut
that was Christiansen's headquarters. The Colonel was playing the
role of the kind, forgiving father to the prodigal son. Eyes concerned and benevolent, voice tolerant, engaging smile. Virata
looked much younger than his thirty-two years. He was very
lean, soft-voiced, and with large, dark eyes.

Christiansen said, "I've looked forward to meeting you, Mr.
Virata. I've heard a good deal about you, and, of course, we
fought one another. You ought to be on our side, I mean the free
world, and tell the people of Asia of the benefits thereto, if you
see what I mean."

The kindly eye was expectant, the head nodded slightly to one
side in an attitude of friendliness.

Virata's liquid eyes focused on him in obvious disbelief. "You
want me to exhort the Asians in your behalf?"

The Colonel nodded graciously.

"I think we must first define the free world," Virata said. "Free
for whom? For you? Or for all of us?"

"Well," the Colonel said, a little perplexed by the question, "for
all of us, that's what I mean."

"You mean then that the United States will allow Filipinos to own their own resources and energy and production? To try foreigners who disobey our laws on our soil in our own courts? To choose our own allies, or to remain neutral in the world's struggles? To have control of our own air and land and naval bases? I do not think that is what you mean, or if you do, your superiors in Washington will not hear of it. Do you know what it means, Colonel, to give your life's toil to a master thousands of miles away who does not care whether you starve, because he cannot hear your moans in his penthouse? Do you know what it means to have every resource of your land controlled by foreigners? No, I do not think you do."

Virata was no longer a schoolboy, but a very intense man. The Colonel was alarmed, and his face flushed.

"You Americans toss us a little aid, and turn our land into a base for your military adventures. And because the books show we have accepted so many millions from you, and not what we have given in return, you believe we should be humble and persuade others to accept our lot. You have had your revolution two hundred years ago; now you have your own empire, and you want to sit back and enjoy it like a cat with a bowl of cream. But we in Asia have an unfinished revolution. It will not be ended until we rid ourselves of foreign bases and a colonial economy, and each of us has enough to eat. This is a fire that burns in Asia, and you cannot put it out with words or guns. You have not ended our revolution in the Philippines by capturing me, because it is all around you in the hearts of thirty million people."

His eyes were flashing defiantly. He said the words joyously. He breathed quickly. A change had taken place in Colonel Christiansen, too. His words came with difficulty as he said, "That sounds like pretty radical talk." He mumbled, "Socialism or communism."

The captive retorted quickly, "When will you Americans learn that what you call the backward nations are not the same as communism? We are simply asking for our place in the sun, too."

Suddenly, a great gorge of anger rose in the Colonel. He shouted, "Get out of here. Get out of here."

The Filipino looked at him scornfully, and held up his arms to be led out. Christiansen sat with his head bowed, unwilling to look at anyone. The others arose uneasily and left him alone.

## *Chapter* FIVE

A WEEK AFTER the victory in the Philippines, there appeared in the Gill newspapers a notice of interest to some 10,000,000 readers. It was a small box on the front page which merely said, "Madame Frieda Aubaret, the foremost seeress of our times, will prophesy the future of 'the hero with a heart,' Colonel Malcolm Christiansen. Exclusive in all Gill newspapers next Sunday."

Madame Aubaret was an example of Luke Gill's genius. She was a handsome, titian-haired woman who had tried acting in the movies and religious evangelism, and then found her own incomparable niche. She was the oracle of Hollywood. Stars who wished to find out if their public or their lovers would remain constant came to her. Producers in doubt about a new find sought her. Gill hired her to write three times a week for his newspapers, and invented a background for her that would have made Homer proud. At birth, a miraculous omen appeared on her cheek, a certain sign among the Indians of Peru, her native habitat, that she possessed the gift of prophecy. An ancient monk came down from his place of meditation in the Andes and taught the child all his mystic lore. Her list of predictions included the crash of two stars in the universe—it had been quite a show several years before —the flight of man to the moon, the mysterious death of the Russian dictator. All these had come to her as visions.

The three-times-a-week column was a monstrous success. Gill himself boasted, "Frieda's predictions have taken the place of advice to the lovelorn as the number one attraction in my papers. Sex is all right, but it can't compete with miracles."

A copy-desk man with a mild hang-over was the first to see her prophecy. He was assigned to tighten up her loose prose before it was set to print. He approached this chore with both cynicism and glee.

"Well," he said after the first reading, "our Pythia has sniffed too deeply of the steaming vapors of the cave. If the readers buy this, they will believe anything, and why am I toiling at a copy desk when I could be deluding them just as well as she?"

That Sunday, millions of faithful subscribers leafed back to the page opposite the want ads to read:

I have had a vision of our great new hero with a heart. I saw Colonel Christiansen striding straight and tall over the burned earth of our American hopes and dreams, and, lo, there sprang up green grass behind him. He walked straight toward some distant goal, and I strained my eyes to see. What was that shining white temple before him? Ah, at last I saw. It was our beloved White House, and I saw him walk through its sacred doors. Is this the ultimate destiny of the hero whom fate has chosen, just as another great leader was found in an obscure manger many centuries ago?

Luke Gill was delighted with the column, and told a staff meeting, "More people will talk about these paragraphs than anything the President says at his press conference."

The prophecy had an extraordinary effect on three men. One was Father Werther, the priest whose darkly shining eyes reached ardent and burning into the spirits of his huge audience. He was a little addicted to mysticism. It helped bridge so many gaps. Also, the Father had a hot and impatient fire of conquest burning within him. He wanted to lead a crusade against the dragon of Communism; he would walk barefoot over the Carpathian Mountains gladly if the troops would follow. But the troops were reluctant. Sometimes his rage was so great against those he felt stood in the path of holy conquest that the Bishop had to caution him gently. The Father decided after much meditation that the Crusade needed a political and military leader. True, he had many friends in political life, governors and senators who freely admitted his friendly mention of them was responsible for their sitting in high office. But none of them had any great sway over the public. This he had to gloomily admit.

But, ah, Colonel Christiansen was different. Here was a hero!

Here was one who had already matched his strength against Communism and won! And, there was this hint of divine intervention to lift him to the Presidency. Why not! Father Werther knelt in the cold, little chapel at dawn after a day of fasting—he found this was a great help to receiving inspiration—and awaited a higher wisdom. Yes, he would elect this hero and send him on the Crusade. Thus the world and the soul of Father Werther would be saved.

So on his next Sunday television program, the priest in his high, hypnotic tones praised the greatness of Malcolm Christiansen, "a leader sent to our wilderness." "If you feel that he is truly destined to restore the glory of America, tell your own local political leaders. Tell them this is one time the people will be heard," he cried, and this order remained like a lighted fire in many minds.

Jefferson Lawrence was not a follower of Father Werther. He was the best corporation lawyer in the United States, a small inconspicuous man with a near-bald head, and cold, rather lonely eyes. His grandfather's name was Lazarus, and he was a full-blooded Jew. His father's name had been changed legally to Lawrence when he entered Princeton. This was important only because it gave Jefferson Lawrence a sense of instability, of not knowing exactly where he belonged or what he believed in. Thus, he was constantly searching for a path or a leader. To him, military leaders had a vague aura of courage and nobility and he had served with a willing eagerness in the legal section of the Air Force during the last war. All he asked was to be allowed to wear a uniform. He was commissioned a captain, but it was embarrassing to send a mere captain to the Supreme Court with the Solicitor. The Air Force made him a brigadier general.

General Lawrence continued to follow military events with poetic faithfulness long after his uniform was put away. He gloried in the exploits of Malcolm Christiansen, and read all of Moonan's series entitled "A Hero With a Heart." When Lawrence chanced to read the prophecy of Madame Aubaret, he decided the time had come to act.

He called Silas King, and made a lunch date with him. King was chairman of the Manhattan National Bank, the largest financial institution in the world, and had been called by President Thompson "the rug peddler of monopoly." Silas King actually was underrated by the President. He was chairman of the political action committee of large-scale manufacturing and financial institutions. Ten to fifteen men touched base regularly with King, and their decisions usually guided the political thinking of the large corporations. He had been an assistant secretary of the Treasury under a Democratic President, but in later years walked on the other side of the street. The sun shown brighter there.

With the first cocktail, Lawrence asked amiably, "Have you found your candidate for President yet, Silas?"

King said, "You know damn well we haven't. I've looked over everything from the boy Governor of Delaware to the fossil who runs the House Ways and Means Committee looking for a dynamic conservative. The only true conservatives are old men with hearing aids. The young fellows are opportunists I would not let in the bank unless the vaults were locked and guarded."

"Have you ever thought of the military ranks? The American people cannot resist a hero."

"I don't know a single professional military man who can do much more than sign his name. I have hired them. You must employ a huge staff to tell them what to do."

Lawrence remarked, "What's wrong with that, provided, of course, you control the staff?"

King looked up from his drink and stared at Lawrence with interest.

"I can see you have an idea, Jeff," he said. "What is it?"

"Malcolm Christiansen, the Marine colonel the press is making so much over these days. He has immense popular appeal, and you are not going to get any fiscal or tax reform without this. Your President has to be above partisan politics and create at least an illusion of leading a crusade. Here, I think, is a Hercules or a King Arthur. Colonel Christiansen is certainly worth investigating."

"How do you propose that?"

"Have Luke Gill bring back this reporter who has been writing the articles about the Colonel. He can give us an idea whether he is a wild man, a radical, or subject to reasoned persuasion. If Christiansen passes this first test, one of us can talk to him and size him up."

Silas King reached across the table and shook Lawrence's hand.

The third individual aroused by the flimsy bit of newspaper prophecy was Senator Maze Bledsoe of Arizona. He was one of those who regards all other human beings as either stupid or dishonest. When he found one who fitted into neither category, Bledsoe was baffled and a hard glaze came over his large and shrewd eyes. President Thompson bewildered and thus irritated the Senator. Bledsoe had decided early that Mr. Thompson was not stupid, so he began searching with infinite patience for that chink in his armor. What was his particular lust—was it women or power or drink or money or friendship? Once he found it, Maze Bledsoe would be able to manipulate the President for his own considerable purposes. The secret remained hidden. Bledsoe's myriad projects were stymied for lack of a lever to use on the Administration, since the Senator was a Republican and the President a Democrat.

Senator Bledsoe had meditated, too. He decided while he sat in the barber chair having his fingers manicured by a plump blonde that he must frighten the President somehow. Then he would be more responsive to the lords of Congress.

The blonde manicurist said, "Say, did you see that prediction by that woman fortuneteller in the *Mirror*?"

"No," he said, admiring the well-rounded contours of the lady. "What did she say?"

"Well, this Madame Aubaret, she wrote that she had a vision and that Colonel Christiansen was going to be the next President. She saw him walking into the White House."

The Senator nodded his big head. When the barbering and manicuring was over, he pulled his huge frame out of the chair, paid for the services and walked out into the lobby of the hotel to get a copy of Sunday's newspaper. He turned back to the Aubaret column, and read it grunting to himself.

That afternoon, Bledsoe went up to Senator Elmer Wingate in the Republican cloakroom and said in his usually hearty manner, "Elmer, how would you like to nominate the next President of the United States?"

Senator Wingate, in the judgment of Bledsoe, was a man who lived in the gray area of not being very stupid or very crooked, but was not brilliant or free from temptation. He was, of course, glad to have Maze approach him. This meant that the Senator from Arizona wanted something done. Usually he paid well for his chores, since he was an influential member of the Appropriations Committee. An item for a harbor or a dam, not very great in itself, but important politically in a state, might become mysteriously unstuck if Maze was paying debts.

Senator Wingate replied he would indeed be delighted to name the next President.

"This is what you do," Bledsoe said. "Read this column of prophecy into the *Congressional Record*, and suggest that in all your wisdom Colonel Christiansen would make an excellent President."

Senator Wingate was pleased with this task. Usually no one paid much attention to him. The reporters regarded him as neither important or newsworthy, and he had been mentioned only three times in the New York *Times* in six months, and in one of those his name was misspelled. He recognized Maze's proposal would probably put him on the front page, perhaps even with a picture, across the country.

During a pause in the leisurely debate in the Senate that afternoon, Senator Wingate arose and asked for the floor. At this, he noticed painfully, ten senators quietly slipped out. Maze Bledsoe, however, made one of his unaccustomed appearances in the Chamber.

"The nation," Senator Wingate called out in his thin voice, "is in that perilous moment of doubt and uncertainty when it cries out, in the words of the great hymn, 'Lead thou me on! The night is dark, and I am far from home. Lead thou me on!'

"We need a leader to arise among us and point the way. I have scanned the faces of the great and near great looking for that leader, but each time I have turned away sad and disappointed. Yes, I have cried, 'Where is that leader who can command all our affections and who can unite us all behind him as Americans, regardless of political or religious faith?'" The Senator looked hopefully up in the press gallery.

One lone reporter sat in an attitude of absolute dejection. The correspondents in this wing of the Capitol were like a flock of geese, they flew with the leaders. If the New York *Times* reporter did not consider a debate or speech worthy of mention, the others bowed to this superior intelligence. He considered Senator Wingate an ass and said so when a gallery attendant disturbed his card game with news that the Gentleman was speaking.

One press-association man asked, "You got any text on his remarks?"

"No."

"Oh to hell with it then. If he can't get his material mimeographed and up here in good time, his prose will go unheeded."

Senator Wingate below went on bravely. "Now, the hand of God, it would seem, has shown us that man. He is defending our sacred way of life on a lonely battlefield. This is Colonel Malcolm Christiansen. I say let us, as one people, nominate and elect him to the Presidency. I ask that the column from the Washington *Mirror* be made a part of the *Record*."

The presiding officer glanced up from a letter he was writing in longhand to his daughter in college and said, "Without objection, so ordered."

The presiding officer had just scrawled out, "The most nonsensical things occur here. At this moment, Senator Wingate, an old political hack, is sawing away at nominating Colonel Christiansen for the Presidency. Isn't that absurd?"

The one reporter in the gallery took notes, simply because Christiansen was news at the moment. He knew if he did not pick up the story, some news editor in a tank town in the Midwest would complain to the AP. So he dutifully dictated four paragraphs.

Up and down the country, editors saw the story as copy boys laid the yellow ticker sheets on their desks. Perhaps they took big draughts from their coffee mugs, made profanely humorous remarks about the wisdom of senators, and clipped the item with their big shears. It would be sent to the back room as a "brightener," a cheerful or whimsical note to brighten the portentous load of death and taxes.

The story touched a deep current unsuspected by Washington. Housewives and mechanics and steel company presidents, troubled and frightened all, wrote letters to editors and to TV news announcers. A Texas oil man announced on a morning program, "Ah'm ready to plank down a hunnert thousand silvah cart wheels to get the ball rollin' for Cunnel Christiansen." A learned paper, "Colonel Christiansen, the Answer to America's Need for Hero

Worship," was delivered by Dr. Ralph S. Halintez of Johns Hopkins before the American Psychological Association. People who had never displayed any interest in politics found the names of their precinct and ward chairmen and insisted the party nominate Malcolm Christiansen.

The Colonel, happily, knew none of this. He was lying in a hammock listening to Mickie's stories or fishing in mountain streams. But there was a change in him, subtle and mysterious as the slow, delicious transformation from girl to woman. His companions noticed that when more attention was paid him—the cable of congratulations from the President, the visit of junketing congressmen to do him homage, the first trickle of mail—Malcolm Christiansen stood up straighter, his eyes were clearer, his voice firmer, his laughter more ringing. He began, perhaps unconsciously, to play a role others cast him in.

Moonan had no idea, really, of how the stew was simmering when he received the cable to drop everything and fly to New York. He accepted the summons with a curse for the whims of publishers who tossed reporters across the world and back again as another man would flex his arms. He was thus surprised when he was met at Idlewild Airport by Luke Gill himself, a small, incredibly dapper man with a waxed mustache, wearing a red waistcoat and derby. He had the hardly contained air of a small boy with a secret.

Mickie said, "If you are here to tell me you've started another war and are going to parachute me into Tibet, I resign."

Gill took him by the arm and said, "Come along, don't make a scene. People will stop and I will be recognized." Once in the waiting limousine, he announced, "You, Michael, have created the next President of the United States. What a darling slogan, 'a hero with a heart.' " He told Moonan of the concatenation of events.

Mickie asked, "What makes you think he will make an acceptable President, much less a great one? You don't even know him."

Gill replied unperturbed, "Some writer or other I read recently said, 'Greatness in the President is largely an illusion of the people.' You, Mr. Moonan, have created that illusion."

They went to lunch with Silas King in a small private dining room of the tower of the Chrysler Building. Jefferson Lawrence was there, and a fifth person Mickie did not know. He was a large, loose-limbed man who looked like the Iowa State basketball coach; he had a crew cut and wore a vivid tie. He was introduced as J. B. Glinnen, known as Jeebie. He was a professional political campaign director.

"What we would like to know, Mr. Moonan," Lawrence said, "is whether Colonel Christiansen has any unusual or radical political or social views?"

"He has spent most of his life in the Marine Corps, and they aren't allowed to have views. His is a clean slate. It's never been written on."

"Does he have any personality quirks or personal scandals?"

Moonan fixed his eyes on his questioner. "When," he asked, "did a personality quirk or a mistress ever keep a man out of the White House? You are not choosing a pastor for the suburban Presbyterian Church or the chairman of the board of a captive company. But, if it will relieve your mind any, the Colonel does not have fits in public nor has he developed a passion for Chinese whores."

"What a pity," said Gill. "Think what pleasures he has missed in life."

Lawrence said coldly, "We are not engaged in cataloging erotica. We are here for the serious purpose of finding a leader for a crusade to awaken the American people to their great responsibilities."

Mickie struggled with smothered laughter, then let it come out in a great burst of sound. He explained, "You are quoting from my third article, Mr. Lawrence."

At lunch Moonan told stories of Colonel Christiansen. When coffee was served, King turned the meeting over to Glinnen. He spoke in a curious mixture of labored phrases and happy vernacular.

Glinnen told them, "It is highly desirable in the age of television to have a guy, I mean a candidate, who makes a benevolent image. What I mean is the dolls have to like him. In Granddad's day, who cared how the Senator looked? If he had a voice like a foghorn that would carry across the county and could yell out those verses from Ecclesiastes and Hosea and acted like he had some brains upstairs, that rang the bell. He could be as ugly as

the barnyard bull, and most of them were. You just look at the
pictures of those senators, or Teddy Roosevelt. Then, they gave
the vote to the girls. That brought in sex with a big S. The first
President the girls helped elect was Senator Harding. He had
showy white hair, a hell of a profile, and what one of the writers
called 'a look of thoughtful earnestness.' And he had a mistress.
He gave the bloomer girls bedroom fever. The dames all went
out to vote, and they swept in old Harding like a bottle on a
wave. Let me look at my notebook, and I'll give you the figures."

He pulled a small black notebook from a pocket and went on,
"Here it is—It was the largest vote ever cast, twenty-five million
votes compared to eighteen million in the election before. Harding
got sixteen million, Cox nine. The biggest plurality in history. So
you see what we're really looking for is a guy, I mean a candidate,
to pull out that woman's vote. So we made some tests. We sent
teams out ringing doorbells of housewives, and polling women as
they left the offices. The question was, would you vote for Colonel
Christiansen for President? The results were highly gratifying to
your cause, gentlemen.

"Forty-eight per cent said right off they would. Forty-three
per cent said maybe, they didn't know, or why don't you invite
me to the bar around the corner and we can talk about it. Only
nine said they would not. Then, we hired the Psychological
Motivation Center to make in-depth studies of women's reactions
to Colonel Christiansen. In ten cities, they showed films of the
Colonel and then turned a flock of psychologists loose on the
girls. They received a distinctly libidinous reaction to Colonel
Christiansen."

"In other words," Luke Gill said, "when the women saw the
Colonel, they felt the mattress under their backs. This is as good
a reason to elect a President as any other, although I don't think
this was exacly what Thomas Jefferson had in mind."

Silas King said with an air of finality, "I think this establishes
Colonel Christiansen as an ideal candidate. Does anyone have any
objections?"

"Yes, I do," said Mickie. "Do you know the story of Phaëton?"
Lawrence nodded his head, but the others said they did not.
"Phaëton was the son of Apollo, the god of the sun. Phaëton
wasn't a god himself because his mama was a nymph. Phaëton

wanted to drive the sun chariot across the skies, and Apollo tried to talk him out of it; said it was a stiff drive with dangers all along the way. But Phaëton had his way. Before he had been gone an hour, he wished he had taken dad's advice. He lost his way. The horses dashed headlong on a wild course, plunging down toward earth and burning the cities and the forests and drying up the streams. Phaëton himself fell out of the chariot and was killed.

"Colonel Christiansen is not a god. A regiment is about his size. He can handle it nicely. And if he gets caught in a dilemma, he has a smart chief of staff he can always radio for advice. I'm not at all sure he could run the country well."

King replied brusquely, "A President should not have to manage the entire country. He can make the speeches, sign the bills, and keep the people in good humor. He has secretaries and commissions and brain-trusters to do the hard work. Government, I believe, should be operated as a dynamic corporation, efficiently, correctly, with a board of directors to create policy, and plenty of autonomy for branch managers. Your objection, Mr. Moonan, is overruled."

Glinnen said to Mickie, "Don't take it too hard, pal. I've never elected a governor yet that I didn't think I could do a better job in his chair."

They talked of organizing a boom. King would find financial backing for a "Crusaders for Christiansen" organization. The title was Gill's. This would be a volunteer group, well staffed by bright young men from industry. Its director, to give it political status, would be the senator who made the speech proposing Christiansen, for President. No one could remember his name. A way would be found, too, to encourage Father Werther. King said, "I have a vice president, named Donovan, with good connections in the Church, advises the Cardinal on financial matters."

The next day Moonan flew back to the West Coast on his way to the Philippines. The plane landed at San Francisco, and he had an hour-and-a-half wait. Troubled in mind, he wandered about the airport. He poked restlessly among the paper-back books. He stared at a new-model car without really seeing it. He looked at glittering gadgets. The relics of a sick civilization.

He was trying to convince himself that Presidents, Emperors,

Sheiks—they were all characters in a Gilbert & Sullivan operetta. What difference did it make how they spelled their names or parted their hair or held their liquor? The golden age of Greece came and went, Rome rose and fell. Alexander and Caesar and Napoleon died, mere dust in the history of man.

No, damn it, that was not true. Men did influence their times. He scuffed at an empty cigarette box on the tiled floor.

Mickie went to the shoe-shine stand inside the busy cave of the men's room. This was one of the sanctuaries where a man could be alone and think. An old Negro with a tired face stolidly polished his shoes.

Two men, their backs to him, were washing their hands. Number one said, "My wife and her girl friends are red hot for this Marine colonel. They think he's going to be President and save the world."

Moonan heard the sound of water splashing.

Number two replied, "I don't know where women get this damned idea. I don't like a military man myself in the White House. But we need a change, and I can't see Senator Fremont. I guess Chris is as good as any."

America, thy voice has spoken. Thy will be done.

Mickie asked himself, Do empires actually rise or fall for such small reasons—a woman's emotional reaction to a hero, a man's desire for change? Is this the curse of man, that he surrenders his fortunes to such minor winds?

He would tell the Colonel to hell with the crew of prophets and operators who wanted him in the White House. To hell with them!

## Chapter SIX

MALCOLM CHRISTIANSEN lay in his hammock furled in sleep. His lips were turned in a faint smile. The muffled noises of pre-dawn were all about him—the plaintive cries of birds coming awake, winds murmuring through the trees, the cooking detail up and clattering about the mess hall, all as though wrapped in a mist.

The Colonel awoke, and looked eagerly before him. The hammock was so arranged that he faced the east, the long, unbroken stretch of sea. From his height, he could witness the dawn. The sky washed now of the blackness of night was a little gray, as though a spring rain were falling. A luminous orange head moved slowly and cautiously above the horizon. Color flamed in all directions, lighting the sky with flushes, giving the water the cast of burnished brass.

This was the good life! Christiansen loved it with the passion of the contented lover. It did not upset his digestion. Here on the mountain was his first and only true mistress, nature. He could lie with her all day and listen to her whisperings at night. His companions were all men; this he appreciated. The Colonel did not trust women with their fussy ways. If they could come to your bed and go back to the harem, they would be all right. But no, they tried to take over your life. They talked too much. They cried. They hovered and patted. They spoke a strange tongue and they were forever laying their traps for men. He had no need here to watch out for their nets as he walked the woods.

Too, his duties were not demanding. He had no ambitions to torment him and only a few regrets.

Colonel Christiansen was sorry he had had to part as he did with his father. Every small-town railroad station reminded him of the incident, every sight of rain pouring in a sheet off eaves recalled it. But time and distance and contentment helped to hide this memory. He regretted his marriage to Ada Mae was not more successful, but this was not very unusual. He knew few men who remained happy with their wives. Ada Mae was a bright, pretty face he had looked at so long it had no more meaning to him than a billboard passed every day. He thought of her in terms of her voice. It was the endless honeyed drawl of the South.

The Colonel had been told of Madame Aubaret's prophecy, but he dismissed it as part of the mad carousel of journalism Mickie described in his stories. Christiansen had received letters as a result of Father Werther's telecast and Senator Wingate's talk. He turned them over to a lieutenant, his public relations officer, to answer. The Colonel read two of the letters from the priest's constituency; that was enough. They had an eerie, goose-flesh quality about them. Christiansen wanted nothing to do with violent views. They alarmed him, just as some of his mother's relatives did as a child. He would creep away from their loud, wild voices and rush to his room under the eaves or out on the prairie to hide among the tall stems of wheat.

None of these thoughts bothered him now. He sat up to watch the spreading sunrise. He remembered Mickie was returning today. That would be fun.

Shortly after noon, Moonan came down the road from the airfield like a charioteer. He stood up in the jeep, waving a new fishing rod he had bought for Colonel Christiansen in New York. The Colonel knew of his coming by the shouts and cheers of the men. They, too, regarded him as a mascot and bringer of glory.

When the absurd ceremony of presenting the rod and the great laughter was over, the Colonel asked Mickie how his business had been in New York. The reporter looked at him with a half-smile and said, "There are some men—when they see anything fresh and new—an uncut diamond from Africa, or a prayer wheel from a remote and inaccessible area of the Himalayas, or a strange whale-tusk carving by an Eskimo—they must have it. Not because they

are searching for any new forms of beauty. They are just collectors. They must have whatever is rare.

"I was with several of these collectors. One of them runs the
biggest bank in the world, another is the most important corporation lawyer in America, the third is the egotist who pays my
daily bread. They want you, Colonel Christiansen. They want to
pull you from your mountain." (The site of the camp had been
named "Mount Christiansen" by the Philippine Government.)

The solemn tone of the reporter's voice was so out of character,
the message itself so inexplicable, the Colonel said after a short,
dry laugh, "But why do they want me?"

"Each one would like to run the Government, but he has sense
enough to know this is impossible. So they want to have you run
it for them. In other words, they want you to be President."

"They can't be serious!"

"Very serious."

The Colonel stared at Mickie awkwardly, his mouth a little
agape. A sense of great disquiet disturbed him. The leaf torn from
the tree, tossed by the winds. Lost and separated from the sap that
bore me, from the trunk that gave me its strength, from the branch
on which I clung. Man is a tree. The sapling can be transplanted
or the boy sent off to school. Some problems of drainage and
adjustment, but the sapling usually lives. The tree grown has its
roots deep in the soil, the air and the rain and the sun are friends.
The routine of life is established. The raging war of adjustment
is over. You cannot dig up this tree and give it new soil to live
with, new air to breathe. He felt physically ill at this suggestion.
Little aches quivered in his stomach, just as the first day he showed
up at Annapolis.

"There is one way to end the talk," Mickie said sympathetically. "I can write you a statement disclaiming any interest in
politics and insisting you will not accept any political nomination."

Colonel Christiansen hesitated. Must the sailor swear in advance
he will not set foot on the island or touch the virgin thereon?
What purpose is there in sailing, if you must not go here or there
if the wind calls you?

Yet even deeper in his mind was another thought. It recalled
the strong, almost forgotten smell of kerosene and citronella, a
revivalist who preached one summer in the grove back of the

little frame church, the emotions of a boy tossed between fear and joy. The web of each life is spun; the threads cannot be broken. That was the message. You are a reaper, you a carpenter, you a fisherman, you a President. That is the ticket you were born with. Do not try to squirm and curse and try to evade your lot. The web is spun; the threads cannot be broken.

Moonan said, "More girls have lost their innocence from not saying no, than from saying yes. This is the time to call off the wolves."

"Oh, I don't know," Christiansen said plaintively. "I don't know."

"You don't want to be President, do you?"

"There are some things we don't understand," the Colonel said shortly, ending this line of conversation.

My God, Mickie thought, the way this fever strikes men. It turns country lawyers, small politicians, TV announcers, simple housewives, retired corporation presidents into raving, preening maniacs. Demos, where is thy sting? The urge to run for office, to carry the mace, to be addressed as "Mayor, Congressman, Mr. President." Now, here is this very decent fellow, innocent as a child, coddled from the facts of life by the United States Marine Corps, thinking he might be President, sit in that most uneasy of all chairs, breast the crashing waves of pressure and clamor and need and sheer orneriness. Perhaps, I could tell him what I have seen of men in the White House. Poor lonely souls, driven off their courses, sick of it and yet held on by a mighty fascination. No, how would he understand? How could he?

Moonan said, "If you want my advice, stand up and shout No."

The prospect dangled before the Colonel like a hypnotist's glittering ball. Showing this side and that, splendor and sorrow, good and evil, glory and pain.

When he was a boy, he lay on the cool green of a field in summer and looked at the universe. Such a trackless path, so infinite. Where will a boy's life take him before he is ancient? Over what seas, into what palaces? In this United States, any boy can be a millionaire and ride in a Cadillac or he can be President of the United States. And if he is President, he need not worry. He will receive Divine Guidance. That comes automatically with the office. Like a candy ball with every purchase over a dollar at the country store. And he thought of being President and riding in a big car, and getting his instructions in letters of gold print delivered by an angel.

So, half amused at himself, Malcolm Christiansen walked to the edge of the camp and stood alone staring at the southern sky. He waited and watched and listened for a word. A strangely moving feeling—what is it that comes over you in the presence of a vast mystery?—possessed him. And he took that for a word. It said yes.

But the next day, in the noonday brightness, he was not at all sure. He told Mickie to write out that statement and leave it at his headquarters. He would look it over.

So, while his thoughts were teetering back and forth on the edge, Ada Mae sent him clippings of Madame Aubaret's columns. Ada Mae took great stock in them. One column, and the Colonel little knew how much of it was prophecy, an editor's idea, a woman's feelings, said: "I have been asked, 'What will Colonel Christiansen contribute to mankind as President?' The message I received is that this man of the sword will restore peace to the world. I saw him approaching from down a long path, and he was heralded by a dove. It flew ahead as if to guide him . . ."

He accepted the miracle gratefully. Have you ever been lost in a fog with a platoon of men? A low branch whips at your face. Your foot stumbles in a hole. You hear the curses of other men through the thick air. But worst of all is the feeling of where are you going, where will you end up? And finally the gray curtain lifts and you see a path, and you know you've been going in the right direction all the time.

Now, Madame Aubaret was telling him that a leader is plucked out of the forest, and set in the right direction. Call it divine guidance if you want to. You don't buck this kind of thing.

The dove of peace. His father, his final entreaty. Malcolm Christiansen had been walking in the right direction all the time. Could he be sure, dead sure?

The Colonel asked Mickie, "Do you think this woman who writes those prophecies knows her stuff? Is she smart?"

"She must be. She makes a better living than I do."

"I don't mean that. Does she really look into the future?"

Moonan shrugged his shoulders. "Who knows what another can see. I can't get behind that veil. But I'm not going to say it can't be done ever. I'm Irish, and we all believe a little bit in magic."

Mickie arranged for the Colonel to meet her. He was flying to New York to receive the "Freedom Award," and could see her then.

On the flight, Colonel Christiansen felt an unfamiliar edge of excitement and elation. He had flown the ocean many times, indifferently, leaning back and falling to sleep, hardly noticing the toss of the seas, the sweep of the night. This time he saw such details as the fantastic play of light on the aluminum wings, the splendid gold of the sun, the cold glory of the moon. He had to talk, to speak, to share the mood.

"You know," he said, "when I was a little kid, my father took me to the state fair, and it was the first time I ever saw what was around me. You know, the way the wind brushes over a wheat field, damned beautiful it is. And the notes in a meadow lark's song; they're like the notes of a flute, you know if you've ever heard one. And the clouds were giant statues of ships and horses and things. That was the beginning of our friendship, my father and me. He loved the things of nature, and we'd go on walks along the creek, and he told me about birds and flowers. Every time I go out now and look for birds, I'm walking with him again. Those were some of the happiest times in my life.

"He was a wonderful man. Once you knew him, you never forgot him. I met a lady in San Francisco once, and she asked me if I was related in any way to Nils Christiansen in North Dakota. I said yes, and she told me, 'He was the kindest man I ever knew.' Those were her exact words. He got a lot out of life. He could sit for an hour watching the bees working on flowers."

The Colonel broke off into an abrupt silence. He ended it by asking, "Would you say a man was crazy because he was a pacifist?"

"No," Mickie replied. "I think we're all pacifists at heart. But when the band begins to play, most of us are afraid to be called yellow or tagged as a heretic, so we join the parade. For myself, I don't like the smell that comes off a field of dead men. I don't like the screams of the wounded out there in the night. I don't like to see a school hit by a bomb. Yet here I am."

Colonel Christiansen had not listened closely. He was too far gone in memory. He simply said, "My father was a pacifist."

The plane stopped at Hawaii for fuel. The Colonel was asleep. Moonan left to buy a newspaper. The headline on the Honolulu Advertiser was: BIG WELCOME FOR CHRIS PLANNED IN 'FRISCO.

The boys are really serious about it. They're going to make themselves a President, and don't spare the razzle-dazzle. Serve the people a new hero fresh from killing the infidels.

As the plane began lowering for San Francisco, Mickie told the Colonel, "There is going to be a crowd down there. For you. Plus an army of greeters and photographers and reporters. There will be a microphone set up for you to say a few words. So when you leave the plane, smile and wave your arm. Shake hands. Smile. They will lead you to the microphone. Look serious. Tell them you are happy to be back on the dear soil of America, and that the men who really deserve this welcome are the boys out there fighting for freedom."

Christiansen had a moment of fright. Maybe this was a horrible mistake. He wet his lips nervously.

"Oh for Christ's sake," Mickie told him, "get out there and smile."

His legs carried him to the open door of the plane. He heard the sound of the crowd shouting and Mickie behind him saying, "Wave your arm." His arm went up. His mouth twisted into a timid smile.

What Malcolm Christiansen saw before him was a bright blur of faces in the late afternoon sun. He heard a sound like that of a heavy wind moving through the tops of a mountain forest. First plaintive and remote, and then, as it moved closer and swelled in volume, with a song of its song. It could be a roaring, raging chorus or strangely gentle. What he heard now was a new song. The voices were human. A long sigh moved swiftly through the crowd and exploded into cheers.

The effect on Malcolm Christiansen was as though he had been touched by a live wire. Startling. Thrilling. No man, no woman had ever called him so, had needed him so, had been so unafraid of its passion.

Moonan watched the timid smile come alive, grow warm and exciting. My God, he told himself in awe, this fellow really has it. The touch. Other men would have crawled on their bellies across the burning embers for it. Clay or Taft. But fate hands it carelessly to Malcolm Christiansen. He is the Messiah.

Mickie wondered with an odd start if this was the way Rome fell, when men lost their faiths in themselves to govern, and called upon an idol to rule them.

The party, greeters and Colonel and photographers, moved to the accompaniment of an American Legion fife-and-drum corps to the roped-off area where the crowd had gathered. The cry began anew. Hands applauded tirelessly. Voices cried out. Like swells in the sea, each one louder, each one drawing a deeper draft of desperate hope and joy from the crowd. Colonel Christiansen waited, the priest before the altar listening to the divine voices, until the applause flagged. Then he waved his hand for silence and said, "I am happy to be back on the soil of my beloved America. But your cheers really belong to the men back there on the mountain who did the fighting for freedom. I was just their commanding officer."

The thunder of acclaim boomed again. Modest Hero! Leader of Noble Men! Re-creator of the American Dream! Hail, all hail to thee!

Malcolm Christiansen rose and soared in spirit, cut free. No longer bound to the little rut of life most men must follow from cradle to grave. This must be another sign. God was sending his signals and he was receiving them sweet and clear. This was the role He had picked, letting him wind his way up the slow side roads. Now, here he was out of the fogs and mists of the lowlands, up on the clear heights where the ranges stretch like giant waves forever.

Colonel Christiansen smiled on the crowd. An editorial writer that night pondered over "the glimpse of heaven that comes with the Colonel's smile. It is out of this world."

He walked through the airport, aware of people pausing to stare at him, of little bursts of applause following his steps and drowning out the announcements on the loud-speaker system. Ticket agents simply put down their telephones and gazed. Redcaps halted. Hurrying passengers suddenly froze.

A man moved out of the throng and, stopping before the Colonel, said awkwardly, "I thank you for protecting my boy. He is Private Pedersen, and he is in your regiment. You will protect us all, the way you took care of him. God bless you!"

The photographers moved in quickly, and the air was bright with their flashes.

Mickie noted, The myth is growing. A disciple appears and reports a miracle. Christiansen has protected an American boy from the bullets of the enemy, the diseases of the area, and the travails of military life. Not God, not the Marine Corps, not the boy's own constitution and good luck, but Malcolm Christiansen.

The Colonel thanked the man, but Moonan saw that he seemed a little pale and shaken. He stepped quickly up to Christiansen and said, "What was it?"

"That man, he looked like my father."

The reporter looked back. A lean, blond man, might be a farmer or small-town machinist, the look of uncluttered space, gentle eyes. You could find a thousand like him a few miles up the coast in Washington. A coincidence.

But not to Christiansen. Not in his exalted mood. This was another sign.


The Colonel had lunch at the Union League Club with Silas King and a small group of his friends. Ordinarily, he would have felt meek in the presence of a Silas King. He was Success, the sweet, sweet American ideal. He must be worth at least a hundred million dollars, wouldn't you say? And he made it all himself, didn't have any part of it handed on by Daddy. He moved and talked with confidence and energy. When he said, "I talked to the chairman of the Fed Board this morning, and I think there will be some relief on the interest rates," the others nodded their heads solemnly as if this was the best of all possible oracles of finance.

King shook Christiansen's hand heartily, and said, "Colonel, you've given America a damn well-needed shot in the arm. We have been slipping back on the road to debt, the welfare state, and higher taxes. We were too tired to fight. But, you've been an inspiration, by God. We feel that with a man like you at the helm, we could get back on the highroad again."

Colonel Christiansen accepted this calmly and with a pleased smile. He no longer saw himself as Malcolm Christiansen, a just-fair Marine officer who would be lucky to get a star before he retired. He was a blade plucked from the rank field of mankind.

He was a savior who could feel about himself the warm cloak of, what do you want to call it, luck, divine guidance, the golden fleece. These princes might well come to him with their frankincense and myrrh. He liked Silas King. He was a real fellow. Some of the others were a little pompous, and all they talked about was net profits and depreciation allowances and per-man output. But King found out the Colonel liked fishing, and they had a good time comparing notes. The banker said the first moment they had time, he wanted to take the Colonel south to his place on the ocean where the surf fishing was, well, you couldn't describe it; you just will have to come and see for yourself. But imagine it, standing knee deep in the warm surf at dawn, casting your line far out, and the exciting struggle with the fish. Hell, that's sport!

Christiansen reluctantly was pulled into a conversation about the size of the Federal debt. Abominable, wasn't it? Now, what do you think, sir, would be a good method of reducing that mountain?

The Colonel half laughed and replied, "Well, that isn't in my field, and all I know is what it takes to run a regiment. But I'd say this, it will take leadership and inspiration just like anything else to cut down this Government spending, and I think you gentlemen could make a very good example."

What was that?

"If the companies doing business with the Government would figure out real closely how much it costs to make the product and pay their men and their bills and their debts, and then turn the rest of the money from the contracts back to the Treasury, I think that would be pretty big."

There was an awkward silence in the richly paneled room. The motor manufacturer, a tall man, looked curiously at the Colonel as though he were an animal in the zoo. The steel man lifted his eyebrow. King slapped Christiansen on the back and said, "Now, you leave the Colonel alone. He isn't an economist. He's a public symbol. What is important is that he have the right kind of people around him. Right?"

The others nodded.

"What we need in this country is a change at the front office, and the one man capable of making that change is our guest."

Christiansen knew he had said something that made the others restless and a little shy. But he knew, too, deep down and with a sense of confidence and joy, that these people needed him. They would have to come to him and put their offerings before him. This did happen, too, before the luncheon, the good steak, the fine cigars, the wine, was done.

The steel man said, and they all grew still, left their discussions of capital gains for the nonce, "Colonel, I think we can be frank. We want you to be the President of the United States. We think you are the only man alive who can persuade the people to support a sound economy. We can offer you our almost unlimited backing for the nomination and election. We can provide for you the best brains in management to run the United States Government. We can guarantee a favorable attitude on the part of most of the press and the radio and television. No man ever had such an opportunity before. Are you with us?"

He was, of course. But he wanted to play with them, just as the woman does her lover. He smiled at them as they sat straining for his answer, letting their cigars burn.

"Gentlemen," he said, "you have paid me a great compliment by suggesting I be the President of the United States. But I am only a soldier. I know nothing of running a Government. I have had no training in it. I am sure you can find someone better prepared for this big job, and let me go back to my pasture."

He was besieged again by their entreaties and arguments. The passionate lover was swearing his devotion. The Colonel's leadership and inspiration was what was most needed to arouse America. He could call upon business, manufacturing and finance, press and radio, advertising to provide him with their finest brains. This they would do gladly. This would be a crusade in which all America would join. In the end, he said he would consider this, and there was applause and toasts. The seduction was well under way, heigh ho, to the mutual pleasure of all concerned.

The next evening at a reception prior to the awards dinner he met a great many more people. Silas King kept bringing them up—the president of a great labor union, a university president, senators, the Chief Justice of the Supreme Court. It seemed to Christiansen that he was a witness at his own birth. A new Malcolm Christiansen was being born, one who had only a physical bond with the baby grown to a child and a boy in North Dakota, and a man in Marine uniform. This was Malcolm Christiansen, the President of the United States. He could see the new man in the deference on their faces, their obsequious remarks, their quick smiles at his every word. This would never have happened to the old Malcolm.

As they were about to move into the banquet hall, King whispered to him, "There's a chap here who could be a great help to us. Has a large following. Father Werther. Has a television program. Don't guess you ever saw him. A little queer. But be nice to him." He gave the Colonel a friendly pat.

Father Werther was a short, round man with a large head and a fantastically gloomy air, as though he spent his life in the farthest reaches of a remote, sunless forest. But when he spoke, the gray unlit screen of his face became bright with action. The action would be one of those ferocious dramas of hate and primitive justice in the Old Testament; you sensed that before he finished a sentence.

He shook the Colonel's hand limply, as if this gesture were totally unimportant. He launched out, with no invitation or prompting into bitter words, "Colonel, there can be no peace until every soul is saved from communism, brought back to the Church. The communists must be destroyed, burned out, dug out until the earth is pure again. But my voice is not enough. Would you believe it, there are men who wear my habit who see no sin in what they call coexistence. Colonel, you must join me on the crusade."

Christiansen was surprised by the violence of the man's words. He unconsciously backed away while saying, "I can assure you, Father, that I agree with you that communism is indeed an evil and must be taken care of, and I want to talk with you at some length about this."

The award dinner was in the large banquet hall. Colonel Christiansen looked down on an immense sea of faces. After the baked Alaska was eaten and the dishes removed, the lights dimmed. Chairs scraped around to face the stage. The house melted to fitful coughs. The Chief Justice introduced "the hero who has added new luster to the stars of the United States . . . who has exhibited the same leadership and courage as George Washington at Valley Forge."

Malcolm Christiansen came to the rostrum. This was his first major speech, his first step as the new man. In truth, he felt a momentary uneasiness, as if he were shaking internally. His mouth was suddenly dry. He wondered in a flicker of panic if he were the usurper, and would be damned for the arrogance of his crime.

The applause began. It was a clap of thunder to revive the spirit. Then, the downpour. Stand in it, be drenched by it, breathe it, glory in it, lift your face to it. It was in this mood that Malcolm Christiansen began, a slight tremor of emotion in his voice:

"Ladies and gentlemen, freedom is the soul of our nation." (Pause, damn it, pause—that was what Mickie said. He made a black mark there.) "From this spirit has flowed our American progress, our strength, our prosperity, our devotion to God. When it is restrained, life loses its joy and meaning. Freedom is the right of men to choose their own worship, their own leaders, their own way of life, their own livelihood." (Pause, count one, two, so the applause can roll up.)

The writer of the speech, Mickie Moonan, stood in the back of the hall. He said aloud, "Gorgeous claptrap." People nearby glared at him ferociously.

"Freedom in our time is endangered by a philosophy which demands that the state, and not the conscience of the individual, control all and give all, and that its officers be endowed with the powers of a Pharaoh. With this, I emphatically disagree . . ."

A rally of hand-clapping moved across the hall like a gale.

". . . Out on the plains where I was born and raised, we were taught that each man was his own master and responsible as such to God . . ."

Halfway through the speech, a complete silence drenched the hall. Even the waiters came and stood quietly around the walls.

". . . Mankind's goal must be peace, freedom and security for every man. With God's help, this will be done."

The audience sat enchanted, hardly knowing the end had come. Then it scrambled anxiously to its feet shouting and applauding madly. The savior has come to free us from our worries, bombs, cancer, airplane accidents, juvenile delinquency, racial trouble, pregnancy, old age, bad breath, piles.

Colonel Christiansen stood smiling in the glare of the floodlight.

He was buoyant with the rapture that comes when speaker and addressed have reached the height of excitement and adoration that lovers know.

Moonan stood in the rear of the hall. His hand trembled as he tried to light a cigarette. What have I done? he asked himself. Who do I answer to?

## Chapter SEVEN

THE WAVES of applause grew fainter. Mickie thought of the tide moving out to sea. The spotlight was turned off and the center lights on. Only a few desperate claps of applause were left. Chairs scraped. The audience began flowing slowly and awkwardly, some to the platform, the others out the exits.

Moonan stood against the wall. He watched Christiansen greeting those whom Silas King introduced to him. The fellow had it, that was all.

A familiar voice said to him, "Splendid man you have there. The stuff out of which American legends are made . . . the Anglo-Saxon face, a touch of homespun, a military hero whose victories are vaguely fictional, experience nil, intellect if any carefully concealed. Top it off with a speech-writer who has a middle-class mentality."

It was, of course, Jerry Branson. They had covered together the fighting in Africa, the Argentine revolution, riots in Paris, a lynching in Mississippi.

"Your man is in," Branson said. "The people are tired of brains and the truth. An unfortunate combination."

"What are you doing here?" Moonan asked.

"Came to observe the opulates invest a new idol. Very interesting group—the opulates. They have a deep and touching faith. In money. Nothing it won't do. It will save your soul, enrich your sex life, hide your warts, keep you alive long past your span. They have a simple test for picking candidates for public office. Do you believe in higher interest rates? Only one answer accepted."

The next day, Colonel Christiansen was initiated into the profane mysteries of politics. The ceremony took place in King's office, a place of rich, mellow, polished wood and the aura of good cigars. No one asked the Colonel whether he wished to run for the Presidency. Silas King spoke with a briskly confident air that did not allow any uneasy questions.

"Your only opposition at the convention will be Senator Frank Fremont."

"From Nebraska," Glinnen offered.

"Only a limited following. Too old-fashioned. We will have the delegates sewed up. The nominating process, Colonel, is much like a proxy fight. If you are well organized, have an attractive product, an aggressive air, and sound financing, you can't be beat. We gear our campaign to winning over the delegates who control the most votes. We won't worry about the man from Latimer County, Oklahoma; let Fremont have him. Our targets are in New York, Pennsylvania, Ohio, California, Texas, Illinois, Michigan—the big chunks.

"Now, no delegate is an island. He has strings to him. His local political organization, home-town sentiment, and the way he makes his money. Take this Union County delegation. The chairman is in the construction business, and gets contracts from the state and county. The Governor wants to be re-elected; he doesn't have much popular following, so he wants a name on top of the ticket that will pull him in, too. 'The hero with a heart' is just what the doctor ordered. So the Governor sends word to the contractor that if he wants to get the road contracts, he will be for Christiansen. And when he goes to the bank to finance a loan for new equipment, the president tells him his friends in Wall Street are very strong on Christiansen. They think he will cut down the cost of government and reduce taxes."

The Colonel said, getting very much in the spirit of the ceremony, "Well, I'd sure like to cut taxes. Do you think that's possible?"

"Certainly," replied King. "We will reach an understanding with Russia and reduce the military budget by at least fifty per cent. There is your tax reduction."

"Will you campaign on that issue?" Mickie inquired.

"Look pal," Jeebie Glinnen said scornfully, "you don't use issues any more. That's old-fashioned. Who in the hell wants to hear the Colonel talk about taxes and aid to black savages in Africa or farm payments? They're sick of this crap. They want this guy to get out there and tell them things are going to be O.K."

Glinnen wanted to know the Colonel's political background.

"Well," he replied with a smile, "it's pretty mixed up. I only voted once. That was in South Carolina, and I registered Democratic down there so I could vote for a friend of Ada Mae's. My father was a Progressive, I think that's what they call them. My Mother's father was the Republican committeeman for North Dakota."

Luke Gill thought that was perfect. The ideal candidate. He could bring in Democrats and Progressives to the safety of the Grand Old Party. He had a slogan, too.

"We should give this campaign a spiritual touch," Gill said. "There is a fantastic number of people who go to church and like the spiritual touch. We'll call the campaign 'the Christiansen Crusade.' Salvation, serenity, and lower taxes."

Colonel Christiansen and Mickie were driven uptown by King's chauffeur. They sat in silence for several blocks. Mickie said a little savagely, "You don't owe Silas King or Luke Gill or J.B. or me a thing. Not a frigging thing."

"What are you talking about?" the Colonel asked.

"If you want to be President, and God knows why you should, you don't need any of us. We're just leeches you picked up in the shallow water. Don't fool yourself that Silas King is interested in a crusade for anything but a sound dollar. It's a common obsession with bankers. If King or Gill, either, read Matthew lately, they would regard Jesus as a troublesome radical and Pilate as being too soft. They are glad the Declaration of Independence is old enough to be regarded as an antique. Jeebie wants to put his thumbs under his suspenders and tell how he elected a President. And I enjoy my boasting, too. I think you ought to know what kind of a medicine show you've joined."

The Colonel said, "You newspaper fellows are always looking on the dark side."

"Perhaps we've seen a little more of the dark side of man," he replied. "Did you ever sit in a police station on the lobster trick and watch the humanity roll in? Or see an informer pouring out his guts? Have you ever covered a race riot? Did you ever see a hungry mob trample the young and the old in a rush for food? When you are President, you'll get a whiff of the rank smells of the world. And you'll burn candles to take the smell away, turn on the air conditioning, pour yourself a drink, but the smell is still there."

Colonel Christiansen said uncomfortably, "Mickie, you sure got up on the wrong side of bed today. You need to laugh. I know what the medicine is. Tell that story again. The one about the gangsters and the Yiddish jokes."

# Chapter EIGHT

AN AIRPLANE swooped gracefully in the blue skies over Chicago trailing a cloud of white smoke behind it.

People stood along the street and at the lake front's crowded beaches watching.

"What do you think it is?" a lady asked the man at the outdoor flower stall. The airplane had just executed the sign of a cross in the still sky.

The man, a little, dark Italian, said, "Don't know, ma'am, but it might be an ad by the Jesuits to get the people back to the churches. They're very smart."

The plane dived like a hawk on a downward air current and began spelling out in huge letters "Join the Crusade." There was so little wind the letters stayed remarkably in place. The lady nodded, cheerful and birdlike. "Oh, we know now," she said smiling on the florist.

Two teen-age boys swam out to the float, pulled themselves up and watched the exhibit. "Boy," one of them said, "those Chris people really put on a show. Did you hear about the one they had for the delegates at the Blackstone Theater last night? Bud Dent, you know him, got a delegate's badge from a drunk in a bar and went to see it. Some of the best figures in Hollywood out on the stage flouncing their tails and singing jingles about Christiansen."

In one of the small, poorly-lit bars on a side street not far away from the hotels, a bartender listened indulgently to a debate. A lean, tailored individual wearing a stunning blue button with gold writing, "Christiansen Crusader," was arguing with a broad-faced Western type whose celluloid sunflower had the slogan, "Fremont, Flower of the Prairies."

"Look, my friend," the Crusader said patiently, "how is it possible for this Fremont fellow to win the nomination? Nobody wants him. Colonel Christiansen has blazed through ten primaries, winning every one of them. You can't tilt the blinds shut on that, you know."

The Fremont flower said loudly and belligerently, "You stole them. You had all the press and TV on your side, hammering out all the time about that God-damned hero with a heart, and not a word about what a job Frank Fremont was doing in the Senate. But I'll tell you who is for him. It's the fellows who have labored in the party through all the bad years while you johnnies were making money and hobnobbing with Democrats. We are the party!"

"You *were* the party," the Crusader corrected him blithely. "The old order changeth."

A river of people flowed through the two floors of the Crusade headquarters. They came up the crammed hotel elevators, and they tramped up the stairs. They consumed gallons of Coke, they picked up thousands of buttons and pamphlets, they talked to anyone who would listen, and they rested their tired feet in countless chairs and couches. Big men in Western hats looked for familiar faces and when they found them, boomed out, "Remember me? I'm Jim Haston from down near Stillwater. Met you at the Sheriffs' Convention. Remember the Little Red Bar and that stripper?"

Shortly after midnight three press-association men and Moonan played bridge in an alcove of the Crusaders Press Headquarters. They were just off the big ballroom where reporters, college students and other uninvited guests visited the bar—the whisky was all gone—and watched the television set.

A tall, rumpled, angular white-haired man with a somewhat wild look came into the alcove and demanded urgently, "Do any of you gentlemen know how I can reach Malcolm Christiansen?"

The dealer answered, "We are not gentlemen, and I understand the Colonel is in a private conference with the Divine Spirit."

The old man said, "I am his Congressman, Edmund Kunkel of North Dakota, and I have an important message for him."

"You can give it to me," Mickie said. "I work for him."

The Congressman hesitated, looking doubtfully at Moonan, and then his words poured out, rushing all together, "I want to beg Malcolm, I've known him since he was a little boy in knee pants, I want to ask him not to do this to Frank Fremont. The Senator is the great hope for America. He's the Moses of the conservative movement, and he's worked hard and with no rewards. When the Easterners gave up, Frank kept the party going. No man is better prepared for the White House. I have a proposition for Malcolm. I want him to step aside and be Frank Fremont's Vice President. I'm sure it can be arranged."

"What's the matter?" the dealer asked. "Don't you believe in General Motors and the Mellon bank? Six hundred millionaires can't be wrong."

The Congressman stared at Mickie. Mickie said, not unkindly, "I'll tell the Colonel of your message." Representative Kunkel left as abruptly as he came. The game went on.

The dealer asked, "Mickie, how did you ever let yourself get mixed up in this outfit?"

"Look at the interesting types I meet. Congressman Kunkel, the John Brown of the old guard . . . Father Werther, a hair shirt with a Cadillac . . . Senator Wingate, the Cicero of the Senate men's room . . . Larry Sweeny, rajah of the labor movement, willing to trade a wage increase for a country club membership . . . Professor Enger, brains for hire—he'll prove anything you want by a guaranteed mathematical formula . . . Mrs. Emily Jones Hamptson Green, eternal womanhood, outlived three husbands, still in the market, funds unlimited . . . Solomon Johnson, public benefactor, turned his thefts or a portion thereof to public works. Endowed the salon of the fanciest whorehouse in Dallas and a Baptist Divinity school."

The dealer asked, "How soon are you going to wrap up the nomination? I'd like to get one good night's sleep."

"Patience," said Mickie, sagging in his chair. "There have to be some conversions. But I have faith in Silas King. How can you lose with a man who has a line on every mortgage in the country?"

Upstairs in the penthouse, Silas King and the president of a steel company were talking to the Governor of Pennsylvania. The conversation was reasonable and leisurely, and carefully skirted the edges of politics. The men drank an extremely good blend of Scotch whiskies King had made up especially for him. The Governor was in good humor. He had agreed to accept a law case that would mean $40,000 a year for at least six years after he left the statehouse in January.

Not a word had been spoken of the crucial Pennsylvania delegation.

Silas asked benignly, "Governor, what do you think of our man Christiansen? We want your honest opinion."

The Governor accepted a light and blew out a small cloud of cigar smoke.

"I've always said he had great political charm. But I have a lot of hard-headed Dutchmen to convince. Will he stand by the party? Will he have reliable men to advise him?"

The steel company chairman said, "Dan, I think you know me and what I stand for. I am completely convinced that Colonel Christiansen would be the kind of President we've all been dreaming about through these God-damned years of the welfare state. What particularly convinces me is that Silas King is going to be chairman of the board of the next Administration."

King looked at his watch and said bluntly, "Governor, when do we get your delegates?"

The Governor answered, "When do you want them?"

"On the first ballot."

"All right."

They all shook hands solemnly.

In another room of the penthouse suite, Senator Wingate and Jeebie were talking to the National Committeeman from California.

"Damn it, Bert," Jeebie said, "you know that a third of your delegation isn't worth what you're asking. We can't give you the job of Attorney General. We can pick up more delegates than that with the Postmaster General, and he doesn't do anything but pass out mail."

"But think of the psychological effect that early in the voting. California is fifth and the first big bag of votes."

Senator Wingate said, "Your price is too high."

The Committeeman sighed vocally. "I should take my hat and go," he said plaintively. "The Fremont crowd will give me anything up to Secretary of State and polish my shoes and cut my hair in the bargain. But I love this Christiansen."

Jeebie remarked scornfully, "Those fellows with Fremont ain't going to have the chance to give away anything, and you know it, Bert. You'd better come along with us while we're still passing out coupons."

"I'm going to make undying enemies for this, but what about half of our votes on the first ballot? I just can't go any farther. What do I get?"

Senator Wingate looked at Jeebie. "How about Secretary of the Air Force?"

At two o'clock in the morning, King and his leading agents met in the penthouse for a count of delegate strength. The windows were opened to blow the tobacco smoke out. The men sat for the most part in their shirt sleeves. King had his rolled up like a gambler at the dice table.

When each had reported, Jeebie—adding up the strength—shouted, "We're over the line, boys. There won't be a second ballot. We got it."

The cheers were moderate. They were too tired.

Luke Gill commented, "The stage is set. The lines are written, the lights turned on. Bring in the hero, innocent and pure, in his shining armor. I suggest our theme song be, 'Onward Christian Soldiers.' "


Malcolm Christiansen was at that moment sleeping in the guest cottage of a large estate near Lake Forest. He was unaware of any of the stratagems executed to win his nomination. He lay secure in the belief that a great call for him had sprung passionate and demanding from the people, and the Grand Old Party was responding like a lover to the kiss. He did not watch the struggle of the nominating and balloting the next day. While the nominating speeches were made, he was sailing on Lake Michigan in a catamaran. Thus he missed the bitter and even tearful denunciations of the "Christiansen steam roller" and the "hypocrisy of calling this black operation a crusade." These words, of course, came from the Old Guard.

He took a nap after dinner when the balloting began. He awoke about nine o'clock and strolled along the lake front. The night was warm and close, and he stood letting a slight breeze cool him after a short walk up the beach. A new moon was over one shoulder, but far out on the lake lightning flashed through clouds. He watched the distant darkness suddenly become brilliant with flashes of color and fade abruptly like the flames of a mighty forge. The Colonel was so absorbed by this sight that he no longer felt a part of the world, and, in truth, this was to him the ideal state—to be able to see without taking a part in the distant conflict of nature. He would not want to be in this storm, forced to flee under cover from its pelting rain or counting the seconds between the flash and the thunderous clap. He wanted to be right here on the pebbled shore of a calm lake feeling a light breeze on his face.

The convention and his role in it seemed far away until his host came looking for him with a flashlight. He shouted, "Congratulations, Colonel! You've been nominated. They want you at the hall."

There was a dull boom of thunder far out on the lake. A distant flash of lightning briefly lit the dark sky. The water lapped softly against the sandy shore. A gull swooped screaming from the left. The wind blew warm and gently. An airplane droned overhead. But these were but background impressions, hardly felt at all. Malcolm Christiansen experienced a joy so fierce he might have been a sleeper awakened by the sting of a wasp.

By God, I made it!

His host was plainly startled by the look on the Colonel's face. He led the nominee back to the house. A helicopter was waiting on the paved area in front of the garage. Christiansen put on a dark civilian suit and with Ada Mae and his host climbed aboard. His typed acceptance speech was in a loose-leaf notebook on his lap.

"How do you feel, Colonel?" his host asked.

He shook his head. There were no words he knew to describe his joy. It was so uncertain a visitor, a butterfly fluttering on a bush, that any word might drive it away.

The helicopter whirled aloft. The city below was an electric flower garden, beautiful and dangerous. One miss in the engine, and a plunge down into the garden of lights. He thought how close we move to disaster at times. Yes, even Malcolm Christiansen. Desire and fear mixed in the same sweat. Adultery in the high grasses of a sand dune. His passion and the major's wife. How bright her image was at this moment. It stayed with him until the helicopter landed safely on a roped-off area behind the huge convention hall.

Policemen struggled to hold back a crowd. Their hands were locked in a human chain, and their faces were sweating and intense. The Colonel stared at the crowd in amazement. The people looked hardly human. The face of an older man in a wrinkled white linen suit covered with convention badges was a red rubber mask changing its shape and features. A fat, bald fellow with huge shoulders stood stolidly in place wearing an expression of pain and shouting at regular intervals. There was so much noise his words were unintelligible. Three pretty girls, their hair disarranged and their cheeks red, swayed as in a trance, like the Indian snake-dancers. Others waved their arms and cried out. Yet they were merely human beings who had lived through four days of the fantastic rites of a political convention.

Cameramen in shirt sleeves stood on ramps putting the scene on films.

Malcolm Christiansen's spirit was pulled, dizzy with excitement, into the crowd. Their cries drove away the major's wife, any thought of danger, a slight ache in his shoulder, and all mortal ideas. He became the priest-king surrounded by his wild worshipers. He stood straight and tall and waved to them. He would have walked into the crowd had not someone pulled his arms and said authoritatively, "This way, Colonel." He went through a lane held open by police and into the rear of the auditorium. He heard now a deep chant intoned over and over again, "Can't–miss–with–Chris! Can't–miss–with–Chris!"

Jeebie, wearing dark glasses and a long string of badges, greeted him with the cry, "Pal, she's all yours."

The Colonel was taken into a space behind the platform, and from there heard the sound of the gavel pounding hard on a wooden disk. A stentorian voice proclaimed, "Ladies and gentlemen, the next President of the United States. . . ."

The crowd would not let him finish. It rose to its feet with an immense inchoate sound. Without syllable, without meaning it rose and trembled the rafters. It was, perhaps, man's endless yearning for the sunshine he never sees. The organ entered the arena of sound, trying to drown out all else with the state song, "North Dakota, North Dakota, where blue skies brighten your way." The aisles on the convention floor were choked with persons waving banners and signs and crying aloud.

The presiding officer banged mightily. He called out testily, "The people of America are waiting to hear Colonel Christiansen. Back to your seats and be quiet." He smacked the gavel again. Obediently, like children, they returned and sat down noisily.

Jeebie pushed Christiansen forward. He marched ahead into the glare of the spotlights. His shoulders were back in the best paradeground manner. His head was high. His eyes were magnificently afire. His familiar crooked grin greeted them, his children. The crowd was silent momentarily, too moved for sound. Then it burst into a deafening roar. He raised his arms in entreaty. He started to speak and his voice broke. He bent his head, for tears were in his eyes.

Mickie Moonan was quickly by his side saying, "Count five and begin." That did it. His voice came out huskily, "If ever a man stood humble and thankful before God and his country, it is I.

"You have asked me to lead a crusade, and, with the blessing of the Almighty and your help, we will win. . . ."

On the second row of the platform, an alert, bald little man who smelled of cologne and whisky said enthusiastically, "Christ, this fellow is terrific. Why, we'll elect the whole city council this time!"

## *Chapter* NINE

THE DELEGATE from Rocky Ford, Colorado, had a damn sight more sense than all those bloody fools tramping up and down the aisles yelling and getting their feet stepped on. This he made known to the lady from Pueblo who sat exhausted and deafened on the seat beside him.

The Rocky Ford man was standing on his chair above the sea of pandemonium and watching the platform with high-powered binoculars.

"This is the way to find out the low-down," he shouted to his friend. He swept the platform with his glasses and stopped suddenly a little to the right and rear of where Christiansen stood waving at the demonstration. "Some trouble here. The Kansas Governor is in a huddle with the boys running this show. There's Glinnen, the crew-cut fella with the dark glasses. He's Christiansen's manager. And Silas King, the New York bank roll. Senator Wingate, he's the chairman of the Crusaders' organization. Luke Gill, the publisher, and a fat fella I don't know. The Governor is talking fast, big emergency. The others look worried. I'll bet something's gone wrong."

Indeed it had. The Governor's hoarse voice was saying, "The Fremont die-hards are going to take a walk. I got this from one of my boys. Told me I could have his hotel room. They're packing their bags and going to hold a press conference, and say they have been driven out of the party by Wall Street."

Jeebie said in melancholy resignation, as if he had expected catastrophe all along, "They will wreck the party; split it right down the seams."

King asked belligerently, "Where did they ever get this idea?"

Gill offered an answer, "*The Iliad*. Achilles pulled the same act on the Greeks."

Silas King suggested that he talk to the ringleaders and tell them frankly their course was unwise and unprofitable.

The Kansas Governor did not think that would be effective. "These are the people who have stood up against every kind of pressure. They aren't backing down any now."

The conversation was going on against the bedlam of organ music, singing and cheers for the new nominee.

"There is only one way to stop the wreckers, and that is for Senator Fremont to ask them to stay with the party," Moonan said.

The Governor was pessimistic again. "I hardly think that will happen," he said. "I talked to him this evening, and the Senator is pretty sore."

Mickie looked at the Colonel smiling and waving at the tumult. He proposed, "The best salesman is Colonel Christiansen. Let him go over now to Fremont's place, and ask for his support and advice and appeal to his party loyalty. It will be pretty hard for the Senator to turn him down."

The Governor agreed. "Yes, that might work. Frank's trouble has always been that he was never able to stay a son of a bitch very long."

The delegate from Rocky Ford noticed that Jeebie went to Christiansen, spoke to him, and he joined the group. "They're leaving the platform," the delegate shouted his advice. "What do you suppose is up?"

The five slipped out of the auditorium into the hot, still midnight air. The city was a muffled roar, almost quiet after the noise within. Luke Gill decided not to accompany them. He explained, "I don't have the knees for genuflection."

The limousine sped down nearly deserted streets. Men sat on their steps in shirt sleeves. Children played around a street light. Young people stood in listless confusion outside a tavern shut now for the night. A tired old woman hobbled along the pavement holding a paper bag. The police siren and red blinking light preceded them, but few looked up in inquiry.

The limousine drew up to the curb of the block-long hotel on Michigan Boulevard and Jeebie gave a last word of advice, "Colonel, just be sweet and reasonable and friendly with the Senator. Appeal to him. We need your help, and all that kind of talk."

Christiansen listened intently. This was his first assignment. He was the plebe again given his first watch. He was sure that if this Fremont was flesh and blood, he could overpower him with good will.

The four walked confidently into the lobby. The management had prudently removed the carpets, vases and chairs. The tiled floor was strewn with leaflets, confetti and one pink paper horn. An immense campaign picture hung from the ceiling, a stiffly smiling face framed by cardboard goldenrod and entitled "Pride of the Prairies." The picture tilted at a grotesque angle, one of the guy wires having come loose.

A limp human form stretched out flat on a wooden bench. The face was hidden by a straw hat with a green band bearing a political slogan. A large, unsteady individual, coatless and with red suspenders, was crossing the lobby. He stopped and paid his obeisance to the hanging picture by a low and almost disastrous bow.

Silas King addressed this nomad, "Where is the headquarters of Senator Fremont?"

"No Fremont," he replied wagging his head sadly. "Dead. Killed by Wall Street." His eyes focused on them narrowly.

"Come on," Jeebie exclaimed, "It's up there on the mezzanine."

The Colonel walked up the stairs brimming with innocent vanity. He had no apprehension of the spilled cup of bitterness he might find in this naked place. He thought of himself as going on an errand of mercy, of being greeted with a touching gratitude. How many victors came to the sullen campfires of their vanquished and offered their hands?

On arriving on the mezzanine, he saw perhaps twenty men milling about disconsolately or talking with a conspiratorial air. Their faces showed the strain of the long, futile campaign climaxed now by defeat. One of them was tearing the delegate's badge off his suit. He threw it on the floor and spat on it. His eyes were red from weariness and anger.

There was a sudden stillness when the foursome entered the area of the Fremont headquarters. The conversation ceased. Eyes were fixed on the invaders suspiciously. No one cheered, much less greeted Colonel Christiansen. He could not realize that his mere presence there, cheerful and whole, was to these men a monstrous injustice, a sin on the whole world of men. He looked into the faces of four of them, searching for a spark of friendship so that he might respond. These faces were like those in an Old Testament tableau found in antique Bibles, stern and unforgiving. They seemed to accuse him of a crime, what crime he did not know, could not faintly guess. He waited for Silas King to take command of this parlor and put it in the proper mood to receive the visiting kings.

But it was Jeebie who, seeing an old political acquaintance, asked, "Congressman, where can we find Senator Fremont? Colonel Christiansen has come to pay his respects."

The Congressman stared at him, at first uncomprehending. Then, without saying a word, he turned his back on Glinnen. The silence was dense and forbidding, as though a hedge of thorns separated the two groups. Colonel Christiansen felt a startling uneasiness and with it an aching tiredness. His physical system had at this chilling contact aged and sickened. His stomach had little gripes of pain. His head was hot. His legs were tired. He wanted to sit down.

Silas King was becoming angry. A stain of red was moving up his neck into his face. Mickie moved ahead, noted a door into an office and waved them on. The Fremont partisans made way reluctantly for them. One almost blocked the Colonel's path, but thought better of it and skulked off to one side.

Frank Fremont, when they broke in on him, sat alone at a desk. He was writing in longhand on a yellow lined tablet. He had a spare figure and keen features. His gray hair was so light as to be almost silken and was brushed sparsely across the large dome of his head. His eyes, when he looked up at the intruders, were like those of a man trapped in a consuming illness, one that he knows will kill him, and, in fact, is giving him more pain than seems just or allowable by a merciful God.

The Colonel had the feeling he would not dare close his eyes, for if he did he would lose all understanding and be drawn into the terrible wisdom of the man before him.

Jeebie said, "You remember me, Senator? J. B. Glinnen. I ran the Northwest campaign tours two years ago."

Senator Fremont nodded gravely, but as though conserving his energy as a sick person will do.

"My friends here, Colonel Christiansen and Silas King, have come to pay their respects to you, Senator."

Fremont arose and walked around in front of his desk. He was a taller man than he seemed. He was in his stockinged feet.

The Colonel approached him with an apologetic step and held out his hand. Senator Fremont accepted it. His hand was cold. Christiansen said in embarrassment, "Senator, I'm a great admirer of yours, and I hope you'll be on our team, and help us get this Crusade off the ground, you might say."

The Senator spoke in strong tones of despair, "I cannot believe you are a friend or an admirer. There must be another reason for your visit. For if you were an admirer, you would not have let me die so miserably as I did today. You would have spared me some of the torture." He broke off and swayed a little. The Colonel looked at him in alarm.

Fremont spoke again, "Pardon me, I should not have said this. It was not your fault." He laughed, a dry, bitter laugh, " 'Time and chance happeneth to them all.' My time and my chance have passed, that is all. Please sit down."

There were only three chairs. Silas King was left standing. He stared pointedly at Mickie who pretended not to notice. Glinnen stood up and offered his seat.

"What is it you want?" the Senator asked. "Is it advice?" The Colonel nodded dumbly. "Then, let me tell you this. Fame is a coin without lasting value. You cannot cash it when you need it most." Christiansen noted how dry his voice was, like crumbling dust. "Let me tell you of a story. It is of a boy who wanted to be President. He studied and trained for it like the acolyte for the priesthood. He spent hours when other boys were playing, reading history and political science and international affairs. He felt he should have practical experience in politics, so he began on the lowest possible rung. He worked hard and became a member of the City Council, then Congress, and finally the Senate. He spoke and labored for what he thought was right and just. He obtained a fame and was addressed as 'Mr. Republican.' But when the party assembled to choose a President, it passed him by. There is a lesson to this, and all men should know it. 'What profit hath a man of all his labor which he taketh under the sun?' "

The Senator walked with great dignity back to his desk. The Colonel saw that he wore plain black socks. This was a fact that moved through the shock he had sustained. It was, in effect, a piece of armor, for he kept repeating in his mind, "Fremont wears plain black socks . . . plain black socks."

Senator Fremont said, "You have your advice. Is there something more?"

Jeebie looked at the other three. None said anything. So he blurted, "Yes, Senator, there is. We have a report that a bloc of your supporters are going to walk out of the convention, and hold a press conference and denounce the nominee. This could split the party wide open, Senator, and cost us the election. Will you tell them to stay put and support the rule of the majority?"

Fremont said nothing for several seconds. Then, as though to himself, he said, "I am not a vengeful man, or am I? Is this my party, my bride any more, or have you stolen her from me and changed her? You call upon my loyalty to the party, and true, this I have preached. But now, do I believe it myself? Can I be loyal to a party that is not me?"

Colonel Christiansen wrenched out the words, "Senator, it sure is your party. I don't want to change it any from the party you have worked for. I want to do just as you would."

Silas King looked at him sharply.

"I wonder if you are free to do as you wish?" Fremont asked.

"Yes, of course I am," Christiansen replied. "You name what you want. I will put your men into the Administration and have them carry out the policies you would approve. I will consult with you."

King could stay out of the debate no longer. He said, "The Colonel, you understand, Senator, has an obligation to all those who support and assist him. What we want to know now is—are you one of that number?"

Fremont raised a pencil and dropped it on the desk. He did

this twice as if it were an exercise in bringing himself under control. Finally he said calmly, "I will not desert my party, Mr. King, and I think I have given it longer and truer service than you. But I feel a responsibility for it. You have invaded the party with your hero and your money and your slogans, as the Assyrians invaded Babylon, and you have won a battle. But I will not let you destroy its soul. That is all I have to say. Good night!"

Colonel Christiansen stood up because he wanted to escape from the room. He could no longer endure it. There must have been a look of rare anguish on his face, for the others stared at him in alarm. Mickie took his arm, and they walked out into the mezzanine.

It was no longer full of silent men. They were gone. But in their place was a crowd, a mob really, of reporters and cameramen. They had a hungry, wolfish, resentful look as though they had been driven from their stolen meals and stood now snapping and unfed. They clamored for news, "Did he promise to support you?" "Did you offer him a Cabinet job?" "Is the Old Guard still going to walk out?" "What did you tell him?"

Colonel Christiansen looked at them with both anger and fear. How dare they snarl at him and yap at his heels? He forced his way through them wordlessly and plodded heavily down the stairs. Silas King and Jeebie rushed to flank him.

Moonan remained to talk to the press. He said, blinking his eyes as flash bulbs went off, "Colonel Christiansen told Senator Fremont of his great desire to have him on his team and to benefit from his counsel. The Senator assured the Colonel of his loyalty to the party, and the two had a fruitful discussion of campaign issues."

When he finished, questions flashed against him. He replied with a flare of temper, "That is all I have to say. This, after all, is Senator Fremont's office and any further word should come from him."

Christiansen walked unsteadily across the long lobby to the door. He had a feeling of loathing for himself. It was the same kind of revolting shame that followed him after he masturbated in the wheat field as a boy and the next Sunday heard the preacher say, "I have found thee, because thou hast sold thyself to work evil in the sight of the Lord." He had been found out now.

King helped him into the car and he sat back exhausted as the siren screamed and they moved away. They had gone only a few blocks when the Colonel said thickly, "Stop the car. I'm going to be sick."

The brakes were applied. The tires squealed. Christiansen got out and walked with King to the park. There he leaned against a tree and retched. The damp, acid smell steamed in the warm night. The Colonel finally stood up and wiped his mouth with a handkerchief. The act purged him, removed some of his guilt. He felt only that he was tired, very tired.

They took the Presidential nominee back to the lakeside estate. He said nothing until the limousine stopped on the gravel drive, and then, "What a hell of a way to end this day, with the taste of vomit in your mouth!"

On the way back to Chicago, Jeebie said, "Silas, you're going to be playing wet nurse for four years. I've seen that kind before."

"No one is perfect," King replied shortly. "I'd like to get in a steam bath, and then get in bed and sleep for a hundred days."

"We still have to figure out the V.P."

"You know my feelings."

King's choice was a white-haired Senator with a distinguished profile, a conservative voting record, and an interest in an insurance company. "We want someone who will be safe if there is an act of God," he had explained. "No Teddy Roosevelt. No wild man."

Jeebie objected mildly, "But he is a nonentity, Silas. There won't be any dames panting to get to the polls and pull the lever for him. The second man on the ticket ought to drag in voters you won't get any other way."

King replied, "We have enough glamour. I want to be safe."

When they reached the penthouse, a caller was waiting. The Irish policeman downstairs had sent him up, and he told them half jokingly they would receive their reward in the Good Place. He informed Silas King his name was Feighan, that he was a police-court judge in Detroit and had come with a message from Father Werther. He was smoking one of King's better cigars.

"What does he want?" King demanded. He did not schedule time for idle conversation. There was work to be done before the convention was all tidied up, the ticket completed, and everyone off in fighting fever.

"Well," said Feighan, "Father is a strange man, if you'll pardon me speaking of a saintly creature, and what he wants is not always so clear you can pass it off one, two, three. His feelings are deep. They come, you might say, from quite a distance." He cast his glance upward cheerfully, as though to indicate he, Mr. Feighan, personally did not consider heaven such a gloomy place at all. Women and song and good liquor. "Father is very worried. He does not think the Party has the proper understanding of the menace of atheist communism, and he may find it necessary to tell his beloved children to stay home and not vote as a protest. Such a protest, he believes, would only have to be once. The politicians would then be anxious to see the light."

King looked at the visitor crossly. He plainly thought this was a felonious pressure, and was puzzled how to deal with it. Clerics were not in the habit of telling him how to run his bank.

Feighan was not concerned about the impatience of his host. He blew out a ring of cigar smoke and admired it.

He said, "Father is of the opinion Governor Boxell of Rhode Island as the Vice President would provide that needed knowledge of evil. Otherwise, the Colonel, good man that he is, might wander off the path from sheer innocence. Sheer innocence."

King replied, "I do not need any advice on how to choose a Vice President. And I do not believe that the Cardinal, whom I know very well, would appreciate Father Werther trying to tell us who to run."

Feighan said cheerfully, "Oh, the Cardinal is against communism, too. I thought you knew that. You won't shake us on that." He picked up another cigar from the box, put it in his pocket and stood up. "I've done my bit. See you in church."

Silas King was outraged and said so when the door had closed on the visitor. "We have worked to set up a tight operation. We have our man nominated. And then, big bites are eaten out of the pie while we watch. First, Senator Fremont. He is the loser, but we tell him he can have anything he wants because a few soreheads threaten to pull out. Now, this priest tells us who to name for Vice President. Before we are through, ten more will raise their clubs over our heads. We'll turn our pockets inside out and sign promissory notes. No. This is where we stop."

Mickie had come in and was willing to argue with King about it. Just for the fun of it partly, partly an old mystique, too, fear of purgatory. It was associated with the cold dampness of the old church where the nuns bustled their charges on crisp winter mornings in St. Paul.

So he said humorously, chuckling slyly at himself and the world, too, "The parish priests and the cardinals and the Pope, too, want to be sure there are strong men who will thrust Satan down to hell and keep him from rising up and snatching souls. It isn't that they see any lack of strength in the Colonel; they don't know whether he will recognize Satan when he sees him. They know Boxell will. He's been finding communists in the most unlikely places because he has such sharp eyes."

Silas exploded, "What a devil of a way to decide on a man who might rule all civilization!"

Mickie said wryly, "One of our famous Irish writers said, 'The building up of a civilization is at once the noblest and most practical of all enterprises in which human faculties are exalted to their highest.' Don't you feel the inspiration from taking part in this exercise, Silas? Think how historians of the future will describe the soul searching, the patient testing of men and ideas before the leadership and program of the Christiansen Crusade was begun."

Jeebie had not said a word the whole time. Now in his voice that so reminded everyone of a pool hall or a locker room, he said, "I think this Boxell would be a good guy. Do you know why? I'll tell you. I've never won a campaign yet that we didn't have someone punching the enemy and confusing him, so that he misses his strides and acts confused, and the voters sense it. They won't vote for a guy who acts like he don't know the time of day and gets easy rattled. The voter is strange, like a woman, you might say. He claims he don't want any fighting over him, but you just stage a dignified campaign and watch the vote drop down. They don't come out unless the blood is stirred. It's all fine to get them to feel gooey all over about a guy like the Colonel. But that ain't enough. They've got to hate the son of a bitch running against him. That's where this Boxell can come in. Oh, I know him. A tough guy on the make. He's slugged his way up where he is now, and he's going further. He will cut President Thompson, trip him up, and let him fall on his face. And our Crusader can be traveling that highroad."

Mickie sided with him not because he liked the Governor, he said, but it was good politics. King said he never hired over-aggressive young men, you could never trust them. But he agreed to let Christiansen make the choice. The two men, King's candidate and the Governor, would have breakfast with the Colonel the next morning.

The next morning, a blur of sunlight from a slanted blind touched Colonel Christiansen's closed eyelids and lightened his sleep. He was finally awakened by a mourning dove. The plaintive, melancholy notes tore away the shreds of sleep, and he opened his eyes and saw that morning indeed had come. Ada Mae was up and gone. He washed, shaved and dressed with the quick efficiency of the old soldier and a man who hates to be alone.

Silas King greeted him at the foot of the stairs and said cheerfully, "Well, Mr. President, how are you feeling?"

Christiansen smiled and said, "I don't know. Haven't had my coffee yet."

King clapped his hands like a rajah in a movie and said, "Coffee for Mr. Christiansen." The butler came with rapid soft steps bringing a small cup. It was good. Silas took him to one side and said he had two potential candidates for Vice President; he could look them over, and if he didn't like either, they would bring up others.

The Colonel shook hands gravely with Senator Forbes and Governor Boxell. The Senator, addressing himself mainly to King, told of his efforts to have Congress pass a Constitutional Amendment limiting the powers of the Federal Government. The Colonel was not only bored, he was irritated. He could imagine the two being together on official occasions, and Forbes steering the conversation around to himself with a lot of gab about a Constitutional Amendment or some such thing that featured him as Number One.

Governor Boxell, by contrast, was solicitous of Christiansen. At the time of meeting, he spoke in richly reverent tones, "Sir, it is an honor to meet the man who has given such hope and inspiration to America." His eyes dropped humbly, as though dazzled by brilliance.

At another point in the conversation, Colonel Christiansen said he did not know what kind of a campaigner he would be; this was all new to him. Senator Forbes looked him over coolly and suggested there were professionals who could teach you the tricks. There were these tricks of how to stand an audience on its hair, how to silence the heckler, how to end on a note of prayer.

But Governor Boxell said, "The Lord, sir, is on the side of some men, and they need no instruction. They are the chosen ones. I believe that of you."

The Senator looked at him with amusement. Ada Mae giggled. Silas' ears turned red. Mickie said it was always touching to watch the devout at worship, and described in detail the adoration of a god made out of an old oil drum by the aborigines of New Guinea. "A little worship is a dangerous thing," he said in a paraphrase. "I would trust an atheist or a true believer farther than a Sunday worshiper. 'And when thou prayest thou shalt not be as the hypocrites are: for they love to pray standing in the synagogues and in the corners of the streets, that they may be seen of men.' You didn't know I had any store of Biblical wisdom, did you, Colonel?"

When the two guests departed, King tried to sell his produce. The Senator had experience and the respect of the financial community. But Colonel Christiansen said no he had decided. He wanted the young man. He thought of him as a colonel does a trusted, faithful, energetic captain, or a father a favored son. There was an argument of sorts. Christiansen grew cold and stubborn, and King, more perplexed than anything else at this undiscovered lode of contrariness, gave in.

"All right," he said, "it's your bed. You have to sleep in it. But don't blame me if the springs creak."

The Colonel immediately was warm and forgiving and talked excitedly of the campaign, apparently having forgotten the Fremont incident. King looked at Mickie in questioning surprise. He smiled back blandly, as though saying, "This man is a stranger to me, too." There are in every man many unfrequented back roads. You never have time to investigate them all.

## Chapter TEN

THE SOUND of hammers chattered cheerfully across the golden prairie.

They added a fresh note to the rural concert of mechanical reapers wheezing and clattering through the wheat fields and the flutelike cries of meadow larks. A tara-ta-ta-ta of busy hammers was answered in the distance by the sweet songs of larks or the shouts of men, and under all this music the sound of the reapers.

The sky was clear and the air so light, as occurs when the first shock of cold strikes the northern plains in late summer, that sight stretched almost forever. Across the level land, against the bright blue sky, farm buildings were scattered like ships on a wide sea. There were, too, lanes of utility poles where mourning doves sat and cooed softly, and far to the right an anthill of sturdy frame houses and small brick buildings. This was the town of Deslacs, North Dakota, where Malcolm Christiansen spent his early life.

The hammering came from the old Lemcke farm. Farmers drove by in their dusty cars and slowed down or even stopped to stare curiously at the colossus of wood taking shape. It was great wooden stands, like those at the Grand Forks fairground, rising as an ark in the desert in a wheat field. The trumpets of a loud-speaker system were being hoisted on wooden towers. Red, white and blue bunting decorated part of a platform, giving it the look of a half-dressed doll a child has left on the sidewalk. Workmen struggled, with many shouts, to erect a huge colored photograph of Colonel Christiansen cemented to a beaverboard frame. Over the picture in huge red letters were the words, "A Hero With a Heart," and below, "Our Next President."

This spectacle created both interest and humor among the neighbors. Many knew him as a schoolmate or as "Nils' boy." Reverence is not produced by close acquaintance with even the gods, and the thought that Malcolm Christiansen might be President was so incredible as to be funny. The widow Muller, who knew about people and was quite old now, had said he would never amount to anything because he had no character. "That boy," she told his many aunts, "will always have to be led. He cannot walk anywhere without being taken by the hand." The widow was hard put now to explain why her judgment had been so wide of the mark. She protested she had not erred, that she was sure "he is still being led around like a prize bull with a ring in his nose."

Farmers walked over from nearby fields and came up from the road to watch this temple and its idol come into place. One old-timer in a broad-brimmed hat curled up at the edges stared at the huge photograph and said several times, "Well, I'll be damned!" A man who had ridden out from town—he did not have the red, windburned face of the farmer—saw the picture being hoisted and said, "I never thought I'd see the day when they'd put him up for President." He shrugged his shoulders in a gesture of the futility in describing the impossible. But there it was!

Malcolm Christiansen was coming home to open the campaign. He had not wanted to and invented excuses, "It isn't a good place really—just a wide spot in the prairie. . . . The weather turns bad this time of the year. . . . There aren't enough people thereabouts to make up a good crowd."

But they told him he was arguing against a law of the gods. A candidate for President always returns home to start the campaign. This ritual invested the candidate with a mysterious knowledge of the people and the earth and the evils that must be exorcised to make life worth while.

The Colonel could not explain what he feared was not bad weather but ghosts. Yes, ghosts. The ghost of the little boy that was himself. The ghost of his father, who must be waiting still, pale and desperate, for him to return and renounce the military life. What could he tell these ghosts when they asked him what he had done with himself? He could only say, "Wait, wait. I will pay all my debts when I become President." He would be eagerness itself to put away his sword and bring the blessings of peace. He would make up for all the lost time. But Christiansen would rather make these promises from a distance than be confronted by ghosts on their own heath.

The politicians overruled him. They were professionals and they were organizing the campaign the way professionals always dreamed they might, and never had the chance. Candidates in their own vanity insisted they knew best how to stir the people. Christiansen was not that way. He said in the beginning, not so much humbly as gratefully, "I don't know anything about politics, and I'm going to let you fellows run the show."

So the professionals, burning with the pure, fierce flame of the desire for perfection, plotted the campaign. They consulted polls and listened to the pounding of the electorate's heart. There were slogans to be shouted and sung and whistled, accusations to be shaped to stir the serpent of doubt. The composite Id of America would be motivated into love, honor and obey Malcolm Christiansen, "the hero with a heart." These priests believed that words, expressions, profiles were more powerful, more meaningful to the people than deeds. They admired the proficiency of the medicine show and saw no reason why such salesmanship could not be created for politics, too.

But even in heaven there are arguments, it is said. The professionals rowed over the substance of Colonel Christiansen's first campaign speech. One school espoused by Mickie Moonan said the Colonel should speak "in splendid generalities."

"Paint life in its most glorious hues, throw in a good line from George Washington for patriotism, and who cares about crop controls or water conservation or postage stamps," he said. "You don't stop and ask for the menu before you knock on the pearly gates. You hear the distant music and the coy laughter of the girls, and who but the devil cares whether the eggs are poached or fried."

Jeebie agreed with him. He said, putting his thumbs in his vest to give himself an air of authority, "I'm against rushing out with fifteen programs and policies in a campaign. All you do is make half the folks sore at you. Listen, if you promise one hundred per cent farm price supports, then the housewife complains. She thinks you're going to raise the price of groceries. You can't win that way. Now, I've studied the American voter; he's my business, and I can tell you this—all he wants is to be assured things are going to be O.K., and you're going to keep the wolf off his doorsteps. You make a lot more mileage out of digging up those old speeches of G. Washington, or Jefferson and Lincoln, and even Roosevelt, the Democrat one, and changing the words around a little."

But they were overruled by sheer weight of numbers.

There were the experts on labor and agriculture and resources and taxes, all of them a bit fanatic and with a pet scheme they had worked on at nights and hid under the mattress for the great day when the party might come in again. The showdown came over the price of corn.

The Congressman from Ohio—he was chairman of the House Agriculture Committee—came to the headquarters. He hunted down Jeebie and Mickie and said with serious simplicity, "There is only one thing we care about in the Middle West, and that is the price of corn, hogs and wheat. Christiansen must not come to North Dakota and leave without promising good prices. Otherwise, many of us will not be around in January to help him, and he might not be giving the orders himself."

So, grumbling and complaining and saying this was a hell of a way to start off a Crusade by talking about the price of bacon, Mickie gave way. This would be a farm speech, and if the farm experts could leave off arguing with one another, they could tell him what to say.

The Colonel reported in at the New York headquarters after his vacation, "radiant with innocence and morbidly healthful." This was the comment of Mickie, who, after a summer in New York haggling with politicians felt like "a flabby, mad woman you'd find hiding in a cave after a battle."

The headquarters was in great confusion. Public relations hardly spoke to research. Agriculture and labor were carrying on a feud. The head of the speakers' bureau was having a messy affair with his secretary, a congressman's daughter. The Vice Presidential nominee was quarreling with the treasurer over funds for his campaign. Everyone was upset and on edge. This was partly because the great race was about to begin, and no one was really ready. But most of all, the headquarters was without a unifying force. Colonel Christiansen had ceased to be anything but a face smiling out of posters, a voice flowing out of recording tapes, words on a press release.

Then, this day he appeared. He announced himself with a glowing smile, peered into rooms and waved to workers. He told Mickie, "You look as fat and lazy as a frog on a lily pad. I'll bet you haven't done a lick of work since I left."

Mickie immediately felt less grumpy and said, "I've been dealing with minor mutinies." They grinned at each other, and found the sight so hilarious, they exploded with laughter.

Christiansen's presence had a magic, inexplicable effect on the whole headquarters. Typists who had been complaining they were going to resign came out in the hall with happy eyes and applauded him. Jeebie dropped a monstrous grouch he had been carrying around. The stock-room boys volunteered to work late that night. A contributor who dropped around suspiciously to see what was being done with the money wrote out a new check.

The receptionist, a motherly-looking woman with a soothing voice, said to the Colonel, "Wherever you are, Mr. Christiansen, the sun shines brighter."

He liked that, of course. He had been fishing and relaxing since the convention and felt well. He looked forward to the campaign as a great adventure, sailing from one cheering crowd to another.

Their plane, the *Crusader*, left Idlewild for North Dakota on a mild, hazy day of early autumn. It was a jet plane, painted blue and with a crusader's shield and cross on the side. It was blessed by a priest, a rabbi and a minister and dedicated by Christiansen to "the search of peace and freedom for all mankind." At the moment of saying these words he felt a mysterious quiver of warmth. And he heard his voice as if he were standing at a distance.

Christiansen was in good humor during the two-and-a-half-hour trip to Bismarck. When he looked down, and the clouds had drifted away and they were over the puddles of the Great Lakes, he began to grow excited. Ahead lay the golden stretch of prairies, and, even if he had not visited them in years, he felt a stir of sentiment. Perhaps it was simply the thought of a return to childhood and innocence. He never inquired deeply into the source of his emotions, but accepted them like the weather.

They landed in a blaze of a perfect fall day. He stood at the airport feeling the sun warm and welcome on his face. The air was clear and dry and the sweet smell of cut clover faint in the wind. The engines of the plane were turned off, and he could hear the sound of a tractor in a nearby field and a thrush's call. He was almost sorry that he had ever left, but Christiansen remembered he was returning, as if to a shrine, to begin the crusade for peace and freedom, and this would be the way his father would want it. He would forget and forgive the scene at the railway station. The old scar would be healed, and need never wake him with its ache again.

He spent the night at a rancher's estate. The big house was one of the frequent anomalies of upper-class American life. Instead of the traditional ranch house with its beamed ceiling, it was a replica of the modernistic house that sits on a cliff looking down aloofly on Los Angeles, even to the furnishings and the art. The latter was modern Japanese. The servants, too, were small and Oriental. The whole scheme was a rebellion against the vast, flat space of the plains, and was plainly the work of the hostess. She, like so many other women who, to their surprise, have received the gift of wealth and leisure, was bored. She had no intention of having affairs with other men, so her romance was interior decorating. Thus, at this stop-off, Christiansen lost the rapture of return to buried memories.

That night he went over his speech with Mickie. He was disturbed and unhappy at the section on farm-price supports.

"I don't understand this. Why do I have to talk about it?" he asked. "Why can't I talk about the way I think the world ought to be?"

"I agree with you, but all the farm people came in and insisted; said it was necessary to get the rural vote. But if you want to cut it out, I can write something more general."

"No," the Colonel said unhappily, "leave it in. The politicians think they know so much about the voters, and sometimes I don't believe they know anything at all. But they're the experts."

The next morning the landscape was gray, covered over by a chilling mist that moved in during the night from the Canadian lakes. Distant buildings were gray ghosts. All sound was muffled, drenched by the moisture. A dog howled nearby, and it was indescribably mournful.

Colonel Christiansen was tormented by uneasiness. He had wandered, not meaning to, not wanting to, into a day from the past. This rare mist, rare because the winds which sweep across the prairies seldom allow mists to settle! The dog's mournful howl!

On the drive to Minot through the mist, the Colonel sat silent and Moonan knew something was wrong. They stopped at the Courthouse to pick up the Governor and a group of state dignitaries. No crowd greeted them, and Christiansen had to wait in the car while someone hunted the Governor. (He was holding court in the sheriff's office.) Governor A. K. Hockaday was a huge, unworried man with a crushing handshake and a booming voice. Colonel Christiansen stood stiffly while the Governor introduced the state officials, "Judge Harry Schumann, polled the biggest vote ever recorded in Mountrail County. Expert on common and uncommon law, eh Harry? . . . Will Anthony, the best square-dance caller in the twin states and our nominee for Lieutenant Governor. Give 'em a call, Will. . . . You know the Congressman. . . . Do you want me to warm up the crowd for you, Colonel, or do you have enough fire in your gospel?"

The little caravan of Buicks, Plymouths and Fords drove across the level countryside the twenty miles to Deslacs. Off the road about five miles out of town was a gray blur. Here again, he stumbled on a painful moment from the past. It was like a raw place of red earth that is never quite hidden no matter how much brush grows over it. You come close enough and you'll see the slash of red, crumbling dirt that will grow nothing but weeds where once a field of grain waved. This relic was the old cottonwood grove where they held the camp meetings, perhaps did yet. By night, and the kerosene flares on the stumps, this place was a scene from hell itself. And that was what the preachers and revivalists shrieked about. So vividly, so spitting with emotions that the people moaned and sometimes stood up and talked in strange tongues. And a boy, six or seven or thereabouts, would feel right down to the bottom of his stomach the horror, the terrible horror of it. You had to be saved, you had to come to

Jesus, or five minutes after you died, you paid for every sin—and they had the ledger books up there and every lie and theft and sin was written down. With what a sense of liberation and joy they sang the old hymn at the end:

> "Oh marvelous grace that has rescued me
> Oh joyous moment when Jesus I see
> Oh happy day when like Him I'll be
> Five minutes after I die."

And how awful it was for the little boy to discover that he had a deep streak of sin in him. Despite the warnings, despite the hot breath of hell breathing on him, he would still lie. And he wondered if he alone of all boys was this bad until one day Jimmy Grimes told him he was the same way. He knew he was damned, but he still wouldn't admit to his pa that he took his pipe out and smoked it and lost it. The fear of the paternal swat on the bottom was stronger than of hell to come. There was always the chance that somewhere along the way boys would do something noble and be forgiven all. They would save that pretty little girl from Bismarck visiting her aunt and uncle from drowning in the creek. Surely that would erase all those check marks in the ledger. But when you went back into the grove again, and the faces were strange and weird in the light of the torches, and the preacher cried out his awful description, then you were scared again.

"You've got to get right with God or die in the flames of Gehenna shriekin' and groanin'."

There was another part of this holy rigmarole that remained stuck to him, too. A lady who spoke in the Unknown Tongue. If you understood it, you could tell how high the winter snows would pile up or whether there would be a dry spell next summer or who was going to die next. She stood up with her lips frothing with spit. She uttered a series of throaty groans and grunts. The others shouted, "Hallelujah, glory, glory," in high excited voices.

Then the preacher clapped his hands and cried, "She's got the power. She's comin' through to God. She's got the prophecy. She's a-sayin' Christ will float high over the sinful earth, and the wind will pile up snow this winter, brethren, and kill the cattle of the sinners." And there was a blizzard that winter, and cattle did die, and there had been sin.

At the Lemcke farm, he got out stiffly and walked through the moist, heavy hanging air to a large canvas tent. There the ladies were having a chicken dinner for the more important people. The Colonel hated this moment. Yet there was a bit of fatalism in it. He was bound to come back here and see these people he had tried to forget, and look them in the faces. It was an act of absolution and simply had to be if he was going to be anything more than just a soldier dressed in a fancy uniform. If he was going to follow the trail his father had always pointed out to him, he had to return and take his medicine. So, a bit stiffly, unsmiling, he shook hands, heard himself called "Mac," and listened to anecdotes that were not exactly complimentary to greatness. But there was a truce. No one blurted out how his father had faded after Lieutenant Christiansen went back East, or any hearty, unthinking recollection that Nils was a pacifist and here was Malcolm made his fame as a soldier fighting the Communists and was about to be made President, and you never could tell. Once or twice, he felt in his quaking stomach this was about to happen, but always the talker was diverted.

When this ordeal was over and the photographers had their shots of the Colonel talking with Aunt Bessie, the stout, cheerful lady in the gingham apron, he was taken over to meet the farm leaders. He put his head to one side—he had learned to do this to signify earnest attention—and all the time was thinking that he had come back and it wasn't as bad as he had thought. Of course, one reason for that was that none of the outsiders knew the secret language of looks and key words that passed between him and his cousins. When the old man talked of "the brown shed," the reporter who was asking so many questions had no way of knowing this was the little shop where his father preached, if that was the word for it, pacifism.

The farm leaders told Christiansen how hard it was to make any money out of pigs, and he agreed and said it was high time they had a Secretary of Agriculture who had the farmers' own interests at heart.

Outside it began to rain. Ten thousand people were caught in the cold drizzle. The Colonel appeared under an umbrella and waved. The crowd sat huddled together in the miserable rain, and just one section made any effort to cheer him. It was identified by a now limp sign, "Crusaders' College Corps." Governor Hockaday was not satisfied, so he shouted into the microphones, "Let's show the folks across the country what a big welcome the home folks can give. Come on, neighbors, a great big 'Hi there!'"

His voice squeaked and boomed through the loud-speaker system.

The farmers and their wives and children sat in unmoving waves on the stands. Rain soaked the big pine planks and dripped on the wheat stubble below. The television crews turned up their coat collars and swore at their fate. The floodlights were turned on experimentally. The voice of the master of ceremonies bounced through the loud speaker in a series of squawks. He introduced the local candidates. They stood up, waved their hats, smiled uncomfortably, and sat down again.

Colonel Christiansen opened the black leather notebook on his knees. He looked through his speech for a few words to give him a flow of strength, to open up a valve of emotion. He needed this just as a motor requires extra effort on a cold morning.

Now it was two o'clock. The red eyes of the television cameras turned on. A producer waved his hand. Governor Hockaday said, "And now from the great and happy state of North Dakota, we present our famous son and the next President, Malcolm Christiansen."

The Colonel stood in the thin rain. His uncertain, boyish smile, entreating indulgence, appeared on screens in cold-water tenements, remote farmhouses, and darkly lit bars. A mother feeding her baby in a Los Angeles suburb had the volume turned too low to hear the words, but she had a moment of compassion for the lonely face. Oh God, how lonely are men! An invalid in a Boston hospital, so weary of the old sights and sounds and smells, and of life itself, felt a companionship with him. A truck driver in an Atlanta tavern looked up from his beer and said, "That guy looks kind of drawn through the wringer."

Christiansen tried to overcome a feeling he had defied the gods too far; he had allowed men to worship him, and now the penalty. A little fear crept into his voice as he said, "Fellow Americans, I am happy to return to the dear familiar scenes of my childhood. The Crusades of old were born in the villages and courtyards of

Christian Europe, and our modern crusade for peace and good government must spring from the grass roots of American life. . . ."

He looked up and saw the gray, rain-washed prairie, a long line of telephone poles, and the blurred collective faces on the stands.

The Colonel stopped momentarily at the close of the first paragraph, according to the instructions in parentheses on the page. There were scattered hand-clappings. Someone shouted, "You tell 'em, Chris!"

He plunged gloomily ahead into unfamiliar words and terms on farm economics, "I favor a constructive and expanded soil conservation program which shall emphasize improvements of a permanent nature, and shall restore to the soil the noo . . ." He halted and stared at the word. It puzzled him. He tackled it again, stumbled, and the third time said, ". . . shall restore to the soil nutriments of definite value."

The Colonel became engaged in a furious, frustrating war with meaningless words. They reached out to trip him. He fought with them grimly. They were the enemy. So were the speech-writers, the politicians, and even the audience. His voice became harsh and complaining. Looking up from the pages, he saw here and there people were getting up on the stands and leaving. A little file of cars was visible moving down the road.

In desperation, he abandoned the speech. He remembered what he had heard from the farm leaders at lunch, and he called out, imploring and earnest, "I want to tell you I am for high farm prices and prosperity on the farm, and don't you believe anything different. My folks were farmers, and I know that when the price of wheat went down I had to wear my old clothes another year. I went around with patches on my pants and my sleeves. So you can be sure I'll go just as high as the next man on farm price supports. I don't know too much about the economics of this sort of thing, but I'll tell you this, I'm not going to hire some fellow from a college to tell me. I'm going to get real dirt farmers for my advisers."

There was a shout down front, "Pour it on, Chris. Pour it on."

Colonel Christiansen exhausted his mind and in desperation turned back to the speech. He stumbled over several paragraphs, reading one before realizing he had said this before. He raced frantically ahead, hoping only to get through this dreadful chore.

He finally reached the end, "And so, ladies and gentlemen, we dedicate this crusade to the common people of the earth, and pray God for its success." He sat down perspiring, feeling it damp on his forehead and under his arms. He knew, too, that his arms were trembling. Worst of all was the black knowledge that he had lost his audience; it sat bleak and soaked before him, unaware or not caring that here was a leader, sent as Moses was, by divine accident, to lead them back to Israel. All they wanted was to get out of the rain and be warm again, because the cold had soaked through and their feet and thighs and noses were frigid. He understood what feeling, if any, they had for him was one of dull disappointment. They had come to witness a miracle, and it had not come off. This was the way he felt himself, cheated and robbed of a great experience. Where had God been this afternoon? Why had He deserted him?

Christiansen sat half listening to the coarsely cheerful voice of the Governor, and wishing there was a place close by where he might urinate.

The Christiansen party set off soberly for the ride back to Bismarck. They got in the cars in a careful, joyless way, as old people do. No one spoke except to comment a little bitterly on the weather. They stopped at a filling station, and the Colonel went in to use the bathroom. As he stood in the close, ill-smelling little room, he could hear Mickie talking over the pay telephone.

"Hey, Jeebie? How did it come through?" he shouted. "Oh." His voice dropped discouragingly. "Oh." Gloomier yet. "Well, hell, it was the rain. How can you stir up a crowd when they're sitting cold and wet? And it was that damned speech. We never should have put all that farm price formula junk in there, you know that. What I want to do is tear up the Los Angeles speech, knock out all that stuff about promising this dam and that. Will you stand by me? O.K. We'll get it booming yet." The telephone was hung up with a clatter. Christiansen flushed the toilet, washed his hands and dried them on paper towels. He took more time than usual to dry his hands, so that a decent interval would elapse between the telephone conversation and his arrival on the scene. This way, there was less chance that Mickie would mention it. He was suddenly angry with them. He felt an urge to shout, "To hell with you all!" Everyone, the weather, the speech-writers, and the audience had let him down. So, to hell with them! But he restrained himself and piled back in the car.

On the way to Bismarck, he complained they were traveling too slowly. The driver pressed harder and harder on the accelerator. They rushed along the rain-slick road at eighty miles an hour and higher. The car trembled with the vibration, and the driver clutched the wheel tightly and drove with a set, grim face. The Colonel pretended not to notice. He was enjoying the discomfort of the others, and had no sense of personal danger. He had only one thought—to get away from this place, to put it far behind. It had humiliated him, and he never wanted to see it again. His penance was done.

When the plane shot off the prairies and climbed up into the Western range of mountains he felt better. He was free from the ghosts. Christiansen was in good humor when they came down in Los Angeles where, Mickie said, life was played as if it were a love affair that will end when the first cock crows at dawn. A huge, noisy, adoring crowd was gathered to greet him at the airport. There was a jazz band and pennants flying, and he was yours truly, sincerely. Christiansen was taken in tow by the movie people and roared off in a Jaguar with a red-haired actress and a producer.

Moonan took a taxicab to the hotel. There he and the chief speech-writer, a young Presbyterian minister who hoped best to serve his Master and his fortunes in this role, went to work. Mickie produced a bottle of whisky, unsealed a hotel water glass with a few mild curses, and poured himself a drink. The minister refrained. Mickie felt discursive after the drink had warmed its way through him, so he said, "Reverend, a political campaign leaps clumsily from crisis to crisis. We are now standing on the brink of crisis. Our candidate at his first big showing in this campaign was a dud. We are at the moment in possession of a whited sepulcher, 'beautiful outward, but within full of dead men's bones.' "

He poured himself another drink. He explained he did not really like the taste of the stuff, but that he had to get the dampness and gloom of North Dakota out of his bones. "I don't have any cheering crowds or movie starlets to warm me," Moonan said.

"I'm just the creator, and I warm my soul from a bottle." He put his bulk down in the chair.

"Reverend, we have a whited sepulcher on our hands. What do we do with him? I say nothing. I am convinced the American taste is for a whited sepulcher. We are tired and nervous from the doers. We are weary of being nagged and exhorted to keep up with the Russians, and not doing very well, either. We would like to have a President who will bloviate handsomely, who will tell us we are great people and kind people and noble people and brave, too, and stop worrying us about being laid low by a nuclear weapon in the night. We want Father to tuck us into bed, say our prayers with us, and tell us all is well, all is well. Then we can attack our little pleasures of frigging and falsifying with a fresh and inspired spirit.

"So, with this in mind, Reverend, let us proceed to the business of preparing the sermon."

# *Chapter* ELEVEN

Across the rich, murmuring land went Malcolm Christiansen selling what one newspaper described, its newsprint heart brimming with gratitude, as "faith in the American free enterprise system."

The people poured out of their suburban Brook Havens and Holly Tree Hills and Saunder's Mills in wide, panting streams of cars, choking the roads to see the Crusader. They came from the soursmelling tenements, hopeful yet suspicious, too, for they had been tricked so often by mere politicians disguised as saviors. In the rural heartlands they listened to him stolidly yet sympathetically, for the farmers were sick of all the forms and obeisances and God-knows-what the Government demanded of them.

He painted the intoxicating picture of a land free as in Jefferson's day, strong as the pioneers, yet full of the cream of wealth and soothed by the music of safety. And the Colonel was the truest believer of all. Each brilliant snatch of autumn color, each star-festooned heaven clear in the crisp night, each cheering crowd, each flowering shop window reinforced his belief.

Following on this path was the lingering, yearning cry of "Chris . . . Chris . . . Chris!" Someone in a crowd, perhaps even a member of the party claque, would shout the cry, and it would be echoed and tossed back and forth.

And then came October. Gales piled up crashing waves off the Carolinas. The trees turned brilliant in the notches of New Hampshire. The heat was turned on in apartments in Philadelphia, and with the warm air came a smell of dust gathered all the summer. Roadside stands sold jugs of cider and bright red apples. Snow fell silently on the stern mountains of Wyoming. The rich smell of burning leaves filled the small towns.

The board of directors of the Crusade, those who had a special interest in Colonel Christiansen, met in New York to hear reports. The politicians spoke with the enthusiasm of missionaries. Huge crowds. Enthusiastic workers. Many conversions. Money flowing in. Chris was wowing the voters.

Jeebie introduced Dr. Allen Glasspole, chief of research for the Psychological Motivation Center. This small, puffy-faced individual was a magician; he looked deep into the minds of men. His organization had interviewed in depth some 25,000 representative voters.

He spoke precisely and through his nose. He said, "Our project shows that Mr. Christiansen is accepted by eighty per cent of American voters as a well-meaning and possibly heroic figure. But this does not mean that eighty per cent, or even fifty-one per cent, will vote for him. The American voter is essentially a shopper. He wants to find out what he will get from this candidate that he will not get from that. Will his taxes be lower? Will his old-age pension be higher? Will he have to pay a cent more for postage stamps? Mr. Christiansen has made almost no impression upon the voters in this highly practical area. There is lacking a strong motivation to cross party lines and vote for him."

There was silence. King bit off the end of a cigar. Jeebie rolled uneasily in his seat and ran his hand over his stiff hair. Lawrence looked stern and melancholy. Gill whistled the Gilbert and Sullivan tune, "Here's a Howdy-Do."

King asked matter-of-factly, "What do we have to do?"

"You must find an issue that is intensely meaningful to many millions of voters."

"Have you found what it is?"

"Yes, sir."

"Shoot."

"Our surveys have discovered the most unpopular act of government is . . ."

Luke Gill said, "The income tax."

"No, sir, that is not it. The most unpopular act is the peacetime draft. This interferes with the family life and the sex life and the economic advancement of millions of Americans. The first group is the draftees. They are taken from their regular pursuits at a critical time. It is a time when they wish to take a wife, enjoy the connubial pleasures, and start a career. Instead, they spend three years at unpleasant, boring labor and at low wages. They are removed from friends and familiar scenes and often are sent abroad where they are objects of derision and actual hatred. The second and not inconsiderable group are the girls who feel they are cheated out of a man, and that the man desired may take up with strange women and bad habits while in the service, and thus be of little worth when he returns to civilian's garb. Third are the parents who invariably feel the youths are either too young to be thrust into this coarse life or too valuable to society or as breadwinners. Finally are the employers who object to having this highly desirable pool of young labor not available.

"Everyone who has any thoughts on this subject feels strongly. We estimate that there are ten million in this category."

"Just a minute," Lawrence spoke up in alarm. "What of the very valid reasons for a peacetime draft, the protection of the free world?"

Professor Glasspole replied, "This does not show up as a motivating factor in favor of the draft in our studies."

Silas King's eyes were knowing and shrewd and eager, like a hound catching the scent of a rabbit. "Well," he announced cheerfully, "this is it. Colonel Christiansen will promise to throw out the peacetime draft."

"I have a slogan," Gill said. " 'Keep the boys home.' Must be some good popular tune we can sing it to. Get people singing and humming these slogans, and you can't lose. That is what the churches found out with hymns and the cigarette people discovered years later."

Professor Glasspole stated, "Colonel Christiansen would, of course, be the perfect figure to declare the draft should be ended. The people would have faith in his judgment as a military leader and thus any fears that are aroused could be easily suppressed."

Jefferson Lawrence alone objected. Solemn and unsmiling, he said, "But gentlemen, we must maintain our protective forces and show the world we mean to secure the rights of free people."

King said simply, "Oh for God's sake, Jeff, first things first. We have to elect this man now. When we are in, then we can worry about defense. We'll give you that job."

Everyone understood that Lawrence wanted above all things to be Secretary of Defense. He did not object further.

When the idea was broached to Christiansen, he listened uneasily. Then he shrugged his shoulders in patient resignation and said, "I rely on you fellows to tell me what to say, because you know politics isn't my game, and even if I have individual objections, I'll swallow them for the broader cause, you might say, of good government and peace."

Mickie observed it was as if during his thirty-two years in uniform the Colonel had hung untouched, unfaded in a dark closet in a cellophane bag. He wondered at the shallowness of the track the military dogma had made on this man's spirit. He went to the church faithfully, knelt in prayer, loved the incantations and ritual, but had no belief. Yet, Moonan reflected, wasn't this true of all of us. Who among us has deep and utter faith any more?

The new doctrine was thrust out first in Louisville and by chance in the armory with its old cannon on the lawn and military trucks neatly drawn up in rows in back.

The audience sat quietly and attentively as Colonel Christiansen led up to his point. Then, the actor knowing instinctively which were his best lines, his voice became louder, clearer and firmer. "The time has come when we must insist that the best years of our youth no longer be spent carrying a rifle, digging latrines, or at a foreign outpost." They did not quite know what he meant. Surely he would not be so daring? "There is no military justification for continuing the peacetime draft."

He was speaking his next sentence when the knowledge broke on the crowd, and it responded with a roar so joyful the Colonel could hardly believe his senses. The professionals in the crowd recognized this was the issue; their boys were in. The rest saw a long-neglected hope spring to life. ". . . Certainly there is no human justification for such a waste of talent and youth. I promise you solemnly that if I am elected President, the peacetime draft shall be discontinued."

They would not let him speak further. This hall of war echoed with wild acclaim. The burdens of defense, all the loose, unpromising sacrifice of money and effort and men, had become too great to bear, and, like a cripple at the shrine walking without his crutches, here was the miracle. Malcolm Christiansen, the object of sudden, fervent adoration, would have given anything for this favor. He had discovered the most luscious fruit on the tree of life, mass worship.

After the meeting, Colonel Christiansen and Moonan were driven to the old resort hotel at French Lick, Indiana, so the candidate might have a night and day of complete relaxation and privacy. The drive added to the enchanted feeling the world held for the Colonel that night.

The moon was up late and, crossing the Ohio River, it poised over the dark outline of a tobacco warehouse. It spilled over on the roof of the warehouse and the middle flow of the river. They left the main highway, and came on the quiet, fragrant, slightly rolling Indiana countryside. The air was full of the smells of burning leaves, new-mown hay and moist earth. When they paused at a crossroad to check the map, they heard the regular, cheerful whir of locusts.

They were on their way again with a shifting of gears. Soon there was a change in the sound of the tires on the pavement. They were slowing down for a village. It was an old town fast asleep. Giant trees, planted perhaps by Johnny Appleseed or one of his kind when this was a dirt road, laced across the street like the beams of a cathedral. Out of the night rose the shapes of slumbering houses. A light breeze ruffled the curtains of a second-story window as they passed. Who nodded behind these waving curtains? What dreams refreshed the weary heart?

The next day, while they were resting at a guest cottage on the grounds of the hotel, a special military messenger brought a package for Colonel Christiansen. It was from General Barrow, the chairman of the Joint Chiefs of Staff. The letter read:

Your speech in Louisville came as a thunderclap to those of us who share the responsibility for planning the defense of the free world....

"Whoever invented that phrase, 'free world'"? Mickie asked the Colonel rhetorically. "It's the neon sign behind which we do the grubby business of running an empire."

. . . I can excuse this on grounds of ignorance, and therefore am providing you with a top-secret report of our global commitments and strategic plans. I trust after reading this report, you will see fit to announce your support for the Selective Service System of obtaining needed military manpower, and thus prevent an immediate deterioration of our overseas position.

I have written this letter on my own initiative without consulting my colleagues, the Secretary of Defense, or the President.

The Colonel read the letter. His long and eloquent lip turned up in exasperation. His forehead gathered in a frown. He sighed gustily and said nothing for a moment. Then, as though trying to free himself, he said, "Same old General Barrow. Treats everyone like reserve majors. No one can ever be right but him."

The report was encased in a black leather notebook and was 116 pages long. Christiansen made no effort to read it. It lay unopened on the table.

"Do you want to look at the briefing?" Mickie asked.

He shook his head.

That evening after they had gone, a cleaning woman found the notebook still on the table, and took it to the manager. He placed it in the safe and wrote the Colonel. There was no reply, so in January he burned the contents and gave his schoolboy son the notebook. The leather was too good to waste.

# *Chapter* TWELVE

"THERE COMES a time in every political campaign," Moonan said, "when the tide begins to turn. Slowly, almost against its will it starts moving into the mud flats. Perhaps the tide has altered long before you knew it and was on its new course. But it has to make its presence known dramatically; you have to see the water flowing up against the rocks and tossing on them, and hear the water roaring into the dry channel before you believe it. Then all the wise guys, the politicians and reporters, will nod their heads and say, 'I saw this a-comin.' It was back there in Topeka."

He said this a few days after the Louisville speech.

Window stickers of blue and gold, "Crusade With Chris," appeared on Fords and Plymouths and Chevvies and not just Buicks and Caddies and Mercedes. Ladies collected "Dollars for the Crusade" in front of suburban supermarkets and in the drab streets of the working class. True, there were sighs and murmurings. President Thompson said in Spokane, "Certainly I should like to drop the draft, too. But I am not only running for office. I am the President of the United States. That is my highest obligation. I cannot honestly stop the Selective Service and at the same time and of honest mind insure the safety of the United States. This is a painful truth." A retired Supreme Court Justice told a law school audience, "A profound sense of inadequacy haunts our time and place in history. We seem to have lost the noble purpose that began our American experiment. We are willing to settle for any jot that will give us a moment more of freedom from the problems that crash about us."

Colonel Christiansen journeyed about the land in a triumphal procession, as a beneficent king receiving the gladness of his subjects after granting a general amnesty and an extra allotment of grain.

He experienced the slow, smoky warmth of Indian summer in Tennessee. The mists crept out of creeks at sunset and lay damp and warm and fragrant on the fields. The mornings began with a mysterious promise, so the early riser was excited by the prospect of the day. He felt the blustering winds of winter in Omaha. Shuddering gusts struck his hotel penthouse, and looking out, he saw people far below struggling against the gale. He saw the snow falling softly in Idaho. He sat on the warm sands of California with the sun on his face. He watched the southward flight of birds in Pennsylvania. He spoke again and again and again to crowds that were all his. He made them laugh and cheer and sigh with lines provided for him. Each day, his faith in himself grew taller.

Then the glorious pageant was over. He left the final rally at Madison Square Garden wet with perspiration and so charged with excitement and radiance that Mickie said, "You glow in the dark."

Bundled up and in a limousine bound for Silas King's place in Connecticut, the Colonel experienced the letdown that comes to a fighter after the bout is over. The dressing rooms are dark and empty. The wild flight of adrenalin is grounded. Reality sits leering in a corner. He regretted too that the outrageous love affair between himself and the public was, if not over, at least in a different phase. They would not be able to caress each other in public as often. And he would change from the lover to the husband who has some slight obligation to pay the bills and keep the woodshed full. Thinking of this latter prospect made him sulky, so he taunted Moonan about his obesity.

Mickie had his own raw thoughts, and he flung back, without thinking, "That may be so, but I haven't any mortgages coming due in January, and you do."

What did he mean by that? the Colonel demanded.

Mickie was sorry he had spoken, but he had to finish what he began. He said, "You have bought and paid for all the votes you will get. A simple cash transaction. Repeal the draft, one hundred per cent price supports, less taxes, peace, more security, more water for the West and more power for the East. But you've borrowed, and the devil will get it out of your hide, as a priest once told me."

Christiansen said with great assurance these were details that men like Silas King and Jefferson Lawrence could work out.

Moonan laughed. He was a mass of shaking, gelatinous flesh erupting in chuckles.

The Colonel told him to be quiet.

The creditors began lining up almost as soon as the votes were counted. At the victory celebration, just after President Thompson conceded, Senator Maze Bledsoe backed Silas King up against the bandstand and told him that, by damn, he wanted the oil imports cut down and named an explicit figure. King told the Senator in a pleasantly negative way there was nothing doing. Bledsoe, shouting out above the band, said all right, by God, just see where he would get when he came before the Senate Appropriations Committee. The senators weren't privates first class in any children's Crusade. They had their own kingdoms, and you had to pay the toll to get through. They expected the promises to be paid off, and pronto.

The Irish judge from Detroit showed up with a list of 253 names Father Werther demanded to be expelled from the Government service as "traitors and heretics." The judge was a little drunk and said amiably enough that the Father, God rest his soul, was a little mad and if his wishes were not complied with, there would be hell to pay.

Silas King grumbled that everyone who put a nickel in the Crusade thought this gave him the right to ten jobs or ten contracts.

Mickie told him, "Silas, I thought you, at least, knew that no one except the priests and children went on the Crusades to propagate the faith. Adventure, women, trade—that's the bait.

"You should set up a priority for the new Administration. Give up TVA to private initiative the first week, the national forests the next, and on down until the rural electric co-ops are dissolved and Western Union has taken over the Post Office Department. This will make it easier for the Congressional investigating committees to schedule their hearings."

King replied, "You are not very funny, Mr. Moonan."

Finally the "Christmas Tree Crusade," as it became known in the press room, was forced by the crush of business to close its New York offices. The traffic was forbidding. One Texan complained, "This here place is like the bellowin' of bulls and the stampede and dust at a roundup."

Too, reporters stopped visitors and asked for names and missions. They often obtained completely frank information, for the businessmen, without their public relations men and lawyers plucking their sleeves, were boldly innocent.

Colonel Christiansen was bored with New York. The people were used to him. He did not stop traffic any more when he walked briskly to Central Park. He was accosted, but by the hapless legion of beggars, job-seekers and persons with mad schemes. One old fellow with piercing eyes presented him with a plan to destroy communism by drilling through the earth and coming up within the Kremlin walls.

The Colonel asked Silas King, "When can we get on with the peace crusade? I don't feel I'm doing enough. Maybe I ought to fly to Moscow or India or someplace like that?"

King knew Christiansen fairly well by then, and discouraged him. He did not want the Colonel wandering off by himself in strange lands, much less talking to the Russian Premier, Radilov, whose shrewdness in bargaining was legendary. "Chris is like a woman who doesn't know the meaning of sin, and thinks that sleeping with a man is being courteous and friendly," he told Moonan.

Out of the whole group of Crusaders one man alone, Jefferson Lawrence, was concerned by struggles for power splashed on the canvas of the world. In Europe, the long shadow of Russia darkened the ground like a roof overhang all the way to the Elbe, the deep Bohemian forest, the Austrian Alps, Thrace, the Rhodope Mountains, and the Adriatic Sea. Its underground runners disturbed the soil of France and Italy and Greece. Any night millions of its shoots might spring up and choke the grain. No one knew for sure the designs of this giant, this ogre, good fairy, or what do you think, Mac. It was the Russia of the Czars, modernized, disciplined and with an intoxicating goal, "The International Soviet will be the human race." Yet, it was the same moody "I love you" one moment, "hate you" the next, open and cunning, trusting and suspicious, true and false, wildly romantic and plainly practical Russia of old.

There was, though, a counterpoise. Cut the rope holding it back and Germany would spring at the jugular vein. The aim would be true. This would be reflex action, without fear or thought, a mystic knowledge buried deep and primeval in the genes and living in the very air. Was the seed planted in some ancient war long before men chronicled their bloody deeds? Did the Huns and the Indo-Europeans clash and grapple like animals in the Pripet Marshes thousands of years ago?

So many argued, as their fathers and grandfathers and great grandfathers had argued in the parliaments and chancellories of Europe, "The Germans will take care of this monster. Just give them the sword." These were those who feared or hated the Russians as sworn enemies of their system or because the Communists had created their own dogma and worship. These debaters were even now forging the sword, preparing it for the Germans. Others, like the Norwegians and Dutch and Belgians, cried out, "Beware! The Germans will destroy you, too. They cannot be trusted. They grow mad when they have the heavy feel of the sword in their hands and see fresh blood drenching the wound."

All the while the ancient, oppressive urge of *Lebensraum* slumbered and awoke, slumbered and awoke in the fertile lands along the Rhine.

In Asia was the most terrible struggle of all, for it was man's struggle against himself. Could he stop breeding long enough to grow food? The silent writhings in the night of man on woman were creating new victims for famine; a billion were starving.

There were two arenas in Asia. The boundary was the giant, mist-veiled mountains of the Himalayas. Beyond the peaks, almost blinding with the sun bright on the snow, to the north and east, was one pit. This was China, 650 million human beings. They were driven, just as the Pharaohs drove the long columns of laborers to build the giant tombs. But the Chinese were driven to hold back the fury of the floods, irrigate new lands, reclaim the soil, plant and reap in perhaps the largest organized human effort of man. The battle was far from over; famine still took her tithe, but there were signs of victory over hunger. This was what caused men in the houses of government, from the Kremlin to the White House, to cry in their sleep. What if China could divert this huge human energy from the desperate drive for food? Would Russia with its 6,000 miles of common frontier rest easily? Would the Pacific Ocean remain an American sea? Would the 750-year-old dreams of Genghis Khan come alive, and the Mongols sweep again over the mountains clear to the Caucasus?

The other arena was to the south. This was India, 400 million human beings who, in the best democratic tradition, were asked to slow the ceaseless spawning and plant their seed in the soil. As democracies everywhere watched in anxiety, the human beings responded reluctantly. Their ways were the old ways, familiar ways, accepted ways. Death, famine, have been visiting the villages for thousands of years. Who is man to change the celestial system and defy its wisdom?

Radilov in Moscow, President Thompson in Washington, Lennox in London, and all the lesser knights followed this struggle closely. For if India fell to hunger, all of South Asia, perhaps Africa and even South America, might turn to China and its bootstrap cure. Over the restless world were millions damned and doomed by wretchedness. They were beyond the call of those who counseled a reasonable pace. They must jump into the sky tomorrow.

Lawrence tried to interest Colonel Christiansen in these scenes. The Colonel fidgeted. His expressive face wore the mingled feelings of boredom, impatience and polite tolerance. He said, slurring even more than usual, "Now, that's very interesting, Jeff, and I'm glad you're well stocked with facts, because that shows interest in your new job, if you get what I mean. You talk this stuff over with Silas. We want to get this peace push moving."

Later, he told King that Lawrence was "deep, very deep." For himself, Lawrence thought what a charming child Christiansen was and wished there was some way he might reach through to him. But he recognized with the unhappy insight of a wise man, this was not possible. He must stand outside, and offer his wares at the door like a peddler.

The group packed up and flew to King's plantation in South Carolina to make final plans and receive the chosen guests. Those left at headquarters could cope with the sparrows and starlings that gather after any political victory.

Each morning at Magnolia Manor, if the weather was good, the Colonel came out after breakfast, climbed into the surrey (often driving it himself) and rode down to the marina on the sheltered cove. There, with much good-natured banter, he and Mickie and whoever else would come along went aboard King's yacht and out to the sea for fishing. Most days he was out until an hour before dusk. His music was the ringing cries of the gulls and the soft murmur of the ship's engines. Perhaps a school of porpoises would frolic off the starboard, and add to the gaiety and humor. The pitch and toss of the waves and the sunlight produced endless miracles of color.

After dinner the men sat around the great fireplace with their drinks while the women played cards and engaged in their own talk in another room. The business, what little of it there was to bring before Christiansen, was introduced then.

The guest one evening was an apple-cheeked old man with a silken fringe of white hair and extraordinary blue eyes. One moment they peered out with a childlike curiosity, the next with a sly craftiness. He was Congressman Burton Gant. According to Senator Wingate, he was one of the most powerful lords on Capitol Hill and would have to be dealt with as King John did his barons.

The Colonel asked him politely, "How many times have you been elected, sir?"

He answered without pride or surprise, "Twenty-three, Colonel. I have sat through the waves of reform, of spending and saving, war and peace like a rock bedded deep in the river. Sometimes the water would cover me, but each time the tide went down there I was as ugly as ever."

"How did you do this?" Christiansen was now interested.

"I will tell you first how not to be re-elected. That is to come panting into Washington with a cause or two to save the world, and an itch to get your name in the New York *Times*. Colonel, a Congressman just can't afford to be a statesman. We leave that to our brothers across the Capitol. They're elected for six years and can play with these strange mistresses. We have to take care of the old lady back home. These days everyone has his business with Uncle Sam, his pension or taxes, loan or subsidy, regulation or contract or draft, flood control or roads. I'll tell you, sir, in these days the voters are a right demanding old lady.

"When I was back home for the election, I saw a fellow I'd fixed up with a job at the Salmon Falls post office, and I asked him if he was out rounding up votes for me. 'Well now,' he told me, 'I don't know. I haven't made up my mind yet.' I reminded him of the job I procured for him and he said, 'But what have you done for me lately?'"

He laughed in a series of little barks.

"What about luck? What part does it play in politics?" Colonel Christiansen asked.

The old Congressman was silent a moment and the pine logs hissed and cracked from the burning resin. Then he remembered the verse and recited.

> "Good luck is the gayest of all gay girls,
> Long in one place she will not stay,
> Back from your brow she strokes your curls,
> Kisses you quick and flies away."

Silas King asked, "Congressman, what is the art of getting bills through Congress?"

Representative Gant sat hunched down in his chair enjoying the warm fire and looking like a gnome.

"I'm not a professor," he replied; "so I can't give you advice and charge you a fee, but I can tell you a story. The last time we had a Republican President he sent a special message to Congress to appropriate three hundred million dollars to help the railroads. It sailed through the Senate and it came to the House and there it sat. The press demanded action. The President made angry remarks about the slowpokes in the House. The railroads issued statements. The bill did not move. Finally, the New York Central sent a young man up to see me. He was a vice president, one of those fellows they have to create influence by buying drinks for reporters and White House secretaries. He'd just come out of a barbershop and smelled real pretty. He wanted to talk to me about the bill. I said if the New York Central was really interested, its president could take the time to see me.

"He came, all right, outraged as hell that his valuable time should be spent talking to a representative from up near the

Canadian border who probably didn't know a Bloody Mary from a daiquiri and never cleaned his fingernails. I let him sit there in my office a bit while I saw a boy from up around Third Lake who wanted to get out of the Army. Then I saw the railroad president. He told me, 'Mr. Gant, I am told on good authority you are responsible for holding up this legislation.' I replied that he was correct. He lectured me. This program had been worked out very carefully with the President and the Secretary of Commerce, and furthermore, the railroad executives had spent a lot of money helping elect the President."

The Congressman smiled at the memory.

"So I told him, 'Sir, you may have the Lord Almighty for your bill, and you may have elected the President singlehanded. But I ask you, What have you done for me? What have you done for my district?' Do you see what I mean? I have a very demanding old lady to feed and satisfy."

Lawrence asked the old fellow how Congress received reforms. He had in mind, he said, ways of streamlining the armed services.

Gant's face in the firelight seemed amused, but, of course, it might have been the way the flames rose and fell. He answered, "That is simple. We do not like reform. It steps on too many toes; it hurts too many people leading easy lives. It is pie in the sky. I say reform isn't worth all the energy you have to use pulling down walls. You want to reform the Pentagon and make it more efficient. How long do you think it would take before they'd find a way to get back to the old paths? Now, it's like building castles in the sand of the ocean front here.

"Mr. Lawrence, you look like a sensible man, so I will just remind you that all the reformers I ever knew or read about died of a broken heart or went crazy. Think of Jefferson up there on his little mountain in Virginia shaking his head and telling himself what a hell of a mess the people had made of democracy. Or Lincoln walking through the hospital wards and seeing all the Indiana and Pennsylvania farm boys busted up and dying because a gang of New England reformers wanted to free the niggers. No sir, stay away from reform. You be tolerant, and the voters will tolerate you."

One day when a northeaster had blown in, and the weather was too rough for fishing, Christiansen went walking down the beach. He was alone except for one of the Negro boys who were always near or by his side. He wore a leather jacket for the wind was cold. It held his pants close to his legs and brushed through his short hair. He had to jump back laughing several times when the waves crashed heavily and washed up swiftly over his path on the sand. Around the first arc of the beach, a mile or so from the manor house, the flat sweep of beach changed to dunes piled up like miniature mountain ranges, a peak here, a plateau there, and all covered with sedge grass leaning with the wind. He thought again of his strange adventures on the low dunes of the coast when he was a young officer. Was it so evil, after all?

That was the way he liked sex—a sudden, daring explosion, a grappling in the sand, and it was over and they went their separate ways cleansed and gratified, back to their own beds and lives.

Standing there in the wind he felt hale, vigorous and potent, and when you felt that way, it was good to be with a woman who felt the same, and invited you but demanded that you fight her for it. No quick end of resistance and then an unmoving lump of flesh. Instead, a wrestling for the prize with the perspiration coming out all over and smelling strong, and the passionate action of the whole body of the woman until it was over and you lay clenched together like two young gladiators. It was strange how well all the minute details of those adventures held in his memory . . . his hand under her back in the sand going numb, a little stiffness in his neck from drawing his head down to kiss her moist lips, the hot sun on his cheek, her low laugh—she never spoke to him, their communication was in other ways—the steady boom of the surf.

He dug his heel thoughtfully in the sand and he had a queer idea. Suppose now his affair with that woman and the voters were all one and the same thing. A quick, hot affair, no kind of deep understanding or even affection, renewed when you had to have each other, wrestling in the sand. And then one day it is over. Both of you over whatever madness it was, and about your separate lives.

He threw the thought aside and walked rapidly down the beach.

# *Chapter* THIRTEEN

THAT NIGHT Silas King did the talking. Not as before when he was the executive organizing the corporation and hiring the help and selling the goods, confident, toughly shrewd and a little pompous. Rather, he was a man talking of a woman he loved once, or thought he had, and who was building anew, out of the broken crusts of memory, a lust too faint to smell, and pipe dreams.

He let his cigar burn down, the aromatic smoke trailing over the room, the long ash collecting while he talked. He was talking of an America that never really existed, except perhaps in the imagination of Mark Hanna and his kind, the manufacturers and bankers turned politicians to make the Capitalist Utopia. His voice was soft and affectionate and yearning in a way that was startling, because it was so out of character.

"Chris, Abe Lincoln was a great President because he emancipated the slaves and gave the Negroes the right to be treated like anyone else. You are going to be even greater. You are going to emancipate the businessman, and save the greatest institution in this man's world, capitalism. Free us, let us get some wind in our sails and by God we'll overtake the Russians any day. But Chris, you have no idea how we've been chained down by taxes and this commission and that—SEC, FPC, FTC—and Congressional investigations. On top of that there's the dead weight of the labor unions. Let a company make a decent profit, and the union chief he's passing out statements that the workers are starving while Mr. Moneybags is raking it in. The Internal Revenue sends in a special squad to see how much they can grind out of you. And the congressmen hold a hearing to find out why you haven't reduced your price to the bleeding consumer. Your profit is a matter of public debate, but when you just break even they say it's because you don't know how to run the shop.

"But take away those shotguns from the commissions, put a little respect for free enterprise in the Internal Revenue, reduce taxes, and watch us go. We'll outproduce, outmarket any country in the world."

"What you want," Mickie said, grinning slyly, "is the right to set your own profit, your own price and your own wages without interferences from labor or government?"

"Yes," King agreed, "that's a fair summation of it."

"Give you ten years of unrestricted power, Silas, and you'll have the sweatshops and the bucket shops back; you'll own all the land, and strip off the Social Security system. Give you twenty-five years, and we'll be back to human slavery. Oh, I'm not saying it is the fault of the capitalist class. A socialist or a communist or a syndicalist would be just as rotten. It's the human inability to handle freedom. Give it to him strong and undiluted like that, and it goes to his head. He begins to think his judgment is infallible, and then he goes a step farther and assumes that everyone else is on a lower, animal level and thus doesn't have to be treated with the same consideration. The only reason you aren't charging twenty per cent interest rates now is because the Government won't let you, and I would be the same way."

King dismissed this benignly, "Your only trouble, Mickie, is that you are a socialist. You reporters all are at heart."

"Until we become editors," Moonan added. There was laughter. King went on, "The first big job, Chris, is to take all the fat off the Federal Government. Boil it down, cook it off, scrape it off. A businesslike Administration. Balance the budget. Who in the hell ever heard of a corporation going on spending more money than it takes in? That's suicide. We can save twenty or thirty billion dollars a year."

"Where is it coming from?" Lawrence asked quietly.

"There is only one place. That's the military. Those useless tanks and planes and air bases, just money drained off the top."

"What of the need to keep up our defenses against attack?" asked Lawrence, the quiet, inexorable prosecutor.

"That is as phony as a three-dollar bill," King replied earnestly, seeking a convert. "The only reason we keep buying all these guns is because we're afraid the Russians will blow us up. And they're just as afraid of us, and they keep putting the steel into tanks, too. Suppose you were a traveling salesman in hardware, and you and another drummer spent all your time quarreling and competing for the same customers and exhausting yourselves with your feud, and neglecting new customers. Wouldn't it be smart if you went to him and said, 'Let's have a drink together, Harry, and divide up this territory. We'll both get rich that way and stay out of the ulcer ward.' All right, this is what we'll do with the Russians. We'll both knock off the armaments and the big armies, and divide up the territory."

"How can you trust the Russians?" Lawrence said. "They are a different kind of human being. They don't have the same feeling about keeping a bargain that we do. You might as well talk to an Indian."

"I don't agree with you, Jeff," King said in oppressively I-know-what-I'm-talking-about tones. "I can always trust a man when I make a deal with him that's to his advantage to keep. If he is making money on it, he won't break the agreement. It will mean just as much to the Russians to cut the military fat off as to us. Perhaps more. The Premier won't have the Red Army breathing over his shoulder and demanding a veto power. I get quite a few stories through trade channels. Premier Radilov asked the president of National Steel if he thought the U.S. would be willing to disarm if Russia would, providing the Germans were disarmed, too, and the money spent in peaceful competition and exchange of goods.

"I know you'll say a Communist is a fanatic, and therefore not a reasonable individual. But the best cure for fanaticism is a five-course dinner. There is not one man in a million who can stand up to good living."

"Yes, even Cromwell discovered that," Moonan said.

Yet the duel, the brush of mind against mind, prejudice versus hope, King against Lawrence, went on for some time, long beyond the interest of Colonel Christiansen. Mickie was interested.

Old Silas, the capitalist dreamer, just as mad as any soapbox orator, against Lawrence. Moonan had some trouble placing this Lawrence in his pigeonhole. There was a distress in his spirit; it flashed up like sparks in a dark room. He was the monk whipped all the way to the monastery by a torment never wholly revealed to his brothers. Then, Mickie remembered thin slices of rumor. Lawrence was married to a woman many years his junior, an artist. The usual trouble.

They were arguing still. Lawrence said, "But how can you be so certain? Life is too unsure. Radilov, whom you seem to trust, might die and the power be taken over by reckless men. They could wreck the world, dig the hidden bombs out of the caches, mount the rockets again."

"Yes, life is uncertain. The wind could blow up a first class storm tonight and raze this house and bury us all. But I don't think it will happen."

This was the part of the conversation Colonel Christiansen took to bed with him. He was awakened later by the sound of rain moving in across the water. It was a low murmur quite different from the regular pounding of the tides. It grew louder and louder and was preceded by the sound of wind lashing the high grass on the dunes and a light dance of rain on the window. Then it struck, driving hard against the roof and windows. Christiansen drew himself out of bed and to the window to close it. Ada Mae drowsily raised up and dropped back to sleep again. He stood at the window. The rain was coming down in dense, wind-driven sheets. Mimosa trees on the lawn were bent over, their fronds in constant wild movement.

Silas King had said he did not think a storm would come and blow down the building, but here was a storm. A warning? Should he have listened more closely to Jeff Lawrence? Could he be right? Oh, to hell with it! You had to put your faith on one man or another. Life, at least in this league, was a gambling hall. You had to put your money down on a painted square or get out. I'll put mine on Silas King.

A heavy gust of wind sweeping from the sea struck an old oak, and the tree crashed over slowly and with dignity, gathering up power lines, before it came to rest on the garage roof. The sound aroused the house. Ada Mae woke up and asked what had happened.

"Is it a hurricane?"

"No," he answered, "it looks like a northeaster. Blowing from that direction. It knocked over a tree and broke down the power lines."

In the instant, he was free of his doubts. Christiansen had a strong love of the out-of-doors in all its moods—the breathless stillness of a sultry summer noon, the brisk and tingling feel of winter, the grandeur of a storm. Here was a mistress indeed. There was nothing of the bitch in nature. So now he wanted be out in the storm, away from the talk, talk of men who had nothing better to do than raise the welts of doubt. He found a flashlight and searched in the closet for the rain gear he wore fishing in the squalls.

The figure with the flashlight was down the stairs and fumbling at the door before it was detected. Silas King, awakened and alarmed by some animal instinct, was out on the stairs calling, "Who is that?"

The Colonel identified himself.

King, barefooted and in his pajamas, came clumsily but rapidly down the stairs. "Don't go out there," he cried. "You're the next President, man. We can't afford to let anything happen to you."

Christiansen laughed at him. King said plaintively, "You don't want me left stuck with Boxell, do you?"

The Colonel did not answer. He opened the door. The rain blew against his face and felt good. He focused the light until he located the utility line. A severed end sputtered, shooting out sparks and small tongues of flame. The oak had broken through the roof of the garage. He closed the door and left Silas King behind it. Christiansen walked, bending his body against the wind, into the downpour. He experienced a physical sense of exultation. Silas King knew his corporations and Jeff Lawrence his law and Mickie how to bang a typewriter, but Chris knew how to operate in a storm. Here was one place where he leaned on no man.

The Colonel entered the garage and looked for the stairs. He located it with the torch. Upstairs he discovered a badly frightened but unharmed Negro who slept there. The Negro was mumbling in a queer accent he could not understand. Christiansen heard shouts over the noise of the storm. He looked out the window and there was as odd a band of wanderers as he ever saw—Mickie lunging about in his pants and a pajama top, Lawrence in a black coat and a derby and King in a raincoat swinging a lantern about wildly. They were shouting for him. He laughed as he stood crouching by the window until he remembered the utility line. He shone his light, pulled open the window and cried out, "Stop where you are!"

A half hour later, they had drinks and general laughter in the manor-house kitchen around a kerosene lantern. Christiansen thought they had never enjoyed such fellowship before. He had forgotten the debate between King and Lawrence.

The storm lasted four days. He grew irritated and had his first argument with King. It was over a letter from Senator Fremont. He complained that the old-timers were not being consulted, and a revolt was threatening in Congress.

Colonel Christiansen proposed that they invite Senator Fremont to Magnolia Manor and ask his advice on major policy and patronage.

"I don't want to have any fights with Congress," he said. "We'll work in co-operation, like one big team. I don't want all the various branches of the government shooting at each other, and I'm for peace in Washington as well as the world. 'Live and let live'—let that be our motto."

Silas King said no. It was the kind of talk that broke up empires. It led to bloody revolutions, and it let the labor unions lean over your shoulder and tell you how to run the shop. The old conquistadores had the right idea. They broke the Indians with the power of their guns; they converted the natives to their religion and held the threat of hell over them, and they defied the great overwhelming number of the natives by the sheer dignity of their contempt. When the Indians raided their outposts, the Spaniards died fighting. This bred respect.

He told the Colonel, "Chris, that's the way to run a business. But again you let an outsider like these Fremont people come in and buy a few shares of stock, and pretty soon they are trying to push you around. There is no limit to the appetite of a minority stockholder if you let him shove you even one foot off your base."

I don't care whether he is right or wrong. If you are the head of the company, you have to prove from the start you are running it."

Christiansen nodded his head without committing himself, merely proving that he was listening, or anyway acknowledging King's right to blow off. Silas said, "There is no such thing as divine right of power. You always have to prove your right to it, no matter whether you are a Holy Roman Emperor or the boss of a street-sweeping gang." He told the story of a friend of his who came in from G.E. to be Secretary of the Navy. He came in the Pentagon, and looked around shrewdly, and soon found out there had to be a quick determination of who was boss, the Secretary or the men in uniform. He deliberately chose when and where and how the test would come. He wrote the Commandant of the Potomac River Naval Command and said that assigned to him on his staff as his driver was an efficient and intelligent young enlisted man, and recommended that he be moved up one grade. Two weeks later, the Commandant wrote back that he was very sorry, but the board had met and considered the case and decided against promotion at this time.

"And when Ted got that letter, he called up the Admiral and he said he thought he had made himself clear. He wanted a promotion. The Admiral said if he would write another letter and demand a promotion, that undoubtedly would occur. 'Oh no,' Ted told him. ' I am not writing any more letters. Once should be enough from the Secretary of the Navy. Admiral, I understand you have several projects you believe are necessary for the Potomac Command. Well, I have looked them over, and they do not impress me a bit. I am afraid I am going to have to veto them.' The Admiral recalled the board, the promotion was passed, and Ted had no more trouble from the Admirals."

General smiles and laughter. Mickie told the story of George Washington called up to the Senate to consult with them. The first President arrived in his full military uniform with his sword buckled on. He was outraged by their questions and marched back downtown and never came back again. "Thank God, for that," Moonan said, "or the President would be an errand boy of Congress, and what a Donnybrook that would be. The President is the one person with enough power to act while Congress debates and debates. The babel of democracy."

Colonel Christiansen heard them out, but they did not change his mind. He said stubbornly, "I don't want to get into any fights with Congress. I respect the—what do you call it?—balance of power. I think it would be best to invite Senator Fremont down here. When I go out to make the peace, I want the senators marching by my side."

"You don't have to let Fremont run the Administration to have Senate support," King said crossly. "You have the biggest club any President ever had. Public backing. One senator dares oppose you on this peace issue, and the voters will murder him. He knows it, too." In the end, Christiansen had his way.

Yet, the Colonel was restless and bored. There was something he missed. He had sport, good friends, the best of food. But missing was the kiss of the crowd. Moonan alone understood the nature of this passion; it was to the Colonel an affair he did not dare admit to himself, for fear it would become a nasty habit and would cause a scene with his wife and consultations with either the family reverend or psychiatrist. But it would be quite all right if an interested friend, understanding the passion and being sympathetic with it, would arrange very casually for him to be left alone in the room with this desired one.

So when Mickie heard of a Negro carnival down the road, he suggested to Colonel Christiansen they take a ride, not saying where they were going.

The car pulled off on the red clay shoulder, and they watched the unhurrying, softly laughing, always murmuring dark people moving among the merry-go-round, the booths with plaster dolls, the cotton candy machine. The women were in bright cotton dresses, the men in faded blue denim, for these were country working people. Christiansen said he wanted to get out and stretch his legs, so this incongruous couple, the man right off a magazine cover, good-looking and erect and benevolent and simple, and the squat, obese companion who waddled a little behind him and revealed anything but simplicity and faith—went among the people. There was a change in the sound, from the bright easy laughter to a silence and a sigh moving in the way a wind does through the treetops. They stopped and looked at the Colonel as men might look at one they thought was a god several thousand years ago when that was more popular than today. He waved and smiled at them. A voice cried out, "Amen," and it was taken up by the crowd.

When the Colonel had soaked this up, as a drunkard his drink, he was ready to go. They were off down the road. The driver, who was a Negro, said apologetically, "These folks around here, they think that you are Mistuh Christiansen the good fellow come back again to keep us from gettin' into a war. That's what the preacher fellow said."

The Colonel pretended to pass it off lightly. But all the while he was thinking that it was little people like this who, by a process that worked better if you weren't too damn smart and skeptical, got the message. You never heard of a Ph.D. having a revelation. But the word of God came to humble people, and this was a recompense for their hard lives.

One more visitor came to Magnolia Manor before the show broke up and moved on. He was an afterthought. He was Moonan's idea, to keep the level in the public-relations cup full and up to the top, almost brimming over. There had been signs of evaporation after Senator Fremont came South and drove such a hard bargain, and in columns hinting that not the Almighty but Silas King was the manager of the Crusade.

"What kind of man is Adam Goodfellow?" King asked Moonan.

"He is enraptured by altruism, just as you are by the sound dollar. He is a man who grew up innocent and stayed that way. He thinks all you have to do to save the human race is tell us all to love our neighbors, and that one day we'll realize the truth of this. He can love and forgive the basest double cross. You know he was just elected Governor of Pennsylvania. He had been campaigning for years for better schools, for hospital care for the aged, or to protect a tiny group like the orthodox Amish sect. He is a huge, stooped character with a cheerful and shuffling walk. He has a big Roman nose and a mop of unbrushed white hair. His support for the Colonel was a real help in many quarters. Gave us a mild glow of good works."

He came to the manor house in the late afternoon, riding in from the nearby railway station in the small surrey like a caged giant. Christiansen greeted him awkwardly, as if he were a curiosity, like a Hottentot.

The Governor put his arm around Christiansen's shoulder and said, "Let us walk off by ourselves."

There was of this man a reminder of his father, almost an odor of unselfishness that was sweet and had nothing of the sour smell of overweening ambition and hostility of man to man about it.

They went down to the dunes and stood for a moment watching the rolling line of surf. The time was approaching for dusk when the winds died and the sun's lingering light gave the water a glimmering tranquillity. A few clouds on the horizon were strips torn from a white sheet and tinted a faint pink. The endless, muffled boom of the tide and the screams of gulls were the only sounds. The Colonel had a desire, not strong enough to burst out, but like the rolled-up leaves of spring on a tree, to tell Goodfellow his doubts. Was it wrong, not only wrong but evil to hunger for the adoration of the crowd? Was he on the right path to peace?

The older man stood, one foot ahead of another. His deep voice said, "Why must men worship idols in their temples when there is the sea? What more proof do you need of a higher intelligence?"

They stood silently. Governor Goodfellow said, "Colonel, we have lost our way."

"Oh, no, I know the way back," Christiansen said.

"I am glad you do. I was not thinking of the path back to the house, but of the way Jefferson saw for America. An enlightened democracy. The slow, gentle process of democracy creating a wise state where men cared for one another's needs, uncovered the secrets of the universe and avoided strife. 'Equal and exact justice for all men, of whatever state or persuasion, religious or political; peace, commerce, and honest friendship with all nations —entangling alliances with none. . . . They should be the creed of our political faith—the text of civil instruction—the touchstone by which to try the services of those we trust; and should we wander from them in moments of terror or alarm, let us hasten to retrace our steps and to regain the road which alone leads to peace, liberty and safety.' Colonel, we have wandered; we have wandered.

"Our energies and talents and resources have been diverted from growth. Our brains are stuffed with the nonsense and untruths that flicker endlessly on the television screens. Government is burdened with petty men. Inspiration is lost, and learning is a vanishing art. The only men who enjoy their work are poets, thieves and pimps. We need a revolution. 'I hold it, that a little rebellion, now and then, is a good thing, and as necessary in the political world as storms in the physical.' "

The old man stared out brooding at the darkening water. He said, "You and I, Colonel Christiansen, are standing on an avalanche. Don't you feel the ground shudder and the snow shake loose? We cannot stop it. This is mankind all over the world throwing off the past. We will be smothered unless we rush ahead. You must lead us, in this spring. The American people will follow you. Just call to them."

The Colonel wanted to respond gloriously, but all he could think to say was, "Well, I'm going to do all I can to get us off on a good start to peace."

"That is good," the Governor said. He turned to face Christiansen. "Let me offer you a humble cup of advice. Peace is more than signing your name to a treaty. It is more than wishes and hope. It is food and water and shelter enough for all. Without these, men will fight. And it is freedom. Without it, there are explosions. Who is to be your Secretary of State?"

"Silas King. He is the best bargainer in the world."

Governor Goodfellow shook his head doubtfully. "I don't know," he said. "There is a man who looks upon the accumulation of wealth as the end-all of life. He is no William Penn or Thomas Jefferson to understand the heavings of men in mass."

Christiansen said he did not think the Governor knew and understood King. He was a good man, really. But what recommendations did Goodfellow have?

The old reformer spoke with the passion of the evangelist who no longer has to think of his lines, he has said them so often. Change the income tax to erase special benefits. Melt down the military establishment and turn its gold to school, medical research, housing, recreation, old-age assistance, consumer protection; recognize and give heed to the faint heart-beats of liberty wherever they existed by giving a helping hand; find water for the deserts. . . .

Colonel Christiansen dug in the sand with his heel. He had lost the old fellow.

The day was fading quietly. Gray folded over the sea. An evening star shone faintly. Malcolm Christiansen, with his unforgettable enchanted air of glory wrapped about him, watched the water move up the beach in the changing tide.

The Governor was not aware that his audience was gone. He said bravely in his deep voice, "This will take courage, and the people will not always understand you. This is the loneliness Lincoln knew. But history will love you well."

The Colonel stared at Goodfellow, partly in irritation, partly in despair. He said unsteadily, "I don't understand all this."

He turned and walked away from the beach. The old man followed shaking his head. Soon the tide came up and buried their footprints.

# *Chapter* FOURTEEN

THE WASHINGTON weather forecast for January 19 was "fair with moderate temperatures."

The day began obediently. A late-rising sun climbed slowly up the hills across the river to the east. Then it touched the dark, barren limbs of the elms along Constitution Avenue with faint bands of gold. The flags on the Capitol waltzed languidly in a slow southern wind. Government clerks lingered outside, reluctant to plunge into their marble caves of paper work on so fine a morning. The rising young men with dispatch cases and morning newspapers tucked under the arms allowed their puritan gazes to wander lightly over the shapely legs of secretaries clicking down the street in outrageously high heels.

It looked like a beautiful day.

At midday, the huge weathervane on the tower of the Smithsonian wheeled around and pointed northwest. The flags began a frantic dance, whipping with every gust. No one loitered, but walked hurriedly and with coat collars up. The face of the traffic policeman at Fourteenth Street and Pennsylvania Avenue grew red with cold. Gray clouds sailed low across the sky in a race to the sea.

An immense cloud, dark as fury, rode on the wind to Washington and was left there when the fickle gusts stopped as suddenly as they came. At two o'clock, lights in the Government buildings turned on. They were like torches in a forest at dusk. At four o'clock, when the homeward-bound rush started to poke across the bridges over the Potomac River, snow fell. It made a soft sound brushing against windows and gathering in corners. By dinnertime, snow covered the streets and sidewalks and was still coming down.

A sage at the Press Club bar remarked, "It is Fate, crying her last frozen tears for Matty Thompson."

This, it was agreed, was a fairly good way of putting it. Matthew Thompson was sleeping his last uneasy night at the White House. He would turn his bed over to Malcolm Christiansen the next day.

Colonel Christiansen awoke the next morning at seven thirty. He was staying at a high-walled estate on Foxhall Road. He was tired and his stomach was not happy. Little twinges racked him, and he lay still, hoping they would go away. If they did not, he had stuffed a bottle of paregoric in his bag. He was afraid some damn thing would come up to bring these gripes on.

Christiansen had left South Carolina happy, healthy and tanned, riding in the private car of the president of the Atlantic Coast Railroad like an Oriental prince. The southern sky was clear and warm. How calm, how friendly was everyone. What a sense of happy adventure lay ahead of them, just as on his boyhood drives across North Dakota with his father. The American Legion band played a marching song with great emotion, the people shouted encouragement in their soft voices, the engineer tooted three times, and the wheels began to move. Pretty women threw kisses, and the journey was on.

Just south of Richmond they ran into the gray skies and snow. The train slowed down to enter the onetime capital of the Confederacy. Old, grimy brick buildings stared forlornly as if they had passed the point of hope and were waiting only for the wreckers. People walked heavily and without joy. And then there was this incredible sight.

At one point the railroad tracks ran parallel to a dreary street of small houses. The train was going so slowly that those on the street and the passengers in the train could exchange penetrating glances. Here it was that some dozen or more human scarecrows stood in the thin snow, glaring at him like condemned men, and holding homemade signs. They were all old and ragged—men so fragile you wondered how they stood up in the wind and old crones with no trace of their sex at all but their skirts. The signs said, "Pray Help Us, Colonel. We Are Starving. How Can We Live on Our Old Age Pensions!"

He could not avoid them. There they were, staring malevolently into his very spirit.

The Colonel could do nothing but snarl at Silas King, "What in Christ's name can I do about their pensions? That's up to Congress."

King said, "They shouldn't allow such things to happen. This is a public nuisance, and they should be arrested."

It was then that Christiansen's stomach began bothering him.

Now, here it was the morning of his Inauguration. He pulled back the curtains and looked out. Bless the day! The sky was clear and the wind was gentle. Those were good omens, weren't they?

He wished with all his spirit the day was over. There would be so many people to shake hands with and say a few words and smile to. It was like running a series of 100-yard dashes. Why wasn't it possible to induct the new President by simply swearing him in before his family, and letting him go about his business? He asked Silas King this, and his friend replied too many people had waited too long for this event. It was a national holiday and must be celebrated.

The Colonel sighed and climbed out of bed. He opened his bag and found the paregoric. The soldier's friend. He unscrewed the cap and took a swallow.

He and Ada Mae had breakfast with the Kings and their host and his wife. Silas was extraordinarily solemn, as if perhaps he was having second thoughts about this venture. Their host remarked about "these perplexing problems," and, "What do you intend to do about the German crisis?"

Christiansen left the table rather abruptly and went to his room to dress in formal clothing. He looked at the striped trousers and morning coat and grumbled to the valet, "You'd think I was going to a funeral."

He was invaded by melancholy. He sat on the bed and put his shoes on. He pulled too hard and a lace broke. He snatched off the shoe and flung it angrily across the room. It almost hit Mickie Moonan as he opened the door.

Mickie put his head to one side and said, "Colonel, your aim's bad. You need relaxation. How about you and me ducking out right now and going to the races? I know a little track over in West Virginia where they are so backward the races aren't fixed."

Christiansen's face split into a great grin.

"Can't you see them up there at the Capitol? The top hats bobbing around, and the ladies shivering in their fur coats and wondering what the cold wind is doing to their make-up. And everyone thinking, 'What's keeping Colonel Christiansen?' So finally here comes Judge Herring looking like an apologetic coyote, and he says, 'I'm sorry, ladies and gentlemen, but the Colonel has gone off with an Irish tout.'"

The idea was so absurd that Christiansen laughed.

Mickie had not finished his tale. He said, "We had a mayor in Chicago, Joe Clancy was his name, and he had been a fireman. The time came for him to present his program to the City Council, and no Joe. The reporters were there with their notebooks and the photographers and the Good Government League, and the Councilmen in their best ties, but no Mayor. So they telephoned his office and they didn't know where he was, and they tried his house. The only person home was an old lady who cooked for them, and she was a little hard of hearing so she screamed at them, 'If you want Joe Clancy, call Engine House Fifteen. He's either back there in the corner playing checkers with Al McGuire or out ridin' to a fire.' They found him at a two-alarm in the Loop."

When Christiansen left the house for the ride downtown, the air was crisp and clear and exciting. The sky was an untouched turquoise, and the dimensions and shapes of objects were very sharp. Looking down the hill at a sea of roofs that cut into the air with a marvelous clarity, he thought of farmhouses etched out of the northern prairie by the dry winds.

The sun glittered on the snow tossed on the branches of trees, roofs, mounds of bushes, and the lawn. He scooped up snow, molded it into a ball, shouted, "Catch," and threw it lightly at Mickie.

The Colonel threw a second snowball before he stepped into the limousine. The car rolled through the gates where a police escort was waiting. Ada Mae chattered. He looked over the speech cards written in extra large type. They had checked the speech on the train, and Christiansen had crossed out the words he found hard to pronounce.

He and Mrs. Christiansen were going to the White House early, because Ada Mae wanted to look over the house and talk to Mrs. Thompson of housekeeping problems.

They came to the White House and waited awkwardly in the entrance hall. He was the stranger in this room with its great glittering chandelier and red rug and smell of furniture polish and flowers. Yet he felt like a passenger on a ship well out at sea; you do not belong to any country, there are no ties tugging at you, and it is possible you will not reach any shore.

President Thompson and his wife came to greet them. The President might have been an officer going home after a tour at a Godforsaken desert base, and shaking hands with his replacement. He was quite cheerful. He gallantly complimented Mrs. Christiansen on her hat, and told the Colonel how much he admired his air of sincerity.

"I would like to have your secret," he said smiling. "I get the disconcerting feeling that my audiences think I am trying to put something over on them."

They laughed and were at ease.

Ada Mae asked, "Are the servants at the White House right dependable?"

The President answered, "Oh very much so. They carry out your orders implicitly. But you see the trouble actually is in deciding what orders to give them. Shall they clean the Blue Room or the Green Room? And sometimes you forget and give them conflicting orders, because there is so much to do you cannot keep up with all the household crises."

Was there an edge of laughter in his voice? Christiansen could not be sure. He distrusted smart men, because they had so many little ways of laughing at you, and you could not always detect them.

The two women left together to look over the house, and President Thompson led the Colonel into the library. Soon they were talking as old acquaintances about the Army-Navy game last year and the mannerisms of certain generals.

Christiansen asked him, "Mr. President, I am confused. Why are you so cheerful at this time when you are stepping down?"

He had no intention of being rude. But the question bothered him so he must ask it.

Thompson looked at him. He replied, "To sit in a house and see it tumbling down day by day, week by week, year by year . . . it is an excruciating experience. I have had enough of it."

There was a silence, and Christiansen could hear the grandfather clock in the hall ticking loudly.

The Colonel spoke awkwardly, "How can it be so excruciating, as you call it? You have a good mind. You are trained in this sort of thing. You have good assistants."

The President said, "Colonel, I am out of my time. I would have been a good James Madison, a part of the exciting current of youth and revolution, yet with a Jefferson before me to lay the foundation. You see, Colonel, Mr. Madison did not have to manage a huge bureaucracy that lies in your path like a sick cow and will not budge. He did not have to juggle like so many balls all those who have acquired the right to tell the President what to do. There are the congressmen, and how many foolish and vain little barons they are. You must treat them ceremoniously and circumspectly and yet wage unceasing war upon them. There are the lobbyists; I think more than twenty-five hundred divide their time between buying drinks and writing reports to stir up the troops back home. There are the dyspeptic editors who have to grind out so many editorials every week. There are the prime ministers of our allies who regard every concession to our own people as a traitorous blow to them. And, of course, that great dumb giant, the voter.

"Colonel, in a few hours, I can take off my bland look and frown if I want to. I can tell a man I do not like that he is a fool. I can take two drinks after dinner without receiving a petition from the WCTU signed by three thousand virginal old maids."

He smiled a thin, ironic smile.

Colonel Christiansen said, "Well, of course I am not going to try to run this whole thing by myself. I don't have the training or the inclination you might say. I have a team of good men, and they are going to co-operate with Congress, and I am going to devote myself to peace."

Thompson looked at him tolerantly and replied, "Colonel, you are a decent fellow, and I wish you well. I have had a little experience with peace, too. She is a wild and commanding mistress. You spend your hours wondering anxiously when she will leave you. At times when the shadows grow long and she seems about to go, you wish in your madness that she would go once and for all and not torment you so."

Colonel Christiansen stood up, and said, "Well, thank you very much, sir."

The new President was sworn in from the top of the long steps of the Capitol. A sharp, cold wind breathed across the plaza and blew his fine hair as he stood bareheaded. Overhead, small clouds raced like frightened children. He saw them first over the tip of the Senate Office Building, and they were soon gone. In his mind's eye, he could see them fly south to the winding river, throw a swiftly moving shadow over the tideland flats, and then be off to sea.

President Christiansen had no sense of physical existence. He did not feel the stinging wind, his black overcoat heavy on him, the thin paper of the family Bible on which his hand lay, nor the unfamiliar grip of a stiff collar on his throat.

He saw, as though from a distance in time, the depthless sea of heaven the color of a cornflower, a thin trickle of mucous running from one nostril of the Chief Justice, the terribly solemn face and red ears of Jeff Lawrence, figures frozen in stiff poses, the gleaming marble pillars of the Supreme Court, and the green dome of the Library of Congress. None of these created any flow of thought; they might have been brightly unreal scenes on post cards.

Then his eyes caught sight of a huge beech tree on the lawn of the Capitol. Its winter limbs were like arms lifted in prayer. This struck a well of emotion. It spurted out, and he had a sense that this very act of standing bareheaded with his hand on a Bible was an answer to prayers of the world's millions, they who wanted peace as much as bread. He wondered if he was really the same creature who came bawling from his mother's womb on a suddenly cool night of early fall, who was reared in a flat, hard country among the fields of wheat and wind-scorched frame houses and barns and stores and churches, and thrown into a military school and there initiated into the orderly society of soldiers.

The Chief Justice was now speaking the oath of office. President Christiansen's mind dipped into memory, did so effortlessly as a hawk swooping on a down air current with its wings outspread. What he recalled was not important, or so it seemed—eating a vanilla ice cream cone as a small boy at a country dairy as his father stood smiling beside him. Why should such a simple moment be so wonderful that the memory of it filled him with joy? He did not know. . . . The stale, hot, unctuous air of late summer in the small church two counties away where his mother often took him, the rustling of the stiff dresses the women wore to church, the congregation bawling out the hymns, the nasal voice of the minister, the buzzing of a fly, the threats and promises of the Bible, the fiercely whispered words of his mother, "Sit still, Malcolm." He had never liked the name "Malcolm" since, and much preferred "Mac" or "Chris." But women, Ada Mae included, seemed to think a man should be called by his whole name even if it were Archibald. This remembered scene made him feel vaguely unwell, bloated and listless and peevish. . . . Coming on the body of a Communist soldier lying in a water-filled rut in Korea. He had on his quilted uniform, and it was not ragged yet so he must have been a new recruit, a farm boy from a distant province, say Kwangsi. Christiansen stood tired and unshaven looking at the body and wondering by what decree did the farm boy lie in the rut on a muddy road and he walk by.

This made him very curious. Was it all a game, and one side permitted to win the game this one hundred years and the other the next? Would his son's son one day lie in a muddy road and a Chinese soldier wonder in passing at the fate that placed them thus?

Malcolm Christiansen realized with a start that the ceremony of investiture was over. He was the President. He had said the words. The Bible was closed and withdrawn. The Chief Justice put on his hat and wiped his nose. Mr. Christiansen began the words of his Inaugural Address.

". . . And so, we will begin the Crusade for peace. And our motto shall be those blessed words, 'Glory to God in the Highest, and on earth peace, good will toward men.' "

The hushed pause, now so familiar to him, followed. Then the applause and cheers spilled over him. The President noticed that even the Chief Justice was a little sentimental, tears watering his eyes. Mr. Christiansen drew himself up even more erectly and bowed his head graciously.

On the platform with him, a quietly melancholy little man in a top hat, looking very much like a manservant in a British play, had different reflections. Jefferson Lawrence thought of the lines of T. S. Eliot:

> And indeed there will be time
> To wonder, "Do I dare?" and, "Do I dare?"
> Time to turn back and descend the stair,
> With a bald spot in the middle of my hair—
> Do I dare
> Disturb the universe?
> In a minute there is time
> For decisions and revisions which a minute will reverse.

The new Secretary of Defense was afflicted with doubts. This, he recognized with a wan smile, was to be expected. He leaped into events in moments of high spirits, and when they had subsided and reason took their place, doubt moved in. He wondered now, looking at President Christiansen, how this foolish, make-believe crusade would end, led by a lovable child who fancied himself inspired by the Lord. Lawrence inwardly cursed himself for not protesting, crying out, standing in the way of the disarmament program.

Mickie Moonan, on the other side where he had a good look at the new President's face, thought, "He does it well, damn well, and who is ever to know the difference? As long as he looks that nobly and speaks so firmly, they will never know."

And Silas King, hardly listening at all, for he put little value in words, sensible man, was counting up what might be done with a tax cut, how the dividends might be distributed so none would fall into undeserving hands.

That afternoon, President Christiansen stood in a wooden stand in front of the White House. His feet were warmed by electric heaters and he drank steaming cups of hot coffee. He watched the parade, as a boy would a circus. He grinned happily at the beautiful lines of soldiers stepping smartly as they passed him, at cowboys on prancing ponies, at shapely girls twirling batons, at the ornate state floats. He applauded in delight at the one from Georgia. It was a peach orchard with lovely ladies tossing peaches to the crowd. And the soldier President had a moment of rare sentiment. This was when his Marine regiment came marching by with a new flag, a gold crusader's cross on a blue shield. No one had told him of this. He heard the cheering crowd long before the regiment reached his reviewing stand; in fact, as it turned the corner coming into Pennsylvania Avenue by the old bank. The roar grew into a mighty ovation of thanks. This time it was he who felt the quickly roused tears on his cheeks.

Toward the end of the parade, as the huge moon rocket was rumbling by, Judge Herring slipped in the back door of the stand. He had been in the White House keeping the shop. He whispered in the President's ear. The British Prime Minister, Hugh Lennox, was most anxious to talk to him. Herring explained that in the Communications Center in the White House sub-basement there was a closed television circuit with London, and the two leaders might use it for their talk. Would the President care to set up a time? An hour from now? Two hours? All this spoken very deferentially. Why not now? President Christiansen responded. He was becoming bored with the parade. It was too long. Others were leaving. He could see them straggling out, walking with tired feet, across the park. Come on, Silas, the President motioned, we have work to do!

The three of them, like three boyish conspirators on their way to a secret meeting place in the woods, went back to the White House. "Thank the Lord for the British," King exclaimed. "I was about to freeze." He stamped his feet on the plastic-tiled floor of the entry to the West Wing.

Mr. Christiansen added, "And I was getting pitcher's arm from waving to every governor!"

Judge Herring led them obsequiously to the elevator and told the operator, "Communications Center."

The car slid effortlessly and noiselessly downward. President Christiansen had not begun to think of what in the world the Prime Minister wanted. His mind was on the Georgia float, the tingling feeling in his fingers as they warmed up, and the desire to go to the bathroom. The elevator door opened smoothly, and

Mr. Christiansen said, "First things first, Judge. Where is the head?" Herring looked bewildered. "All right, you landlubber, where is the can, the john?"

The elevator operator pointed down the hall. "First door to the left, gentlemen."

As they walked, Judge Herring said, "All reinforced steel and concrete down here. This is the impregnable bunker. Only a direct hit would destroy it. Food for two months stored here. An auxiliary power plant with a gasoline engine. Soothing music."

Herring pushed open the door. They were met by the familiar antiseptic smell. The President stood at his stall, sighed in relief and said, "But what would you do when you had to go outside and breathe the poisoned air?"

Herring replied, "I haven't gone that far in my briefing yet."

The Communications Center was a small routing and reception room, and in a fan around it there were rooms for receiving and transmitting by radio, teletype, Morse code and television, and for decoding messages. Also several studios. The routing room, which they first entered, was occupied by a lieutenant and enlisted men armed with pistols, the guards and messengers. They all arose quickly and saluted. Mr. Christiansen nodded his head, "At ease." Herring said they wanted to be taken to the television studio to talk to the British Prime Minister.

The studio was inelegant and functional. They sat at a table and looked at a screen ahead and a little above them. Just above the screen the lenses of the cameras were visible. The officer in charge of the center, a colonel, explained that the photographed image of the speaker on the other end of the circuit would appear on the screen while simultaneously they were being photographed. All of the major capitals of the world now had such equipment.

This new toy at his disposal fascinated President Christiansen. He asked a good many questions and even went into the little room behind the screen where the photographers worked to see what their picture would look like.

"Silas," he called out, "look pleasant. You're like a man waiting for his case to come up in court."

"How can I?" King replied dourly. "The British probably have a hot potato to toss to us—at a cost of several billion dollars. They never waste any time. This is a genius of theirs."

"What do you mean?" the President asked absently. He was still looking at the equipment.

"Very simple. They find a crisis that must be solved in forty-eight hours, and we wind up paying the bill. Winston Churchill took that little haberdasher we had for President in the late forties, Truman, like Grant took Richmond. Overawed him. Not me. I would have said, sorry, Mr. Prime Minister, but we are not paying this bill."

"I don't think I know about that."

"When the second World War was over, Britain was on its tail financially and overcommitted. There was trouble in Greece, with the Communists likely to take over. This would have broken the British command on the Mediterranean. So Churchill whispered in the haberdasher's ear that Russia would come charging out of the East, and sink all the fleets in the Mediterranean, and it was true that Stalin was acting a bastard at the time. So we wound up paying the bill for Greece and Turkey, and that was merely the beginning. I am afraid really to look up how much money we have poured down this drain simply because Churchill was so impressive and this man Truman so impressionable. We could have paid off the national debt." He shook his brightly gleaming bald head in melancholy movement.

Within a few minutes, the engineer turned off the lights in the studio. A figure appeared on the screen, presumably Hugh Lennox, the British Prime Minister, a bulky, loose-limbed individual wearing a double-breasted waistcoat.

"My congratulations, Mr. President, and those of the British people." His voice rather reminded Mr. Christiansen of a jeep moving slowly over a gravel road. "I regret interrupting your festivities."

"Oh, that's all right," the President said. "I was getting cold and tired of standing."

"We are very much concerned by a crisis that has arisen."

Secretary King's foot nudged the President's. Steady, old boy. A chill began at the base of Mr. Christiansen's spine and moved up his back. He could feel goose pimples on his arm. Crisis! What terror had broken loose in the world? He was not sure he wanted to hear it right at this moment.

Mr. Lennox said, "Our intelligence chaps have discovered a

small American atomic weapon, apparently stolen from your stockpile in Germany, in the cache of the *Freiheitbund*. This is the unofficial militia of that terrible Gottfried fellow. We have recovered the weapon. We have also obtained copies of a rather violent plan by the Bundists."

The President said a little crossly, "I don't understand this. Who are these people, and what do they want with our bombs?"

The Prime Minister's eyes widened in a look of polite surprise. He explained, "Mr. President, Gottfried is a neo-Fascist—I believe that would be correct—who has organized the youth in semi-military battalions. He has been telling mass meetings that the youth must reunite Germany by force. The theft of an atomic weapon is proof of the reckless character of this moment. You give a German a bomb, Mr. President, and he is under some mystic compulsion to throw it. This is exactly the plan with the stolen bomb. They intended to blow up the principal Russian military installation in East Germany. Carry the bomb in a bag, just as in the cinema. A bloody business."

President Christiansen was panting asthmatically as he breathed.

Silas King asked, "What would the Germans hope to accomplish? They would be wiped out in retaliation. This is wholly impractical."

Prime Minister Lennox said, "Why does a shark strike? If we can get our scientists to find the answer to that, perhaps we shall begin to know why wars break out to the great amazement of the historians who look at the facts afterward. And you know there is another interesting bit of data about the shark. Apparently it has some mechanism by which it can detect slow motions in the water, such as those made by bathers. A trace of blood in the water makes the creatures uncontrollable. They will attack anything in the way. They are known to attack boats."

Secretary King said straight, blunt, pragmatic, "Now, that is fine, but what will the Russians do?"

The Prime Minister replied politely, carefully avoiding any show of emotion or even an interest whipped up uncommonly, "I am afraid the Soviets will be up to a bloody act if they discover the theft or the existence of the plot. They are rather suspicious, and might feel called upon to wipe out a spot of West Germany as a form of necessary reprimand. And if they find this was an

American nuclear weapon, your Admirals are likely to spot Soviet periscopes off Boston and in the Gulf of Mexico. Quite messy, don't you think?"

Mr. Christiansen went through the uneasy motions of the early stage of seasickness. He could see, oh how vividly—that was his curse—the periscopes off Staten Island.

King said, "There is only one thing to do. Go to the Russians immediately. Make a clean breast of it. Impress them with our sincerity, frankness, and that sort of thing. And search for a way to harness the Germans."

The Prime Minister looked mildly surprised. "Well," he said, "that sounds sensible, and might appeal to the Russians. They like to feel a member of the family. Seem to resent the casual way a British chap calls up an American chap, and straightens out a family quarrel in a few minutes. They have to go to long and boring conferences at Geneva, where the world press stares over their shoulders, and they have to maintain their party manners or be regarded as crude Slavs. Quite a strain."

Mr. Christiansen discovered the shock, the sickness, the dizziness were over. Instead, he was mildly lightheaded as after the first drink. No great sense of concern. Thanks to Silas King. No crisis too great or too little, just give me a ring, Silas King. This man was going to be the best Secretary of State since . . . hell, who were the Secretaries of State? This man was going to be the best Secretary of State in American history. Throw away the striped pants and tea cup approach. Direct action by Silas King. As American as the mail order catalogue, the supermarket, the Coke machine.

The British Prime Minister had been talking, and the President had lost track of what he had been saying. He tuned in late to hear, "The Premier, Viktor Radilov, is a very clever chap in, I would say, an American way. No connection, but you may find him difficult to pin down. That must be the ballet dancer in the Russian character, dodging nimbly and gracefully. The German Chancellor is a frightful old fellow who is always bellowing about the insults his beloved Germany has received from the Russians or the British or the French, and demanding apologies. And he runs to the cardinals for divine intervention and a Papal blessing whenever he gets in a tight squeeze. A man his age should be writing his memoirs and indulging in eccentricity. The Germans are remarkably vital, but they need a little mixing. That is the secret of our Royal Family."

The transatlantic conversation was over, and they were riding in the elevator again when a new reaction struck the President. It hit him suddenly. Who in the bloody hell was responsible for the Germans getting one of our atomic weapons? President Christiansen felt the need to chew him up, to show there was a new exec around. God damn lax administration. Sentries fraternizing with the Germans. Might have blown the world up.

Upstairs, President Christiansen curtly motioned to Judge Herring and told him to find out who in the hell was in charge of the safekeeping of our nuclear weapons, and get him to the White House right away. He wanted also the head of our intelligence service. Not the new director, but the manager of the operations, the civil servant. They were located and came apprehensively into the President's office with the crate of his belongings still unpacked, a dusty spot on the wall where the picture of Franklin Roosevelt had been, still not replaced.

The President said coldly to General—What's-his-name—Ferris, "What kind of an outfit are you running, Ferris?"

The General, who had come from a celebration at the Army-Navy Club where many drinks had passed down the hatch, let his smile slip and replied, sir, it was a good operation so far as he knew.

Mr. Christiansen said furiously, his forehead flushed with pink, "We have just been advised by the British Prime Minister, no less, that an atomic weapon was stolen from our stockpile in West Germany, and has turned up in the possession of some young fellows. This could have led to a war, and it still may. I want to find out who let that weapon get out of our hands and all the circumstances, and I want that security system tightened up. This is a rotten disgrace."

The General started to speak, opening his mouth and letting a syllable slip out.

The President waved an angry finger at him and said, "I don't want any alibis."

The General said nothing. Mr. Christiansen turned on the Central Intelligence man who was nervously rubbing his hands.

"This is a fine outfit you have. We have to find out from the British about the theft of an American nuclear weapon. We might just as well disband your agency, and pay the British to get our intelligence for us."

"Sir," said the man under the red glare of the President's anger, "we are not supposed to watch the Germans. They are our allies. Just the Russians and the Chinese and the Bulgarians, and . . ."

President Christiansen shouted back at him, "I want you to watch everyone who might start a war. I don't give a damn whether you think they are our friends or not. A German with a bomb is just as dangerous as a Russian with one."

Secretary King watched this scene with a shrewd narrowing of his eyes. This was a different man from the mild Colonel who said he didn't know anything about farm prices or interest rates or foreign policy, and was grateful if you told him what to do. When this kind lost his temper and began ordering others around, his wind was up. He was losing his investment and scared about it. What big investment did Malcolm Christiansen have? How little he knew of him. A mistake to be caught by surprise by his moods like this. But there was so infernal much to do, the time was eaten up, gone, and here was a stranger sitting in the White House. King was surprised and uneasy; there was a very deep point in Chris he had never touched before. It was sensitive and reacted just like a hair trigger. Bang, off went his temper. That would have to be watched carefully. In an angry, upset mood the President could do something mighty foolish.

Late that night, after the Inaugural Ball, the President and his Secretary of State talked to Viktor Radilov, the Soviet Premier. Mr. Christiansen had been impatient all through the ball, wanting to see this man. What manner of man was he? What intimate glimpses could be caught on the screen of his opposite, the one on whom the peace rested? And finally when the studio was dark and still, a figure came before them on the screen, watching them as closely as they watched him. Radilov had a long and narrow face with fine features; the clipped, erect, disciplined air of one whose mind controls his emotions and lets them out only when they are useful.

Seeing him, assimilating his personality in one or two swift glances, President Christiansen decided he must now or never break through to the stranger on the screen. The President was like a traveler confronted by a deep and trackless forest which he must penetrate before night falls. He plunged in, not the least frightened but sure he would find the way.

Mr. Christiansen said, "Mr. Premier, I am Malcolm Christiansen and I am the new President of the United States. I want to report to you important news I have received just this day—one of our nuclear weapons has been stolen in Germany. It was taken by the young fellows who believe in a man they call Gottfried, who I understand is a bad character. Furthermore, the plan of this man is to blow up Russian barracks in East Germany. The British discovered the theft and recovered the bomb. I have this afternoon ordered an investigation and a tighter security system. I am sorry this happened. This is my Secretary of State, and he echoes my thoughts. I am pretty new to this whole business, but one thing I do want to do is to prove to you and your people we want peace just as much as the next fellow, and probably more."

Deep in the woods, the President paused. He looked anxiously in the Premier's eyes for a clue. The eyes, they were not cold exactly, but violently dispassionate. For a moment there was nothing in those eyes but the collection of knowledge, the quick, orderly sorting, the cool analysis. And then, Mr. Christiansen knew he had found the right path out of the forest; there was a faint light ahead to guide him.

The Premier began speaking, but what he said was more or less unimportant. President Christiansen knew, and he knew the Russian knew he knew, that words are nothing but masks. Either the mask is gray or it is illuminated by a light from within, and from this light there is friendship or another passion.

Malcolm Christiansen was elated. He had come frightened, driven by his fear to this room, not knowing where he was going. Yet within a few minutes, he and this other very important man had settled a great question. They had decided to try and be friends. And it was all so easy.

## *Chapter* FIFTEEN

Jefferson Lawrence sat behind a desk that was much too big for him. It emphasized his small stature and his humility. The desk with its carved legs and drawer fronts was the gift of the Shah of Iran to an earlier Secretary of Defense, and was a token of the Shah's gratitude to the American military for helping suppress an uprising among the northern tribesmen.

Lawrence was reaching a painful conclusion—he must make up his mind on whose side he was playing.

He was now an intruder in this huge five-sided building squatting on the Virginia earth. Its corridors were at almost any hour swarming with men in smart uniforms with rows of decorations across their chests who greeted one another as fraternity brothers meeting on the campus. You could not travel far down a hall without seeing military displays—models of battleships, tanks, planes or missiles. They were encased in the manner of a jeweler showing off his finest gems, both arrogantly and tenderly. The new Secretary of Defense was treated by the generals and admirals with what he recognized as condescension. There is a way of saying, "Yes sir, I agree fully, sir," that plainly means, "If you are stupid enough to want to do it this way, all right. But time is on my side. You are a passing visitor to this scene, and you will go and I can do things as I have always done them in the way which is, of course, correct."

The Joint Chiefs of Staff were now seated before his desk. Lawrence, used to making quick judgments about men in the courtroom, had them, at least temporarily, tagged. The Chairman, an admiral, was slow and ponderous and stubborn. He did not even recognize new ideas; so far as he was concerned they did not exist. The Air Force General would have made a good used-car salesman. He was expert at meeting conflicting arguments and skillfully turning them around to his favor. The Army General was solid and quiet. Secretary Lawrence felt that alone they might get along very well. The Navy Admiral was aggressive and blunt. These four men were products of a system which takes boys at an age when they are too young to think for themselves, feeds them a little education and a heavy ladling of simple doctrines and stiffens them with discipline. Pressed in this mold those who could not conform dropped out or were not promoted.

These four, so different in weight, shape, color of eyes and hair had a startling sameness, like the flashing of the sun on four gun barrels.

The Admiral said heavily, "Mr. Secretary, we feel that the morale of the armed forces would be seriously impaired if General Burnside was removed from command of our Air Force in Germany and disciplined. We believe that he has not been sufficiently implicated in the theft of the bomb to be so harshly penalized."

Secretary Lawrence made a decision. He would restrain his lawyer's instinct to argue and debate. He said simply, "Gentlemen, I am sorry this is your viewpoint. I respect it. But the decision has been reached by the Commander in Chief."

"Suppose," the Air Force General said with a studied casualness, "that the Commander in Chief did not have all the facts when he made his decision? Suppose all those facts are now made available to him?"

"No, gentlemen, the decision is irrevocable. The orders of a commander are not like a lawsuit to be pressed all the way to the Supreme Court. It is Almighty, it is autocratic, and it is final." He spoke pleasantly.

The Army Chief of Staff said, "I think what we all fear is the slap at General Burnside will weaken Germany's faith in us. This is the real issue. It is his testament that Germany is the strongest brick in the allied wall against the East. If Germany is breached, the Western Alliance will be a box of loose sand. And the Germans are realists. If they see Russia is going to be the master of Europe, they will find a way to accommodate."

Secretary Lawrence felt a sudden twinge at the word "accommodate." His own life was a process of accommodation, accommodating to a series of clients, to good news and bad alike, to weather, to his wife's damning indifference. He had failed her.

There had been a scene the night before. He was in the library reading *War and Peace* and had lost all trace of time. Claire was out. He did not know where. There was a commotion in the street outside the house so loud that it pulled him away from the exciting words, "One of the most conspicuous and advantageous departures from the so-called rules of warfare is the independent action of men acting separately against men huddled together in a mass. . . ." He lifted his eyes from the book and listened. Cars were screeching to a stop and horns honking furiously. He returned to his reading. ". . . But this kind of warfare does not follow any rules of war, but is in direct contradiction to a well known rule of tactics regarded as infallible. This rule lays down that the attacking party must concentrate his forces in order to be stronger than his opponent at the moment of conflict. Partisan warfare (always successful, as history testifies) acts in direct contradiction of this rule . . ."

There were loud shouts and now a banging on his door. He put the book down regretfully, for he had found that literary adventure was always more satisfactory, at least to him, than the real. He saw the butler in the hall and told him, "See what it is."

The door was opened. He heard the polite murmurs of the butler, gay young voices, and Claire's. He would know hers whispering in a crowd, every intonation. He would still every thought and almost the beating of his heart to hear her. The hall was full of a flowing stream of young people. They were intoxicated not so much by drink as by themselves and their youth. This was so like Claire, who lived with a quiet, solemn old man and who feared the damning passage of time, to surround herself with the young. She hated the threads of hair turning gray and every little line on her face.

Jefferson Lawrence tried to return to his reading. "The so-called 'partisan' warfare had begun with the enemy's entrance into

Smolensk. Before the irregular warfare was officially recognized . . ."

Someone was pounding popular melodies on the piano, and they were singing loudly—shouting really. What must the neighbors think? A deputy secretary of State on one side, the Secretary of Commerce a few houses down, a Presidential assistant across the street.

He must talk seriously to Claire and tell her that she, too, had responsibilities as the wife of a Cabinet member, as the wife of a lieutenant of the Crusade.

Even as the words came to his mind, he knew he would never have the courage. For she was like the bluebird who comes to the window sill of the invalid. He needed this vivid touch of beauty, and would do anything to hold it for his own, to see her occasionally, to share her moments of contrition. And he knew, also, that she could not do without him. For she would explode in the air as a Fourth of July rocket.

Lawrence sat quietly in the library until they were gone, trying to read, and doing very badly at it, of Denisov's attack upon the French. "He went up to Peyta, got off his horse, and with trembling hands turned over the blood-stained, mud-spattered face that was already turning white . . ."

Claire came in the library. He felt her eyes on him. He kept his on the page, not reading. He no longer knew how to talk to her. She left the room, her dress making a swishing sound as she moved.

This was accommodation, living with what you desired and hated and feeling the deeps of humiliation. He told the Joint Chiefs of Staff now, "The Commander in Chief is seeking an accommodation with Russia, and it is your duty to co-operate with him."

The slight Secretary of Defense, bald, mild yet with a sort of starch in him that no one was able to analyze, arose from his place behind the desk. The interview was over.

The Joint Chiefs got up stiffly and left through the door to the right. There was no hearty male conversation. Just a departure.

Secretary Lawrence looked at his office again, at its huge emptiness. He suspected the planners had especially designated this hall for the Secretary of Defense, for its great unfilled space would create the need for friendly spirits to fill it. A Secretary with no friends in this monstrous building would be solitary indeed.

Later in the day, at five thirty, when the parking lots surrounding the Pentagon were almost cleared of cars, Lawrence called General Anderson, the Army Chief of Staff, and asked him to step over. The Secretary had coffee on his desk and poured a cup for his guest. Then he asked, "Tell me, General, what is this all about?"

"Mr. Secretary, there is alarm in the services all the way from the Pentagon to the most remote base. Our religion, you might call it, is being destroyed, and by one of our own priests." General Anderson had a plain face and this gave an added earnestness to his words. He looked up inquiringly at the Secretary. Lawrence nodded his head approvingly for him to go on. "We've been taught the only way to keep freedom and wealth is with a loaded gun. When I was a young officer, I had a colonel—you will not find his name in any military history or as the author of a textbook, but he was a great soldier and teacher. Our infantry camp was a wild area just twenty-five miles from the city, and people who had grown tired of their dogs, drove them out and abandoned them on the edge of our camp in a woods. The Colonel took several of us lieutenants in two jeeps and drove into the woods where the dogs roamed. From a paper sack he threw out meat scraps, and told us to watch what happened. A dog with the keenest nose, a hound, an old basset, smelled the meat first and the closer he came the more excited were his sounds. This attracted the others, and within ten minutes there was the god-damndest dog fight you ever saw. The stronger dogs tore the meat away from the weaker ones. The poor old basset was left bleeding and hungry. It was a terrible sight to watch.

"The Colonel turned to us when it was over and said simply, 'Never forget what you saw today. This is why the United States must be always strong and ready to fight for its bone!'"

"You see no difference between men and dogs then?" the Secretary asked quietly.

General Anderson thought a moment. "Not enough to change the meaning of this story. Men are easier to discipline. They quickly learn the power of force. I will not shoot my enemy, because I know I will be subjected to the humiliation of a public trial and probably sent to prison or be killed myself in the gas chamber. But nations are harder to discipline than men, since they are easier to inflame into anger and they are not as reasonable. They do not understand the consequences of war or other violent actions. I can tell you with a fair degree of accuracy how many men would be killed, how many cities ruined, how many billions spent on any military engagement. But this would not deter a nation once it is aroused to the holy spirit of war. And, I can tell you the consequences if we disarm and throw over our best ally, Germany, but this will not halt a nation when it is filled with the fervor to repudiate war. These are sicknesses that come over nations. We in the military must do our best to keep an edge of sanity on our security."

Secretary Lawrence took a drink of coffee and said mildly, "So you have become the priests, the only true believers?"

General Anderson smiled. "Priests are men, too," he answered. "They have the same faults as anyone else. We have our own self-interest at stake—I'll admit that. If we disarm, promotions will be much slower. Life will be harder and our vanities will be damaged."

"Let us get to the present problem," Lawrence suggested. "What do you think the consequences will be if Germany is disarmed and we reduce our military spending a third?"

"Have you ever seen two men face each other with loaded guns? Well, I have. In fact, I was one of the men. I was out on patrol in France and became separated from my men. I had my automatic rifle under my arm and with my finger on the trigger was going through a ruined village. It was the half hour after sunset and I went inside an old building; it must have been a store or garage. I rounded a corner and saw a figure before me. It was a young German officer. He had his weapon in a position to fire, too. We stared in amazement at each other. I do not know what went through his mind, but I know my own thoughts: I can pull the trigger and kill him. But before he dies he will kill me, too. Neither side will profit. I backed carefully away and around a corner. When he saw what I was doing, he retreated too. Not very military, but practical. This is the position of America and Russia. Neither of us is going to pull the trigger, because we don't want to commit suicide. This is what the megaton bomb has done to warfare and the relations of states."

The Secretary asked, "Would you give the order to fire missiles with nuclear warheads if a Russian invasion fleet landed on the New Jersey coast?"

The General rubbed his forehead with the palm of his hand. "No," he concluded. "I would not. Never so long as there was any hope. But if we were defeated and our homes burning and our future impossible, then I would. This means the need for mobile forces for a limited war are our first priority."

"What does all this have to do with disarmament and Germany?"

"Russia has immediate and limited objectives. She can now win them without danger of megaton attack or resistance from us. That is, if we sterilize Germany and disarm ourselves. Russia wants to rid itself of its fear of Germany. There is only one way— to take over and control West Germany. Strip it, wash its minds."

"How would this be done?" The lawyer had to have his facts and chew them.

"Oh, I think it is easy enough to forecast, Mr. Secretary. There would be the usual heavy artillery of propaganda attack. This would be followed by efforts to create trouble and dissension and break open the regime. At the proper time of unrest and chaos, Communists and East German partisans would seize control of Government buildings and proclaim a revolution. Who would there be to resist? Not an army. Not the United States forces. Not the British. NATO would have to hold meetings and conferences, and by then the revolutionary Government would be recognized by Russia and the deed done.

"The loss of West Germany to the defense and the economy of West Europe would be fatal. Italy and Austria and France would topple over. Spain would be lost. I leave you to imagine the effect upon the United States if the wealth and industry of Europe belonged to the Communists. We have to keep West Germany on our side and militarily strong."

"Aren't you afraid the Germans will explode out of control? After all, the young followers of Gottfried did steal a nuclear weapon, and did intend to use it."

The Army Chief of Staff replied, "I do not think it is fair to judge a nation by one incident, sir. The officers I know are, of course, bitter against Russia. But they are patient, too. They know they must outsit Russia. They believe the East German Republic will erupt again and again, and one time the Soviets will not be quick enough with their tanks."

"These are dangerous games," the Secretary said soberly.

"I do not know of any safe way."

"No," Lawrence replied with a slight smile, "we coexist with danger these days. This, I may tell you privately, is my chief concern. I am afraid the people will be so soothed by the President's honest search for peace they will think danger has been miraculously removed from the human scene."

Across the river, on the high reaches of Foggy Bottom, stretches another huge theater of government. Leave the large, barren lobby and take an elevator with scarcely noise or motion up to the fifth floor. Out and turn left all the way to the glass-enclosed reception room. It looks like a window display in a furniture store, modern decor, paintings designed to give an impression of wealth not recently amassed but mellowed with age and culture, and, to complete the picture, a beautiful young lady. Her sole function is to welcome people, and make them feel happy with her smile. She was so successful the Nicaraguan Ambassador implored her to be his mistress and the Iranian Ambassador offered to marry her to his son. She had a way of hearing when people were coming in and looking up with a charming smile. It was the whish of the door and the sound of footsteps. Messenger boys and department assistants walked with a different step from important people who had a measured, meaningful tread of authority.

This afternoon, she looked up with an especial smile and said prettily, "How good to see you, Mr. Smallwood."

Anthony Smallwood was, to his associates in the State Department, the most important man in the foreign service. He had the gravely courteous air of an usher at an Episcopal funeral and he rather needed his hair trimmed. He was an assistant secretary of State and the constant thread of foreign policy through three different administrations. Along Embassy Row they said, "Presidents may come and go, but Tony Smallwood stays on forever." He knew where all the treaties and codicils were hidden and kept his eye on the young men coming up in the Department. A slight, disapproving nod of his head and careers were dashed forever, at least in the foreign service.

Smallwood was coming now to visit the new Secretary much as the tutor calls on the new boy at school. There was much a Secretary must learn, and Anthony Smallwood was the man to teach him. There were things one did and one didn't. These were as immutable as the tides.

Silas King was waiting for him. King thought of Smallwood as the manager of a very old factory he had taken over. He was an old-fashioned patriarch to whom the employees brought their marital as well as their fiscal problems. They had been doing business in this shop a long, long time their own way, but times were changing. And Silas King was the man to change them.

The Secretary of State spoke with cordial authority. "We have an ambitious program of foreign policy, Mr. Smallwood. You've probably read of it from the President's statements. We are going to break the ice and begin conversations with Russia in the near future."

Smallwood murmured, "Ah?" The tone was slightly questioning, slightly skeptical, but very polite.

King continued his exposition. At every pause, the Assistant Secretary murmured, "Ah?" The effect was to create an almost maddening desire to say something to evoke another response, even if it was indiscreet. This, King decided, was the technique. He abruptly said, "What would you think would be the earliest date for a meeting between the President and the Soviet Premier?"

Smallwood sat up, as if suddenly coming awake, and said, "Ah yes. We must first recall the Ambassador from Moscow for consultation on the preparation of issues. Then our ambassadors from our allies of NATO, SEATO, and the others must come home. We should consult with them on the possible reaction of the governments where they are accredited. One must not say anything to Moscow that might be misinterpreted in Ankara or Bonn or Kabul. This would upset the delicate balance of relationships. There is an ecology of politics, you know. Then, by all means, a meeting of the foreign ministers of the major Western powers, to be followed by a conference between the foreign ministers of the United States and Russia, to report back to the allied foreign ministers. Finally, a meeting of the heads of state of the allies, and exchanges of papers and views. After these are sufficiently studied, then a date could be set for the conference between Mr.

Christiansen and Mr. Radilov. Possibly a year and a half from now."

"My Lord, man," King replied, "the world might be blown up by then."

"Ah?" the Assistant Secretary murmured. This time there was a slight note of defiance, as if to say, "See if you can get it done, then. And when you can't, then you will have to come back and ask me politely to do it my way."

King understood what this "Ah" meant. He knew he would have to bring in his own manager and understudy this fellow and then hustle him to a branch factory, so to speak. It meant, too, that he would never have the full obedience and co-operation of this department with all its experts and high priests. He would have to run it with a few of his own boys and a bull whip.

Even at that, Silas King, hard and shrewd as he was, underestimated his opponent. Three days later, the news that the President was considering an early meeting with Radilov was leaked to the New York *Times*. The Secretary of State then received a long file of politely complaining ambassadors and cables from abroad. What did this mean? How will it affect our relations with you, our foreign aid, our this and that? They tried to smother him with their inquiries and alarms. Newspaper correspondents in Bonn wrote excitable stories, not quoting anyone, but the wise hands knew the source was the German Foreign Office, saying this would undoubtedly drive Germany into the Russian camp.

On Capitol Hill, old Crankshaw rose to make one of his rare speeches in the House of Representatives. Crankshaw had been in Congress so long that even the ancient colored man who presided over the public toilet could not remember a time when he was not there. Crankshaw was the chairman of the House Armed Services Committee, and his Congressional district in southern Illinois was crammed with defense contracts. He was sometimes called the "co-chairman of the Joint Chiefs of Staff."

"Mr. Speaker," he said in his cutting nasal twang, "there is a great ugly fowl named the goony bird, and it is close to extinction because of an idiosyncrasy. It has developed a keen appetite for its own eggs, and they must be snatched from the nest by goony enthusiasts before the predatory act.

"I am reminded of the goony bird and its unfortunate taste by

the rumor that the President of the United States is going to meet
the Russian Premier, Comrade Radilov. Nothing could be more
suicidal than for the American nation to agree to disarm, as the
Soviets have been calling on us to do for twenty years. Lay down
your arms, little dears, Moscow coos softly, and we will eat you
up. We must never cut our armed strength, or allow the United
States to fall behind in any weapons category, or we too shall fall
prey to the fate of the goony bird."

The *Congressional Record* listed laughter and applause at this
point.

Public attention was next diverted from this stream of thought
by what appeared to be a leak to Reuters, the British news agency.
The story stated that a nuclear weapon had been stolen by a group
of German youths aligned with Gottfried, that the bomb had
been recovered after a pitched battle in a youth hostel in Leipzig,
and that the Bonn Government was refusing to round up the
thieves.

It was at this point that Silas King decided delay in setting a
date would create more confusion and struggle between all the
forces involved. He personally called the Soviet Foreign Minister
and proposed three different dates, and received a favorable and
definite reply. The Secretary went to the White House, and talked
with Mickie before seeing the President.

"Mickie," he said, sitting down in the worn leather chair, "You
can't even do a simple thing like arranging to meet the Russian
Premier without setting every dog in town to yapping."

Moonan replied, " 'The old order changeth, yielding place to
new.' But not very quickly or easily. It oozes out drop by drop.
Your trouble, Silas, is that you are a revolutionary. You're up on
the barricades waving a red flag."

"All I want to do is reduce taxes, and any damn fool can see you
can't do that unless you make a deal with the Russians and save
twenty billion dollars on military spending. What's so subversive
about that?"

"It's change, Silas, and anything new is subversive. Galileo was
accused of heresy because he said the planets revolved around the
sun, and the earth wasn't the center of the universe. Your trouble
is that the world has been going along quite comfortably divided
between the Whites and the Reds, and you want to break up the

game. For a whole generation people have amused themselves plotting and scheming and making up ghost stories about the other side and breaking every known commandment because it's for a good cause. You are creating a lot of problems. And all this for a tax cut. Is it worth it?"

He heaved with sputters of laughter.

The Secretary looked at him, wondering if he were being laughed at and said, "You don't understand the value of money. No one does any more. That's the trouble with the world."

Mickie issued a statement in the President's name saying he and the Russian Premier were meeting to talk over common problems and giving the date and place. That would end the pulling and hauling over whether to meet or not to meet. On the story of the bomb theft, he gave orders that no one in the Administration should say anything but "No comment," and this would apply to inquiries from Congress, too. He knew that silence would destroy any story. Reporters, like anyone else, grew tired of asking questions when there were no answers. They would go back to the card game and the endless story-telling and name-dropping.

It was true the reporters had hot flashes of resentment toward Moonan. They gathered around him in an angry circle when he ventured out in the lobby and accused him of holding back news. (He had a theory that when news people came together in search of a story, a mass passion came over them and their glands worked too hard.) When their words became too violent, he said, "Look, lynching isn't allowed on federal property. If you want to string me up, you'll have to catch me out for a walk. Nothing more is going to be said outside the statement. Period." He elbowed his way through the crowd and went back to his office and shut the door.

Within fifteen minutes there was a long-distance call from Luke Gill. His voice, smooth and friendly, said, "We miss you back here, Mickie. No life and no good reporting. I haven't been able to dig up a line on the stolen bomb. That's quite a story. What is the real information? Off the record, of course."

Mickie said, "You can turn off your tape recorder, you pirate. I'm not going to tell you anything."

President Christiansen was the only one untouched, unscathed, undamaged. He was muttered at by a few heretics, but believed capable of only great, humane and wonderful thoughts. It was all right to criticize his priests, for they were, after all, men. They lied and cheated and lusted and envied like other men. But not God. No one said he was appeasing Russians or cutting off needed employment in defense plants. He was the prince of peace. And to make it certain, Frieda Aubaret announced in her column, directing her words directly to the President, "You have crossed the chasm, and the fires are smoldering and dying and the grass growing wherever you step."

## Chapter SIXTEEN

THERE COMES a time when God must talk to His people and answer their questions. Silas King thought that hour had arrived.

He stopped in one morning and said, "Chris, you must set the record straight. I have to spend my time assuring the ambassadors that you and Radilov have not hatched up a scheme to cut off their handouts. They come to me in a sweat afraid the cold war will end, and we'll stop foreign aid and the Russians won't ship them steel at a discount."

They were having coffee in the President's office. The steam rose slowly from the cups. The morning was clear and bright with the sun. Mr. Christiansen could hear the wind in the trees and imagine them tossing their branches with each gust. He judged the wind to be from the northeast. He could feel it brush against the windows on that side. A rosebush scratched against the pane with every push of the wind. The President listened to the outdoor sounds along with the conversation, so that he did not hear all the words.

Judge Herring stood under a portrait of Washington in uniform. He could fly if his secretary motioned to him urgently from the doorway. It might be an important Senator on the telephone who could not be kept looking at the clock. He said, "Congress is waiting for word from you, too, Colonel. They are like children in a kindergarten. If teacher does not tell them what to do, and tell them plainly and firmly, there's hell to pay."

Mickie sat comfortably in a large overstuffed chair. He said,

"And I've a bunch of howling wolves who descend on me twice a day, and want to know when the President is going to have a press conference."

Mr. Christiansen knew they were each pushing him a little bit, that it was part of a game they all played skillfully; he pretending not to notice what they were doing, and they pressing ever so slightly so that he would not take fright. There was that risk, of course. He was skittish and would shy violently if a strange idea was thrown suddenly at him. He said he wasn't so sure he liked the press conference. This business of having a lot of know-it-all strangers come and interrogate him, and ask difficult and stupid and hurtful questions—no, that did not strike him as helping anyone.

"How does this bring us peace, Mickie?" he asked. He was almost certain Moonan could not answer this.

But Mickie sat smiling. He said, "Colonel, look at it this way. With those television cameras up there in the back of the room, you aren't talking to press at all. You're talking to Mamie Jones as she's flopped down in the chair after cooking for the mister and five kids, and you're making her feel better. And you're talking to the guys in Casey's bar. You won't be using the stilted language of the speech-writers. This is an everyday conversation between you and the millions watching that screen. You give them the message. You make them feel better about the lonely business of living.

"You come out before the audience with a little statement you've prepared in advance, and that sets the tone. Then, we'll have several questions planted in the audience, and you'll know the answers down to the decimal point. This proves you are on the job and know what's going on in every corner of the shop.

"When questions fly in and you don't know what in molasses they're talking about, you simply say, 'No comment,' or 'I never comment on matters before Congress,' or 'It would be harmful to our efforts to improve the peace if I spoke on this subject at this time.' You make these negations with quick authority, and that will be enough to shut up most questioners. But if any persists in this insolence, you look at him as if he were a juvenile delinquent and you've got the audience on your side. And you have to remember, too, that most people don't give a damn about the details of government. All they care about is whether they are going to be blown up with a megaton bomb, the size of their tax bill, whether Junior is going to be drafted, their pay check, job security, and old age pension. They want to be reassured that everything is jim-dandy."

Moonan looked around him triumphantly, searching for any questioning voice.

Judge Herring said, "You sound as though you had a prejudice against the democratic system."

"Oh no, I like it very well. The trick is simply knowing how to get the people to want to do what you believe is in your best interests. This knowledge used to be the sacred property of the Church. Now it's available to anyone who can rent the brains of the public-relations technicians and buy or wheedle free time on the air. The public is quite a tractable beast if you know how to handle him."

Mr. Christiansen was listening despondently. Now his face suddenly brightened. He held up his hand for quiet. The others looked at each other in surprise. The President heard it clear and sweet. The cardinal had come back, after all! There was his note. And, pulling back the curtains to look out, Mr. Christiansen saw him on the rim of the bird-feeding station, a brilliant scarlet flash on the drab lawn. Day before yesterday, the President had first heard him and rushed to the window to see him flying off. The sight was extraordinarily bright and joyful, since he had been talking to a long-faced delegation detailing all the dangers of dealing with the Russians.

In the hope of bringing the cardinal back, he had obtained sunflower seeds and three bird-feeding stations. He had waited all day yesterday for the cardinal. He thought he heard him once, but looking out, missed him. Now, the glorious bird was there.

This world within a world—a red bird cracking a sunflower seed on a feeding station hanging from an oak limb and a man watching him with delight and reverence—was reality. All the rest were dim shadows and voices talking not very clearly. He watched the plumed head dip down for another sunflower seed, seize it and look about alertly for foes. Birds were his companions in lonely, festering moments, meadow larks on the Dakota prairies, cocky little English sparrows when he was a plebe in the old town on

Chesapeake Bay. Now in the most lonely time of all—he had to admit it—here was the cardinal.

All he wanted to do, the President told himself standing at the window, was to get rid of this cloud of war that hung heavily over the world. Once that was gone, well, things would be better. The people of India would find something to eat. Wheels of industry would turn.

He had no great personal hatred for war, as had his father. But then his brother had not been poison-gassed and suffered a long time dying. Colonel Christiansen regarded war as one of the disagreeable things of life, of which there were many—such as women who talked all the time. War invariably meant bad weather, bad food, worse smells. And the hell of seeing a man you had bunked with moaning with pain or simply dead with his eyes open, and your own fright over whether you were next. Yet it was strange how quickly all this passed; how the human mind holds only so much and spills over. So he at this minute could not remember in any detail at all that rotten time on the beach at Korea. He had a general knowledge it was rotten, and that was about all. Still, he kept remembering over and over again his father's face at the railroad station, as a man in a story recalls an old crime.

The world to Malcolm Christiansen was the storm raging outside the camper's tent. He was safe within. He could hear the rain driving hard on the canvas, but he was dry. He could feel the sides bellow in the wind, but he was snug and untouched. But let the storm hurl down the tent, and he was exposed to all these attacks, drenched, wretched, afraid. He could curse his lot into the raging night, and no good would come of it, only, in the end, despair.

Here he was now, given to understand, sold a bill of goods that looked fine in the catalogue, that he should trade in that soldier's tent and accept a much better model, tailor-made for the President of the United States. And it was true this was a flossier model shelter and had many attractions, but there were times when the wind blew up the flaps and he stood staring at a world that would frighten the boldest man. No storm ever presented such a wild scene—man fighting man madly for food, for a few pennies, for power, and nowhere the smiling face of God. If you looked long enough, you began to doubt that peace was probable, or that there was any order or sense to it all.

Judge Herring asked him patiently, in his old man's voice, "Would it be all right to set the press conference for Thursday morning, say at ten?"

The President said shortly, "Oh, all right." He knew they would keep after him. If not Thursday, Friday or Monday or Tuesday.

The National Security Council was waiting for the President in the Cabinet Room. Sitting with the awkward air of men who have not made up their minds what mask to put on were the Vice President, Secretaries of State and Defense, and the director of Central Intelligence.

The wise men, the staff of the Council, were more at ease. These were the brains, often the philosophers of national policy, whose names and faces were unknown to all but a few. One had wandered up the ranks through Military Intelligence, but now all the brass was rubbed off. Another, a onetime Wall Street banking partner, had abandoned his old life because of a fascination with this new world of secrets and violence. These men had worked for two other administrations. They could tell where Kabul was, its strategic imports, how many agents the Communists had there, and the strange complexion of its government. They knew the stresses and strains, the rubs, the aches of the world.

The wise men were curious about the newcomers. Would they upset the delicate balances?

Secretary King asked Lawrence, "How are your generals taking the austerity program?"

Lawrence replied with a slight smile, "The Pentagon, Silas, is like the carnivorous flower, Venus's-flytrap. Its beauty and exotic perfume attracts the insect. As soon as the insect alights, the plant closes its petals, seals it in and eats it at leisure. Venus's-flytrap takes, I believe, about a full year to digest the insect. I am being lured into the trap. The generals believe that during the process the Christiansen Administration's military reforms will be thoroughly eaten up. I am deluged with attention and kindness, rather than rebellion. I sense, though, there is not overwhelming enthusiasm for austerity."

"The military," King remarked sarcastically, "is the seventh heaven of the welfare state. Free education, room, board, medical care, pensions, vacations in foreign lands, state stores to buy goods at a discount. A boy with no skill or special ambition can join the Army and in fifteen years be in charge of spending more money than the president of General Motors."

The civil servants sat quietly. They had heard this talk before in other Januarys.

Secretary King asked, "Jeff, how do you feel the military people react to you?"

Lawrence replied, "I am much afraid that in private they sing the verse from Gilbert and Sullivan:

> "Of legal knowledge I acquired such a grip
> That they took me into the partnership,
> And that junior partnership I ween
> Was the only ship I ever had seen.
> But that kind of ship so suited me,
> That now I am the Ruler of the Queen's Navee!"

He added, "I should have at least been the commander of the American Legion or chairman of one of the big military supplying firms. This way, as a rank outsider, my education must proceed from scratch. I am sure there is a section right now working out the exact number of man hours that will be required to convert or digest me. And my telephone conversations are all possibly being stored on magnetic tape, so that a military psychologist can evaluate me and find my Achilles' heel."

President Christiansen came to the meeting several minutes late. He asked, "What are we here for, Si?"

The Secretary of State explained this was the first meeting of the National Security Council. Military policy and foreign programs were reviewed here and meshed together. The President set the goals, the team moved in behind.

"Oh yes," Mr. Christiansen replied. "Very good. Well, gentlemen, I don't have any big speech to give you, except this. Our goal, as I guess you know by now, is peace. That's what the Christiansen Crusade amounts to. Silas King is the chief of staff. He will work out the details, and I want you to regard his orders as mine. And, Jeff, I want you to make sure the military people don't block our path. I'm sure we'll be successful if we put our hearts and souls to this great task."

"Now," he said smiling, the long crooked grin, "I've got some good news for you myself. Cardinals and song sparrows are coming to my feeding stations on the back lawn. I think this is a pretty good omen for us."

It sounds so plausible when he says it, Secretary Lawrence thought. It is Christiansen and his kind who lead men along the primrose path.

> Do not, as some ungracious pastors do,
> Show me the steep and thorny way to heaven,
> Whiles, like a puff'd and reckless libertine,
> Himself the primrose path of dalliance treads,
> And recks not his own rede.

Lawrence asked, "Mr. President, I believe I can deal with reasonable men, for they do not want to die. They are willing to join in a compact for survival. But what of the odd man who believes he is doing God's will, or the will of his ancestors, or whatever idol he kneels before, and that if his will is not allowed, he must pull down the temple as blind Sampson did?"

King answered him, "Jeff, you are always the lawyer, thinking up impossible situations and prodding others with them."

"Impossible?" he asked. "Every revolution, whether it is communism in China, or nationalism in Africa, or the mystique of Gottfried believes it has a divine license. Think of all the wars and killings we Christians perpetrated before we grew older and more sedate. This is what concerns me. I don't doubt that the United States and England and Russia could reach some legitimate accommodation. But if we give up our guns, who is going to protect us from the Sampsons? Or what will happen if Russia sees itself pressed by a new Hilter; will it care anything for its promises to us?"

He thought but did not say, because he saw the look of pain and anger in the President's eyes, that war, why, it is a human exercise as natural now as eating and sleeping and copulating. To be sure, it is possible to go without meat and sleep and sex, but for how long? Men organize their societies, nurse them to virility, then they must fight, exhaust themselves perhaps for centuries, and then build themselves up again to explode anew.

The President was addressing him earnestly, "Jeff, you can do anything you believe in. You've got to believe this is possible, and when you do, it will be easy. That is creative thinking—I think that's what they call it. We must be one big team of creative thinking."

The civil servants were a little surprised at this. They had never heard quite this before, remaking the world by creative thinking. The oldest and wisest, Morgan—he had been in intelligence so long he could not be identified in any other way, as ex-insurance salesman, banker, congressman—thought of what a queer kettle of fish this was. The faith healer, Mr. Christiansen, believing his foolish dreams as so many simple, trusting souls do. The capitalist, Silas King, with his own pipe dream—balance the budget, reduce taxes, and all is well, all is well. Jefferson Lawrence, the romantic rubbed a little with the rasp of disillusionment.

Radway, the intelligence director, read a paper on "The German problem."

Secretary King watched the President's eyes and hands. First alarm sprang into the eyes; the hands clasped suddenly, followed by a slow relaxation. Then the hands played restlessly with a pencil with growing signs of irritation; the pencil stabbed sharp dots on note paper, was thrown down once, and picked up again. The Secretary broke into the reading of the paper, saying, "I think we understand the drift of your report, Radway. You have copies for all of us? Fine. Now, I want to offer a simple and direct plan for dealing with the Germans. Disarm them! Get the Russians to agree to a permanent arms embargo on both Germanies. This will save us both a lot of money and concern."

The Secretary beamed in anticipation of praise for his brilliant idea. The President smiled at him, and the Central Intelligence man saw which way the wind was blowing and smiled, too. He said, "Capital idea."

Secretary Lawrence, his air of modesty a shield, said quietly, "Silas, I seem to be cast in the role of the devil's advocate. But let me point out that Germany is the forward wall of our defense line. Germany could hold off a Communist attack from the east for days, weeks, months, and give the rest of us a chance to arm. Otherwise, all Europe might fall and leave us isolated and alone."

"What makes you think Russia is going to attack the West?" King demanded. "You are taking this on faith, like a Bible story."

"No," Lawrence replied, "I am trying to be a good gambler and look over all the risks first. All the record of Communist statements and creeds seems to point to a new explosion if the capitalist world fails to fall from its own rottenness, as they say it will. They must make their prophecies come true. Maybe they will decide that the danger of mutual destruction is too great to go to war. But we do not know this."

Radway was eager to come to the assistance of Secretary King. He said importantly, "Mr. Lawrence, there are some competent students of the Soviet phenomenon who believe that the aggressive tendencies were largely protective. It is contrasted to the juvenile delinquent who is afraid of the world around him because of his insecurity. But as his security increases, he becomes less combative. Thus, if we follow this, disarming Germany will make Russia a better member of the world community."

The President suddenly sat up, pointed his finger at Morgan, the civil servant, and asked, "What do you think, you, the fellow with the green tie?"

Morgan replied, "Mr. President, the strain of living in an armed world can become intolerable to any nation, and it may break the strain by firing a gun into the air, even though it knows this may be suicidal. For this reason, any plan, plot or scheme to persuade, force or coerce nations to disarm is all to the good. So far as trusting either Germany or Russia, or, for that matter, Nigeria, they are all human, and I would not trust any nation or man if the iron is pressed to his back."

"That is good," the President said, speaking with the curt and undeniable air of command of the trained officer. "Silas, I want you to go ahead and see what we can do to disarm Germany. Is there any more business?" There was none.

Silas King on his way out saw Moonan and informed him of the decision. An hour later, Mickie called in the New York *Times* man at the White House and told him the Administration was thinking seriously of a plan to disarm Germany. This was a device to prime the pump of world opinion.

There was a brief lull. London had nothing to say except "Keen interest." Moscow Radio reported the story without comment. Peiping in its regular stereotype warned this might be an imperialist plot to lull "the forces of peace and progress." Bonn was silent.

Congress brooded over it. But the next night, Father Werther delivered an impassioned appeal "not to turn Germany over to the devil." He cried, "One people and one people alone have not faltered in their heroic resistance to atheistic communism. These are the Germans. Their Christian zeal and resolution is an inspiration. Now, they are to be thrown to the wolves, stripped of their arms. I ask all of you to write the President and your Congressman in protest . . ."

The following day, Capitol Hill roared with speeches. Several nervous senators called Judge Herring and said they thought it might be politically unwise to press this disarmament scheme.

The Judge hunted down Senator Fremont by telephone and reached him in the senators' barbershop.

"What do you think of the plan to disarm Germany, or more to the point, its effect on Congress?" he asked.

Fremont replied as the lather dried on his face, "Judge, if the President and Secretary of State have good and sufficient reasons to disarm Germany, I say go ahead, and don't worry about Congress. Congress is not supposed to exercise the right of veto over the Executive on foreign policy. We would be in damn poor shape if you let five hundred and thirty-six men try to dictate policy. Our reactions on The Hill are too quick, like those of a teen-age boy at the sight of a pretty pair of breasts."

"But do you think there will be much trouble over this?"

"Congress will go just as far as you'll let it go, you know that. We have a natural antipathy to letting you fellows downtown run the Government, and if you let us, we'll turn the tables and give you orders. But if, right now in the beginning, you assert the authority, oh, there will be murmurs on the floor and curses in the cloakrooms, but we'll behave and thank the good Lord we don't have to make these awful decisions of whether to trust Germany or Russia. My advice is not to give an inch. And put the President on the air with a report to the people, and explain this is his first step in nailing down the peace."

Later in the day the German Chancellor was quoted as saying he would never permit the disarmament of Germany. "Can a father allow his children's arms to be cut off for fear that one day they may strike out in anger?" The British Foreign Office expressed cautious approval. "The sooner massive steps toward disarmament are taken, the safer the world will be." Moscow was friendly. "The Americans are showing a spirit of peace and good will under President Christiansen." Peiping still thought it might be a trick, but worth the risk of a trial.

The reactions were studied. Silas King came to the White House to present the report to Colonel Christiansen. He listened with an air of boyish trust, and said, "Well, Si, I don't like to get into a fight with Congress or make the Germans unhappy, and what I really would like is a plan that will make everyone happy, because that is the theme of this Administration—make friends."

Secretary King explained that this was fine, everyone agreed that making friends was a worthy objective. Yet somewhere along the line you had to make decisions and not everyone would agree. But with the President's powers of persuasion, he could win them all over to the reasonableness of his position.

Mr. Christiansen's face brightened and he said, "You do whatever you want, Si. I trust you entirely. I'm going out now to take a look at a pileated woodpecker."

## *Chapter* SEVENTEEN

AT NINE o'clock in the morning, they began lining up in the dark hall. The first ones hung their coats, damp from a light snow spreading over Washington, on wire clothes hangers. The others folded their coats in little piles along the deeply worn tile floor. Then they took their places in the queue strung out along the middle corridor all the way from the heavy oak doors of the Indian Treaty Room to the elevator.

This was an ancient building filled with ghosts. The tall, lonesome figure of Abraham Lincoln walked its halls deep in sorrowed thought. The tiled floors were trod by generations of generals and admirals and ambassadors. It had graceful stairways, high ceilings and fixtures that gave each room an air of antique dignity. The doorknobs were handsomely and richly engraved. Each suite had its own fireplace, installed to take the chill off winter mornings a century before. This old relic had been the headquarters of the War Department, the Navy and the State Department during the Civil War and was located just west of the White House. Now its employees, mostly men in tweed coats who puffed on pipes, were an army of Presidential assistants piling up mountains and mountains of paper work on the budget, economics and geopolitics. Some of them on their way to the men's room stopped to stare at this growing line of intruders, and wondered indeed what it was all about. But of course, they told each other, as they squirted the liquid soap and washed their hands, a Presidential press conference!

The reporters read their morning papers, simply stared down the hall deep in thought, or talked.

"Well, how's the Crusade?" a newcomer said as he took his place in line.

"Biggest looting since the Vandals sacked Rome. Admirably organized, too, by the genius of Daddy Warbucks King." This from the tall man with the red vest.

"If any of you read history," said the columnist, "you would know that when Pope Urban issued his appeal for volunteers for the Crusades, he called especially, as I remember it, on those 'who have hitherto been robbers, now to become soldiers of Christ.' The Pope promised that a hitch in the Crusades would be a complete penance for any sin. So a fine body of robbers and cut-throats proceeded to rob and rape its way across Europe and Asia. Why should modern man, I ask you, be any different, especially when he has a special dispensation, too? The benevolent smile of Malcolm Christiansen. Forgives all sin. Forgets all troubles. The smile of Lethe."

A cluster close to the door was discussing a story reported in the Minneapolis *Tribune*. It said that a high-ranking American officer in Germany was implicated in the theft of a nuclear weapon by the Gottfried militia men. The officer, so the article alleged, had become friendly with the Gottfried cause and engineered the theft.

"Where did Reilley pick up that story?"

"He always did have a smell for mischief. Some people are born with it."

"You can lose the sense of smell, though, by prolonged licking of the tails of the high and mighty."

The laughter startled a government secretary picking her way daintily down the hall in very high heels. She wondered if her stocking had come loose, or some other disaster.

Halfway up the hall, a reporter with a loud and complaining voice was talking of Father Werther. "What does he want us to do—fight a holy war?"

The columnist was explaining, "Christianity, Joe, is the most warlike of the religions. Not even the Moslems with all their waving of scimitars ever killed as many heretics and non-believers as the Christians. Mark Twain said, 'Two or three centuries from now it will be recognized that all the competent killers are Christians; then the pagan world will go to school to the Christian—not to acquire his religion, but his guns.' "

"That sounds subversive. Who is this guy Twain? Hadn't we better let the House Un-American Activities Committee get him on the stand and ask him if he is now, ever was or contemplates joining the Communist Party?"

Another burst of laughter.

"Do you think your President will get around to disarming the Germans?" a British chap asked with a slight frown of anxiety.

"Not if it takes any time off from his bird-watching."

The doors opened and the line began slowly to move. Secret Service men scanned the White House passes, checking faces with photographs with a solemn intentness. Reporters wandered down the aisles of folding chairs and sat down in little groups. This was a strange little hall, perfectly square, two stories tall with a balcony running around the second level. The four corners directly above eye level were adorned with plump bronze angels. It was here that the Indian chiefs were brought, dazzled by the white man's opulence and great magic, and persuaded to give away their lands. Now it was turned into a stage. There were wooden platforms in the rear for the television cameras, microphones on the desk in front of the President's seal on the wall.

Here the President held his press conferences.

At this moment, President Christiansen was glad that Ada Mae had made him take one of the pills that did away with the tiny flutterings in his stomach. For this saved him the indignity, the surrender, of having to go by himself and open the little bottle and take one out himself. This way he was under duress. He was taking it not because he was afraid of what might happen at the press conference, but because he had a nagging wife and he was doing it just to please her. He had taken the pill right after breakfast, and felt a curious serenity. He no longer worried about what the reporters would ask him, because it didn't matter. He was sure he was right. God was on his side, and He had a pleasing way of coming in at exactly the right time and saving the day. So why should he be afraid of a gang of reporters?

He was walking across the street to the old building with a Secret Service man by his side and Mickie a few steps behind. They were soon in the warm, dark, musty enclosure of antiquity. In the elevator Moonan told a story he had been saving. Two sailors were shipwrecked on a small island. They waved at every passing ship in vain. They sent out messages in bottles. No luck. They almost lost hope. One day they sighted a bottle twenty-five feet out which was being gently pushed in by the tide. They watched it as though it were pure gold, or at least their one hope of getting away. Every time it seemed the tide would push it away from their little island, they cursed and yelled. When it actually came within wading distance, they were trembling with excitement. The sailor who picked up the bottle and pulled out the paper uttered a monstrous groan. "What's the matter?" his companion asked.

"It's from us!"

President Christiansen laughed all the way from the elevator down the hall to the Indian Treaty Room. His face was split with a happy grin when he walked in to face 269 men and women. This smile dissipated much of the questioning skepticism that had been festering and gathering out there in the dark hall from nine o'clock on. The President could feel the crowded room come to him as he stood smiling at Mickie's joke.

He said, "Good morning, ladies and gentlemen. I'm glad to see you were able to get here despite the snow. I was given to believe by Mr. Moonan that reporters don't move out of doors except in the dark of the moon and in good weather. But I see he was mistaken."

There was laughter.

"Now, I don't have any special message or news to give you, except that I want to enlist all your help in bringing to the people all our efforts to bring peace to the world." He remembered to look at the television cameras, because these were not beady, electronic eyes at all, but millions of people back home looking on him kindly and gratefully. This must be his frame of mind, a good king addressing his worshipful subjects. "What we are trying to do here is make it possible so that no one will have to lie awake at night worrying about being hit by one of those big bombs, and everything wiped out. Now, if you'll just bear with us, ladies and gentlemen, and realize that whatever we do, it will be in that direction. Sometimes, when you are sailing you know you have to tack back and forth and someone from shore would wonder what in thunder you were doing when all the time you were just trying to get the wind right so you would shoot right on back to your home mooring. So bear this in mind. We're shooting for that one port, peace. Now, if any of you have any questions, I'll try to answer them."

They were up all over the room crying, "Mr. President, Mr. President!" The sight was so humorous he smiled. Like mushrooms popping up after a summer rain. He looked over the room and remembered that this tall fellow on the aisle had a question he and the press secretary had talked over. So the President nodded his head.

"Mr. President, I wonder if you could tell us what was your thinking in scheduling a meeting with Premier Radilov?"

"Well, that's simple enough. When you move in a new neighborhood and you find out the fellow down the street is pretty important, but he and the fellow you bought the house from have been feuding, do you think you ought to continue the feud just because you live in the same house? No, you ought to find out what this fellow is like, and see if you can't get along with him, because nothing is so unpleasant as a neighborhood where two families are feuding, and they try to get everyone else involved. So, one of the first things I did when I became President was to call Mr. Radilov and I told him I hoped we'd be good neighbors and that I would like to meet him very soon."

"Does this mean, sir, that you are willing to seriously discuss disarmament?"

"Why, sure. You don't keep a loaded shotgun in the house if you're not afraid someone is going to break into your house. And loaded shotguns are dangerous to have around. Some fellow goofing around might pull the trigger accidentally, or a child, or something like that, and there would be an awful tragedy. So I say sure, let's talk about disarmament. Let's do more than talk. Let's take the fuses out of our bombs and use that material in them for human betterment—that is if Mr. Radilov and his folks will go along."

The British correspondent thought warmly, Gad, this chap is something wonderful.

Another chorus of voices pleading for attention. The President spotted a black and yellow striped tie; that was a cue.

"Mr. President, is it true that there is an American officer, a General Bronk, involved in the theft of the nuclear weapon?"

"I cannot answer your question, because it is all under investigation, and it wouldn't be right for me to comment on anything that is still being investigated. That wouldn't be judicial; I mean it wouldn't be fair to all parties concerned. But I will tell you this—whoever the guilty parties are they will be punished, because we just can't have people stealing atomic bombs and carrying them around in suitcases and shooting them off. Why, that would throw everything into an uproar. What use is there to have an army or a navy or an air force, if some crazy young people steal a bomb and sneak it into your country and blow you up? So I say, let's get to the bottom of this and clean it out. I have ordered a foolproof system of protection and control of all these nuclear weapons."

The cameras whirred industriously. A tape recorder was taking down every word. The audience was hurriedly scratching notes. The bronze angels looked at the scene in plump good humor.

Mr. Christiansen nodded his head again, recklessly without regard to previous instructions. He felt he could handle this outfit. He would take on anyone. This fellow looked like he had something on his mind and was bursting at the seams to tell it.

"Mr. President, a great many leaders of the free world, and I include such illustrious names as Jefferson Lawrence, Chancellor Ehrlich Steinhauer of Germany, and General Ali of Pakistan, have stated that it is not possible to trust the Communist mentality. Therefore, in view of this burden of opinion, may I ask, sir, what it is you hope to accomplish in your conversations with Mr. Radilov, and whether your attitude will be one of skepticism or trust?"

The Colonel leaned forward, his head to one side, listening. His face plainly showed bewilderment. A flush began to rise from his collar to his face. He seemed on the verge of blurting out an angry remark. Mickie watched him with a feverish anxiety. Then the President smiled and he said, "Young man, you write that out and send it to me, and I'll ask the Attorney General to find out just what it is you are asking."

The room erupted into laughter. Moonan thought in admiration, "He does have a way with him. Natural, untutored, platform-deft."

Another question. "Mr. President, suppose the theft of the bomb were really engineered by the Russians and was a scheme to get us to disarm West Germany so they could take it over? Do you think this probability should be investigated, sir?" The reporter sounded miserable asking his question. He fumbled and stuttered. The question had come to him from his editor who, in turn, had been asked it by a prominent local merchant at the Board of Trade luncheon.

"Does this really bother you that much?" the President asked sympathetically. The unhappy reporter said nothing. Mr. Christiansen added, "If it does, I'll use my influence, if I have any, to get you in at St. Elizabeth's." (This was the local mental hospital.)

The audience roared. Even the stoic Secret Service men smiled. The correspondent sat down confusedly. If others had barbed and poisoned questions waiting typed out in their hands and damp with sweat, they hurriedly forgot them. The men could always tell the editors the President did not recognize them; they would give the questions to Mickie at his next gathering. His insults were easier to bear than the President's lightly scattered scorn. So the press conference rambled on, the President exhibiting a cheerful innocence, the reporters a respectful caution. Finally, the cry went up, "Thank you, Mr. President," and the press-association men on the end dashed out the doors to the telephone booths in the hall. Mr. Christiansen watched them with a look of incredulous amusement.

Walking down the hall with his American guide, the visiting British newsman asked, "I say, is that all the questioning your President gets?"

In public, yes, the American replied.

"Somewhat superficial, wouldn't you say? Nothing like the rigging our P.M. gets in Parliament. The Government must present its case, you know, and stand for questioning by the Opposition. All duly elected, so they can ask questions a bit sharper than your lads at the press conference. No one elected them. They stand on thin ice to begin with. They don't represent anyone except an editor or a publisher, and he, I presume, is one of the most conservative members of his community since he is so dependent on advertising, eh?"

His host said it was too bad the Britisher wasn't about when there was a Democratic President. The questioners were really sharp then.

The chap replied, "What a shame, really, there isn't a public forum where the American President must answer the profound questions, the ones that get under the cellophane coating, you might say. Under your present system, you may have a pleasing child as a President and no one will ever know the difference."

Mr. Christiansen was back at the White House. He was met by Judge Herring, who asked, "How did it go?"

Moonan replied proudly, "This boy has the touch. All under control."

The President smiled. He was pleased and happy. This test he had dreaded the way a boy will fret and worry over an expected scolding from his father, and when the reprimand isn't bad at all and he even acquits himself well, then he has a sense of joy that is part relief and part the explosion of the normal enjoyment of life he has been holding back.

Yet there was a question scratching him. He asked Moonan, "What did that reporter mean about some statement Jeff Lawrence made about you can't trust the Russians?"

"Oh, it's probably some speech he made four years ago to a Legion convention. The ghosts of old speeches rattle around Washington for years. Every time there's a major debate, both sides load their muzzles with conflicting statements from Washington and Jefferson and Lincoln."

"Is there anything I have to do in the next half hour?" the President asked.

"Nothing," Herring answered.

"Well, I'm going out and inspect my feeding stations. Get my mackinaw out of the closet, will you Mickie?"

He was soon out the door to the garden, and, flanked by Secret Service men, striding briskly down the lawn.

"Was it really all right?" Judge Herring asked Mickie.

"He had those boys eating out of his hand," Moonan said joyfully. "From all the boasting at the Press Club bar, I thought they were going to try and murder him. Only two tried it, and the Colonel fixed them. Got the laughter going against them. And if there is anything a reporter can't stand, it is being laughed at."

Judge Herring was holding an envelope in his hand and, noticing it now, said, "This is a secret report from the Secretary of Defense. I think he wanted the President to see it before the press conference, but it just arrived fifteen minutes before, and I didn't want to intrude some new material at that late hour."

"Let's see what it is."

"Do you have your Q clearance?" the Judge asked dryly.

"I don't think they'll give it to me," Moonan replied. "My grandfather was in the Irish rebel army, and the security people can't take a chance on me. There might be a Congressional investigation."

They opened the report and read, Mickie leaning over the Judge's shoulder:

In view of your press conference, I thought you should be apprised of the latest information of the Joint Chiefs of Staff on a subject of vital concern.

Within the past two weeks, two Soviet and East German infantry divisions have drawn up to the frontier of West Germany. They are in positions of from five to ten miles from the border all the way from Lübeck to Rehau. Traffic to and from the East Zone is periodically stopped and searched. Communist agents have increased their efforts to infiltrate into youth groups in West Germany and to fraternize with U.S. troops.

The purpose of these operations, in the opinion of the Joint Chiefs of Staff, is (1) to destroy the effectiveness of our missile retaliatory power in West Germany by subversion and swift, armed assault, and (2) to launch an attack on West Germany at a time when the world may be lulled into hopes of peace by negotiations of a personal nature between the United States and the U.S.S.R. . . .

Mickie looked up and said, "Mary, Mother of Christ, when I think of how close this came to the Colonel! If he had seen this, the press conference would have been a Donnybrook." He sat down suddenly and wiped his forehead. "Jeff Lawrence is one of those damn fool romantics who creates more mischief than the greatest villain. A man armed with good intentions is as dangerous as a mobster."

"What do you mean by that?" the Judge asked.

"Why do you suppose Lawrence joined our caravan? For a job? To get his name in the papers? To get his hands on power? To legally steal millions? No. He thought this was a Crusade. He has an urge to associate himself with good works, humanity, all the rest of the words we threw about. So he joins the show and is disillusioned. Silas King, he discovers, wants to cut the military budget so he can save on his taxes. It rubs against his soul to pay money to the Government. So Jeff has to shop around for his own crusade. The military has one tailor-made. They can sing it in their sleep. Lawrence is going to save us all from being murdered in our beds by the Russians."

"Suppose this note is correct?"

"Why do you think my hands are sweating? There ought to be someone around who can tell us whether this memo is crazy or the real thing. Don't you have an intelligence expert tucked away in the closet?"

Herring remembered there was such an expert on the National Security Council staff. He had been there for years. Name was Morgan. He was called to the Judge's office.

Morgan looked the part of a monk whose vast knowledge of men was incongruous with his cowl. He had an untidy gray tonsure and a round face well traveled with wrinkles and furrows. His eyes were cautiously amused and wise.

Judge Herring explained that a memorandum had been received from the Defense Department. He wanted some independent judgment before turning over the information to the President. Morgan put on his spectacles and scanned the report. Then he looked up and asked, "How honest do you want me to be?"

The Judge replied, "That is a strange question."

Morgan said, "Not in this business. Most of our customers for intelligence, as those at a gasoline station, have their favorite blend. The bleak bare bones of truth, decently garbed, or entirely wrapped in a pink cloth of optimism."

Mickie nodded in approval. "I like that." He explained, "We've asked for you, because I don't know whether we can trust a report from the Pentagon. The generals are fighting their own rear-guard action to stop the disarmament of Germany. Give us the bare bones."

Morgan said, "My own judgment is that this is purposely alarm-

ist. This deployment of troops is neither new nor secret. It has
been published in the European press, and, I suspect, on page
seventeen of the New York *Times* opposite the Lord and Taylor
ad."

"Why are the Russian troops there?" Judge Herring asked.

"That is a matter of judgment," Morgan replied. "If you
believe a woman is a witch, whatever she does is evil, even if it
is only baking a pie. If you are convinced the Russians are going
to overrun Europe, you get one answer. But if you are willing to
search deeper you will investigate the Russian character. Not just
the Bolshevik, but the Russian since he drove out the Tatars and
Ivan the Third created the 'third Rome' in the fifteenth century.
Read his history and his literature, listen to his music. You will
begin to understand. The outlines of his soul will dimly appear.

"The truth is that the ancient curse of the Russian is his fear
and suspicion. He feels menaced—by the Tatars, the Germans, the
Turks, the Chinese. This curtain was lifted a little by Peter the
Great. That was in the seventeenth century. He was a vigorous
and curious young man, and he visited the capitals of the world.
The first ruler of Russia to do so. But it takes more than a Czar
and his court or a few hundred Communist comrades visiting the
unknown world to lift the curse.

"Do you know the Russians never lost it, even in the golden age
of music and literature? Tolstoy suspected the West. The curse
came back, of course, when the Communists seized power, and
the Western nations tried to throw them out. Radilov understands his people. He was speaking the other day at Stalingrad—
I have it here: 'As soon as we created the socialist state, the capitalists tried to bring us down with the whip. The French landed
their forces at Odessa, the British at Murmansk, the Americans and
the Japanese at Vladivostok. The Germans and the Polish gentry
invaded the Ukraine, and the tsarist generals began their counter-
revolutionary slaughter. We were torn from all sides. We stood
and repelled the onslaughts. We have now outgrown our fathers'
trousers, and have acquired our own. We have developed our
muscles.' Right there is the spirit of the Russian."

Morgan paused to look at them. He wanted to know if they
were still interested.

Satisfied, he went on, "And you may add to this the Russian's hatred of the German. There is something about them that defies friendship. Put a German and a Russian in a room, do not tell one who the other is and blindfold them. They will smell each other and be fighting in an hour. Today the Russians think they see the rise of what they call German adventurism. And when they are in this humor, they can easily believe we are secretly preparing the Germans to attack them. It isn't rational, but there it is. Many things we do are not rational."

"Let me ask you this," Mickie said. "Are the Soviets going to attack West Germany?"

Morgan smiled a small, wise smile. He said, "I take it you don't expect a yes or no. I'd say the odds are against it. The Russian is pretty cautious about going to war. He will do almost anything—humiliate himself unspeakably—to prevent war from touching his soil. That soil is sacred to him. But once war comes, he fights fiercely. Of course, if the Russian thought he could burst across the Elbe and swallow up West Germany while the rest of the world sat on its thumbs, he might attack. Or if he is convinced the Germans are going to attack him and it is a case of kill or be killed, then the Russian will move."

"How sure are you the Russians are not going to invade Germany?" Judge Herring insisted. He wanted this nailed down.

"You can never be sure of what goes on in the minds of men," Morgan replied.

# *Chapter* EIGHTEEN

MICKIE SAT over his second whisky-on-the-rocks in a little bar next to the funeral parlor on Pennsylvania Avenue. Al's Little Café was small, dark, narrow, and filled with the mingled scent of beer, tobacco smoke, and Italian cooking. Hanging over the bar was an oil painting of a nude Al had accepted from a student at the Corcoran Gallery who needed to eat and drink and was broke. The nude was small and black-haired and elfin, and was called "Eloise."

This was one place where Moonan could go for a drink in a back booth without anyone noticing him, or at least coming up and hanging around and wanting to know all the low-down. The other patrons were taxi drivers and art students and small shop-keepers. The reporters had not yet discovered that this was his hideaway.

His friend Jane was with him. She was wise enough to realize a man could be good company even if he did weigh too much and didn't own the mint. She was the widow of a writer who had died in an airplane crash, and Mickie had found her a job as head of the historical section of the Treasury. This meant sorting out press clippings and the like.

Jane sat receptive and interested. Mickie had a pleasant glow as he said, "You see, both of them, I mean the President and Jeff Lawrence, are romantics. A romantic is one who thinks the world is divinely inspired and all he has to do is find the right key, and then divine justice and altruism will appear. It's like focusing a camera; the distant ship isn't there until you get the focus. You know what I'm talking about. I'm sure all girls feel this way about men until they live with them.

"But when it comes to war, the Colonel knows what it is and Jeff doesn't. Mr. Christiansen knows that a soldier will get the Distinguished Service Medal for conduct that would land him in prison for life or the electric chair as a civilian. He had a mean, unbroken sheer bastard in his outfit, and someone invented the name Trig for him. That's to say, he was trigger happy. He'd shoot at anything if it was the rear end of a horse or his own sentry. He was a wiry, inscrutable, silent country boy from the red clay of rural Alabama, and he spoke with the broad drawl that others normally make fun of. But not in front of Trig. I heard of some that tried it back in the States, and he'd knock them clear across the room. There'd been a pretty bad incident back at the Marine base. A New York kid, a refugee from one of the Harlem gangs, made fun of Trig's accent, and drew a knife. Before the fight was over, the Harlem boy had a concussion and Trig was cut up badly. They caught Trig stealing liquor from the officers' mess, and he got a couple of girls in trouble. The fear of punishment just didn't bother him. It wasn't there. It was left out of him at birth. This is why he made such a magnificent soldier. He wasn't troubled with the ordinary, rank-and-file fear that overcomes and paralyzes and sends individual soldiers and whole companies under fire running in panic. It just didn't occur to Trig that anything serious would happen to him. Do you get the picture of the kind of fellow he was?"

Jane nodded with a pleasant smile.

"All right. There was a sniper's nest in a mountain cave, and it was picking off our men with devilish accuracy. The Colonel ordered that it be wiped out, and I suggested, 'You ask for volunteers, and promise each man on the patrol a quart of whisky, ten dollars and a week-end pass to Davao.' Trig was one of the five volunteers. The patrol snaked around in back of the cave, approached it from above and dropped in suddenly with wild howls. You could hear them from our outpost. There was a lot of shooting. We knew the enemy was subdued, because a flare was fired as the signal. So we hurried over. Two of our men were killed, a third was wounded. Trig and a very black colored boy from

Detroit had killed or put out of action ten guerrillas by grenades and hand-to-hand fighting. When we got there, Trig and the Negro were quarreling over possession of a gold crucifix around the neck of a wounded Filipino. The colored boy had it, and Trig lunged at him with a knife and said, 'Give that to me, you black bastard. We don't 'low nigras to walk on the same sidewalk with white men where I come from.'

"The Negro got a bad slice on his chest from the knife wound."

"What did the Colonel do about the men?" Jane asked in her placid, interested way.

Mickie laughed. "He recommended both of them for the DSM and the Detroit fellow for the Purple Heart, too, for a combat-inflicted wound. So you see Mr. Christiansen knows what it's all about. But not Jeff Lawrence. When he was in the war, he was in Law or Supplies or something like that, and an old buddy of his told me he would come down on Sundays to the Pentagon and read the citations for medals—just like the one we sent in for Trig—and go away with a real glow. These were heroes nine feet tall to him."

Jefferson Lawrence was alone at the small, perfectly appointed table by the window looking out over the river. He had dinner and sat there over his coffee watching the winding pattern of traffic as it crossed the bridge and spread out like a serpent with two heads. Open beside him was *Mrs. Dalloway*. He thought how this dainty, fragile older woman threading her way through the streets of Westminster on a day in June, enjoying the flowers in the shops, the greetings from old friends, but never really drawing a deep, passionate breath, was so like himself. He, and Mrs. Dalloway, too, had never permitted themselves the luxury of joys that dug into the bone marrow of the spirit.

He had not because he was both poor and ambitious. Poverty imposes a kind of chastity on the ambitious. They cannot stop to grasp and embrace and sit in the back seat of cars along a dark country lane. No, they must look the other way and climb one more painful step up the ladder. He made the decision with his eyes open, or so he thought. At any cost, he must leave the dreary Pennsylvania mining town where his father was a pharmacist. And so he had, so he had. At State College, he had no time to walk among the violets on the water's edge. From his room he could look out in springtime and see the couples hand in hand walking slowly, deliciously, across the campus, and he could smell the sweet vernal winds. He was not stone. He was not unmoved. He had to teach himself patiently that these traps were not for him. He must mentally pull the blinds and close the window, so that all that existed was in the books before him. At law school, the same. More of this stamping down of human emotion as a young lawyer in New York. By the time he was prosperous enough—his goals were high—he was bald and afraid of women. The only one who would have him was his cripple, the strange unhappy woman who became his wife. Perhaps it was right; perhaps it was just. He had dared to defy nature, to turn his back to the Lorelei, and he was punished. Like Mrs. Dalloway, with her regrets about Peter Walsh, he had his moments of melancholy over a youth too well spent. If he had had a son, he would tell him, "Gather ye rosebuds while ye may . . . This same flower that smiles today tomorrow will be dying." But then his son could afford it.

Lawrence was waiting for Bill Boxell. The Vice President had called and asked if he could see the Secretary at his home. He said the matter was urgent. The Secretary was uneasy about the visit. He did not like Boxell. He suspected something underhanded and furtive about him. Lawrence could not put his finger on it precisely, and this worried him. When you disliked or distrusted a man, you should have a reason. Human nature was not a piece of meat you could tell was bad by its smell. Lawrence stared a minute at the lighted ribbon of traffic, hoping that a clue to his dislike of the Vice President would appear. It did not. Therefore, he decided he was unfair to the young man and should make an effort to understand and sympathize with his point of view.

A half hour later the Vice President arrived. He looked very carefully at every piece of furnishing, as though hoping to store this information carefully in his mind. He observed the Florentine vase in the hall, the Renoir painting in the library, as well as the long shelves of well-bound volumes; the pattern of the Oriental rug, the delicate cut-glass chandelier.

He said to the Secretary, "I understand you came from a little Pennsylvania town near Wilkes-Barre. How did you find out about this?" He waved his arm around at the furnishings.

It was not a discourteous question, Lawrence decided. This young man had so little time to learn he had to be curious; he had to find out. The Secretary did not tell him at what cost, at what loneliness, he learned these things. He merely said, "Any good decorator these days can make you a tasteful home."

The Vice President said, "If you hear of any names that would fix me cheap in return for advertising they decorated the Vice President's home, let me know. I can do business with that kind."

Again, Lawrence thought a little sadly, these were the fees of poverty and ambition. Boxell did not have the chance to grow up graciously. He had to acquire everything he was going to get in four years.

They had brandy in the library. Boxell looked at Lawrence with a searching glance, the kind that a prosecuting attorney would give a man on trial. What are your weaknesses? Where will you break? How best to destroy your peace?

The Vice President said with a slight bluster, "There isn't anyone who loves the President more than I do. Old Chris is my ideal. At the same time, you have to face facts and realize that a man who's been in the Marine Corps all his life doesn't understand much about politics. What does a monk know about sex?"

Lawrence listened with the practiced, deceptive calm of the lawyer, but his face was in the shadow.

"So, we have to protect the old man for his own good. You see what I mean. Congress is full of politicians, and if you want to get along with them, you have to be politic. This is why I say we just can't go ahead and disarm the Germans and pull down our own defenses. Let me tell you what happened to me today. A fellow came up to me, a Senator, I don't have to tell you his name, and he told me, 'I love the President like a brother, but God damn it, he's crucifying me. I've got a quarter of a million Germans in my state, and those krautheads tune in on Father Werther every night, and if he tells them to go out and piss in the public square, that's what they do. He's telling them now to write letters to their Congressmen opposing the disarmament of Germany.' And another one comes to me and he says, 'Look here, there's a mill in my state employs five thousand people making uniforms for the Navy. The owner is my best campaign contributor. They are threatening to cut his contract in half because of disarmament. And I have an air base and they want to close it, too. Damn it, Bill, they're going to bankrupt my state and throw me out of office.' So, Mr. Secretary, let's get the President to go slow."

Jefferson Lawrence was trained to listen to men and detect what was actually on their minds, what thoughts the words masked and muffled. Senators had come to the Vice President with a proposition: you get the President to back down, and you have my political support. You save my political hide, and a deal's a deal.

The Vice President said, "Father Werther told me, 'I can get my followers to switch right back to the Democratic Party if you people go ahead with this scheme of appeasing the Communists.' I told him I was not going to let any appeasement go on while I was Vice President." Having said this, Boxell seemed to realize the boldness of it and began a futile, fruitless, long explanation. Lawrence sat placidly as if he had heard nothing, detected no strange howls in the night.

When it came time for the Secretary to reply, he was troubled. He wanted to be honest, to show this young man that part of being "quality" was being honest in your responses to important questions. He found himself telling the Vice President of the troop deployment on the German border. Then he said, "I can tell you, as I have the President, that I am concerned. Not for the reasons you give. They are legitimate to your sphere. My reasons fit mine. They are that I do not want to risk the defense of my country on the hope that the Russians do not want war. I think the best guarantee that I know of against Soviet aggression to the West is a well-armed Germany. I am engaged in trying to convince the President of the wisdom of this course. If I do not succeed, I shall have to support him or resign." This was as far as he had gone in his thinking at the moment.

Jefferson Lawrence went to the library and finished *Mrs. Dalloway* before he went to bed. And when he had finished and put the book back in its place, he remembered with terror that Virginia Woolf's penalty for being able to write this exquisite prose was death. She killed herself. He, Jefferson Lawrence, did not want to die. Yet, he was afraid that, in a mood of lost hope, he might choose it. Death was such a cheap painkiller. But it was not noble. It was not noble. He repeated this in his mind several times.

The next day, there was a display of thunder and lightning in the Senate.

A Southern senator whose drawl was somewhat fictitious since he had spent most of the past thirty years in the Mayflower Hotel or the Capitol, orated, "A grave and tragic threat hangs over the free world. The grim Mongolian face of Russian imperialism, coupled with atheism, is lined up solidly along the border that divides the free world from the slave. Yet even at this hour of peril, we are preparing to dismantle our defenses. American troopships are on the high seas preparing to return U.S. troops from their place of duty. We are thus inviting the invader to take over Europe and bring the field of battle closer to our beloved land."

The Senator said this with a happy vehemence. He considered himself personally wronged. He was a Democrat and had enjoyed the ladling out of 500 jobs in the Administration. This was cut off by a Republican victory, which, he did not hesitate to say in the cloakrooms, "was won by that pusillanimous promise to protect the young men from the perils of military service, including seduction by foreign women."

From the other side of the aisle, a figure arose and asked, "Will the distinguished Senator from Kentucky yield?"

He would, indeed, to the honored and respected chairman of the Armed Services Committee, who, although of a different political faith, was nonetheless a Christian and a patriot.

The Chairman replied, "It is indeed an honor to be so graciously referred to by the distinguished gentleman from Kentucky who is himself a patriot and whose words just uttered show his devotion to his country. I wish to advise the Senator that in view of the information to which he has alluded, namely that Communist troops are drawn up along the frontier, I have recommended to the President that he cancel all orders to bring the troops home, and that they remain canceled until the Soviets remove their armies from these highly belligerent positions."

The Chairman had not made any such recommendation; he was acting by sheer political instinct. He recognized the Administration had blundered, and he wished to take credit for correcting it from the Republican side of the aisle. He would write his recommendation and send it down by messenger later in the afternoon.

A few minutes later, Senator Fremont hurried into the chamber and, dryly rasping, said, "Is it proposed that the United States adopt far-reaching policy on the grounds of rumor? This is absurd. Someone whispers in the cloakroom that Russian troops are on the border, and we, United States senators, react like children frightened by the tale of a ghost. I think we should have confidence in the President of the United States who not only enjoys the trust of the people, as evidenced by the vote they gave him, but who is an accomplished alumnus of the military himself. If there are dangers to our security, is it likely that one of us would know more about it than the President?" He looked scornfully over the row of senators, and his eyes rested a moment on the Chairman of the Armed Services Committee. The Chairman bowed his head like a chastened boy and decided not to write to the President, after all. The Chairman, like so many of his colleagues, had come to the resigned conclusion years ago that Frank Fremont always knew what was best.

But it was too late. The hounds were aroused, pulled from the leather couches and the card tables of the Press Gallery. This was flame, fire, disaster—Russia and Germany lunging at each other, troop shipments home to be canceled, bulletin bells ringing on the teletypes, breathless announcers breathing the catastrophe into microphones with the same cheer with which they hailed the joys of the laxative they advertised.

Thus, inevitably, before the hounds were winded and tired of the chase, they came to Mickie Moonan. What was all this stuff about Russian troops poised on the border, and the recommendation of the Chairman of the Armed Services Committee that troopship sailings be halted?

Moonan had, of course, seen the report on the ticker of the brief Senate debate. But he said, to get the record clear, "Where do you get this astounding information?"

From the Kentucky Senator and the Chairman.

"I'm not aware that the gentleman from Kentucky is capable of speech," he said, standing huge and grinning. "I thought that what passed from his lips was old gristle softened up by sorghum molasses and back-creek whisky."

Mickie stood ponderously, listening to questions with the drowsy air of a sleepy old bear watching the cubs at play. Then he said, yawning slightly, "I don't know what is so new or startling or exciting about the Communist troops. The New York *Times* reported this on page twenty-seven last Sunday. This is what they thought of its importance. I am told this is a regular practice of the Soviets to hold maneuvers with the East Germans near the border."

"What comment does the President have on these troop movements?"

"Why should he have any comment?" he retorted, holding the hounds at bay. "This would be a silly business if the President of the United States passed out a handout every time troops maneuvered anywhere in the world. This would take up all his time, and have the world trembling like a bowl of jelly in a railroad diner."

"But this is important; the Chairman of the Armed Services Committee said so in the Senate."

"If it is that important, he would have communicated his urgent feelings to the President. This he has not done. You're just trying to make war scare out of Congressional chatter. You ought to know better than that, Bob."

This was the ritual of the press conference. The thrust of the fencer, the parrying, the thrust, the parrying, and the counterthrust. Moonan was not going to let them get anything out of him, and they knew it almost as soon as he opened his mouth. But they had to keep up the game until a decent time had elapsed and they could troop back in a loose, straggling crowd and telephone their offices and say, "It looks like we've overplayed the story. The White House doesn't show the least concern, and, Christ, they ought to know, if anyone does."

But there were some who detected in the few hours of confusion the real rift, the deep, unclosable gap between the fighters and the pacifiers, and they wondered where, in the end, the President would stand or sit or straddle. But for most it was just a note on the spike, "Check Chairman on letter to President," or "Get background story on E-W tension at German border from Pentagon," or "Ask Secretary of State at news conference what he's doing re frontier mess."

The President had to be told, of course. Judge Herring and Moonan agreed that Silas King was the one to tell him. The President believed that nothing could go wrong if Silas handled it. His prosperous, shrewd, but genial face, the good quality of his suits and shirts, his expensive shoes, the way he made short, snappy gestures with his right hand, the easy assurance in his eyes and voice, and even the rich aroma of his Havana cigars, dispelled the President's doubts.

And, he had a kind of affection for King. Mr. Christiansen liked to hear again and again the story that Mickie told of Silas.

"Now, Colonel, I won't swear under oath to the truth of this story, but it was told me in good faith in Pittsburgh," Moonan said. "You know Si was head of a steel company. The union had been bargaining with him for weeks and not getting anyplace, and finally in exasperation the union president said, 'Mr. King, your company keeps making more and more profits. What are you going to do with them? Don't forget, you can't take it with you.' And they swear that Silas replied without batting an eyelash, 'Well, then, I won't go.'"

The Secretary of State told President Christiansen casually about the troops, some of the background of the trouble, and said he, Silas King, was not worried. He put his thumb in his vest to show his contempt for the worriers. Of course, there were people up there in Congress who had nothing more to do than cause trouble, and they were asking that the troopships be held in port.

Mr. Christiansen heard this with a sense of shock. The morning sunlight was coming through the Venetian blinds in bars and for a moment it seemed as though the bars wavered. This was the physical reaction. Much deeper was the alarm, the quake of the ground beneath him. For he understood, even through these casual words, how close to the edge of the pit he stood. If he leaned out too far he would be sucked in, and not himself alone but all of civilization. The path to peace that seemed so easy in the dark had become alive at noon with dangers on every side. Who was he to think he could succeed?

# *Chapter* NINETEEN

THE BITING winds of winter blew all through February. President Christiansen could hear them at night storming through the tops of the elms and oaks. They whipped his face as he walked along the towpath or inspected the bird-feeding stations. And when he looked up, he saw the winds drive clouds across the sky like fleeing cavalry.

Never, it seemed to him, had winter been so long. The days lumbered along, each filled with a vague threat of unexpected danger. He would wake up suddenly, fully awake, at three o'clock in the morning and hear the wail of a siren as an ambulance or police car drove swiftly in the lonesome streets. After it died away, then the winds, sullen and steady. He lay awake listening to the sounds until imperceptibly they died away and he fell asleep.

True, there was no definable danger. The Soviets quietly withdrew their troops from the border. A date was set for his meeting with Radilov. The Germans were behaving. China was quiet. Steel production was booming, and merchants reported the best January and February in history. But people were restless. They did not know how to sit still. Silas King had to have a second highball before dinner. Jefferson Lawrence sat moodily at Cabinet meetings as though his mind were a thousand miles away.

In those wide-awake moments in the middle of the night, the President often had the impression, fleeting but sharp, that a vast conspiracy was at work all around him. Mischief was breeding, and he was purposely kept in the dark. It was so much like the conspiracy of silence when he was a boy. He could feel it then by the extra attention paid him, the kind and even pitying glances spent on him by teachers and aunts. This was the time when his father was attacked by the American Legion post as a pacifist and probably a Communist. He heard the news only when some older boys taunted him, "Your old man's a red." He did not know what "a red" meant, but by the tone of their voices it was bad. So he did the only thing he knew, he leaped at them with his fists flying. They knocked him down and rubbed his nose in the dirt and sat on him while he cried, "He isn't a red." He could, at the remembrance of the incident, recall the gritty taste of dirt in his mouth.

The first Friday in March the snow began to fall. At breakfast, he saw it and mentioned to Ada Mae, "Looks like March is coming in like a lion. That means it will go out like a lamb."

She chattered, "Malcolm, I don't believe those old sayings about weather any more. They made them up before those big bombs. The exploding atoms have changed everything. You can't tell anything about the weather any more. Now, I read a piece the other day in *Reader's Digest,* or, let's see, was it *Woman's Day?*"

The snow was light and mixed with rain and was melting. After breakfast the President put on his mackinaw, gift of the Hudson Bay Company, and went out of doors. The wind was turning then from a sluggish southerly breeze to a cold, moist northeast. He told a Secret Service man, "Bet we'll have six inches of snow before she stops."

While he was in the yard the pattern of the snowflakes changed. They became large and fluffy and clung to his eyebrows. The sound of the snow as it brushed against bushes and tree trunks and the gardener's shed was soft and sibilant. Looking south, he could barely make out the obelisk shape of the Washington Monument, so thick was the snow.

"Don't let the snow break down the azaleas and lilacs," he told the gardener. Regretfully, Mr. Christiansen went back into the White House, stamping his feet in the hall and shaking like a dog. The snow melted into little drops of water on the warm floor.

He stood before a good, roaring log fire warming his hands and asked Judge Herring, the faithful servant, "Well, what do we have today?"

There was a meeting of the National Security Council.

"I thought that wasn't until tomorrow," the President said.

"It's been moved up because of the events in Iran."

"What events?" His back was to Herring.

The Judge disliked such moments when, by sheer accident, he had to explain bad news to the President. The accident being that Mr. Christiansen did not read the morning paper very often and then only the sports and the comics.

"There has been a change in the government." That was enough for the time being.

The President had to stop and think where Iran was. There were two countries in that general area they called "the Middle East" and their names were so much alike, Iran and Iraq. One was ours and one was theirs. Which was which he could not remember. This was unimportant, because the experts knew. He went to his office where they were awaiting him. Jefferson Lawrence who always looked a little sad, as if he were apologizing for the bad conduct of the world, was sadder than usual. The Central Intelligence man looked like a junior officer expecting to be given one hell of a chewing out by the General. Silas King was frowning. Morgan alone was the same, the monk who was surprised at nothing, beyond the pale of hurt and outrage.

The map was unrolled. Morgan was given the task of reporting the events. He stood, a rather untidy man with a pointer in his hand, and trousers that bagged in the seat. Morgan said, "Iran, or Persia as it was once called, is strategically located. Across the northern mountains is Russia. To the east are Afghanistan and Pakistan. To the south the Persian Gulf and across it Arabia. To the west is a small sector of Turkey and a long frontier with Iraq. The Russians for centuries have coveted Iran, because of the Persian Gulf and its threat to the old enemy of the Czars, Turkey. Iran is the site for five of our intermediate-range ballistic missiles. At about two o'clock this morning, a junta of younger Army officers seized control of military headquarters and the royal palace. The Shah is under arrest, and Colonel Hajir has been proclaimed chief of state. His Minister of the Interior, Ahmad Iqbal, had been a member of the outlawed Tudeh Party which was in part infiltrated by Communists trained in Russia. Colonel Hajir has made no pronouncements of foreign policy. A broadcast by him announces agricultural reforms, recognition of the Kurdish minority, and the liberation of all political prisoners. Moscow gave diplomatic recognition to the new regime an hour after the coup was accomplished."

He paused.

Mr. Christiansen stared hard at the Central Intelligence director and asked coldly, "How did this happen?"

Secretary King said, "It isn't his fault, Chris. There are fifteen or twenty countries that could blow up tomorrow. We can't sit on all the lids." He added, "If we knew how. We're living in a time of revolution. The question is what do we do now. The loss of Iran to our team would be a tough blow. So I say let's rush in and recognize Colonel Whatever-his-name-is, and try to save the oil leases. We can even do some fast bargaining with the Russians, if we have to. Take out the missile bases if they leave the oil leases alone."

The President turned to Lawrence. He sat mysteriously brooding with his chin on his clasped hands. He was trying to organize his thoughts, but he could not escape the conviction that he was, not inferior to other people, but not allowed to know their pleasures and joys. He had forfeited this right. He said, "Mr. President, it is my duty to talk to you in terms of the defense of the United States. Iran was a key pivot of our defenses. Our missiles from there could strike at southern Russia all the way from the Ukraine to the giant industrial complexes at the base of Lake Baykal. They could command the inner reaches of China. From all available information, the new regime in Iran is oriented toward the Soviet Union, and would then be inclined to turn the missiles away from Russian soil . . ."

Secretary King interrupted him, "We haven't established that the Russians are mixed up in this, but what if they are? Suppose an enemy had missiles planted in Mexico aimed at us? Wouldn't we try to overthrow any government that permitted this and seize the missile bases?"

Lawrence listened with an air of polite concentration. He then went on quietly as a trained lawyer who is stopped by an objection, and then is permitted by the judge to continue. "The loss of Iran immediately threatens the political stability of Turkey and Pakistan, our two remaining allies in this part of the world. Their days are then numbered. Arabia will totter and fall away from us, and all of northern Africa will be exposed. This is not to mention our favored position in oil and other resources. I recommend that we move immediately to declare this an illegal revolution, rush in troops from Turkey, Pakistan and the Persian Gulf, liberate the Shah and have him make whatever agricultural and other reforms are necessary."

President Christiansen looked at him dumbfounded. In this quiet, unpretentious way, war was made! Five men sitting easily in a pleasant room while the snow fell heavily outside and others went about their business with no thought that the great, shattering explosions of war soon might be heard. History was a fraud then. War need not be made at hot haste when the tempers were mad, but by men just as cool as these. You might talk in low voices and reasonably while you planned the landing on distant beaches. Thus, the infinite savagery of the battle is created without even the dignity of passion. Mr. Christiansen could easily envision the scene—the landing-ships moving toward the Persian beach. One struck by a direct hit. Wounded men screaming in the water. Troops in nearby ships cowering and praying in panic that nothing like this would happen to them. But wait, there were other pains waiting for the doomed. The mortar and machine-gun fire stopping the first wave of attackers to strike the beach, so that hours later when the tide came up it pulled back with it the helpless bodies of the fallen.

The President stared at his Secretary of Defense.

Silas King said, "Just because you are Secretary of Defense, Jeff, doesn't mean you have to declare war every time you lose a cannon. We are not going to defend every rocket site, and you had best make your generals and admirals understand this."

The debate went on for half an hour, and by the end the President was hot and feverish. The decision was that the United States would immediately recognize the new regime. An assistant secretary of State would be sent to bargain with Colonel Hajir for the best deal possible and would be prepared to offer economic assistance for the agricultural reforms.

"If the Shah doesn't have the sense to run a good show and risks a revolution, it is not our fault," King said.

Mr. Christiansen was ill off and on during the day. Not only was he feverish, but he experienced hot, flashing pains in his chest. Ada Mae spied him wincing and by constant nagging had him describe his symptoms. She called the White House physician, Dr. Boyer, and he ordered the President to take the medicine he prescribed and go to bed. He fell asleep as he was dreaming all over again the sequence of the troop landing on an enemy beach. He did not awake until midmorning of the next day. He opened his eyes and was surprised. He had been living in a boy's world, and should have seen on waking the low rafters of his attic room, the railroad calendar on the wall, and the land outside the window in the gray early morning stretching like an endless sea all the way to China. But instead, he saw the white Colonial fireplace and above it a portrait of Herbert Hoover that Silas had given him because he thought it would be an inspiration or a reminder.

Once this surprise was overcome, the President examined the room. Dr. Boyer was standing near the bed watching him.

"What are you doing here?" Mr. Christiansen asked in genuine astonishment.

The physician said the President had gone to bed ill, and he and two specialists just wanted to examine him and make sure he was all right.

Mr. Christiansen replied that he was all right and didn't need any sawbones to tell him that. There was a brief, mild argument, and he gave in because in the Marines, too, when the medic gave the orders even the General had to gruffly do what he said.

The physicians listened and checked and pounded and did all the mysterious things that men of medicine do in their rituals, and he accepted this supinely without any feeling at all, except perhaps a very faint amusement. When it was over, the one the others looked to with respect—a little, wiry man with a goatee—said he did not see a sign of injury.

Mr. Christiansen thought the time had come when he could ask, "What is this all about?"

The goatee replied, "You showed symptoms of anginal attacks, that is a heart attack, when Dr. Boyer put you to bed. There was evidence of a spasm of the arteries. But our examination has shown this was a pseudo-anginal attack, and was caused by extraordinary tension rather than by a true heart attack. Did anything disturb you yesterday?"

It all came back to him then, not with the full shock of reality, but like an incident, say, a dog being hit by an automobile and seen from a distant window. He experienced a mild stomach nausea.

"Yes," the President replied, "it did."

The goateed specialist said with a grimace of humor, "My dear sir, I advise you to avoid troublesome subjects. Surely you can arrange for the world to accommodate you thus."

After the doctors left, Mr. Christiansen arose and looked out the window. What had the morning brought him, what gift of weather? A gray sky could turn him back to bed, unwilling to look at the dreary face of the day. But this morning, the sun was out. Gleaming, from tender yellows to dazzling gold, sunlight flashed on a heavy coat of snow. It must have fallen steadily. The bushes were bent with the weight. The lawn was completely covered. Snow caught in the crotches of trees and on the long outstretched branches.

The President was excited by the sight.

"I have to get out there," he said.

He put on his boots and mackinaw and with two Secret Service men beside him tramped through the more than ankle deep snow to the gardener's shed. Mr. Christiansen armed the agents with large sacks of bird food. He took the snow shovel and cleared three large patches on the ground. Bird food was strewn abundantly. He was exultant in his work and at the end stood and watched the birds swoop down and eat hungrily. He grinned happily and said, "There is a good morning's work. Those cardinals would have starved without this emergency feeding."

The President came back to the White House in such good humor that Judge Herring canceled an appointment he knew would have been unpleasant. He explained to Mickie, "The Colonel is so like a happy child when he's in this kind of a mood that you tell yourself, 'He'll find out the troubles soon enough. Why spoil his day?' "

As March continued, Moonan said, "Time marched on all right, but on the wrong side of the street, running into light poles and small children." In Germany, Gottfried was lighting flames by his speeches. The Fatherland must unite and throw out the foreigners, he shouted, and time, that fiend, was stealing days away from the Germans. Two officials in East Germany were assassinated, and members of Gottfried's DRP underground were implicated. In the West, a pacifist preacher was driven out of his church and beaten by a mob. Swastikas appeared on walls, and once again a nameless terror awoke in the hearts of the Jews. They had thought all this was past, and their children could walk the streets without fear. Now it was coming back like a mist slowly moving across the fields at night. The German military, according to the *Blaetter Fuer Deutsche und Internationale Politik*, were secretly agreed that democracy was not for Germany and merely awaiting the death of the old Chancellor to install a Caesar.

The United Nations nuclear test control system detected two large man-made explosions in China's remote Sinkiang Province. This was coupled with vague reports in Delhi that China was experimenting with an explosive more powerful than the fusion of hydrogen atoms. China denied this, and held up the inspection teams six weeks before they were allowed in. In Africa, the long bleeding nights of civil war in Algeria stirred with a new frenzy of violence and torture, and the whole continent shook with rebellions. A Labor M.P. told Parliament, "We have allowed the white man to become a symbol of evil in Africa, and we will need more than a faith that God is kind to the Anglo-Saxon to protect us." In South America, the Communists cast the largest vote of any party in Brazil.

The Russians, too, had their spasms of pain. The outbursts were muffled, but they were there to show there was no tranquillity anywhere, to prove that Marx was just another romantic. In Moscow, the chairman of the Communist Party secretariat for the European "comrades" said, "There is no pleasing these people. They cry for bread, and we give them bread, and there is always a new demand. We give them apartments, theaters, sport arenas, and they are not satisfied. Damn them, what do they want?"

In the United States Senate, during the debate on the farm bill, Senator Fremont arose. Others, talking of it afterward, said he seemed tired and less tolerant than usual. His dry voice cut like a file as he said, "The gentleman from North Carolina wants an easy way out of the farm problem. This is the age of the easy way, and that is our curse in America. We want easy credit, easy religion, easy virtue, easy living, easy war, and easy defense. From every side the people are besieged to obtain on easy payments gadgets to make life easier. I hear no entreaties to make life bolder or richer. And we, the gentlemen of the Senate, are not immune. In the cloakrooms the talk is not about where America is going or where it should go, but about the gilded parties that the two social rivals give at their respective estates in Spring Valley and Georgetown, or of the gallery of pornographic photographs the Postmaster General is always glad to show his friends.

"We have become rotten with prosperity and our new slaves, the machines. Rome fell when it came to the stage of letting the slaves fight its battles, write its literature, manage its businesses. We have been degraded by the slaves of metal. I am reminded of Cicero writing his friend Atticus before the fatal plunge of the Roman Republic, 'Anything more corrupt than the men and times of today cannot be conceived.'"

In the third week of March, the north winds vanished. Malcolm Christiansen was awakened in the night by the sudden silence. He pushed open a slat in a Venetian blind and saw the trees silvered in the moonlight as tranquil as a sleeping sea. Not a twig moved.

When he wakened again at a few minutes after seven, there was a slight, murmuring breeze in the trees. It was from the south. He opened the window and smelled the sweet, soft earth smell come all the way from the fertile Carolina piedmont. The President said, "Thank God, spring has come!"

That week he received an unexpected visitor. The Indian Ambassador came to Silas King and said the Prime Minister, Dr. Gangju, was in Canada attending a Commonwealth conference and would welcome the opportunity to call on the President informally, not as a chief of state. No ceremony, just an opportunity to meet this interesting individual who also had such high hopes for peace. It was arranged. The press knew nothing about it until Dr. Gangju was at the airport on his way back across the Pacific and Indian Oceans.

The President thought of him ever after in terms of his soft, gentle voice with the well-bred Oxford accent, the large eyes brimming with wisdom rather than shrewdness, and his fine dark face. In a way that Mr. Christiansen could not explain, Dr. Gangju reminded him of his father. There was his mildness, the same ability to forget the dirty dishes left on the table and think of the beauty of the skies. They did not go to the office, but sat instead on the back porch where they could see the trees heavy with buds.

Dr. Gangju said, "The state of the world, Mr. President, is no longer the balance of power. We live under the balance of terror. The mightier nations, stronger than ever the world has seen, live in a state of terror of each other. So in spite of their anger and passion and disgust of each other, they restrain themselves, because they see the consequence. And here now, we see this great attempt by yourself and Radilov to find a way of life under this terror. It will not come quickly; you must be patient.

"All over the world masses of people hope there will be a way to disarm and remove the terror, and this cannot but move governments. This is the current of life that is convulsing humanity. This is the only way there can be a future."

President Christiansen felt safe talking freely to him, and said, "Yes, I understand that, all right. But you have no idea how many people here, important people, mind you, don't agree. There are senators, and clergymen, and even my own Secretary of Defense, who say we should go on treating the Russians like they were the enemy, and be ready to fight them."

The gently murmuring voice of his guest replied, "Oh, I have that problem, too. I have these surges of emotion and slogans and fists pressing at me. For the first time, two major powers of Asia face each other across an armed border. For the first time, we Indians have a great power sitting on our borders and watching us. It is immaterial whether we are friendly or not. We are sitting on our haunches staring at each other with nothing separating us. We face each other in anger one moment, in friendliness another, but we are going to be facing each other not just tomorrow but for hundreds and hundreds of years. Neither China nor India is going to walk out of Asia. And we are not going to settle anything by fighting. The shooting of guns is not important in the greater race.

"You see, mighty waves of changes are coming over Asia. This is the real battle. You see in China a revolution, one of the most basic in history and involving six hundred and fifty million people.

We see mighty changes in India, involving four hundred million, not with those abrupt and violent methods of the Chinese, but still tremendous and revolutionary changes taking place in the whole structure of life. This change is the major event of the world.

"What troubles me, Mr. President, is when I see the emotion and enthusiasm that must be used to push ahead the changes—make our land more fertile and build our factories—turned into wrong channels. The jingoists, they stir up our hates so easily that we are lost and diverted, and in the end all we do is kill and kill and kill and perhaps slip backward. So, how are we to live together, people of different systems and religions? Are we to live in permanent hostility or are we to find some other way of existence? Perhaps as people who tolerate each other. This is what you, more than any other man alive, can help to bring about. You are at the top of the hill when the people look up. They see you, and they put their hope in you."

The President had a feeling of extraordinary joy, as he had experienced before when tramping through a dark mountain forest to find himself suddenly in a clearing where a stream ran softly in the sunshine. It was a sense of liberation from the gloom and the toil of the climb.

Mr. Christiansen awkwardly put his hand on the Indian's and said, "Thank you so much, Doctor."

# *Chapter* TWENTY

THE CAMERAMEN set up their equipment on the rain-slick runway. The early morning shower was gone, and the sun shone on puddles. The President's imperiously graceful jet plane, The *Crusader*, was being serviced for the European trip.

The photographers were grumbling as usual. Little Joe, small and dark, limping as he hauled a bag of gear from the station wagon, said, "I don't know why I don't get a hernia dragging this stuff all around. And what for? You'd think we were out to do an original on the second coming of Christ."

"Aren't we?" asked Rod, the worried blond in the duffer.

Little Joe spit on the ground and, acting out in mimicry, said, "Here comes the President in a hell of a grouch. A squirrel has grabbed some food he puts out for those God-damned sparrows. But Moonan, he spots the cameras, and he tells Chris, 'Smile.' So he puts on that grin that looks like a kid with a stolen watermelon, and we turn on the cameras. Then the President gets solemn. That's part of the act, too, and he says, 'I'm going on a Crusade for peace and prosperity.' And Silas King can't bear to be out of the act, so he steps up to the microphone and says, 'And I'm proud to be by the side of this great man.' And you know all King is thinking about is how he can screw those Russians out of a deal at six per cent interest. And the President, hell, he goes along for the scenery."

"Yeah," Rod said, "they promised to show Chris a nightingale next or a trout stream."

"Hey Joe, what kind of a lens are you using?" another shouted. "A zoomar."

Rod said, "You know what I'd do to stop wars. I'd get all these characters who want to start a fight and dump them in the Sahara Desert with nothing but their fists."

"The Desert isn't big enough for that kind of a crowd," Little Joe replied. "You'd have to find room for half the human race." He turned and, noticing Rod's camera, said, "Son of a bitch there, you've stolen my camera angle. Get back." He raised his arm belligerently. There was laughter.

The President left the White House at noon. On Constitution Avenue, he rode under a great arch made by two fire-engine ladders and lettered, "The Crusade for Peace." Government workers had been let out at eleven thirty and stood curiously along the street. The women waved when Mr. Christiansen went by, then wandered off toward the shopping area.

Mr. Christiansen had been aroused by the early morning rain, the drenching pelt upon his windowpane. It had seemed to him a foreboding sign, to awaken the day with a black cloud sweeping out of nowhere, dropping its load, and stealing away before most citizens were awake.

He put on the suit that looked well on television. At breakfast, he tried to read the sports page. Not that he was interested in sports; they bored him. But the reading was like turning on a fan to drown out the sound of the neighbors on the next porch. Ada Mae was chattering as usual. What bothered him was that invariably by sheer accident she touched an area he had boarded up and did not want to enter. That morning she said, "I saw that strange priest on television. He's a weird thing. And the things he said, Malcolm, about your trip. Why, he as much as put a curse on it. They ought not to allow such people to talk on the air and give people such weird thoughts. He gave me goose pimples."

The President himself felt a chill spread up his thighs. He told Ada Mae she didn't have to watch Werther.

"I don't know what else I'm to do when you're playing cards," she replied.

He retired guiltily behind the newspaper. At the same time, Mr. Christiansen was resentful that she raised the issue. Surely the

President of the United States could play cards with his friends to relax him for his great mission! Yet even this stir of indignation did not melt the hard core of his guilt. He had a dry, sucked-out feeling about his relationship with his wife. What had happened to the joys and delights of twenty-five years ago? They were so dim now he hardly remembered them. There had been the small chapel at Quantico, the smell of lilacs. Someone had gone out in the gardens and cut so many of the old-fashioned deep lilacs the chapel was full of them. They went to a mountain hotel in Virginia and she caught a cold swimming in the lake. He remembered her sparrow-like voice hoarse and asthmatic. Oh yes, and her lingerie washed and hung in the bathroom.

There must have been a time when he needed Ada Mae, he supposed. She saw that his clothes were washed and ironed, that his favorite toothpaste was always on the shelf, but she did not hear the incoherent sounds of his soul and translate them into music. She thought they were just symptoms of an upset stomach.

President Christiansen had a light schedule during the day. He signed mail and several bills. He dictated a few letters. He talked over with Judge Herring the system for running the shop while he was away.

Then came the time to leave for the airport. He and Ada Mae and Mickie, of course—he would not be without him—went to the limousine. He noticed the little dabs of color on the lawn, purple, white and yellow crocuses. Their car rolled down the long driveway and turned right on Pennsylvania Avenue. There were people in Lafayette Park sitting in the sunlight on the green benches, taking pictures of each other, feeding the pigeons from paper bags, or striding through in a purposeful manner. A group of Girl Scouts, sightseers, no doubt, looked at the statue of the proud young man, Lafayette.

Turn south past the old Treasury with its gray walls, statue of Alexander Hamilton, and air of utmost respectability. The magnolia would be in bloom in a month, and that Mr. Christiansen enjoyed. Straight ahead to the Ellipse where, he remembered, the sandlot teams played ball in the summer. As a visiting midshipman, he had watched baseball here. Not that he liked the sport, but because he became absorbed in a friendly group. There had been cab drivers and tourists and government clerks shouting and laughing and encouraging the players. The Commerce Department now on the left. Swing right, and the parade began on Constitution Avenue near the Washington Monument. He had pitched pennies down from the Monument as a midshipman and took a local girl once to a nature lecture on the far side of the hill. They had an unexpected revelation of nature, a couple making love in the bushes. The panting, muffled cries went on through the lecture.

These were the idle, passing thoughts of a traveler. Far deeper and more persistent was a desire. The President wanted an augury. He wanted to know before he started how his voyage would end. But nothing at all but crowds of government employees on a pleasant day of early spring. It was a ritual, and they all knew it. The clerks had an extra hour off to wave at him, and he, in turn, smiled and waved at them, and in an hour they would have forgotten one another.

When the President's limousine reached the end of the old Navy Building, the low, ugly, ramshackle affair built in the first World War, a woman darted out in the street carrying a sign. She eluded the first policeman. The car ahead of the President, filled with Secret Service men stopped, and they piled out quickly. Mr. Christiansen raised himself on the seat to see the sign. It was homemade and said, "Save Us or the World Will End."

The Secret Service men caught hold of her. She cried something at them, a fat, middle-aged woman in an old checked coat. The crowd did not understand it at all and laughed as the police carried her kicking back to the curb.

Ada Mae said, "What silly things people will do, I do declare."

Mickie was silent. He knew the President too well to make fun of this omen. Mr. Christiansen smiled as if he, too, regarded the woman as, well, having a screw loose. But he felt much happier, much more ready to pick up and go. He had his signal. The word was given. He knew his mission.

At the end of Constitution Avenue, the short parade was over. The cavalcade picked up speed, went swiftly around the Lincoln Memorial, noted the broad-rumped bronze horses on the bridge, sloped down and onto the highway leading to the jet airport.

At the airport a small crowd of Government officials, ambassadors and congressmen applauded him. To them, and for the cameras and microphones, he gave one of his earnest little speeches.

"My friends, this is really the start of our Crusade. We have been busy getting it fueled up and ready to go, and now we are off. We are going to sit down and talk to those fellows from Russia, and we are going to provide a means for peace and liberty and justice for all men. And here with me is my good right hand, Silas King . . ."

A smattering of applause as the Secretary smiled. He said, "It is a pleasure to serve with so great a leader as our President."

Jefferson Lawrence, representing the Cabinet, presented Mr. Christiansen with the gift of a fine leather brief case with a Crusader's shield finely cut into it and touched with gold paint.

Secretary Lawrence said, "Peace, Mr. President, has been the Holy Grail of all wise and just men. Nearly thirty centuries ago, Homer of Greece foresaw the day when 'joyful nations join in leagues of peace.' And Woodrow Wilson told the Senate, 'There must be, not a balance of power, but a community of power; not organized rivalries, but an organized common peace.' But of all the men who sought this goal, none have ever reached it. It has eluded mankind, and seemed to mock its seekers. But we have faith in you. We know you will not be beguiled by a false peace that only postpones the day of reckoning. We know you will not weaken our strength and trade it away for false promises. We look forward to the peace with justice you will obtain for mankind."

The President, quickly moved to emotion, any emotion almost, had a moistness in his eyes when he responded, "You are all such loyal, fine men, why, I cannot fail."

But later, when the plane was in the air, and down below like a lazy dragon was Chesapeake Bay, he asked Mickie, "What did Jeff Lawrence mean?"

The small crowd of officials had watched anxiously or curiously as the great shining plane sped down the long runway, climbing slowly above a stand of pine trees, and then was safely aloft. Then the crowd began to break up.

Secretary Lawrence stood alone, cloaked in his somber air of isolation. No one came up and clapped him on the back or passed on a piece of gossip. Finally he turned and tramped back toward the parking area. Then it was he heard a booming voice, "Mr. Secketary, lemme hitch a ride with you."

He was confronted by a huge man in a worn, broad-brimmed Western hat, a flapping topcoat and a green silk shirt. He looked at the Secretary with shrewd, direct eyes cupped in sagging pouches. This was Senator Maze Bledsoe of Arizona, the chairman of the Defense Appropriations Sub-committee. Lawrence remembered one of the assistant secretaries telling him, "Maze controls our purse strings, so we have to let him in as a silent partner. There are almost as many defense contracts stuffed in that state as in New York. His per cent, you might say, for getting us the money from Congress. Curious fellow. Tough, earthy with the touch of a showman. Wears those green shirts to create the impression he is responsible for the irrigation projects in the Southwest. He enjoys the name a political opponent threw on him, 'the Big Bastard.' I've heard him tell a campaign audience, 'They call me the Big Bastard, but lemme tell you it takes a big fella to get things done for the little folks.'"

They walked to the limousine together, the Secretary in his precise, even pace; the Senator in a big, ambling stride.

"Remarkable fella, the President," Bledsoe said. "He could charm a rattlesnake." They walked several steps in silence. "Does he have anything under his hat?"

Lawrence replied, "I'm sure you investigated his qualifications before you switched from Senator Fremont to the Colonel."

Senator Bledsoe said with a laugh, "Hell, that ain't got anything to do with it. Frank held up my bill to tap the Colorado River for a couple billion gallons of water for my cotton. I grow more long-staple cotton than anyone in the whole U.S.A. I told Frank I either got my water or I went to Christiansen. He gave me a lecture about ethics in politics, and I told him ethics didn't grow cotton. Now, what about my question?"

"President Christiansen is an extraordinarily gifted individual. I have never known anyone with his capacity to create confidence and good will," Secretary Lawrence replied.

Bledsoe looked at him shrewdly and said, "I getcha. Now, tell me this. Does he believe all this guff about peace and disarmament?"

"I believe he does," the Secretary said steadily.

"Too bad. The generals who turn pacifists are the worst goddam sort." The Senator gripped his forehead in his big hand and massaged the flesh, as if to stimulate his mind. "Mr. Secketary, I can advise you this—we are not going to shut down our military plant while I'm sitting on the Appropriations Committee. I'm not goin' to bankrupt my state so Silas King can pay off those bond-holders who are worrying about the size of the national debt. It doesn't worry me any. We're goin' to vote the money up here for whatever it needs to keep the guard up, and we don't want any cut-rate defense.

"I can tell you this, too. There's damn little sentiment on the Hill for taking the guns away from the Germans. Hell, those fellows are holding the fort for us, so our young fellows can grow beards and recite poetry and chase little girls. We've got to give those Heinies the kind of weapons that will stop and slow up any general attack from the East, and still not start a nuclear war. I don't want any of that radioactive dust fallin' on my cotton patch."

He smiled at the Secretary and clapped a big hand on his knee. "You think this over, boy!"

When Jefferson Lawrence reached the Pentagon, his mind worked with a violent impatience. The Senator had part of the answer. Weapons that would stun and slow down an attack from the East! The Secretary ransacked his mind. He carefully searched each cupboard. He was violently impatient, but he was thorough. Nuclear weapons, they were out, even the little ones. The first time the air was split with the crash of atoms, the timber of survival would shake and crack. He was in favor of dumping all these bombs in the ocean lest some fool use them. But that was another complex question, and he passed on leaving, in effect, the page turned down. Conventional bombs? No, again the danger of retaliation. This weapon must be unseen, like a mist stealing in from the sea during the quiet of the night. The enemy must not know he has been hit until too late. Lawrence finally reached the right drawer, and his drab, melancholy face flushed with a smile of triumph. He called his secretary.

"Send me the top man on chemical warfare. I don't know his name."

That was it, an odorless gas that could be released without detection, and benumb an entire army and yet do no permanent harm. This would be the ultimate humane weapon. Provide the hours needed to stop the chariots and douse the fires.

Secretary Lawrence's fingers played on his desk top as though practicing a concerto. Then they were still, and he smiled. It was a secret smile at himself. What fools vanity makes of men! As if in the rolling surge of history, wave crashing on wave, his steps would be left in the sand merely because he thought of a way to stop an attack on the West in this small insignificant year. Perhaps a bust among the dingy figures of the past in Statuary Hall of Congress? Next to Huey Long? Or Will Rogers? He could see future tourists, a family laden with cameras and little children—the woman would have shorts that were too tight, the man an orchid sports shirt, and one of the kids would peer into a dark corner of the hall and say, "Who for Pete's sake is that?" The mother would read the name and reply, "I think he musta been a Vice President or invented the ray gun."

His secretary some moments later ushered in a portly major general. General Pookey, chief of the Chemical Corps of the Army. He had an eager porcine appearance. No Secretary of Defense had ever asked to see him before. Always the big bomber boys or the missile men were hustled in and out, their chests heaving with decorations. The others stood in line to submit memos to assistants to assistant secretaries of their services.

Secretary Lawrence told him the type weapon he was interested in. General Pookey smiled hopefully and said, "I think the psychochemicals would fit the bill, sir."

"What is a psychochemical?"

The General said enthusiastically, "It attacks the nerve centers of the body and discombobulates them. There is the lysergic acid series. We tried them out on animals, and you may have seen the cat-and-mouse film. We put a cat and a mouse in a cage and injected just a little of this stuff into the cat, and it ran away from the mouse like it was crazy. It went into a panic of fright. You could do the same thing to an enemy base. We could put this lysergic acid in a dispenser that would operate through the exhaust pipe of an ordinary truck, say a laundry truck. Drive around the base and this stuff is not visible and you cannot smell it or taste it. In a short time all the troops from the general to the private are in no shape to fight anyone."

"How wide an area can you cover?" Secretary Lawrence asked thoughtfully.

"We've made tests from planes and ships and have proved that we can lay chemical or bacteriological warfare materials over several thousand square miles. And we have a wide variety of weapons. We can turn a whole state into one big sickbed. We can create hallucinations. Step up the dosage and death occurs. And there are those nerve gases that dry up nerve impulses, so the body twitches and jumps like a chicken with its head off."

"You have quite a chamber of horrors," the Secretary said. "There is a certain moral twinge that comes to the civilian in a casual discussion of discombobulating, as you neatly put it, the human race. It will pass. It will pass."

"Nothing to be ashamed of, Mr. Secretary," the General said sympathetically. "I've seen fellows on hunting trips cry like a baby when they shoot their first deer. But you get over it."

"Yes, I am sure you do," Lawrence replied. "Cicero and Horace, quite gentlemen they were, too, never complained of the mock battles in the Colosseum where hundreds of slaves killed each other in savage fights for the entertainment of the mobs. But, more to the point, can you so compress the nerve gas that it can be fired from cartridges or discharged from capsules?"

"We certainly will find out, Mr. Secretary," General Pookey said happily. "You'll find the Chemical Corps ever ready to meet the challenge. We strive for perfection, whether it be to turn a cat into a mouse or a country into a million lunatics."

Secretary Lawrence stood up to show the interview was over. "It is gratifying," he said, "to see such enthusiasm for your task. I wish it might be spread around a bit. Make me up an enthusiasm gas and I will use it in the schools and temples."

When the General had gone, Lawrence went to the window and stood there motionless. He was not watching anything outside. He was thinking—he knew what he must do; he wished he had the spirit of the Roman Stoic who told himself, "Each task from hour to hour performed as though it were to be the last, free from passion, insincerity, self-love, discontent . . . a manly being, a citizen, a soldier at his post."

He sighed, knowing how difficult it was to bend a man's self to such ideals. He went back to his desk and called for the budget director. He must somehow find a way to keep a hundred million dollars, more or less, free and waiting for his plans.

## *Chapter* TWENTY-ONE

SILAS KING fastened his seat belt and set his jaw grimly for the take-off. He did not like airplane travel, but it was the shortest distance between two points, and time was money. He regarded all travel, just as he did sleep, as an outrageous diversion. You saw one mountain, and you saw them all. Big, useless hunks of rock. The contour of the land and the distribution of water and ore confirmed his belief that whoever set up the earth was criminally careless. If you thought this thing through, you would not have the great waste spaces, oceans, deserts, hundreds of thousands of square miles of frozen tundra.

The *Crusader* shot forward with a giant roar toward a distant clump of pines. Secretary King sat tense, awaiting the fatal mishap. But no, a miracle occurred, the plane rose above the trees and, soaring upward, was airborne. King reluctantly unbuckled his belt. The President and Mickie were playing cribbage.

Moonan became conscious of the Secretary's stare and glanced at him. He made a remark to the President, and they both laughed. King knew the subject; he had caught two words. They were laughing at his habit of carrying a crisp new one-dollar bill in his pocket. This was his St. Christopher's medal.

It was much more than that, if they knew. It was a religion, a hard creed, a modern-day Stoicism laid down by the Secretary's grandfather, old Artemus King.

Artemus came to the birch-tree section of upper Michigan in an old Ford before World War I. No one knew where he came from, but the story somehow circulated that he had been thrown out of a Mormon community in Idaho, and wanted to get as far away as possible from the avenging angels. His apostasy, Lawyer Nielsen said or invented or half imagined, was that he sold his daughter, a girl of wondrous beauty, to a non-Mormon for enough money to buy him a Ford and a good grub stake. At any rate, he bought a country store in Presque Isle County, and from that vantage point, hearing all the troubles of the people for miles around, began acquiring mortgages cheaply and efficiently. Let someone get sick or fall on hard times, and Artemus King was there with a smirk of sympathy and a loan. He had a son, but he was a grave disappointment to Artemus. He went to the state college and decided to be a schoolteacher. Artemus decided there was a basic flaw in the way he brought the boy up, and he would have to discover a new technique for the grandson. He watched the Catholics; they did a good job of holding what they once got. The fact was, Artemus calculated, they got them young and tender and filled them with the gospel before they could acquire foolish notions.

So, one of Silas King's first memories was of one summer at the country store which was trading post, bank and information exchange. Artemus beckoned the boy over, opened the cash register with a melodious sound, and picked out a crisp new one-dollar bill. The old man said, "This is all you need to have or to know. This will buy you twenty Hershey bars or a good knife, or one hundred balls of chewing gum. You never need go hungry or thirsty or be without friends if you have this fine piece of paper. It is artistic and historical, too. Look at that good picure of George Washingon, and the eagle, and that Egyptian pyramid, and all those fancy lines. Feel it. It feels good. Crisp and clean."

Every summer they had this lesson, the old man and the boy, about what a dollar would buy. Artemus would find out what the boy wanted that summer, and tell him how many dollars it would take to buy it. And he further instructed, "There are two ways to earn a dollar. Toil with your hands and your legs and your back, and you'll never make enough. The other is to use the brains God gave you. You don't need many either. You make the money work for you. You loan it out and you charge for it." He took the boy all around the county, and into three beyond, still in a Ford, and showed him all the property he had mortgages on and those he had foreclosed and owned and which were earning for him.

Old Artemus' training was not neglected by Silas. The crisp new one-dollar bill was still the symbol. He thought there was never a painting quite so good as that of the Father of Our Country with his thin lips and big nose engraved on the bill. George looked like he knew the value of a dollar himself.

Silas King never had any occasion to doubt his faith. It was a simple, workable creed—the dollar bill, or enough of them, would buy you whatever you wanted. This was the spirit he was taking to Geneva. He would buy what the United States needed from the Russians, and that was peace and hands off of Latin America. He had bought off every rival in the past, and saw no reason why he could not do the same with the Russians. Sure they were Communists, Marxists, whatever that was, but they were human beings, weren't they? They wanted soft beds, perfumes, their women trim and sensuous, warm clothes. Of course they did. And they didn't have what it takes to buy these pleasures, or enough capital to be able to make them themselves. So, loan them the money, but with an understanding. They were realists. They would know what you were talking about.

Silas King had looked over the world with the knowing eye of the mortgage banker, and he had decided there were only two parts of the world worth exploiting, Latin America and Africa. They had mineral wealth, cheap labor and the willingness now to trade their wretched lot for what the Age of the Machine could give them. Of the two continents, he decided, let the Russians subdue the niggers of Africa. They had prepared for this, learning Urdu and Swahili and grunting languages like that in their universities. Leave us Latin America. We'll go in with a cross in our hand, a Latin phrase on our tongue, and a crisp new one-dollar bill in our pocket.

Secretary King did not like the Germans. They were too clever, and they had discovered the secret. Build up your industries. Sell your goods and services a little cheaper than the competitor, get on the ground floor with technical advisers, and in this way spread your power. They were dangerous, because they were so foolhardy. When they could not get what they wanted by clever dealing, they tried to get it at the point of a gun. Disarm and boy-cott the bastards—that was King's formula. He knew the Russians would like that line of talk. And, he could get the support of the Jews. They had influence and enough fear and frantic anger to be a steady flame on parliaments and banking institutions.

So Silas King had no secret qualms about his mission. He did not offer any humble prayers.

The pilot, an Air Force colonel, entered their cabin to describe the flight plan. He said, "We are taking a new, direct route with-out the necessity of a stopover before we reach Geneva." The Colonel showed them the route charted on his maps. "If we don't hit any unexpected head winds, we can clip an hour off the record. I understand this kind of thing impresses the Russians. We will be riding above the clouds over the Atlantic, but there will be breaks where you will be able to see below."

The President went forward to watch the navigation and to look out from the broader scope of the pilot's curved windows. Mickie stretched out to nap. King smiled slightly as he sat com-fortably. He wondered what old Artemus would think of the little boy off to make the biggest deal in all the confounded history of man.

The Secretary sat alone, seeming to look out the window, but actually playing his favorite game. It was much like playing checkers with himself. He was horse-trading with a rival, this time the Russians. He allowed his mind to play dumb, to be sur-prised by a colossal move of the Russians. Then, skillfully, blandly, he planned the counterstroke. He always thought ahead, "What is it these bastards want more than anything else?" There was in every man this secret pride or lust, and all you had to do was dis-cover it, and you had your deal made. You didn't trade him dollars or acres, you gave him whatever it was that burned the hottest in his soul. Since all you wanted was dollars, you had the ad-vantage.

Silas King scorned the trappings of diplomacy, the fawning elegance of manners, the great parties, the special kind of wit, and attempts at charm. "Hell," he once said, "if a man wants some-thing from you, he doesn't care if you are a hare-lipped ape. Some of the meanest men I know are the most successful operators. And they didn't go to Harvard either."

President Christiansen's talk of peace and good will was, to his Secretary of State, hurrah music. That was it, hurrah music. You fed it to the crowd to keep it happy and out of your hair while you were at the bargaining table. But it had no place once inside that room.

In midafternoon a steward brought the Secretary a message from the radio officer. Moscow had just announced it was offering West Germany a favored trade and non-aggression pact. King showed it to Mickie.

"What do you think?" Moonan asked.

"The Germans will never accept it. They will haggle with us for better terms, and threaten to sign up with the Russians. They've been playing us that way for twenty years. Scooped up billions from the Treasury with this game. Every time one of those roaring Russians gets mad and shouts, the Germans hit us while we're frightened and upset."

He looked so outraged, as if this was a personal affront to him, that Mickie laughed. The Secretary stared at him, not quite sure why the other was laughing. He decided this was the time to tell an anecdote, try it out really.

King leaned back easily, the amiable fellow in the locker room, and said, "In my home town, Flint, that is, there was a peculiar German baker. Heinecker, Hans Heinecker. Every five years he bought a new car, and his haggling soon involved almost the entire business community. He would go first to Sid Foster and tell him he wanted a new Chevrolet. What kind of deal? Heinecker listened with his dumb Dutch air, and didn't say a word. He put the figures down in a little notebook, nodded his head and walked out. Next he went to Gus Morgan two blocks away and said Sid had offered him this kind of a deal. What would Gus do? Gus would give him the line about Hans being a good member of the business community and his bread was the best in town, so he would give him a little better offer. It was written down. He went to every damn Chevvy dealer in town, not once but several times, until someone practically gave him one. One year the dealers thought they had him. They had lunch and agreed over Scotch and soda on one price, and to hell with the Antitrust Law. He still beat them. That crafty old man went to the next county, to Owosso, and got a lower bid than at Flint. He made the rounds again. Al Hays was loaded up and had a note due, so he cut his price, but made Heinecker swear not to tell anyone. I saw the check."

Mickie bubbled with laughter, spitting it out through his mouth and nose and trembling with glee.

"You like the story?" the Secretary asked, "or is it just your time to laugh? I sometimes think you are like a dog who has to piss every so often or he feels badly about it. You have to laugh."

"No," Moonan replied, "it's a good story."

"I may try it out on the Russians then."

The midafternoon dinner was awkward. The President and Mrs. Christiansen and the Secretary and Mrs. King ate together. There was nothing in common to bind the four of them. Mickie might have brought them together with his stories and spring of humor; but he was eating with the crew, the translators, two State Department experts, Morgan, and the Secret Service men.

Mr. Christiansen escaped to the cockpit. There was peace. No noise but the soft, infrequent voices of the men and the electronic buzzing and clickings. Through the broad sheath of windows, heaven lay close and naked. Night had come. On one side, a bright moon—almost full—shone on the raft of clouds floating below. He thought of moonlight falling on a field piled high with snow and the wind still. This was a precious moment. The boy was safe in bed under the rafters. The blizzard had come and gone. The air was quiet, and the stars swam in the night. The emptiness of space was lit with a thousand thousand dazzling little lights. He looked with the hopeful faith of a child, thinking it was proof, or at least evidence, that there was a God and He had things well in hand.

"I heard a Methodist bishop say we ought to be preparing missionaries to send to other planets," the President said to the crew chief.

He replied, "I wonder what the missionaries would tell those creatures they find."

Mr. Christiansen said maybe they would try to put clothes on them. There was quiet laughter.

The clouds drifted away, and they were over land.

"An edge of Spain," the pilot said, "Next the Bay of Biscay, then France and Switzerland." He showed the President the route on the chart. Mr. Christiansen looked below and saw the Gironde River, a twisting serpent across the west of France. The *Crusader* was descending from its great height. The radioman was chattering almost constantly with the ground. The pilot was alert, watching his vast instrument panel, giving instructions, and checking with the navigator. There was a series of bumps, as a sledder experiences going down a knobby hill.

"We're ahead of schedule. About twenty-five minutes," the pilot said.

Within minutes, the plane was skimming over the mountain heights, silent and brilliantly white in the moonlight. They were the breathless crashing waves of a great sea stopped in motion, frozen. Mr. Christiansen felt a spurt of awe so strong as to hypnotize him against a background of sensations—a nagging desire to urinate, an apprehension over his meeting with Radilov, irritation at Ada Mae, and a suspicion Jeff Lawrence was not playing on the team as he should. The great plane wheeled and Lake Geneva came in sight as they crossed low over a towering range. They seemed to be gliding in like a hawk to its prey. There was the familiar touch of the wheels on the runway and the long, screaming ride over the cement before they finally slowed enough to taxi in and come to a halt.

To the right was a huge plane with wings swept back like those of a soaring eagle. The pilot said, "That's the new Russian jet. Fastest thing in the air."

"Do we have anything like it?"

"No, Mr. President, the budget people cut it out of the appropriation."

Mr. Christiansen looked enviously at the Soviet plane and said, "Well, the budget boys must know what they are doing."

The time was close to midnight, but a crowd of several hundred stood in the clear air awaiting him. A wind was blowing off the mountains, and the air was cold. This was evident in the way the mechanics scurried around with their heads down, and those who stood waiting to see the American peacemaker had their coat collars turned up. The lights of the airport were bright and a little unfamiliar after being up in the sky these several hours.

The President went to the bathroom and then let the steward

help him put his overcoat on. He stood in the aisle a moment by himself to summon up his spirit. His spirit was something he had to summon, and he had little tricks to do this. He told himself these people out there had great faith in him and believed he was going to bring peace to the world. Otherwise, they would have stayed home around their fires watching the television or making love or counting their money or grieving over their wretched lot. But they threw this aside and braved the cold, because they knew—some sixth sense told them—he was the fellow who was going to save mankind from its ruin.

With his spirit thus coaxed up the stairs from its cellar, President Christiansen walked out on the ramp smiling and waving. There was a cheer, and it reached him just as the wind cut his face. The photographers were there, of course—God knows where these people came from, did they spring from the earth?—and his eyes were dazed by their lights. He shook hands with the welcoming committee. He did this impatiently, wishing it would be over. He did not fly the Atlantic for this.

He stepped into a limousine with Ada Mae and the Kings, and they were off to a villa which, he was told, rested on a terrace above the lake. The car was pleasantly warm. He was a little excited. The view of the lake was beautiful. He felt an ache of desire. He was not sure what he desired, except that it be exciting.

His face looking eagerly out the window of the limousine was not that of an ordinary tourist. All the strange emotions and desires had quite blotted out all the things the tourist sees and jots down in his mind to write his aunt about.

The villa was large and white and elegant. He was told it had been owned by a financier who blew his brains out. Something to do with a woman. Silas shook his head in disbelief.

They were all installed, the luggage taken out, the place inspected. The President was having a drink with Silas and Mickie in his sitting room. Mr. Christiansen sat in his stockinged feet. A Secret Service man knocked and entered with a most surprised look.

"What is it, George?" Moonan asked.

The agent replied, blurting out the words, "Mr. President, the Russian Premier and his Foreign Minister are downstairs to pay a call on you."

How wonderful that was, the President thought. Just at this

time when he was so excited and did not want to go to bed, here
they were.

"Show them up—no, I'll go down and bring them up."

Off he went down the hall in his black silk socks, no coat or
tie. Mickie looked questioning at King. He shrugged his shoulders
as if to say, "What the hell." So, like two children following their
leader over some absurd path they went after him.

The President went down the marble stairs—they were an exact
duplicate of those in a famous palace in Rome—without a special
plan. All he thought was that Providence had come to his rescue
once again. His silent prayer in the cockpit had been answered!
For what he dreaded, dreaded with a cold, dry fear, was meeting
the Russians in the stiff and formal sessions where he could not
summon up his magic and smile. Now, it was so easy; race down
the stairs, shake their hands in warm greeting, smile, have a drink
together before the fire, talk of the little things all men enjoy.
This would open the meeting with Malcolm Christiansen at his
best.

Mr. Christiansen saw two men below in their long black over-
coats with sable collars. He recognized Viktor Radilov as the
taller—the long angular face, eyes as sharp and inquiring as a
fox staring out of the brush, and close-cut hair. Yet with all this
sharpness there was an aura of the romantic about Radilov. Perhaps it was the color of his eyes, a pale blue, almost violet.

The other was short, with the blunt features of a peasant. He
had a large nose and lips, and eyes that could be humorous or surly
as the occasion demanded.

The President reached out his hand and grinned. He tried to
remember what it was he was supposed to say, and said in greeting, "*Zdrasstwicha, tovarich.* Is that right?"

Radilov said with great animation, "You have won our hearts.
There is a Russian proverb—the way to a man's heart is written
in his own tongue." His own accent was curiously American,
rather than English. He reminded the President of a Czech wheat-
farmer he had known in North Dakota.

The Foreign Minister, Alexandre Vorontzov, was introduced.

"Do not try to remember that name, Mr. President," Radilov
said smiling. "Call him Silvio, as we do. This is from a famous

character by Pushkin who was such an excellent marksman he could shoot the ace from a card at fifty paces."

"Are you such a shot then?" Mr. Christiansen asked.

Radilov answered for him. "He is the best in the world. Alexandre saved my life by shooting an assassin sent to do away with me when we were daring young men thirty years ago. So you see why I must have him by my side—but we are delaying the business of our visit, Silvio!"

The Foreign Minister drew from behind him a flat package done up in wrapping paper.

"We have heard that you love mountain fish, so this day we sent our best fisherman into the mountain and bring you trout for a midnight feast," Radilov said.

"This is great," the President replied. "You will stay for the feast, and I will cook the trout."

Thus, to the great shock of the butler who retired to his pantry and stared out in disbelief, the kitchen of the villa was invaded at one o'clock in the morning. The American President cooked the trout. The Russian Premier said he knew how to prepare American-fried potatoes, and insisted on doing it. A fat man, not identified, made the coffee. The Foreign Ministers smoked cigars and made uncomplimentary remarks to the chefs. There was great laughter. Also an attempt by the two chiefs of state to sing an American melody together.

The scene actually was not that mad. The five men, buoyed up like balloons in a spring wind, came into the large white kitchen. Radilov said, "Mr. President, I know you enjoy fried potatoes. I read much about you. Allow me to prepare them."

Mr. Christiansen replied with a grin, "Now, I'll just take you up on that, because I don't think you know how to fry potatoes the way we do. And, I'll say this, if you do come up with even a fair replica, why I'll learn how to cook one of your dishes."

The two cooks were supplied with aprons, and rolled up their sleeves. Radilov was presented with potatoes and a knife. To the amazement of the three Americans, he sliced the potatoes in the way they are cooked in small towns and on the farms of the Midwest, like cucumber slices.

Secretary King said, "I'll have to hand it to you, Mr. Premier. When you set out to learn something, you surely do it thoroughly.

Those are American fried potatoes all right, the way we had them back home. And you even talk like an American."

"Oh, I had many American teachers," he replied with a curious enigmatic smile at Vorontzov.

"Where did you collect the teachers?" the President asked.

Radilov looked at him as if weighing his answer with a quiet inner amusement.

"You have the quiz games on your television, and I will be the master of the program and ask you if you would guess."

"Would they be American Communists?"

Radilov looked at Vorontzov out of the corner of his eye, and the hearty, peasantlike man laughed in good-humor. The trout and potatoes were sizzling in the frying pan, the coffee was boiling and the smell was very pleasant. The walls of strangeness between the men had miraculously fallen away. They were absorbed in playing a game.

The Premier looked at King and asked, "Mr. Secretary, what do you think?"

"You have been trained by your countrymen who had diplomatic service in America."

"And you," nodding to Mickie.

Moonan said drolly, "Mr. Premier, you sound to me like you learned your English in a Chicago poolroom."

At this the Foreign Minister burst into loud laughter, and Radilov's narrow face itself relaxed into a smile.

"You, my friend, are the most correct. I learned your tongue in an American Legion Americanization course in Detroit, at the Polish-American Club, and at a war production plant. You seem surprised. I admit this is not in any of my country's historical statements. You see, I ate the forbidden fruit of freedom, and this is not well publicized. How do you keep the masses to their socialist tasks if it is bragged that the leader has tasted the apple?

"The episode began in this manner. In the early years of the great war, while Russia was still at peace, I was a student in Moscow. I wrote an unwise tract, in which I criticized in the emotional manner of the young the treaty with Hitler. How can noble socialist Russia, I asked, tie her soul to that of the beast, Hitler? And, more to the point, how can we trust our old enemy, Germany? She will stab us in the back. This essay found much favor among the students and it was reproduced, and, as such things must, found its way into the hands of the Secret Police. But they did not know the author. Soon it became known through what you call the 'grape vine' that they are searching and have narrowed the author down to a medical student at our university.

"Friends come to me and say, 'They will discover you. Flee!' But I am noble and young, and I say, 'No, I will argue my case with the police. I will make appeals to all the authorities. I will arouse the country.' They tell me I am a fool, that I will end up in a pit in Siberia. One night, I am asleep in my quarters. I hear a noise, the creaking of boards. It is too late. A cloth heavily soaked with ether is placed over my nose, and I feel simultaneously a hypodermic needle in my arm. All is blank.

"I awake in a sledge on a country lane, and I would cry out but a hand is placed over my mouth. I look up. It is my friend, Silvio. He smiles as you see him smile now, and he says, 'Be silent, little brother. This is for your safety.' We escape by an underground route, as in your South when the slaves escaped North to freedom. A stop on the outskirts of a village. A warm soup and bread. A fresh set of horses. A new guide. When we are stopped, the guide says Silvio is a doctor taking a desperately ill patient—much shaking of the head and whispers of scarlet fever—to the hospital. Close to the border, a guard is suspicious. He bids us wait while he goes to call his superior. He leaves to march off down the road, and Silvio shows his markmanship. We speed on through the snow like Gogol's troika.

"The two of us embark on a ship at Riga as common seamen. We think the voyage is only to Britain, but it is to Baltimore, a place in Maryland. We pretend we are Poles; we both speak the language, and some fellows we meet in a drinking place say there are plenty of jobs at Detroit making guns to fight Hitler. That is where we will go, I tell Silvio. We will so fight Fascism. A Pole who tells me he hates Germans says let us all go to Detroit; he has a car. So we travel in a majestic old car, a used Packard which drinks gasoline like a thirsty dog in summer. It is easy to travel in your country, Mr. President. No one says, 'Where is your passport? Where is your work card?' They say, 'Have a Coke.' Consequently, Silvio and I go to work for the Consolidated Brake and Shoe Company in Hamtramck helping to produce the tank tread. We become Americanized by the American Legion, and at the Polish-American Club. I can narrate for you the Oath of Allegiance and the story of George Washington, and sing to you 'America, the Beautiful,' and also other songs which are not so auspicious which are rendered when in a state of near intoxication.

"When the Fascists attack Russia, Silvio and I vow we will return to fight these German beasts and for the glory of the social motherland, and so by various means we returned after a year and a half in America."

This tale was spoken with the intensity of a rushing train. There were no pauses where anyone might interrupt. Radilov's voice had a spellbinding quality, ringing with excitement. So it was that when he finished the silence was stunning.

Finally, President Christiansen broke it to say, "That is a gripping story and it moves me to hope that our friendship will be very good."

So the meeting ended in a spirit of fellowship with Radilov and the President singing "America, the Beautiful." There was no word of the business of the conference, the fate of the world.

When the Russians departed into the bright, clear night, the three Americans sat in a still excited mood and had a nightcap. By Swiss time it was three in the morning, by theirs six hours earlier.

"What a fellow Radilov is and what a dramatic story he told," Mr. Christiansen said.

Silas King said dryly, "The only difficulty, Chris, is that there isn't any such company as the Consolidated Brake and Shoe Company in Hamtramck and never was. I ought to know. My father was superintendent of schools there then."

## *Chapter* TWENTY-TWO

MALCOLM CHRISTIANSEN awoke too early. He usually did. The villa was quiet except for a muted clatter below. He supposed it was the servants in the kitchen, and he envied them their cheerful, nonsensical chatter—the high cost of eggs, the death of the butcher, the way a wealthy gentleman was carrying on with the café singer.

He put on his bathrobe and sat on the edge of his bed looking at the lake. The sun was coming up and piercing the mists of the mountains. The lake immediately in front of the villa was touched with light, while beyond it was still the subdued color of dawn. A large sailboat was slowly moving out from its mooring. The sails were raised; they flapped listlessly, then a breeze caught them, and the boat was in motion. It left a small trail in the still water.

What did these sailors care of war or peace, or whether God was securely on their side? All they wanted was a good wind and a clear sky.

The President had a moment of revelation sitting in his green plaid bathrobe on the bed, and it gave him a sudden, violent twinge in the stomach. The truth was that last night, it was not he, the charmer of the American masses, the "hero with a heart," who had won the personality contest. It was Radilov with his story. True or not—he did not care. But the Russian had stolen all the attention and glory, and Mr. Christiansen sat spellbound like a little boy at the circus. Was this the way to get the Russians to agree to marvelous concessions, so that peace would be painless and acceptable to Father Werther?

President Christiansen stood up. He must not sit still and think like this. He should shave and brush his teeth and put on his clothes. By that time, someone should be awake and they, too, could talk about the changeability of winds and women's hearts. The President wished Mickie was up.

Mr. Christiansen went downstairs in the little European elevator, and had breakfast with a Secret Service man. To his surprise and delight, the thin slice of ham was cooked exactly right. The coffee was excellent. The agent was a good companion and regaled the President with the story of a gang of counterfeiters. Mr. Christiansen arose from the table in good humor.

Silas King, meanwhile, sat on a stool in his dressing room. He had on a red satin dressing gown with black lapels and his shorts. He roughly pulled on a sock.

Beside him, on a table, was a tray with a glass almost drained of orange juice, a plate with evidence of bacon and eggs, and a cup half filled with cold coffee. A file of dispatches with the "Top Secret" stamp showing lay on the dresser.

A Venetian blind was slightly crooked, as though it had been pulled up in a hurry.

Moonan, fully dressed, was standing in front of the window eating a piece of toast with marmalade on it.

Morgan, the National Security Council man, sat in a corner.

Secretary King snapped a garter shut and said in a perplexed growl, "God damn it, why does all this have to happen just now? Why isn't it strung out?"

Mickie rumbled out a belch and said, "Maybe this is the work of God testing the faithful."

"Well, He can stop it. I don't have time to play Job." Another garter was snapped.

Morgan remarked in his deep voice, "In this business the trouble comes in bunches. Let there be a riot in Bechuanaland, and I'll be deviled if the King of Arabia—the man we're counting on to keep the Middle East straight—isn't poisoned by a jealous wife, and the Japanese elect the wrong party, and the Indians and Chinese patrols shoot at each other in the Himalayas. Human madness is contagious."

Secretary King laced a shoe and stamped his foot on the floor.

"Contagion, hell," he said. "The Russians stir these things up to keep us off balance. It's an old trick—calling the mortgage."

In the silent papers, strewn so carelessly on the dresser, was an account of a violent night at the Panama Canal Zone. Fifty thousand Panamanians had marched into the Zone and staged a sit-down strike. The United States Governor, a retired general, ordered the troops to drive them out. Fire hoses and tear gas were used. This enraged the demonstrators, and several thousand stormed two Government buildings, wrecked them inside, and fired on the troops. A miniature civil war ensued. The morning saw thirty-one dead, several hundred injured. Demonstrations were being staged all over Latin America against "Yankee imperialism." . . . The Ambassador to Manila had cabled that a storm was rising in the Philippines over Senator Evangelista's resolution calling on the United States to vacate Clark Field. It would be defeated by a two or three vote margin and only after damaging debate and editorial comment.

Reading this, King said in a series of explosive bursts, "I don't know what has happened to the world. When I was a kid, we didn't spend a cent on foreign aid, and everyone loved us. Now, we are a son of a bitch, and we've been passing out money like a drunken sailor."

Mickie said mildly, "When you were a boy, Silas, we weren't trying to run the world. We're in the same business as Caesar, and if we don't have the cast-iron guts for it, we'd better retire. The Russians would be glad to take over."

There were other unwelcome tidings in the dispatches. In Germany, Gottfried told a huge rally that the Germans were "destined by God to destroy the heathenism of Russian Communism." This sore, Morgan observed, was not through festering.

Moonan was called out of the room by the communications office—the White House was on the telephone with an urgent message. While he was gone, Secretary King talked to the State Department. Morgan sat placidly while King exploded into the telephone. This was an old experience for him—the violent shock at the first encounters with the wretched behavior of mankind. He told himself, no wonder the average American diplomat prefers to stay in his air-conditioned compound with his frozen steaks and Coca-Cola instead of mingling with the natives. Only the missionary with his stubborn, foolish belief in the goodness of man can endure them.

Mickie came hustling back into the dressing room, his heavy jowls moving as he walked. His face was a little red. He said abruptly, "Silas, an insurrection is being organized back home! Judge Herring has just talked to me. Item Number One, General Corning, the Army Chief of Staff, told a Senate Committee, prompted by Maze Bledsoe, that the United States must not be lulled into disarming either ourselves or our friends because of sweet words from Moscow. Number Two, the Vice President is telling everyone that it was a mistake for the President to sit down with the Russians. Three, Bledsoe is organizing the opposition to whatever treaty we bring back. Four, the missile manufacturers have a full-page ad in the leading newspapers on the theme don't let down your guard.

"This might blow into the kind of revolt that killed the League of Nations. How many senators will vote for a treaty that will throw ten thousand out of work in their state?"

The Secretary slapped his palm several times against the arm of his chair. He said, speaking flatly and dryly without emotion, "There was a half-wit who lived near my Grandfather's store. They couldn't let him out alone, or sure as sin he would step into a trap set out for fur. I found him in the woods once howling in that crazy way of his, his leg in a trap. I can see his face very clearly, and I wonder if I look that way."

"Has something else happened?" Moonan asked uneasily, knowing there had.

"Yes. Our seismograph station in California has detected a man-made explosion. Bigger than a hydrogen bomb. They've pinned it down to an area of Soviet Asia—Turkestan. This means they have deliberately broken their word to test a new weapon, a giant new weapon!"

He pounded his fist loosely on the edge of the chair, and asked, "How much of this can we take and stay here?"

From the corner of the room came the deep voice of Morgan. "A man can take many blows and still live, Mr. Secretary. This is the most surprising fact of life."

King looked at him gratefully. "All right," the Secretary said. "I'll take your word for it. Our first problem is, how much of this shall we tell Chris?"

"Nothing," Mickie said spiritedly. "Nothing! Our only chance of getting free of all these traps is that wonderful miraculous personality of his. And you know how he collapses when he hears bad news. Like a girl who's been seduced and abandoned."

Secretary King took off his bathrobe and held out his arms for the valet to put on a shirt. He nodded his head in agreement.

That afternoon, King and the President drove across town to the Soviet villa.

Mr. Christiansen was quiet all the short drive. He was consciously trying to tap the springs of emotion that lay within him. Ah, here was one! He was a boy again, seated on the hard plank bench of the outdoor evangelist chapel. He heard as though muffled in a dream the aroused, unnaturally excited voices singing:

> "Rest on the promises, beautiful promises
> Rest on the promises, the holy promises of God . . ."

They were wafted into heaven itself by the hint of those promises, and then brought crashing, screaming to earth by the shrill warning of the preacher, "And there were voices, and thunders and lightnings, and there was a great earthquake such as was not since men were upon the earth . . . And the cities of the nations fell . . . And every island fled away, and the mountains were not found. And there fell upon men a great hail out of heaven, every stone about the weight of a talent . . ." The little boy recalled by memory shivered with the horror of it. That boy had wet his pants a little while the world was ending. Perhaps that was the way it would be—the terrible, the brilliant flash in the sky, a mass wetting of the pants, and the end.

His mind, like a drunk wavering down a street, lurched into an unexpected hidden lane. He thought of his fierce, joyous pleasure with the Major's wife on the Carolina dune. He could even feel the sand gritting on his bare arm beneath her quivering, bare buttocks. What a thought to come to him now! Mr. Christiansen tried to shake it, to retrace his trail of memory back to the chapel in the grove.

The President was so engaged that he noticed little on the drive, not even the splendor of the Soviet villa and its red carpet from the driveway across the columned portico and into the elegant entrance hall.

Radilov greeted him gaily, "Quite a palace for a pig, eh? Who would think this of the Communists?"

Silas King said matter-of-factly, "Why not? Mr. Christiansen's father was a mechanic. Mine was a schoolteacher."

The guests were ushered into an eighteenth-century drawing room with an immense cut-glass chandelier and a Da Vinci. Toasts were given.

When Mr. Christiansen began to speak, he knew the spirit was with him. He had that peculiar glow of energy and ecstasy that comes to the weary soldier with a shot of straight whisky.

He said, "Mr. Radilov and Silvio, the four of us are just about the last hope of the world for peace. If we can't make it, well then the millions who inhabit this earth will have to pack up their hopes, and get ready for the big explosion that will end everything."

The President was so affected by his own words that moisture gathered in his eyes.

"You know we have to do a lot more than just say we won't throw any missiles at each other. We've got to figure out a way for all the nations, little or big, black or white or yellow, Jew, Catholic, atheist, or what-have-you to stop fighting. And that's a big order. But I think it can be done. ("Rest on the promises, beautiful promises . . .")

"I'll tell you why. Back in the frontier days of America, it wasn't safe to go without a gun. You'd get in an argument with a neighbor over a stray, and he'd shoot you, or with a stranger in a bar, the same. And robbers stopped the stagecoaches and stole the money and jewels. I guess the mortality rate was pretty high. But then more people began to move in and settle the land, and they decided this was a pretty poor way to live. So they enacted laws and appointed sheriffs and made murder dangerous. This is what we've got to do—make it plain that shooting a cannon or a bomb is a world crime and will be punished, and we've got to disarm at the same time."

Radilov came to the President, and threw his arms about his shoulders and embraced him. He said in an outburst of excitement, reminding Mr. Christiansen very much of a Polish speaker at a political rally in Chicago, "You have touched our hearts, Malcolm Christiansen. You are one of us, for war is the evil enemy of the Russian people. Twice in one generation, our fathers and our brothers have been destroyed, our cities razed, our farms burned, our women and children carried off as slaves. Our noblest writer, Tolstoy, has said, 'War is such a horrible, such an atrocious thing, that no man, especially no Christian man, has the right to assume the responsibility of beginning it.'"

The two men stood close to each other, like the bellows and the forge. Their foreign ministers could feel the heat of the flames.

"Here you see a man . . ." The Premier put his hand dramatically on his chest. ". . . a man who has been twice driven to the gates of despair. My father was lost in the slime of the Pripet Marshes when the Germans invaded our land in the first World War. And my dearest brother, Pyotr, was a partisan fighter in the Ukraine and was killed by the Huns in the second World War. My soul dried up when I heard that the cherished comrade of my boyhood was dead. I went out into the night, and I walked for miles in the snow and I cried until I had no more tears.

"Do you wonder that I awake in the night and hear the guttural curses of the Germans and the screams of my people? The Germans have twice taken us to Golgotha, but never again. I say they must be disarmed. They must be prevented from ever holding a weapon again. Let them go back to their novels and their symphonies!"

Silas King looked at this scene through the eyes of disbelief. Even the setting was unreal. Like one of the operas his wife insisted they attend. No people who were getting down to business ever talked this way. Chris was hamming it up, and the Russian doubled him. Just like a tenor and a baritone in a flighty Italian opera. At this point the old ladies in the boxes would be breathing hard. It did not occur to King that either the President or the Premier believed a word he said; instead, they were a couple of kids putting on a show.

The Secretary said with the hearty amiability a good salesman uses on an evasive customer, "Mr. Radilov, we appreciate your sentiments. This makes our job easier. I have with me here a series of proposals, carefully considered steps in the direction of disarmament, trade, non-aggression, economic zones, and political activity." He opened his dispatch case and produced a thick sheaf of papers.

Radilov spoke excitedly, the tenor protesting the enemy is at the gate, and we must fly, Esmeralda, we must fly. He said, "Mr. King, we must pull up our socks and quicken our pace. We have not the hours to mull over distant problems. Germany at this moment is planning war. The Federal Minister, Herr Oberstadt, has declared, 'Over there in Russia the soil is waiting for us. There we must strike roots.' Can you doubt that intent, Mr. Secretary of State? Now, I will make you a proposition. If you will agree to disarm Germany, I will reduce the strength of our armed forces by one-half. Put that in your pipe and smoke it! What do you say?"

Silas King was used to sitting on the country club patio or in a board room in negotiations that were interspersed with conversation on the quality of the whisky, the state of the greens and the Republican prospects at the next election, so he was suspicious of the Russian's proposal. He told himself, "This fellow is like a Jew peddler. He's trying to flimflam us."

Radilov suddenly seemed to become aware of the striking difference between the President and his Secretary of State. He addressed himself to King, saying, "Do you know, Mr. Secretary, that it is calculated that in the last six thousand years, man has been exposed to nearly fifteen thousand wars? And in these wars four billion people have been slain. And the cost has been equal to a strip of gold twenty-five feet thick, six miles wide, stretched over the entire equator."

King replied, "There is not the slightest disagreement among us on the waste of war. But Mr. Radilov, you are asking us to make all the concessions. Of course if Germany is disarmed, you can reduce your armies and use the manpower and investment to improve your country. What is our reward? Violent attacks from members of Congress who regard Germany as our best bulwark of defense against you. We must return with a specific and trustworthy machinery which will keep you from attacking us."

Radilov threw up his hands. His voice was harsh and metallic as he said, "You Americans! How can you think we have any stomach for war? My country lost twenty million souls in the last war. Most of them were men and boys. Do you think we have forgotten that lesson so easily?

"And yet before the war was even finished, you began to say, 'We must beware the Russians,' and stacked the Germans' arms so they might be turned against our hordes from the East. How could we have overrun Europe? Our troops would not have fought. We had no supplies. What must we do to prove we are peaceful? Do we have to throw away all our guns, so the Fascists can rise up in Germany and Poland and Hungary and attack us?"

"It would have helped," King replied, "if you had been less doctrinaire and more tolerant of the priests in eastern Europe."

Radilov faced him directly and said, "How can we be sure of the loyalty of these people if their souls are in pawn?"

He paced the length of the room. The heels of his black shoes made little impressions in the heavy rug. His image flashed back and forth in a large gold-framed mirror. The petals of a delicate white flower in a red vase trembled each time he walked past.

President Christiansen watched the flowers. They reminded him of raindrops hanging on a linden tree after a rain. The flower was a safe shore for the President's thoughts. He did not want to be out in this troubled sea of debate, at least for the moment. Wait until the storm had worn itself out.

Secretary King said, "Mr. Premier, you have asked what you can do to prove your peaceful intent. For one thing, you can keep your word on agreements already reached."

Radilov stopped pacing. Mr. Christiansen looked in surprise at his Secretary.

The Russian asked, "What do you mean?"

King said, "I mean the explosion of a new super-weapon in Soviet Asia. How did you think this could not be detected by the seismographs?"

Quite unexpectedly, the Premier's great show of ego collapsed. He sat down. He seemed very tired. He said in a low voice, "It was those damnable Chinese."

"The Chinese?"

"Yes. In the Takla Makan Desert. Your engineers should have located the area by now. Now you know why we are so disturbed. The Germans menace us from the west, and the Chinese build huge weapons on our eastern frontier. How can we breathe? For God's sake, if you are a Christian and believe in the principles of that man, help us and save the world!"

Mr. Christiansen felt as though he had been hit from behind and spun around.

"You mean," he asked, "that the Chinese might attack you?"

Radilov addressed him gently, as one does a child who is loved. "Mr. President," he said, "if you wish to read the future, learn of the past. In the year 1218, Ghengis Khan and his Mongols swept into Turkestan, just across the border from the Chinese bomb test. The great city of Samarkand fell. The Mongols drove to the Black Sea and the Dnieper River. In 1235, another invading force from the East took all of Russia and ravaged Poland. Today, we and the Chinese sit along a six-thousand-mile border watching each other and reading history."

"But you are fellow Communists."

"Do the Christians ever fight one another?" Radilov asked ironically. "A man's religious or political beliefs do not change his nature or his needs. We must all eat, drink, sleep and defecate. And if we are hungry, and our neighbor grows tomatoes in his garden, we will steal them. The Chinese keep themselves hungry by their insane breeding. In another hundred years, there will be no one but Chinese. They look at our green fields which we have irrigated, and they pant at our frontiers. And now you Western-ers, you point a cannon at our back by arming Germany. Poor Russia!"

The President said calmly, even a little sternly as if to strike dumb any objections, "We will disarm Germany. You can count on that."

Secretary King looked at him in amazement and exasperation. What did Chris mean giving away his best card just at the moment when a flaw, a gnawing weakness, was exposed in the enemy? This was the time to drive a hard bargain. Now they had thrown away Germany and would have to appeal to the altruism of the Russians. Silas King did not think much of that.

Radilov emotionally grasped Mr. Christiansen's hand and pressed it.

"Spasibo, spasibo!" he said. "You have brought to the world the spirit of peace."

The President had no clear idea of why he made this offer. He had a feverish sensation of well-being, as the patient when he first breaks out of the world of illness and is aware of dear and familiar things. For a moment, Malcolm Christiansen was in boyhood again, in the little room under the eaves. The delirium of flu cleared and he saw his father by his bed. And as he opened his eyes, his father smiled at him and said, "You're all right now, son."

Silas King's shirt collar felt too tight. He was swollen with outrage, not so much at the President as himself. He had been outwitted by a Russian peddler. Radilov had divined the secret of Malcolm Christiansen. This came as a thundering clap of knowledge to the Secretary of State.

He sat pounding his right fist loosely on the arm of his chair. He discovered he had oddly lost the power of revving up his mind and finding a new angle. He was simply too outraged.

Then to his surprise, he heard Mr. Christiansen say, "Now, Mr. Radilov, we've got some problems and we'd like your help on them. We look on the Americas as, well, one big happy family. But the Communist agitators are stirring up the people in South America not to like us, and this is all very unfortunate."

The Russian Premier replied, "Mr. President, you have become our brother. We cannot allow any to speak ill of you." He spoke rapidly in Russian to the Foreign Minister, and told Mr. Christiansen, "Your name will be honored throughout the socialist world. Any who attacks you will be pointed out as a counter-revolutionary."

Silas King was a realist. When by an off-chance he was defeated in a plan, he had the good sense to keep his eyes open and wait for opportunities. They were always around waiting to be picked up by the fellow with keen eyes. And old Artemus King had sharpened his eyes so he could spot an opportunity just as some other boys he knew in upper Michigan could see a deer running through the brush a half mile away at dusk. He was ready to accept the Russian's gift and to understand that it was a loan really. A loan that could be recalled if the United States became careless about its promise to disarm Germany.

## *Chapter* TWENTY-THREE

THE PRESS party at the Soviet villa filed in respect past the great sturgeon, sampled the caviar, admired the lobster from the Black Sea, and headed for the bar. Smiling young Russian officials stood everywhere eager to reply with facts and figures should a correspondent inquire about the virgin lands or freedom of worship. Radilov himself had not yet arrived, so there was no central focus. The press flowed into three separate seas.

In the first were those frantic souls besieged by foul-tempered editors who kept cabling, "Get the news!" So they scurried about glass in hand, either apologetic or mildly belligerent, haunting anyone who looked remotely like an official spokesman and pitifully begging for some crumb to satisfy those evil, dyspeptic editors who held the whip over their heads. "But don't you have any idea what they talked about?" they insisted to a bland Soviet third secretary who pretended not to understand or to the "Voice of America" man who was dismally aware his suit was long out of fashion.

In the second sea were those in search of a clever line to embellish a dull dispatch. If they listened carefully in the right group, they might pick up a brilliant *mot* and store it preciously in the memory until they could get in a corner and hastily scribble it down. This line would then be utilized the rest of the year, like a second-hand coat that is treasured until it falls apart. These seekers encircled Paul Carter, the American columnist. He was a tall, stridently thin individual who wore a habitual air of indifference or condescending amusement. His face, as a rival once exclaimed gleefully, reminded one of a bored horse. But Carter had a reputation for brilliance and learning, and foreign ministers gave interviews to him.

The third group swirled giddily and unashamedly around the beauty. She was Anna Yashin, the niece of the Foreign Minister. She was one of the rare beauties who is unaware of her exquisite charms, and so is not eternally dropping her eyes, quivering her lips, showing her profile and behaving like the coquette. She was black-haired with flashing eyes and a sturdy figure. The conversation in this circle was very animated but dull, for who can marshal his thoughts and speak wittily in the presence of beauty? The brain thickens, the tongue stammers.

Radilov arrived at about seven thirty and strolled from group to group being introduced and making remarks. He was obviously in high good-humor. When he met Carter, Radilov said, "Mr. Columnist, I have read your dispatches and you say we are here to trick the Americans. There is a saying in my country that when a man slaps you, before you strike him back ask him his reason. He may have good cause. So I ask you, what trick am I playing?"

Throughout the room, there was a movement toward the little group. Those close by overheard Radilov and immediately pressed in. Others, looking out of the corner of their eyes, noticed the closing in, and, with the curiosity of the crowd, joined in. Anna, for all her charms, was left almost alone.

Carter covered his embarrassment with a haughty gaze and said, "Mr. Premier, you are trying to persuade the United States to disarm Germany while you give nothing in return."

"Oh, so that is it. So you think the disarming of Germany will benefit no one but the Russians? Do you remember a place called Auschwitz? This was where the Germans exterminated four million people. These were not soldiers they killed in battle. These were plain people, Jews and others who did not hold with their fascist beliefs. Do you think these same people can now be trusted with atomic cannons and germ warfare? Is any corner of the world safe from such bestiality once it is armed?"

"There are some people," said Carter, "who regard Russia and Germany as two monsters, each checking the other. What if one of them is reined? Will the other leap on the world and subjugate it? You have asked questions. I answer you with two more."

"You are a lively fellow," Radilov said in appreciation. "I suppose now you will go back to America and run for President, because you have been bold enough to ask the Russian Premier a question or two. But that is all right. O.K."

There were several claps of applause, mainly from the young Russian officials, and laughter. A photographer climbed on the bar to look down on the intent faces. Radilov was smiling. Carter was tense and uneasy. He was not prepared to argue dialectics with the high priest of communism.

The Premier continued, "The great issue for the world is the survival of mankind, and you invent fairy stories to put me off. When, I ask you, has Russia gone invading and plundering across the land?"

"What about Poland?" a voice in the crowd asked. "Poland 1939. You struck a dying man."

Radilov searched the group as if hunting for the questioner. He replied, "My friend, I will not call you comrade, for that you obviously are not, when a fiend is approaching your children with a knife upraised, you hide them behind whatever barricade you can find, even if it is your brother. This is not the way things are written in the books, but it is true. The urge for self-preservation is both wonderful and terrible. We knew that the Nazi monster was going to attack us. We were not ready. We played for time. We stormed into Poland to gain ground between ourselves and the Huns. War and the fear of war causes men and nations to commit fearful acts. If you have ever been on a battlefield, friend, you would know this behavior is not limited to the soldiers of any one nation. The madness is universal. But let me add this, neither the Russians nor the Americans, so far as I know, ever destroyed whole villages or tried to exterminate a race of people. Yet this was done by the Germans whom you now enfold in your arms and give atomic weapons."

A young journalist who had learned Russian just in the hope of meeting such a young lady as Anna Yashin looked at her enchanting eyes and asked if the Premier habitually argued with his guests.

"Oh yes," she answered in a pretty, accented English. "Comrade Radilov is a champion talker, do you not think?"

The Premier was saying, "I have studied the causes of war as Dr. Freud analyzed the sex urge, and I hope you will listen just as attentively as you would to a discourse on the erotic habits of the female glowworm. The day when a nation will go to war to increase its power and prestige is gone with the suits of armor and the trireme. War is too expensive and too dangerous; you do not take it on lightly as you would a walk in the country. No, the causes of war in our times are fear, hunger and madness. Let me illustrate by a story the lesson of fear. When I was a student, there was a serious and nervous fellow named Yury who lived down the hall on one side and a very loud and careless student, Aleksei, on the other. Aleksei was forever making bold remarks, but he was really a kind and humane person. Yury had a violin and when he was troubled he would play the violin, and not very well. This reacted on the nerves of Aleksei and he shouted, 'If you do not stop this screeching I will kill you with my hands.' Aleksei looked capable. He was strong and had large hands. Other students thinking this was a great joke would remark whenever they saw Yury, 'I understand Aleksei is planning to kill you.' They even in the careless humor decided on a time, the anniversary of the Revolution. Of course, Yury did not take these remarks seriously at first. But, as I have said, he was a nervous and imaginative fellow, and when he lay awake at night exhausted by his studying he would remember the remarks and the strong hands of Aleksei. He was badly frightened one night quite late when he came home from the symphony and Aleksei, who had been out drinking, stumbled into the hall at the same time. Aleksei playfully reached out to clasp him, and Yury ran away making strange noises, his heart beating in terror. He began to believe that Aleksei was going to kill him. This was very real to him. He read it in Aleksei's eyes and in the motion of his shoulders as he walked, and even in his rough, careless songs. Yury decided his only hope of living was to kill Aleksei first. He secretly obtained a pistol by saying he was going home and that bandits menaced the people in the country. He studied Aleksei's habits, when he went out and returned, when he walked down the hall to the toilet. He planned to hide in a stall in the toilet and shoot Aleksei as he came for his morning duty. He steeled his heart against this abominable act by telling himself this man was determined to kill him with his hands. On the appointed morning, he was waiting in his hiding place and when the familiar figure arrived, he fired the pistol. Fortunately, his aim was less sure than his intent, and Yury broke down and

cried, 'I have lost. Strangle me now and put me out of my misery.'
Aleksei who had a great sense of humor roared with laughter at
this bizarre attempt at murder, and then told Yury he had no
intention of harming him. They became fast friends once the fear
was removed.

"Thus it is with nations. You Americans are afraid of us, and
we Russians are afraid of you. A few of the generals of both
countries speak in their usual belligerent manner; each of us thinks
the other is about to attack; we are consumed with fear and plot
feverishly how to destroy the other.

"Hunger eats away the sanity, as fear does. An Arab sits under
the blazing sun hungry and homeless and looks at the green fields
of Israel, and he undergoes a chemical change. He is consumed
with a desire to make his revenge. His own life is so wretched and
worthless, he would rather be dead than alive. Perhaps his children
or their children will eat the wheat and grapes that grow in Israel
if he attacks.

"And then there is a madness whose roots are mysterious. They
are ancient and mystic. They overpower a nation with a passion
for murder. Such a passion deep in the spirits of the Germans has
led to two wars in one generation, devastation, mass murder. When
will it strike again? I am afraid that time will be soon unless
Germany is disarmed."

Carter had recovered his composure during the telling of the
story. He lit a cigarette to show the Premier his hand was not
trembling, and asked with an air of indifference, "Sir, how do you
square your pacifism, as you have expressed it tonight, with your
frequent statements that communism will control the world?"

Radilov laughed and, pointing through the crowd at Anna with
her faithful group of admirers, said, "I am counting on the beauty
and eloquence of our Russian women to convince you non-
believers. And if this fails to move you, there is your own stomach
that will prompt you. You will eat better under communism. You
will not worry about unemployment. Your lives will not be at the
mercy of greedy monopolies. How can you doubt this? Our economic growth has far outstripped that of the capitalist nations."

An Indian correspondent said seriously, "I will admit, Mr.
Premier, that your economic progress is very attractive, but we
are repelled at one aspect of it."

"What is that?" Radilov asked curiously.

"It has been obtained without compassion, and at the expense of human dignity and freedom."

"My dear sir," Radilov replied with relish, "you cannot enjoy freedom or dignity if you are starving and victimized by selfish economic groups and corrupt officials. And any great human effort, such as we have seen in a lifetime in Russia, must be marshaled and organized and disciplined. It cannot be achieved by merely wishing it, by merely saying to your citizens, 'You must do this because it is your duty.' It is human nature to do what is customary and what is easy. You must propagandize, and you must punish the slacker. You must show your fist, if needs be. This is unfortunate. I wish that God had made man more reasonable, but we must take what we have. We in Russia have as our goals peace, prosperity and freedom, but we are honest enough to say we have not won the heights as yet. The sons and grandsons of the peasants who resisted collectivization, of men who died in Siberian mines, will enjoy a freedom and a dignity that will make the sacrifice of the past seem more logical. The American will cringe at the memory of his violent war of extermination on the Indians, yet he will say the end justified the means. He will say the earth is more abundant, the life is richer and better because of this. We Russians can say that in a generation or less."

The Premier paused a moment, then told the Indian correspondent, "If there is another method of winning great progress in a short time, let me know it and I will argue for its adoption in the Communist circles."

In a moment of silence someone on the edge of the crowd said in an aside, "He sounds like a Jesuit arguing Catholic theology to a non-believer." Radilov overheard it and answered, "I admire the Jesuit. I wish our Communist missionaries were as thorough and as trained in logic. Send me Jesuits and I will give them jobs in our universities as devil's advocates."

"Does this mean that the grandchildren of the Bolsheviks will enjoy religious freedom?"

"What a strange choice of a word, 'enjoy.' Perhaps you mean by that the sensation of an opium smoker. Why should we Communists permit opium simply because it allows the smoker to escape in a dream away from life? No, we want our comrades to face and get good out of life. I do not understand the Christians. They do not have a deep faith in their God. They must pray to all sorts of little gods to reinforce his will. Yet, they desire that everyone else believe in Christianity. Our Buddhist and Moslem and Hindu friends do not demand we go to prayers with them. But you Christians are forever urging us to set up religion. I say we do not need it."

Mickie Moonan came in quietly and stood near the buffet, unable to decide whether to have something to eat or join the crowd pressed around Radilov. An acquaintance who covered the State Department came up to Moonan and said in disgust, "This man is a menace."

"Who is?" Mickie asked.

"The Russian—Radilov. He makes clever speeches, and these foolish people think how charming he is, and even applaud him. Why people from some of the best newspapers like the *Herald Tribune*, are right there in the front ranks fawning over him. No one stands up for principles, or for the Christian religion, or for patriotism any more."

"Why don't you take him on then, Bert?" Moonan asked.

He decided he was horribly hungry, and turned to look for a canape. Bert followed him and explained, "It is better to keep one's dignity than debate with a man like that. Camus said, 'The problem is to serve human dignity by means which remain honorable in the midst of a history which is not honorable.'"

Moonan did not reply. His mouth was full.

Someone else in the crowd was questioning Radilov, who stood with his arms crossed and a smile both triumphant and ironic.

"You talk a great deal about peace, Mr. Premier, but what about your missile-launching sites along the Baltic Sea, in the Carpathian Mountains and in the Thuringian Forest? Don't they constitute a danger to peace? Aren't you afraid one of your men will carelessly push the button?" the questioner inquired.

The faces in the crowd were set in attitudes of interest. A mouth was open here, a head bent there. Smiles were frozen from the last sally of humor. There were frowns of intense concentration on the question and the answer. A pipe had gone out. A thumb and forefinger held a nose thoughtfully.

Radilov said, "I will be honest with you. Of course they are a threat to peace. Any instrument of war in the hands of man endangers peace. But we have these missiles to stop anyone who might think Russia is a nice dish for the taking. The presence of these missiles will make anyone think twice before sharpening his sword for the Russian head. Now, I will do this—if you disarm Germany, I will remove the missile bases, for there is no longer need of them. I do not fear war from the British, or the French or the Belgians, or the Swedes."

This statement was greeted by a drawing in of the breaths and tensing of the reflexes. One reporter made as if to casually slip away and beat them all to the phones. But the Reuters man, a stocky Scotchman, reached out and grabbed him and said gruffly, "No one leaves until this is over." Sheepishly the other murmured in French about *la toilette*, but remained.

A Czech correspondent tried to draw the Premier out on "the weaknesses of capitalism as exemplified by American civilization."

Radilov replied genially, "Why should any good Communist ask me that question? He should know the answers himself. If you want to know about America, go there, or, better yet, since time is flying and your education is in immediate need of knowledge, go see Mr. Moonan. He is the gentleman over there enjoying one of the great luxuries of the world, Russian lobster."

The Premier broke free of the crowd saying, "I have consumed enough of your time when you should be at ease with nothing more on your mind than a pretty pair of shoulders or the flavor of a good wine."

"What about vodka?" a voice shouted.

"I do not drink vodka. It has been the curse of Russia. Those with miserable lives, instead of trying to better them have lost to the degradation in the bottle."

There was a rush for the door as those who wished to file bulletins raced to telephones. The young Russians observed them with good-natured wonder, shaking their heads.

Gradually the party re-formed its former circles. Her admirers all returned to Anna. Those in the same sea with Carter said to one another, "Isn't that fellow Radilov incredible? Simply incredible. A magnificent showman!" A casual-looking fellow exclaimed, "Can you imagine what life will be like when the Communists spread their tide over the world? No whisky. No mistresses. No splendid near-naked women on the beach or the stage. Everything very earnest. You will spend your vacations working on the communal farms. Television commercials replaced by slogans for the revolution. The national heroes will be the prize worker at the Gary steel mill and a Texas steer. No satire. The party secretary will replace the psychiatrist's couch and the confession box."

This horrible description evoked a deep groan.

In the third sea, the anxious correspondents pressed the young Russian men into corners and asked, "Where are the missile stations?" . . . "Where is the Thuringian Forest?" . . . "Do you think he really meant to give up the missiles?" . . .

At the American villa, President Christiansen was having an after-dinner drink with Silas King and Morgan. The latter was saying, "If you had a good day today with the Russians, Mr. President, tomorrow will be difficult. This is a part of their usual tactic. They must test the enemy and search the blackness of his soul, *à la* Dostoyevsky. They want to find out if we are really in earnest with peace or toying about with it. If we are not, they think, we shall become enraged by their highhandedness and walk out. So, when they become grim and tight-lipped, then is the time to exercise all the charm and smiling good-humor and tolerance."

"Why do they act like that?" the President asked, stretching out his legs before him.

"Hmm. You might compare them with the barbarians deep within the jungles of the Amazon who, when they are driven out by hunger, are deeply suspicious of all other men. They do not trust them, and must test them in their own curious way."

Mr. Christiansen rattled the ice in his glass abstractedly. He said, "Let me tell you what we'll do tomorrow. Instead of having a formal meeting, I will take Radilov for a drive in the mountains, and we'll talk in an informal manner, don't you see?"

He looked up and, smiling, said, "If only we could reach some simple way of making sure of disarmament—like having the heads of state of all the nations take lie-detector tests under the auspices of the United Nations."

King swallowed hastily and coughed. When he had finished sputtering, he said weakly, "Chris, nothing like that, please."

The next afternoon, the long black Chrysler limousine, with

its escorts, headed up the slowly winding drive past the terraced rows of villas, then orchards, and toward the French Alps.

As they rode along commenting on the scenery, Mr. Christiansen noticed a quality, or lack of one, in his guest that had escaped him before. Radilov was not, could never be, smooth. There was an essential roughness to him that neither time nor events could rub off. He was like a certain Congressman from Detroit who, despite his expensive clothes, could not hide a crude vigor. It was too powerful to be held in.

The President asked, "What do you want for your country, Mr. Premier?"

Radilov replied so quickly the thought must have lain at the top of his mind, "Russia must move ahead swiftly, as in that famous passage from Gogol . . ."

The Premier recited in a voice that was so intense Mr. Christiansen felt a little uncomfortable: "And, Russia, are not thou too flying onwards like a spirited troika that nothing can overtake? The road is smoking under thee, the bridges rumble, everything falls back and is left behind! The spectator stands still struck dumb by the divine miracle; is it not a flash of lightning from heaven? What is the meaning of this terrifying onrush? What mysterious force is hidden in this troika, never seen before? Russia, whither flyest thou? Everywhere there is earth flying by, and the other states and nations, with looks askance, make way for her and draw aside."

Radilov was silent a moment, and then said, "I read this passage when I was a student, Mr. President, and I vowed this was my goal, this was my sacred oath." Abruptly he asked, "And what is your goal for your country?"

Mr. Christiansen briefly was confused. What was it indeed? He had heard Silas King talk often of "sound money . . . private initiative . . . reasonable profit." Someone else said "full employment" or "civil rights." But none of these had a meaning that really moved him. Into this urgent void came the sound of his father's voice, and the President replied, "To live in peace."

The Soviet Premier looked at him and searched his face. He repeated, "To live in peace, eh? That is all."

"What would you strive for if you were in my place?" Mr. Christiansen asked a little belligerently.

"Hmm. If I were President of the United States, I would try

to erect its walls and furnish its chambers in the image of Abraham Lincoln, and make this the ideal for freedom and knowledge for the world and for history. In this way America would be known in the future for something more than the Ford car and the atomic bomb and the lady with the magnificent bust. I would make of every child an educated man or woman who loves, who worships freedom and learning, and so even when the splendor and richness of my civilization had declined, the world would still be in awe of what I had achieved."

The President said in surprise, "I didn't know you felt this way about freedom. Why don't you do something about it in Russia?"

"You forget," Radilov replied, "you asked me what I would do if I were in your shoes. I have a different clay to work with. My people are young and possessed of a youthful vigor that must be forced into correct channels. Yours is an ebbing civilization, the tide is running out. Oh, I have read Spengler's *Untergang des Abendlandes* and his forecast that the European-American society is in decay and will be followed by the emergence of the Russian, and then we, too, will rot away. But before I die, I shall write a letter to my successor and ask him to pass it on and on down the line, saying what we can do to prolong our hour in the sun, and then when we are dying to be noble and great nevertheless."

"Well," said Mr. Christiansen, "I've never read this Spengler, and I don't believe what he says. Why we've got the highest standard of living ever achieved, the highest productivity per man, the greatest productivity per acre, the best housing, and all this sort of thing. Our Army and our Navy and our Air Force are second to none, if you will allow me to differ with you, so how can we decline?"

"Babylon fell. Rome fell. It is a process of nature just like life and death."

Their little caravan was winding smoothly up the mountainside. They moved into the area of the immense stands of pine. The air was sharp and pungent with the scent of pine needles. Radilov pointed ahead where the Alps towered like ancient monuments to the sun. He said, "Up there are huge sheets of snow and ice that break loose and come crashing down on the village. The avalanche. When the avalanche begins to break loose, there is a terrible sound of groaning and cracking, and when they hear this the villagers are struck with terror, and they flee if there is time. In the world today, there is the same sound."

A small twinge of fear gripped Mr. Christiansen and he asked, "What is this sound you speak of?"

The slightly metallic voice responded, "The preparations for war. You and I can halt this avalanche. Are you for it?"

"Yes."

The Premier clasped his hand tightly and said, "Peace must have its salesman; it will not come without it. The man Jesus was the salesman for social justice. Without Him and His chroniclers the word humanity would have no meaning. He was a great revolutionary. Now, there must be a leader in whom the world has faith who says how peace can be won, and of the heroic efforts and sacrifice needed. The world will never trust me, nor any of my people. But they have only to look at you and they believe you. They must be made to believe it is not impossible."

The limousine had stopped, and the two heads of state got out, buttoning their coats as they did. The air was cold. The height and the almost unimaginable majesty of the scenery had a dizzying effect. The air had a taste of purity like spring water, clear and cold and invigorating. Downward, captured in the sloping valleys, were little villages and green pastures. In the sunlight the snow had melted and streams gushed out of crevices and sparkled in the light. Above were the towering giants, the massive, snow-drenched peaks under a pale blue sky. They were the titans guarding Valhalla. Here was a wild and startling grandeur, and yet, curiously enough, serenity.

Malcolm Christiansen had a peculiar illusion, that not only was he at a great height, but that his life itself had ascended to a new and towering level. He stood in the cold wind not even noticing it, aware only of a sense of power. Peace lay in his hands, awaiting his bidding!

Radilov narrowed his eyes against the glare of the sun on the snow and looked at him with a curious smile.

# Chapter TWENTY-FOUR

JEFFERSON LAWRENCE sat before a microphone hunched and penitent, like a prisoner in the stocks. His mouth was dry, and he reached out for the glass of ice water before him.

On either side of the Secretary of Defense were eager and anxious assistants. They bent toward him as though blown by a storm. Immediately in front of the Secretary, a woman press photographer on bended knee raised her 35-millimeter camera, aimed and shot. The click was audible during the pause.

The Senate Committee hearing room was so jammed that a senator had to have the guard clear a path for him to reach his seat. The spectators sat fiercely intent, the press a little more indifferent but with pencils in place waiting for the answer. Smoke from many cigarettes and pipes drifted lazily to the green ceiling. A panel of green marble ran around the walls and broadened behind the committee bench.

There sat Maze Bledsoe, huge, amiable and leering. His dewlaps hung with an air of ponderous amusement. He said in an easy drawl swollen with inference, "Did you hear the question, Mr. Secketary, or do you want me to give it again?"

Lawrence nodded.

"All right, I'm askin' you, do you think Germany is important to the defense of the citizens of these United States?"

Secretary Lawrence said quietly, precisely, and with a hint of agony, "May I be excused from answering that question?"

Senator Bledsoe grinned at him.

"Nope."

A senator several seats down from Bledsoe cleared his throat and stated meekly, even apologetically, "I think the Secretary should have the right to determine what questions he chooses to answer in view of the present situation."

Bledsoe regarded him with contempt and said, "The senator from Ioway has been here less than a year. I would advise him to read the rules before he interrupts the chairman. Mr. Secketary, will you proceed?"

Very quietly came the reply, "I would have to say yes."

Senator Bledsoe winked slyly at the press tables.

"All right, lemme read you a statement by one of our ablest columnists: 'An alert, well-armed, well-disciplined German military is the best possible deterrent to the frightful Soviet strength rolling west in a wave of blood and terror, for the Russians have a handsome respect for the Teutonic spirit. The Kremlin does not really believe that either the United States or Great Britain would risk wiping out the opulent life by firing its nuclear warheads at an advancing Communist force. But the Soviet strategists have no doubt about the Germans. By the best military judgment, one German division can hold back four Soviet divisions. The Russians would never trust a satellite division in combat with the Germans.' Now, Mr. Secketary, would you have any serious quarrel with that statement?"

"Senator, I have no way of reading the Russian mind, so I cannot tell you what the attitude of the Kremlin is toward the United States or Germany."

"Aside from that."

"I would have no quarrel with the statement."

"Mr. Secketary, do you believe that Congress has the responsibility to tell the American people the truth as we know it?"

"Yes, sir."

"Are you satisfied that the United States can adequately defend itself without the aid of an armed Germany?"

"Senator Bledsoe, the problem of defense in the world today is to be sure that any potential enemy is too frightened to attack you, that he is convinced that if he strikes, you or your allies will kill him automatically and without pause. He must be convinced that you and your allies not only have the capability, but the will.

The will is as important as the capability. Fright or panic will petrify the will. I have seen evidence of this in the courtroom, of a bank teller too frozen with fear to press the alarm bell when the bandit thrusts the pistol at him, or of a woman who is so drowned with panic she cannot fight off her rapist."

"Do you think that Germany would hesitate to attack if we were hit by missiles?"

"No, sir. The Germans realize their existence as a free nation depends entirely on us. At least, this is my opinion. I would not be so bold as to suggest my judgment is invincible."

Secretary Lawrence looked up with a shy, half smile. The patient photographer clicked again.

Maze Bledsoe thoughtfully stroked his eyebrows with the thumb and forefinger of his right hand. His large, derisive voice went on. "Mr. Secketary, we've heard it suggested in various public statements and discourses that the Russians sincerely desire peace. Let me now quote from a statement made by one of those Russian fellows thirty years ago: 'War to the hilt between communism and capitalism is inevitable. Today we are not strong enough to attack. Our time will come in twenty or thirty years. The bourgeoisie will have to be put to sleep. So we shall begin by launching the most spectacular peace movement on record. There will be unheard of concessions. The capitalists will rejoice to co-operate in their own destruction.' Now, Mr. Secketary, do you think we can rely on the Communists to keep the peace?"

Lawrence replied precisely. "Senator Bledsoe, my job is to prepare for the worst possible eventuality."

The Secretary hesitated, took a quick drink of water, and then, his pale face alive, intent, pleading, said, "Senator, we can start on the premise that we are all agreed on the urgent need for peace. The American people are faced with the most difficult and far-reaching decisions in their history. They must decide what course to follow in the quest for peace, and what tools to insure the successful pursuit of that course. Soviet Russia and its Communist allies represent at least a theoretical threat to our existence, to our homes, our churches, our capitalist society, our free institutions. The Communist powers have the tools to destroy us if they choose. We in the military do not know what is in the Communist heart. We have to assume that a man holding a gun at us may pull the trigger.

"Some people may be willing to pay a steep price for peace, that is at the expense of their human rights and freedom. Others say peace is valuable only when coupled with human dignity.

"There is not much any one man, such as myself, can do to change the course of events. All he can do is to be true to what he believes is right and be willing to stand by that conviction. Thus, he will encourage other men and perhaps influence his times . . ."

He stopped, as if made mute by the greatness of the issue. The hearing room immediately was filled with the sound of applause. The Secretary dropped his head, the figure praying at the altar. Senator Bledsoe let the applause run its course, then banged his gavel and said indulgently, "No displays from the spectators, please."

The reporters were busily scribbling, trying to get the precious words down. A radio engineer motioned with a nod of his head to indicate he had the entire colloquy on tape.

Jefferson Lawrence's heart beat rapidly. He thought it must be throbbing so loudly it could be heard in the room. This scene he had lain awake the night before planning and rehearsing, just as he would an appearance before the Supreme Court. Each expression, each pause, had to fit into the entire scene for its most dramatic impact. He arose pale and sleepless, but with an elation he had never known before. Finally he had found a role that did not shame him!

So it was now, in this crowded chamber, veiled with tobacco smoke, silent after the applause, that Secretary Lawrence sat listening to his heart.

Senator Bledsoe looked down from his seat with a magnificently malevolent approval. He had God-damned well taken the play away from the President's television speech tonight from Geneva. With this kind of testimony in the record, the Senate would never accept a plan for disarming Germany without cast-iron guarantees which, of course, Russian would not give.

That night, Bledsoe stood in line waiting to pay the cashier at the Methodist Building cafeteria. He sucked his teeth noisily and nodded familiarly to a Supreme Court Justice greedily attacking a piece of chocolate cream pie.

The cafeteria and its building, a prim citadel of Wesleyan modesty across the park from the Capitol, were favorites of congressmen, justices, and scholars from the Library of Congress. They ate roast beef rare, talked in lowered voices in the lobby, lived in the apartments upstairs, and exchanged greetings with the jolly Methodist Bishop on the elevator.

Bledsoe reached the cashier and towered above the register. He carelessly drew a wad of bills from his pocket and let a twenty-dollar certificate flutter downward on the table. The Senator said, "For me and my assistant." He looked knowingly at the cashier and dropped one eyelid slightly. The cashier, a ministerial student, blushed and looked irritated. Senator Bledsoe always did this to him.

The object of the Senator's leer was his secretary, an extravagantly beautiful Mexican-American girl who stood beside him. She had jet-black hair, startling red lips, a vacant, doll-like expression, and breasts that brought startled looks to even the Bishop. A colleague once said ruefully, "Maze hauls Rita along to take your mind off your business while he skins you."

The Senator scooped up the change and slouched out of the cafeteria. He belched contentedly as he picked his hat off a hook. Congressman Allen who was always trying to make friends with important people came up to Bledsoe in the hall and said, "Maze, we've saved a place for you before the television set in the lobby."

"Well," the Senator said in a patronizing air, "That's mighty nice of you. Do you suppose the old boy is calling for reinforcements?"

He sat down in the proffered overstuffed chair and spread out his legs. Rita was squeezed in between an assistant librarian and a lobbyist for second-class mail users. Later, neither could remember a word the President said in his address.

The audience watched in bored silence while an agitated announcer begged them to buy a laxative. Then, there was a flickering, and the warm and earnest face of Malcolm Christiansen appeared.

Bledsoe remarked, "Looks like my pop come to tell me the facts of life."

Congressman Allen laughed excessively and said, "By God, Maze, you've got the power of description. I was beginning to blush, and didn't know why."

The Methodist Bishop went "Sh."

The steady eyes of the President of the United States probed deeply into the souls of his watchers. The voice, tones of firmness, vigor, and optimism, said slowly, "My fellow men." A pause. "Many years ago, long before we ever dreamed of the hydrogen bomb, there lived a wise ruler. His name was David. David wrote down his thoughts as they came to him in the silence of the lonely fields where he tended his sheep as a young man. These are called the Psalms, and men have ever treasured them. There is one line that I think characterizes our efforts here in Geneva. It is, 'Seek peace, and pursue it.' " Pause.

"To seek peace, you must have it in your heart. You cannot go to your neighbor and say you want to settle a dispute over the fence line unless you really mean it. This has been the trouble in the negotiations between ourselves and Soviet Russia for a generation. We have both come to the conference table with pistols in our hands."

Mr. Christiansen pulled the lobe of his left ear with his hand and smiled. It was the sun appearing from behind the clouds. The little group in front of the TV set smiled too.

"At Geneva, I approached Mr. Radilov, the Soviet Premier, and in the words of the Holy Writ, 'I give unto him my covenant of peace.' He responded in kind. We talked as men who want the great adventure of living to continue. We agreed that war is destructive of everything mankind holds dear. There is no disagreement between capitalist and communist over love of life. Therefore, we have reached certain basic agreements. The dread of a nuclear hurricane need no longer disturb your sleep. . . ."

The group in the dim lobby of the Methodist Building sat spellbound. The end came with a rich and confident smile. The chairs creaked. The Bishop, anxious to get his word in first, said in his best pulpit manner, " 'I will hear what God the Lord will speak; for He will speak peace unto His people.' "

"That's ratin' the President pretty high, ain't it, Padre?" Bledsoe asked. He knew how much the Bishop disliked to be called "Padre."

The assistant librarian sat in delicious silence hoping that Rita would not move.

Congressman Allen asked, "What do you think, Maze?"

The Senator took off his glasses and rubbed his eyes. He replied,

"I think old Chris must have been sold a hell of a bill of goods. In this game, you don't quote the Scriptures unless you know you're going to have a devil of a time sellin' your product."

"Yes," the Congressman replied, "I've done it myself."

"So have I. So have I," said Bledsoe. "And I may have to do it again." He drew out the words. "Come on, Rita. We've got work to do." He winked at the Bishop, slapped the Congressman on the knee and walked toward the elevator.

The Bishop remarked plaintively, "I know he means well."

Secretary Lawrence watched the telecast alone in the library of his great Georgetown castle. He was so familiar with the gloom of this silent room that it no longer affected him.

The set was hidden behind a panel in the wall, so that this symbol of the pitchman and his medicine-man spiel would not intrude upon the rows of books climbing the library. The Secretary pushed the panels back, turned on the set and focused it. He also focused his mind to the lawyer listening dispassionately and critically to his opponent's argument.

". . . This agreement will work, and really banish the fear of the end of the world only if we have faith in it, and try to make it work. Every citizen must do his part. The angry word must not be said. The suspicious tongue must be silenced by patience and understanding. I would hope that in the days ahead we would give medals to the peacemakers and erect statues to them in our parks, for, as the Psalmist has written, 'Mark the perfect man, and behold the upright; for the end of that man is peace.' "

Lawrence thought, This dear, sweet, innocent man. Doesn't he know that the end is not peace at all, but survival? Every form of life is in a deadly conflict to survive. This is the energy that brings on change and evolution. He was reminded of Darwin's description of the fierce struggle between the wasp and the spider; each understood the other must perish if he were to live. Peace was the recess between wars to heal the wounds and restore the strength.

This was a clever and dangerous speech. Mickie Moonan had written it, of course. The Secretary could imagine the fat assistant, his shirt collar unbuttoned, thumbing through the concordance of the Bible looking for the appropriate quotations. The people would be moved by these words, but not Congress, or at least not for long. Disarmament would mean the air base or the small arms plant in the district would have to be shut down, and the Chambers of Commerce would be raising hell and sending delegations to Washington and asking the Representative to get some business there before they all went broke.

The Vice President and Judge Herring watched the telecast together. The Judge had invited Boxell to the Metropolitan Club for dinner, not because he liked him, but because he thought he should find out what he was up to.

The Metropolitan Club was an institution of slightly worn elegance scarcely two blocks from the White House. It was patronized traditionally by men of wealth and social standing. Room was made for those Government officials who were champions of the balanced budget. A large framed oil portrait of Herbert Hoover hung reverently in the lounge. Alexander Hamilton graced the library. Congressman Stuyvesant, a traitor to his class, once wrote the Board of Governors that his room was "haunted by the ghosts of William McKinley and Warren Harding" and asked that they be "properly exorcised so I can sleep without being awakened by their nagging."

The dinner was not too successful. Judge Herring finally had to tell the Vice President, "It grieves the President to hear that you have been talking against his program. He regards you as he would a son."

"Now look, Judge," Boxell said crossly, "you don't need to give me any prodigal-son lectures. My political future is ahead of me. I have to make my way. I didn't have a newspaper chain to turn me into 'a hero with a heart.' When the President goes off on an adventure and doesn't consult me, am I supposed to tell all my friends that he is divinely inspired? Not me. I will have to bear the consequences when the roof falls in."

He stared challengingly at the Judge, but suddenly changed to an aggressive smile. The Vice President arose to greet an older man, one of the wealthy contributors to the party.

"We have just been saying, sir," Boxell said, "how the good cause was kept alive during the lean years by your help."

The other bowed modestly, a look of pleasure on his face.

After dinner, the Judge and his guest went up to Herring's

bachelor apartment. It had the bare floors and severely useful furniture of a monk's cell. There they watched the President.

". . . With peace and good will abroad in the world, there is nothing we cannot do. When men no longer have to support on their backs the heavy burden of armaments, minds and machines can bring the good things of life to the most remote region. Grass can grow in the desert. The hungry can be fed. The poor clothed and housed decently. Education and recreation will be within the reach of every man . . ."

The Judge puffed a pipe contentedly. The Vice President sat forward and breathed heavily.

". . . The golden age stretches out its hand to us. We have but to take it . . ."

The Vice President said in admiration, "Damned if I know how he does it. Pie in the sky, and the people eat it up." He added angrily, "If I said that, half the columnists in town would say I was faking. He sounds like he means it."

Judge Herring said, "Did you ever consider he might mean it?"

Senator Frank Fremont ate his dinner from a tray at his desk. His office—the high-arched ceiling decorated with frescoes by Brumidi, the long sweep from his windows down the green mall to the Washington Monument, was in the old Capitol itself. He enjoyed living with the voices and presences of the past. His desk was covered with chores, letters to be answered, bills to be read, meetings to be called. His work, as he ruefully admitted, was never done. The Gridiron Club kindly made fun of him as, "The old woman who lives in a shoe; she had so many children she didn't know what to do." This was true. His interest in the other ninety-nine senators was tolerant, affectionate and paternal, yet with the stern and severe hand of the parent showing at times. He knew their faults and virtues. He scolded, persuaded and rewarded. Above all, Frank Fremont looked on the United States Senate as the absolute rock of democracy. Presidents could fail. The House could run wild, but the Senate was firm in its faith.

Fremont ate his bean soup and reflected on President Christiansen's trip to Geneva. It disturbed him. The Senate would have to ratify any treaties the President negotiated, and it would fall on Frank Fremont in the end to bring the Senate and Administration together. They were, he knew, miles apart. He had heard that day grumblings of discontent, and he knew there would have to be a great deal of shoring-up. Maze Bledsoe would require his pound of flesh. The reason for his opposition was probably that some big irrigation project was stuck in the Budget Bureau. And the President should call in some of the leading Catholic Congressmen, and explain to them he was not giving in to the Russians, and that really the tide of religion might begin to flow back again into the East. Senator Fremont hoped that some member of the Presidential delegation had sense enough to press this point on the President while he was talking with Radilov. And for senators afraid that disarmament would throw millions out of work, the President should be ready to announce a full public works program in the areas most affected. Big water-development schemes for California, for example.

Senator Fremont sat so long in thought, his steak was cold when he began eating it.

His middle-aged secretary, who was as plain as he was, came in to remind him the President would be on television in five minutes. Fremont wolfed down his apple pie and swallowed his coffee hastily. As a result he felt pains in his stomach all during the telecast.

Malcolm Christiansen's smile, radiant and comforting and confident, entered the room. Why was it that this man could effortlessly call on the good will everyone has stored away? Was it a careless mixture of genes? Or was there a god, a Zeus, with a fine ironic humor who arranged this?

". . . My fellow Americans, I have a special message for you. The safekeeping of the peace will depend, in good part, on you. The treaties we sign here will be returned to your representatives in Congress for ratification. Your voices, your wishes will prevail when the Senate votes on the treaties. I ask you to search your consciences, look at the sweet faces of your children, and decide whether we have been right in trying to bring peace to a troubled world. Then, write your senator and tell him your thoughts . . ."

Senator Fremont was shocked. This was blasphemy, driving that beast, the public, on the Senate! How the cloakrooms would fume and roar tomorrow. What perverseness it was to refuse to allow the Senate in its own wisdom and time and method to decide the future of the world, to harass it with the letters and post cards from home! Frank Fremont did not like this.

Yet, he asked himself, if I had been President and this was the one project I put all my heart upon, would I do the same? No, he decided, this was not the way he would handle it. He would go up to the Hill as a personal missionary, sitting in the big office of the majority leader, drinking a little booze, trading a few jokes, asking the advice of the senators and making them think this was their program. In the end, he would have his way and everyone, or almost everyone, would be happy.

These thoughts must be put away. Senator Fremont knew he had a job to do. He must soothe the wounded vanities of the Senate. He would have to smooth the way for the treaties. Within minutes, his telephone panel was lighted up. Frank Fremont dispensed soothing syrup in his dry and dusty voice. His callers were profane, partisan or plain plaintive. "Let's wait and see how this turns out," Fremont suggested. "Maybe Malcolm Christiansen has done the impossible. God knows, we all hope so."

It was ten o'clock when Senator Fremont had time to call the Under Secretary of State, a former senator.

"What reaction do you get, Tom?" Fremont asked.

"Well," the other replied, "the British are pleased. They can make a lot of savings in their military budget. The French are like a woman who is told her husband was seen having a drink with a strange blonde. The Germans, *mein Gott*, are exploding. They have been betrayed. They will not disarm. They will turn the weapons on themselves first. They will appeal to the United Nations, call on the Pope, and invoke the aid of Thor."

Shortly before midnight, Senator Fremont walked through the gray and lonely main hall of the Capitol, down the great stairs where the huge portrait of a famous naval battle hung, and out into the murmuring night. He was tired, but he doggedly walked the several blocks to his home on North Carolina Avenue. He was short of breath and had a pain in his chest when he arrived. He hoped it was not his heart. He did not have the time for any foolishness like that.

## *Chapter* TWENTY-FIVE

MALCOLM CHRISTIANSEN and Viktor Radilov had a farewell breakfast, just the two of them. They were like two summer lovers
parting, each returning to his familiar rut. The tides were rising,
the vacation money was almost gone, and even the excitement was
fading with the expectance of going home.

The President was vaguely uneasy. He had no specific complaint, only a dim, heavy sensation that ahead of him lay trouble,
a penalty for these days of dreaming so wildly.

Radilov noticed this and said, "What troubles you, my friend?"

"I don't know. It's just that I don't look forward to going back
and having to argue with Congress about this. Some won't like it,
and they'll make crazy statements and disturb people. I don't like
to have to contend with that sort of thing. But you don't have
anything like that to worry about."

"Oh yes I do," Radilov replied quickly. "The disarmament
program will liquidate the jobs of two hundred and fifty thousand officers, and they will complain and plot. Generals do not
like to be converted into farm managers. They enjoy wearing
their bright uniforms and having the women look at them and
thinking, Oh, what an attractive man! And it is nobler to order
soldiers about in heroic tasks than to deal with such subjects as
the disposal of cow dung. Yes, I will have my troubles. I will probably have to be firm and demote some rebels, provide assign-
ments for others in Mongolia, and even reserve a prison cell for
another."

His voice suddenly changed, and becamse harsh and ugly. "Then, my friend, your newspapers will say I am a cruel dictator, another Nero, and have initiated a new purge against innocent and suffering men. I do not understand your press and your congressmen. Nothing I do is right. Yet when I return to Moscow, my enemies will say I have been brain-washed by the magnetic American President, the magic Mr. Christiansen." With this last sentence his manner returned to one of formal gaiety. He smiled and the two laughed together.

The swift transition both disturbed and fascinated Mr. Christiansen. This harsh side would appear without warning and without explanation. The President had a disquieting feeling that this mask was more true than the disciplined enamel and even the exciting tales of this strange man.

President Christiansen wanted to know really what kind of a person he was dealing with. He wanted to know what he wanted of life and how much he would pay for it.

Radilov said, "You see, Mr. President, human nature remains the same whether it is under communism or capitalism. We need to create a great new program for our scientists, to discover the secret elixir of altruism, and then mix it with the breakfast food or strong drink of the populations of the world. I am afraid your Mark Twain was right when he said, 'Man was made at the end of the week's work when God was tired.' If there is to be any improvement, it must come from earthly laboratories."

While they were eating in the American villa, there was a shuddering crash outside and the sound of breaking glass.

"My God, what was that?" Radilov asked.

The President replied this was probably an accident on the street. Radilov stood up and looked out the window. The road was almost straight below about 200 feet. The Premier's face became so peculiarly intent that Mr. Christiansen stood up and looked, too.

A heavy car had rammed into a school bus, which had in turn veered off the road and turned over. The vehicles looked like injured bugs. The sedan was stopped crosswise of the road and a great steam rose from its hood. The right front wheel of the school bus was still slowly turning around.

Children, dazed, bleeding, crying, emerged from a rear door which had been flung open, and wandered without purpose.

Radilov called sharply to his bodyguard and spoke rapidly and urgently in Russian. The other saluted and left on the run. The front door soon closed after him.

The Premier explained in English, still watching the scene, not turning to address his host, "We have medicinal supplies in my limousine. I have sent it down to give help."

He had such an urgency in his voice that Mr. Christiansen said, "I wouldn't worry about this. The kids were scratched up some. But an ambulance will be here, and the police and the authorities will take care of things all right."

People descended on the scene as though they had been watching all the while from behind hedges for just this event. There was a siren and the Soviet limousine came swiftly and stopped. Three of the bodyguards leaped out and began examining the injured children. The two chiefs of state stood watching.

It was not until the police and ambulances arrived and the injured had been taken away that Radilov returned to his breakfast. He poured himself a fresh cup of coffee and his hand was trembling slightly.

This symptom aroused the President's curiosity. Why was it that a motor accident should so upset the emperor of the Communist world, which was itself built on bloodshed? So he asked, "What is the matter, Mr. Premier?"

"Forgive me, it is an old scar breaking open."

"Yes?"

"I come from a small village on the rim of the Sea of Azov. It is a pleasant country, and I have many pleasant dreams of it, swimming in the summer, sledding in the winter, taking long walks in the woods, paying court to a lovely young lady. I married her and we had two children before I was forced to leave the country. My wife and children returned to the village which, because of its distance from Moscow, was less concerned in the edicts of Comrade Stalin. The war swallowed the village. The invaders took it over. But I heard from the partisans that my wife and children lived. I asked to be transferred to the forces on that front, and when the enemy began his retreat back through Odessa and across the Carpathian Mountains in the winter storms, I was in the first party to reach Rostov and my village. What a terrible scene it was!"

He paused, for he was having trouble speaking. There was a moment as Radilov fought with himself, placing the rein on his emotions and slowly forcing them into line. Mr. Christiansen watched in fascination, and himself experienced a similar flood of emotion, the wild flight of terror and stunned disbelief at the sight, whatever it was, and the struggle to control it.

"The invaders had taken away every able-bodied man and woman who could slave for them. The rest? They were driven into the square of the village, children and old people, and machine-gunned. We saw the dead and the dying, my own among them." He gripped the sides of his chair with both hands until the knuckles were white. Then he threw his hands into the air in a sudden gesture. "Do you understand now why I cannot endure the sight of an injured child? Each time I see a nosebleed I think of the blood frozen on the faces of the children of the village."

The President shook his head sadly and said, "I don't know why people behave that way. I don't understand it."

"I will give you an answer. There is a beast in the soul of every man, and it is so easily aroused by hate. It lies in waiting to be called. Men have massacred men without shame for all the sorry history of humankind. Witness the destruction of the American Indians, the Jews of Poland, the Incas by the Spanish, the Russian children."

Later the President described this conversation to Silas King. The Secretary said matter-of-factly, "He probably made it up."

"Why, Silas?"

"They want to get you over on their side and they will tell you anything to do it. But when you want them to do something in return, they squirm, they feint, they object, and, damn it, you never pin them down."

The President had another visitor before he left for the airport. He was the Papal Secretary of State, Cardinal Ganganelli, a tall, austere, dignified individual in his stately robes. Mr. Christiansen was somewhat awed by him.

The Cardinal had come for a report on Mr. Christiansen's promise to intercede with Radilov on religious freedom.

Cardinal Ganganelli said in a voice that was rich and measured,

"The Holy Father is pleased that the two mightiest nations, in terms of arms, are meeting to find a true path to peace."

The President bowed his head in acknowledgment.

"But the Holy Father is concerned over the heavenly fate and earthly consolation of lost souls who are turned away from the Church by the preachments of atheism. He inquires of the results of your intercession with the Soviet Premier."

Mr. Christiansen answered, "Well, I did take this up with him, but he is pretty hard on religion. He claims it splits the loyalties and energies of his people at a time when they have to be given to the State in order to make rapid progress. Those are about his words. I wasn't able to shake him much on that. But I was able to get a clue, you might say, as to why, besides this, he is so touchy about religion. It's this—the Russians are awfully sensitive to criticism. Their hackles rise, Your Eminence, when you suggest they aren't like other men, but are beasts and that sort of thing. I think that in time they would get over this feeling of theirs about religion, if the churches would stop calling them names."

The Cardinal said gravely, "Of course, the Holy Father has considered this course, too. But you may realize, Mr. President, that the Communists are continually agitating against religion. If we fail to observe this and comment upon it, more souls will be lost. Religion, like anything else that is good, is acquired and maintained only by labor and faith and discipline. The Communists offer temptation in material comforts in life. The Church in its ministerings can provide only spiritual comfort from the bruises of life and a heavenly reward to the faithful. Now if we should remain silent and forbear to describe the damnation that comes from following the voices of communism, the tide of faith would, I am afraid, ebb. This is our dilemma.

"The Church has existed under many forms of government. It does not demand of its children that they prefer a republic or an oligarchy, that they choose capitalism or socialism. What we ask is very little—that we have the right to minister to the souls of the people. And thus we do not complain of the economic system or the political theories of Premier Radilov. It is wholly his atheism."

The President sighed. He said, "I have done all I can. I don't know what else to do."

At the airport, the Presidential party was accosted by a strange figure, running rapidly across the cement, his coattails flying, a dispatch case in one hand. It was Dr. Dietrich, the German Ambassador to the United States.

"I am glad I have reached you," he told the President and Secretary King. "I have just flown in. My Chancellor is much concerned by reports of the correspondents and asked me to communicate with you."

The wind had turned cold and tugged hard. Mr. Christiansen had to hold his hat on his head. He wanted to get inside the plane. He asked the Ambassador curtly, "Well, what is it you want?"

"The Chancellor requests assurances that he may place before the Parliament tomorrow."

"What kind of assurances?"

"Assurances, dear Mr. President, that the agreement concluded between the United States and Soviet Russia will not permit the Soviets to consume the German Republic, and that the United States will never agree to stripping the German Republic of its means of defending itself from the aggressor."

Mr. Christiansen said, "Silas, you talk to him. Come on, Mickie."

The Secretary said, "Dr. Dietrich, I don't have time to go into this fully. I can only tell you the United States will protect the territorial integrity of the German Republic. Other than that, you must await details of the treaty when it is presented to the Congress."

He left the Ambassador standing helplessly, his mouth open to ask a new question.

The plane ran into a head wind and arrived back in Virginia late and in a heavy rain. The welcoming crowd had dwindled to a few hundred who huddled under the eaves of the airport and waved a few sorry banners. The President drove immediately to the White House without waiting to make a statement or acknowledge the bedraggled applauders.

On Thursday morning a week later, Mickie looked out the window of his office in the West Wing of the White House. There would be a press conference in about an hour. He could imagine one of the boys leaving the AP office on Connecticut Avenue and walking leisurely down to Pennsylvania Avenue in the spring sunshine. What a sensuous stroll it would be!

The spring wind would blow rapturously, pressing their skirts against the thighs of the pretty ladies. (Nothing was quite so full of ravishing promise as a dress blown tight against a female curve by a spring wind.) And the reporter, after observing these facts joyfully, would stop and look at the covers in a bookstore, and wonder when he would get to work on his own book. The pangs of ambition would stir within him. But not for long. A record shop would call him with its music. He would slow down enough to listen, and walk ahead whistling cheerfully.

All the little stores would invite his attention, bright jewelry, travel agencies with exciting posters, a grocery with foreign delicacies, a café with a thick steak on display along with a bottle of wine, summer dresses on the frozen figures of mannequins, and even a building excavation to watch. He would cross the street and go into the little park at Farragut Square. Surely stenographers would be sitting on the benches in the sun and exchanging confidences, a humorless young mother from an apartment pushing a baby carriage and looking with envy at the free girls, a picturesque old man in a beret feeding pigeons, a young policeman twirling his stick—in short The Spring.

But Moonan thought with melancholy, not for me. I have to help keep the United States Government from running off its trolley. What a dull chore this becomes in the spring!

The President was not in the best of moods. An old friend from his Annapolis days had called him and argued over disarmament. He was connected with a shipyard, and he asked Mr. Christiansen, "What do you want to do, bankrupt the country and throw millions out of work?"

And at breakfast, the President had outlined the details of his treaty to congressional leaders. There were some grim faces seen leaving the White House. Now, the press conference. Mickie made a decision; he would go to the weekly card game at the Chicago *Tribune* fellow's apartment tonight and get damn good and tight.

In an hour's time. Moonan walked across the lane with Mr. Christiansen and tried to cheer him with a little joke he had saved. The President did not laugh very hard. When they arrived at the fifth floor of the old building, a Secret Service man there said, "A big crowd. Had to turn them away today."

They walked through the anteroom. The President unconsciously put on the somewhat stern face of authority he wore when dealing with important subjects. The reporters obediently arose with an awkward movement and the sound of moving chairs. Mr. Christiansen nodded to them. They sank down again to their seats. Mickie sat behind him and searched the faces. There wasn't a one in the crowd who had any honest-to-God affection for Malcolm Christiansen. Let them write freely, no editors running their pencil through the copy, no advertisers raising hell at critical remarks, and they would all say he was a nitwit propped up by his press secretary and Secretary of State.

Mr. Christiansen said forcefully, "What I want to say is this— I am submitting the details of my agreement with Premier Radilov to the Senate this noon. Now—it is divided into several parts. First of all, there is a non-aggression pact; that is, we agree not to attack them and they agree not to attack us. This is the kind of thing we have with all our allies except that we agree to go to the defense of these allies if they are attacked. We felt, both Mr. Radilov and I, that we ought to have some experience getting along with each other, for this will be novel enough, before we talk about mutual defense. And, after all, who is going to attack either of us? Next, there is disarmament. This will be a belt across central Europe that will have nothing but small, police-power armies, no nuclear weapons, no bombers, no missiles, no tanks— that sort of thing. This area covers Germany, Poland, Czechoslovakia, Hungary, Rumania and Bulgaria. We want to invite Austria into this, too, and anyone else who wants to join. Also we agree to reduce our own armed forces stage by stage. You'll see that all in the treaty. Third, we take up economic competition and set aside certain prime market and prime raw material areas which I think Secretary of State King can explain in more detail if you ask him. What we have done, I think, is to get us started solidly on the road to peace. I don't say we've got there yet. But we've started. It's up to Congress next to show its spirit of cooperation and prove we are peace-loving like we say we are. That's about it."

Mickie noted the President was nervous. His hands behind his back rapidly clasped and unclasped. The fingers searched anxiously for one another. The thumb of his left hand continually brushed his Naval Academy class ring as if it were a lucky symbol.

Some twenty reporters had jumped to their feet in the crowded room. Mr. Christiansen nodded to one of them.

The voice said, "Mr. President, your treaty, I gather, assumes that we can trust the Soviets?"

The President pondered a moment. He scratched an eyebrow. He replied, "I'm glad to be asked that because it gives me a chance to answer specifically and let you know exactly where I stand on this. I agree it is very controversial. Now I have friends who feel very strongly you can never trust a Communist, and they give some compelling arguments about practices of deceit and treachery and so forth. Now, on the other hand, there are those who are just as vehement and just as forceful who say you can trust the Soviets if you are always careful to base your trust on mutual self-interest. So, what can be more to the mutual self-interest than saving yourself from being blow up? And I must say that in my personal dealings with Premier Radilov he seemed an honorable man who was really quite sensitive about the newspaper talk and the political speeches that you could not trust him, as if he was some strange kind of beast, you know."

The President halted to show he had finished his reply and looked about the room with his blue eyes until he spotted his next questioner.

"Mr. President, have you set any time limit on when the Senate should finish its action on the treaty?"

"Well, I think we have got to look at this thing realistically, and we have got to study this thoroughly and take our time. But the circumstances are such that we have got to do this thing expeditiously, too. There is no question about that."

He recognized another reporter.

"Mr. President, do you have any assurance that the Germans will accept disarmament?"

"Well, I don't see why not. Of course, I haven't gone into any long discussion of this with any of their people, although I had a few words with their Ambassador in Geneva. But look here. If you were a country with limited funds, wouldn't you like to be able to disarm and cut expenses that way by billions? Especially when we still guarantee their territorial integrity. What more would you want? The Germans can go ahead and develop composers and authors and people like Dr. Freud and all those

German philosophers you have to study in college. I remember what a trouble I had in getting them straight. Whew!" Mr. Christiansen grinned boyishly. The room burst into delighted laughter. Mickie smiled and relaxed. God damn, you couldn't beat him!

"Mr. President, many people ask this question and maybe you can clear it up—why is it that you, a military man, are such an advocate of peace?"

Mr. Christiansen smiled benevolently and then became most serious. "Well," he said, "there are lots of things. My father was a pacifist, you know, and when you get that kind of thinking early it sticks with you. And then a soldier has lots of experiences that make him realize how wasteful war is. Let me tell you of one.

"In this last war or skirmish, whatever you want to call it, in the Philippines, I had a young reserve officer on my staff. A brilliant fellow. When he got through his duty, he wanted to go back to school and be a research chemist. Not perfumes and that sort of thing. He wanted to go into the laboratory and find out what caused cancer and arthritis and ease human suffering.

"One day he went out on a patrol, and we found his body. A bullet through his brain. Life was gone. All our wishing couldn't bring him back. Here he was dead, and all that brilliant promise was snuffed out. Here was a fellow who with all that devotion just might have discovered a cure for cancer. But he was taken away. How can you believe that war does any good when you see things like that happen?"

The President's hands were relaxed. His voice no longer jerked as he talked. The reporters were sitting quietly intent. Moonan could feel the atmosphere change as the lifting of low pressure by a shift in winds. Everyone there, even the stony-faced Secret Service agents staring narrowly into the crowd, was in a dream world of peace where brilliant young men solved the problem of cancer.

# Chapter TWENTY-SIX

"THE STATE Department can think what it wants. Our duty is to assume that the Russians will make every effort, including deception, to avoid carrying out their part of the disarmament agreement. Thus they will be able to seize Germany. I am not saying this will happen; only that we must be prepared for the worst possible situation."

This was said calmly and matter-of-factly. The speaker was Jefferson Lawrence. He sat in his library, drink in hand, the perfect gentleman and host, addressing three guests. They were General Gordon, the intelligence officer for the Joint Chiefs of Staff; General Pookey, the Army's Chief Chemical Officer, and Colonel Brady, a young officer marked for his excellence in operations.

The Secretary said unemotionally—he might have been addressing the court on a question of corporate law, "Our objectives, in military terms, must be to prevent Germany from falling into hostile hands. General Gordon, how do you think an attack would occur?"

The General shifted so that he was sitting on his right haunch. He replied, "I would say, Mr. Secretary, it would come very suddenly, a surprise. There would be some excuse for massing troops along the border, and then a surprise break-through at several points."

Lawrence said, "I thought as much. So what we need is a weapon to stop and cripple the first assault wave. I think I have discovered such a device. I have read the disarmament treaty very carefully. It restricts Germany to small arms and rifles, but does not specify the ammunition. General Pookey, do you have large quantities of nerve-gas cartridges?"

"Yes, sir."

"Please describe the effect."

General Pookey, a big, ponderous man, cleared his throat, and said, "The psychochemicals would make any enemy force tractable for twelve to twenty-four hours. They would lose all will to fight. Or the biological agents will sicken the enemy and put them out of action for a longer period. Very humane." He spoke with the hearty enthusiasm of a feed salesman describing his product.

"I was not aware that humanity had any legitimate function in the science of war," the Secretary remarked with a slight smile.

General Pookey said after a short laugh, "Well, it doesn't really, but this is a very good selling point when you're up before Congress asking for money. We've got a bad name in chemical warfare—a lot of folks remember the boys gassed in World War I —so we have to dress our chemicals up in a humane package."

"Suppose you tell us how the psychochemicals work," Lawrence said.

"This stuff, sir, hits the nerves and senses and discombobulates them. Your hearing would go dead. You couldn't see clearly. Your physical balance would be gone. Your will to fight or make love or the other strong urges would be shot. Just not there. You'd be like a baby. These are the lysergic acid series we think very highly of. We have tried them out on volunteers. This is what we do. We put a big guy in a ring with a little one, and we say go to it, fellows, and a real prize for the winner. So the big fellow chases the little one around the ring. Very comical. Then we give this big fellow just a tiny amount of lysergic acid, no more than on the head of a pin. It takes about ten minutes to work. The big guy then runs away from the little squirt. He's scared silly of him."

Colonel Brady asked quickly, "What about your nerve gases, General?"

Pookey said, "Think, gentlemen, in terms of an electric current which runs an IBM computer. There is in the human system something like that. It is cholinesterase, and it acts as the transmitter of a nerve impulse from one nerve joint to another. The nerve gas stops the production of this cholinesterase, so you do not have any nerve transmission. It's like blowing a fuse on an IBM. If this happens around your heart, your heart constricts and stops. It knocks out the nerve system and paralyzes it, you see. And the beauty of all these agents is, you can't see or smell or taste any of them."

General Gordon asked, "How do you dispense these agents?"

"Many ways. Cartridges fired from an ordinary rifle. From the exhaust fumes of a truck or a station wagon. There is no way to detect in advance the dispensing instruments."

The Secretary finished his drink and said with an air of objective admiration, as if he were discussing a piece of art, "How strange it is that the history of mankind is a progress in new ways to die! We alone of God's creatures have this inventiveness. Think of this art. From the crude methods of the cave man, simply slaughtering his rival with a club or blow, to the intricate tortures of the Turks, to the mechanical inventiveness of modern civilization. Now, we have reached the omega stage where one man can blow up the entire world.

"Is there a perfect way to die? If so, let us invent it quickly. Or if one had the choice, which would he prefer—the way of the ancients, left alone on the cliff to fall from hunger or cold into a sleep from which you would not waken, or by an absence of the nerve fluid, twitching like a chicken with its head cut off?"

"My uncle always used to say," General Pookey replied, "that the only way to die was of a heart attack in a high-class whorehouse in San Francisco."

The officers enjoyed this remark with laughter.

The Secretary quietly and precisely gave instructions. Picked units of the German Army should be armed with chemical cartridges in secret. Colonel Brady would be placed in charge of Operation Citadel.

"It is imperative for the success of the mission that the utmost secrecy be maintained. If, at any time, this operation becomes known, I will accept the complete responsibility."

They had a final round of drinks, and then the Secretary showed them to the door through the dim entry hall. The scene reminded him of one from *Macbeth*, the stealthy plotters escaping to their dreaded tasks after a tryst.

Lawrence returned and sat alone in the library in the semi-dark. Only a reading lamp was on.

What have I done? he asked himself. Can one man change the irrefutable course of fate? Or was he the victim of a sickness, a little more serious, than that visiting his country? He remembered the lines of Euripides:

> For who knows if the thing we call death
> Is life, and our life dying—who can know?
> Save only that all we beneath the sun
> Are sick and suffering, and those gone before
> Not sick, not touched with evil.

Or was he, instead, a modern John Brown? That great bearded madman who tried, in vain, was it, to speed the slow wheels of change. Lawrence arose and hunted among the volumes until he found Stephen Vincent Benét's poem and prayer of John Brown:

> "I hear the rolling of ͟ᴸᵉ wheels,
> The chariots of war!
> I hear the breaking of the seals
> And the opening of the door . . .
> Oh, fairer than the bugle call
> Its walls of jasper shine!
> And Joshua's sword is on the wall
> With space beside for mine."

Yes, Lawrence conceded, he had a little of the madness of John Brown in him. In all these careful, conservative years of his life, he had noticed this, kept it to one side, soothed it by saying, You will have your hour later. The hour had come. That was all.

The Secretary admitted he would like to think of himself, too, as a Pericles crying to his faltering nation: "Do not think you are fighting for the simple issue of letting this or that state become free or remain subject to you. You have an empire to lose. You must realize that Athens has a mighty name in the world because she has never yielded to misfortunes and has today the greatest power that exists. To be hated has always been the lot of those who have aspired to rule over others. In the face of that hatred, you cannot give up your powers even if some sluggards and cowards are all for being noble at this crisis. Your empire is tyranny by now, perhaps, as many think, wrongfully acquired, but certainly dangerous to let go."

He wondered what Malcolm Christiansen would think of these bold words. The Secretary could almost see the very alive face faded by the impact of the words, protesting that was all right for poets, but they never had "nuclear destruction" to contend with. And Silas King would be scornful and say, "Why in the hell do you want to waste your time with books, Jeff? You have to live in the present, and the straight fact of life is we have to cut down our military expenditures, balance the budget, and give the suffering taxpayers some relief." And President Christiansen believed this, too, because it was convenient and fitted in with his own mystic faith in peace.

As for himself, Lawrence thought ruefully, he was another Miniver Cheevy, born too late. He would have made a good seneschal serving a great medieval lord, keeping his swords and shields burnished bright, giving him provisions for his Crusades and amours, living through him the romance that would never fall to a short, mild-appearing, troubled man.

In this mood of self-examination, the Secretary asked himself where, oh where would his little scheme end. He had to admit there is a certain point, an infinity, where the mind cannot reasonably reach. He hoped that with the use of the nerve-gas cartridges the Germans would be able to maintain a wall against the East until such era when time itself eroded the wall. Because time was like the rivers of antiquity cutting the deep ravines into valleys and wearing away the mountains. But who could tell what some crazy, sudden human impulse would do? The Germans might choose to use the nerve gas first. That was a risk.

That same evening, President Christiansen was host at a stag dinner. The guests, carefully chosen by Silas King for their leadership in the corporate world, gathered in the library. They stood on the rich red rug with the great seal woven in the center while the President went among them shaking hands.

Mr. Christiansen was in a good humor. He delighted one group with a story, saying, "Viktor Radilov, you know, is quite a human fellow, and he told me about an American, an Englishman and a Russian being captured by cannibals. They were given a last request before being put in the pot to stew, so the Englishman sang, 'God Save the King,' and the American asked for and got a tranquilizing pill. But the Russian just said, 'Hit me on the head.'

When this was done, the Russian stumbled to his feet, pulled out a gun and shot the cannibals. 'For God sake,' asked the American, 'if you had that gun all the time, why didn't you shoot them an hour ago?' 'What,' the Russian replied, 'and be branded the aggressor!' "

The guests roared happily with laughter. Yes, indeed, who would have thought that this Russian bird had such a sense of humor.

They filed into the state dining room with its silver chandelier, light green walls, gold draperies, marble mantel, and the brooding portrait of Lincoln on the wall. The President linked his arm in friendly fashion with the chairman of the steel company.

Much flattered, the chairman thought he must do something for this warm-hearted, charming man. During the dinner they talked of deep-sea-fishing and surf-casting. When the coffee was served, Silas King rapped with his spoon on a goblet and announced, "The President has a few words he wants to express to us."

There Mr. Christiansen was, his face handsome, earnest and sincere, in the light of the tall candles. He said, "Gentlemen, frankly I need your help. Silas and I have been in Geneva, and we have negotiated a deal that will lift the heavy burden of armaments off our necks and the threat of war off our spirits. But there are a lot of folks who will object and say we shouldn't have done this and give all sorts of peculiar reasons that will disturb the people in Congress. All of you have friends in Congress, and I'd like your help in making them see the light when that treaty comes to a vote."

The other guests looked to the steel chairman for a reply. He said, "Mr. President, there is a question that I am sure comes to the minds of all of us. Where will we sell the steel, if not to the manufacturers of armaments? This is perhaps not a question that ought to be asked when the fate of the world hangs in the balance, but nonetheless it will be asked not only by myself. The unions will ask it, too."

Mr. Christiansen replied, "Well—I have faith that the great free-enterprise system will solve that easily enough. With the freedom and encouragement given capital by us, this should be easy. Don't you think so?"

The chairman pursed his lips thoughtfully.

Secretary King called out, "Let me answer your question, George. One part of our agreement with Radilov is that he will leave Latin America alone. We are going into a giant development program for that area. Public guarantees for private investment. Loans. They are going to use an awful lot of steel and trucks and construction machinery for this program. It will make up for any deficiency in steel purchases for military purposes. So far as I can see, the only companies that will be hurt will be those dealing exclusively in armaments. Du Pont was smart enough to get out of that years ago, and into plastics. And, on top of this, you'll get a good tax cut. It is in your interest to be on our side."

A dignified life insurance president down the table said, "Hear, hear!"

Across from him, a tall oil man spoke up, "I'm like the colored fellow who got a new job as a handyman, and the preacher noticed he was sporting a new tie and he asked him where he was working. The boy told him 113 Pierce Street in Dallas, and the preacher he said real shocked like, 'Well, John, this is very bad. Why that is a house of prostitution.' John told him, 'I don't ask where the money comes from just so as I get paid regular.' I'd just as soon sell my gas and oil to tractors in Brazil as bombers in Omaha. In fact, it's a damn sight more steady and doesn't depend on Congressional appropriations. Mr. President, the Russians and Chinese couldn't use a couple of million barrels of oil apiece, could they?"

The auto manufacturer said jovially, "I'm surprised at you, Ned. I'd have thought you already had scouted that deal and had the order in your vest pocket."

"Who says I haven't?"

A burst of general laughter.

The university chancellor commented, "Mr. President, we have no gasoline to sell and no steel to market. But we have been receiving research contracts from the Government for military projects amounting to forty million dollars a year. The loss of these grants would seriously undermine the morale of the university and, I am sure, retard basic research necessary for progress."

The oil man said, "Thank God, Doctor, the college boy can get back to studying the essentials, the female form and how much beer he can handle."

President Christiansen stated, "We haven't heard from you, Reverend."

A deep, resonant voice proclaimed, "Mr. President, I am a peddler of sorts, too. With every peddler, a favorite device is to tell the prospective customer not only of the benefits of his product, but of all the evils associated with his rival's furniture polish. With peace and coexistence, you have weakened my argument. Therefore, I think it is only fair to ask you to arrange for me to hold a mass evangelist meeting in the Moscow Coliseum."

"That," replied the President, "I will arrange for the seventh Sunday in June."

More good-natured laughter.

The oil man remarked, "Reverend, if you had a crack at those heathens, you'd have work for all the parsons you send now to the back-country churches down South. I'd buy some Baptist stock myself."

The dinner ended with the steel man promising that the guests would use whatever slight influence they had to speed the course of the treaty.

When the men were leaving, the steel man managed to get Secretary King aside. He said to him, "I hear, Silas, that your company has managed to get control of the mine in Bolivia. We were working on that, too. Let me know sometime how you did it."

The Secretary merely smiled and said, "What big ears you have, George."

# Chapter TWENTY-SEVEN

THE CHAIRMAN of the Foreign Relations Committee looked like a bird of prey. His face was very wrinkled, his eyes were sharp and predatory, and his nose might have been an eagle's beak. He alternately nodded sleepily and spoke in an angry Southern drawl as if he were mortally offended.

For some minutes he had been sitting apparently asleep as the Committee gathered to hear Secretary of State King explain the treaty with the Soviet Union. The Secretary had not arrived, nor had most of the members.

But suddenly the Chairman's head came almost violently erect and he stared sharply through lidded eyes at a shape winnowing its way down the chamber. It was Rita, Senator Bledsoe's assistant.

The young Senator from Colorado saw her too and remarked in awe to the white-haired Senator from New York, "I don't believe she's alive! I think old Maze had a sculptor consult volumes on erotica and fashion this creature, and gave IBM the job of animating her."

"If you're a good boy and vote for Maze's bill, he'll let you take her home and find out."

"Not me," said Colorado with a shudder. "You know what happens when the straw gets too close to the flame. And I don't aim to get consumed this early in my career."

His companion said indulgently, "You'll learn to take the accidental blessings of fate more tolerantly as you grow older."

Rita swayed up to the Chairman who was watching her closely.

"Who do you want, gal?" he inquired as he let his hand carelessly graze against her buttocks. She said that Senator Bledsoe wished to speak to him privately in the committee office.

The Chairman followed Rita, hardly taking his eyes off the movement of her hips. He reluctantly greeted Senator Bledsoe, who said, "I didn't want to invade your sacred precincts, Carl. I just wanted to ask if you wouldn't invite some of our boys from Armed Services to sit in when you question Silas King. We've got a little community of interest with you."

The Chairman said crossly he guessed that would be all right, but for God's sake, tell J.K. from South Carolina not to smoke those "stinkin' ceegars."

Then in a burst of animation he said, "Maze, in what slave market did you pick up that gal? I'd like to get one myself. For my grandson, of course."

Bledsoe grinned and said, "Troy. Did you ever hear of it?"

The Chairman shook his head and replied, "That's the way the wars get started, Maze. And we're all for peace these days."

"One more thing," the Senator from Arizona asked. "Do you suppose you might invite the Vice President to be present?"

"No suh," the Chairman said positively. "I don't want that hoodlum in my committee. If he hasn't anything to do, let him go out and rob a bank."

Bledsoe shrugged his shoulders.

Fifteen minutes later, Secretary King, with his retinue of assistant secretaries all a little anxious and trembling inwardly in anticipation of the great ordeal, arrived at the hearing room. They were hailed outside by a crowd of reporters and photographers. They closed in around the Secretary and began asking questions. He blandly waved them aside, and went in. This was to be a closed hearing.

Members of the Committee were seated behind the great curved walnut desk. It covered the entire end of the chamber and was raised so that the witness sat below as in a pit.

There along the bench was John Mahon, handsome and slightly graying, from Massachusetts . . . Richard Lemar of Alabama, lean, tight-lipped and red-faced with a voice, when aroused, that swelled like a bullfrog's . . . Charley Dolliver of Kansas, small, squarely built, a rugged face, unruly white hair and blue eyes . . .

Pasquale Caruso of Michigan, nervous, restless black eyes that darted like insects hovering over the water. Senator Fremont came in late and opened his huge brief case to draw out a note pad.

Silas King looked up at the Senators and said in the hearty voice of a luncheon club speaker, "Gentlemen, no accused ever had a more distinguished jury to plead his case to."

The Chairman ignored him. He pounded the gavel and said crossly, "We are here to study a treaty with our late enemy, Russia, which has been negotiated in Geneva. I think we should make a thorough study of this no matter what the outcry, rather than speed through in high gear against the red lights. It's become so peace is a sacred word, and when it is mentioned everyone salaams and tries to outshout the other fellow in his faithfulness. You can't talk about the subject sensibly without getting truck-loads of hysterical mail dumped on your desk."

The Chairman paused to glare over his spectacles at the Secretary of State. King beamed back at him.

The Chairman grumbled, "They've made peace a saturnalia with all their appeals to the emotions. Mr. Secretary, we will wish to propound certain questions to you, and you had better be ready with the answers."

The Secretary nodded agreeably.

"The stenographer will take no notes. This is all off the record. Otherwise, certain senators would be making speeches to insert in their news-letters, and nothing would be accomplished. Mr. King, you will save us and yourself a lot of time if you will simply tell us what is in this treaty for us."

The Secretary answered, "That is a very practical approach, Mr. Chairman. First of all the danger of being wiped out, all our assets, by Soviet missiles has been reduced to a negligible factor. We have taken out an insurance policy against the biggest danger that threatened us. Let me put it another way. If you were running a major airline, it would be worth a great deal to you to get an insurance policy that would protect you against all crashes. Second, by reducing the danger of surprise attack, we will be able to save twenty-five billion dollars a year in defense spending. This releases a tremendous amount of productive energy into activities that will bring us more dollars. The treaty also provides for an economic exchange with the Communist world, and thus opens up new markets for durable goods. Further, there is an understanding that Russia will not intervene economically or politically in the Americas while we recognize its supremacy in areas now under its control."

"In other words," Senator Dolliver asked, leaning forward with a smile that was not amused, but set, "you have agreed to divide up the world."

"We have established areas of primary influence," King corrected him.

Senator Mahon said anxiously, "Mr. Secretary, I am not in the least impugning your integrity, but what worries many of us is— how can you be sure we can trust the Russians? Their record is not too good, you know. Isn't there some token of reliability, some bond they can put up. It would be very impressive if they would agree to allow the Church to function unhampered in the eastern European area."

Secretary King replied, "I did suggest this to Premier Radilov, and I will tell you of his answer. He said if we would guarantee the Communists would be allowed to operate freely in South America, he would do the same for the Church in the satellites."

The Chairman laughed in a dry cackle and said, "That will take care of you papists."

Mahon said good-humoredly, "I knew I wasn't going to get any sympathy from a Southern Baptist."

Bledsoe spoke up, "The Chairman still keeps his Ku Klux Klan robe in the closet, Jack."

The Chairman looked at him with the humorless and crabbed affection some old couples have for one another and remarked slyly, "I am sure what the Senator from Arizona keeps in his closet is much more interesting."

There was laughter along the bench.

Silas King sat quite unperturbed. He knew that for all their truculence and defiance now, most of these men would vote "Aye" when their names were called by the clerk of the Senate. Oh, they would have to make obeisance to their pet shrines. There would have to be breast-beating and florid oratory on the Senate floor. This was the accustomed show which, so far as Silas King was concerned, was a damned waste of time.

The Secretary could look up on the bench and spot this man

and that who, for all his show of independence, was a slave of public opinion. Malcolm Christiansen could shape opinion with the careless and indifferent ease of a potter molding his clay. There was something for everyone in this program.

Mahon and Caruso would have to have long talks with their cardinals, but perhaps their path could be made easier if the word was passed along that the Administration was not opposed to federal funds for parochial school services. Maze Bledsoe could be brought around by the Budget Bureau temporarily holding up the Gila River irrigation and water storage project. The Chairman's son received a $30,000 fee for legal services from International Exporters, Inc., which depended on the good will of the State Department for a smooth operation.

Silas King believed that every man had a string hanging from him, if you could but find it.

The Chairman asked him, "Now, about all this trade with us the Russians are going to do. Who is going to pay for it?"

Secretary King replied, "It will come out of their treasury."

"Isn't there some loan or gift from us involved somewhere?" the Chairman asked suspiciously. "I've been sitting on this committee a long time, and I pick up my ears whenever you fellows from downtown start talking about all the trade we're going to get. It usually happens that a foreign country comes here with foreign money worth four bits, fifty cents, and the State Department has a scheme to make it worth six bits, and it comes out of our pockets."

Well, the Secretary admitted, there was a loan involved, an extension of credits. He added, "I believe respect and understanding will flow from gratitude."

"Oh yes," the Chairman replied, "that reminds me of a trial back home where a fellow was on trial for raping an old maid. There was no question of his guilt. The act had been witnessed by the old maid's sister who hid in the closet. Well, do you know what that fellow's defense was? He claimed he ought to go free, because he had given the old lady the pleasure of fornication, which otherwise would have been denied her, and had provided her sister with an educational experience. I think this is about the way with us and the Russians."

The chamber roared with men's laughter.

The doors were thrown open shortly after the noon bells rang, and the news crowd rushed in in one great gush. The Secretary's picture was taken shaking hands with the Chairman who said, "Mr. King has made a most orderly presentation and impressed the members of our Committee with his effectiveness as a bargainer. I foresee no problem in reporting out the treaty favorably."

The open hearings took one week, with the Chairman shooing the witnesses through like an impatient mother hen. The Committee voted 15 to 2 to approve the treaty. Senator Mahon wrote a separate concurring opinion, which said, "The Christian evangelism of the President has broken open a spillway through which religion may one day return to eastern Europe. There is no possibility at all, looking at the realities of military facts, in which the great wall of irreligion erected by the Communists can be thrown down by force. But there is indeed a very great hope that under a relaxed attitude and through the mission of men like President Christiansen that the belief in God, so natural to all men, may flow back into these lands and illumine the lives of millions . . ."

The debate began in the Senate in an atmosphere almost of indifference. Only three senators were on the floor when old Ed Stringer stood up and said in his powerful, hoarse voice, "Mr. President . . ." This was Ed's last term, even he admitted that, and he wanted to breathe one last blast of sulphur in this forum. He was a devil's advocate and a sincere one. He believed that what other men professed in great numbers must be false. Therefore he must arise and shout in such a voice that the timbers of the temple would tremble at his opposition.

Senator Stringer began with a crafty diversion, a soft, mellow mood of tolerance, as he said, "There may be some reason to believe that a ray of hope for world peace is beginning to appear in a weary world."

While a row of ladies in the gallery smiled down on this benevolent old gentleman, he said, "This is a welcome sign, surely, no matter how faint . . ." Then his voice roared so that a party of tourists coming down the main hall heard it, "But it could become our deadliest enemy. Because of our overwhelming hope for peace, we could succumb to the fatal disease of complacency . . ."

The ladies in the gallery looked at one another in dismay. Who was this crazy old fool?

Happily, in good voice, old Ed roared on, "We must vaccinate ourselves against this deadly disease, no matter if the Kremlin does approach us with a velvet glove over its mailed fist; regardless of the messages of good will that are aimed at us by the master mechanics of the Communist conspiracy . . ."

When Senator Stringer had spoken for an hour, the Chairman came and sat at his small mahogany desk, and exhibited to all a look of boredom and contempt.

However, he arose after several minutes and stated, "The Senator from Montana (the Chairman refused to say "the distinguished Senator") has made three distinct errors of fact in his presentation while I have been on the floor."

Old Ed burst out in his hoarse boom, "If, as the distinguished Chairman has alleged, I have made three errors of fact, I will admit it. I will confess my sins in public."

The Chairman said dryly, "That, sir, would take too much of the Senate's time. We must approve the treaty this year."

Stringer roared back, "I do not understand the Chairman's great haste to pass this treaty. Two weeks ago he was speaking in the most critical tones about it. I am reminded of a man who ran for office up in my state on the platform that he was a Lutheran and a lawyer. His opponent said, 'Yes, when you are with the lawyers, they talk about you being a Lutheran, and when you are with the Lutherans, they talk about you being a lawyer."

"That," said the Chairman crustily, "is better than being known as a jackass all the time."

Grumbling like an old dog, the Chairman left the floor. He pushed through the swinging doors to the cloakroom where he saw Senator Fremont reading over a memorandum. The brawling voice of old Ed followed him even into this sanctuary, "And, Mr. President, anyone who dares be against this treaty is pilloried in the press; he is deluged with mail from fools, and he gets telephone calls from businessmen wanting to know if he is against a tax cut . . ."

The Chairman complained, "That peckerwood has a voice like a moose in labor."

Senator Fremont looked up and smiled. "What is the difference between a peckerwood and a woodpecker, Joel?" he asked.

"They're both birds, but a woodpecker minds his own business."

Fremont put the memorandum back in his brief case, and said, "What is your time schedule?"

"Oh, we'll get it out of here on Friday. Will that satisfy the Crusader?"

"Oh, I am sure it will. But you know, Joel, I don't like this debate at all."

"What's the matter, Frank?" the Chairman asked in what was meant to be a tone of affectionate concern.

Fremont tugged at his ear and then said, "Joel, this treaty represents the greatest alteration of world power since the creation of the American Republic. Yet none of the speakers so far have done any more than repeat old phrases we have been using for ten years. Such a great event should bring forth the most creative thought in the Senate. We should sharpen our minds, and present to the Executive Branch new thinking for its guidance. This is the great role of the Senate. But we have failed, and I wonder in my gloomy moments if this does not spell the end of our democratic period."

"Hell's bells, Frank, a senator doesn't have any time to think any more. He's too busy arranging veterans' pensions and tax concessions and government contracts. The only fellows who have the time are the freshmen, and no one listens to them."

Senator Fremont wiped his spectacles with the handkerchief from his breast pocket. He replied, "It isn't right, Joel. It isn't right. We are not fulfilling our role."

Their conversation was interrupted by a series of bells ringing on the news teletype.

"That infernal machine," the Chairman said, "they ought to take it out of here. It sounds like a jay bird."

Senator Fremont walked over to the news ticker and read the bulletin:

LONDON: A revolution has broken out in Czechoslovakia. Rebel troops and militia have seized Government buildings and the broadcasting transmitter in the capital city. General Ludvik Drtina, commandant of the Prague military district, gave the orders for the coup at midnight, just eight hours before the Czech National Army was due to be disarmed under the new U.S.-Soviet agreement. The provisional president is Dr. Jaroslav Duris, a former Communist minister who has been under house arrest. The revolt was revealed when the BBC picked up a broadcast from Radio Prague appealing to the United States for assistance in its hour of liberation . . .

The Chairman noticed the intense interest of Senator Fremont and stood beside him reading the dispatch.

It continued:

. . . A portion of the Czech broadcast stated, "The people of Czechoslovakia have broken out of their prison and are returning to democracy. America, land of the free, do not let us be dragged back in chains. Our years of torment are over. Czechoslovakia is once again free."

The Chairman spit on the rug in disgust.

"Frank," he said, "there goes that God-damned treaty down the well."

# *Chapter* TWENTY-EIGHT

AN EMERGENCY meeting was called at the White House for two o'clock.

The long lobby—it ordinarily had the inelegant air and quiet gloom of a second-rate funeral parlor—was now crowded with newsmen and noisy with their talk. Groups made occasional querulous forays to Mickie's office and demanded of his secretary, "When's he going to have something for us?"

She replied steadfastly and wearily, "I don't know anything."

"That's a hell of a way to run a shop."

The milling throng heard the same rumors brought over from the Press Club, only vastly exaggerated. It was reported as absolute fact that the United States had paratrooped an atomic battalion into Czechoslovakia to protect the new regime, that the American troops had been fired on by Soviet tanks, and that a declaration of war against Russia was being prepared, or, in the next breath that the President had already sped away for a second meeting with Radilov.

Secretary King arrived first at the White House. He rushed from his limousine, plowed brusquely through the questioning mob of newspeople, and vanished. One reporter observed, "Old Silas looks like U.S. Steel had dropped twelve points."

Jefferson Lawrence arrived next. He was a decorous figure in a black coat and hat. He greeted the photographers modestly. An anxious young man with a microphone worked his way to the

Secretary and asked, "Sir, will we take military action to protect the Czech freedom fighters?"

Lawrence replied in a low voice, "I have nothing to say at this time."

He walked deliberately through the crowd, nodding to familiar faces (he had made a point of becoming friendly with influential correspondents), but saying nothing.

The Central Intelligence Director ran the gantlet. Finally, there was Senator Fremont and the Foreign Relations Committee Chairman. The reporters managed to stop these two, but the Chairman won their release by saying, "Boys, we know about as much about what's goin' on as a mother-in-law on the weddin' night."

In his office, President Christiansen presided over the meeting. He sank back with a pallid and uneasy face, and his hands continually rubbed the arms of his chair. It was difficult to determine whether he was listening. Mickie thought he was. There was an occasional flicker of awareness in his eyes, distantly focused. It was though the President was reluctant to be actively involved in this crisis. Mickie half expected him to say, "It belongs to the rest of you. Take care of it!"

The Central Intelligence Director reported in a monotone, "The trouble began at Prague University at a poetry festival. . . ."

King said angrily, "That's a hell of a funny place to start a revolution—at a poetry festival."

The Director replied, "Well, Mr. Secretary. You see, poetry has a very honored place in Czech literature. It expresses the highest aspirations for honor and human dignity. At this festival a poem honoring heroes of the past was declared counter-revolutionary and forbidden. Students stormed the office of the rector. He would not see them. The crowd grew to several thousand and sang the 'Internationale' and the 'Marseillaise.' They have very provocative words, you know. The police attempted to disperse the crowd, and the students disarmed them.

"More police were called, and a riot broke out. The students tore up the street and set up barricades. They broke into an arsenal of the student militia and armed themselves. Up to this point, the rebellion was an uprising limited to the university and with no leadership or plan.

"General Drtina then decided this was the time to seize control, or never. He led the Prague garrison and took over the Government buildings. The Russian troops proved tractable and offered no resistance. In fact, the Russian troops turned over their commandant, General Orlov, to the Czechs and recommended that he be hung in the square."

The narrator hesitated, awaiting any questions. There were none. He went on, "The provisional president, Dr. Duris, came to the American Embassy and asked for immediate recognition and assistance. He said this alone would prevent the Soviets from moving in by force."

Secretary King said angrily, "He wants us to break our agreement so he can stay in power."

The President asked in a low, almost inaudible voice, "Have you heard anything from the Russians?"

The Director replied, "Not officially, sir. But there was a Moscow Radio broadcast about twenty minutes ago which denounced the uprising in typical terms. Called it a fascist unleashing of terror instigated by *émigrés* hiding out in Germany. But this is a first reaction, like a woman screaming when a man pokes a pistol at her."

Judge Herring said, "Joel, what's going to happen on the Hill?"

The Chairman said, "There will be a contest to see who can piss the most on the Russians."

Senator Fremont added, "Jack Mahon has already introduced a resolution to recognize the new Czech regime, and I had to find an excuse to adjourn the Senate or it would be on the books now."

Suddenly the dismally quiet figure behind the desk erupted. Mr. Christiansen spoke as though trembling with an inner fury, "Why does everyone call on us when they are in trouble? What business do we have with Czechoslovakia? We can't go out and manage the world. You'd think we had an international rescue service."

He subsided for a moment. No one spoke. Then the President said, "I don't like to see people kicked around or hurt. But damn it, what can we do?"

Secretary Lawrence said with sudden exhilaration, "Mr. President, we could call on the United Nations to provide a force to isolate the nation from foreign intervention and hold supervised elections. We could paratroop . . ."

Silas King interrupted him coldly, contemptuously, "Oh, for Pete's sake, Jeff, lay off dreaming of knights and crusades. We have an agreement with the Russians to give us an age of peace and of prosperity. And you ask us to break it up for some school children whose names we can't even pronounce. The minute any of our troops land in Czechoslovakia, the treaty is off. We are in war again. Our defense budget goes up like a skyrocket. They overturn governments in South America, and nationalize our holdings. There's hell to pay."

The Secretary of Defense said, "But there are principles. The Declaration of Independence declares them, life, liberty and the pursuit of happiness."

"That," the Secretary of State replied, "was written by an aristocratic radical who married a wealthy woman and could afford to indulge in literary remarks. I'm not for chucking overboard a treaty because of Thomas Jefferson."

The Chairman chuckled. The sound was like gravel rattling in a cement mixer. He said, "This is just like a closed meeting of the Foreign Relations Committee."

Senator Fremont's arid twang intervened. "The noble sentiments of Mr. Jefferson are intended as broad guides for human conduct. But, like everything else, they should be mixed with discretion when put to use. The choice before us seems to be whether we wish to risk war, or certainly a fierce economic and political offensive with the Communist powers, over Czechoslovakia."

The President sat apart, seemingly preoccupied.

Judge Herring bowed obsequiously, as though he might be speaking on the Senate floor with its fantastically exaggerated mode of internal courtesy. "I admire the Senator's magnificent way of expressing a situation. You have expressed, it seems to me, the views of the Administration exactly. I see there is nothing more for us to do than to await the unfolding of events."

The Chairman's eagle-bright eyes looked at him with sardonic amusement.

Mr. Christiansen indicated his approval by a gloomy nod. The meeting began slowly, reluctantly, to break up. When all had left, even Mickie off to placate his unruly mob, the President rose stiffly, like an old man.

Hesitating a minute, not sure what he wanted to do or where to go—the outdoors somehow did not attract him; it was too bright, too overdone with spring joy—he wandered about until he reached the library. This had a regal melancholy to it, fit for a king or chief of state who wished to meditate, even briefly, on the sorrowing conduct of mankind. He soon grew tired of this solitary sitting in the shadows and turned on the television set.

Films of the Czechoslovakian revolution were being shown. He had not the will to turn off the set; there existed in the pictures a fascination, and he needed another spirit, a Moonan, to help him throw it off. The President could merely say, "Do you want to look at these, Mickie?" and Mickie would understand from a slight shading of the words and reply happily, "Of course not. Let's get to the pool table and there undertake affairs of state."

The announcer delivered himself of a little cultural lecture so dear to the television public. He showed a map of the ancient city of Prague. He explained it was on a mountain plateau of Bohemia. We all know Bohemia for, guess what? Beer, of course. The city is cradled by deep forests and protected by towering walls of rock. Prague was on the passageway from East to West. Its men have fought the Turks and the Teutons, the Russians and the Germans with equal vigor.

There was a picture on the screen of the city—the Gothic spires of the Cathedral of St. Vitus, the old palace of the Hapsburgs, university buildings six centuries old, the tower gateways and sculptured figures of a famous bridge. The romantic legend of the founding of the city, lean forward while I tell it: beautiful Princess Libusa of Bohemia went into a trance. She pointed to the far hills and a forested height and said, "In that forest you will find a man making a doorway. There you will build a city and you will call it Praha." The announcer explained with kindly patience that "Praha" was the Slavonic word for "doorway."

And now we switch to the present. Here are the wild, pale faces of students in shabby coats marching across the bridge. They are inflamed by a passion which even the film reveals. And listen to their voices as they sing. Does it not pain the heart? Joy that is doomed, doomed before the night will fall! Why is this allowed? Cannot society do something about this, or at least turn off the set?

The students carry old flags—they must have been hidden for

years under mattresses and in closets. They chant a plaintive, roaring chant, which, thanks to our announcer, means, "We will no longer be slaves!"

There is fighting now. A young man with long hair drops, and blood streams from his nose. A terror-paralyzed Communist official stands against a wall waiting to be shot. His face has been torn by scratching fingers of hate. Another figure twitches from a lamppost.

Now, here we have what is the most terrible of all to watch. Drop your head if it bothers you too much. An official of the new regime, his long, equine face drawn with weariness, aware of the giant odds against him, pleads in English, "I make my address to the American people, to their conscience to save us from the blackness of the Communist night." His lower lip trembles. His eyes shine out of deep holes. His voice breaks.

The President uttered a little moan and rose to turn off the set. Then he sat exhausted in his chair, his easy, easy chair. The set was dead, but he could still see the face of that man crying out for deliverance. It was like the sound of a man coming up from the depths of a mine, crying for rescue when all above knew this was impossible.

A Secret Service man came in and said, "I beg your pardon, sir, but they want you in your office. You have a call from Moscow."

Judge Herring and Moonan were both waiting for him. With crisis, the Judge grew more and more like a small bird in his brisk, bright, nervous movements; Mickie was inclined to wear a fixed, gloomy smile. The Judge twittered, "Mr. Christiansen, there are new developments. Students broke into the arsenal and have attacked the Soviet missile base outside of Prague. Heavy fighting is going on. A Russian armored division is moving in from East Germany. Paratroopers are standing by in the Ukraine. And Mr. Radilov wishes to talk with you. They are waiting in the Communications Center."

The President nodded to Moonan and said, "Come with me." They walked silently to the elevator. The doors slid open for them, then just as smoothly and noiselessly shut again. Riding down, the President saw the face again. Right there on the blank wall of the elevator. And he heard the braying voice of the country preacher rising in the still summer air, "And the Lord God called unto Adam, and said unto him, Where art thou? . . . Cursed is the ground for thy sake . . . For dust thou art, and unto dust shalt thou return." And it struck him with the immense start of a sudden heavy blow that perhaps his sins had attracted all this woe. He was not sure how it was done, but had a vague idea from dusty teachings of childhood that sin was like a lightning rod.

His own sins he knew too well. He had repudiated his father. The one mortal who had loved him and understood him, he had walked out of his life. He had simply opened the door and stood waiting in the rain for the train east. And there was the sin of adultery, that fierce woman with the daring eyes.

Mr. Christiansen felt for the moment limp with the knowledge of his own guilt. He scarcely knew when the elevator had reached the sub-basement. Moonan was gently pushing him, and they went toward the mechanical murmurings of teletypes.

The air was stale in this underground labyrinth. All the smells common to men clung there, too tenacious to be sucked out by fans. Mickie himself smelled of smoking too much.

The President asked him severely, "Mickie, when are you going to stop smoking?"

"My God, not until the world cools off."

Their footsteps sounded hollowly on the tiled floor. They were inside the studio now, and the great screen was flickering with lines and patterns. Viktor Radilov then appeared, as in the movies a face emerging from the fog.

Radilov spoke stiffly, the words shooting from his mouth like wooden pellets from a toy that must be wound up every few shots. He said, "I have come to you, as a brother, in the spirit of Geneva, and I ask you to seal off the West German border with Czechoslovakia."

"What is the reason?" the President asked.

"Because of the Germans."

"What Germans?"

Premier Radilov shook his head in disbelief and said, "Mr. President, is it true your intelligence does not know that German bandits, armed bandits, are crossing in the Fichte-Gebirge area into Czechoslovakia and attacking our garrison at the missile base? I see you do not know. This is true. These Germans, the followers of Gottfried, armed—American arms, I may advise you—have taken advantage of the confusion of the revolution to try to seize the missile base, and point the missile at our heart."

Mr. Christiansen asked, "Have you inquired of the West German Government whether it would close the border?"

The Russian said scornfully, "There is no Government in Bonn. There is a trembling old man, an Army which does not obey him, and these ruffians of Gottfried who steal their arms from your depots. If you do not wish war between the Union of Soviet Socialist Republics and your German friends, you had best close the border yourself and within this day. I think you understand. We will not permit the missile base to fall into German hands."

The President wondered how you prepared the body and the mind for such shocks. They dropped on you with the ferocity of line squalls. He asked, conscious of the stupidity of his question, "But what about the revolution?"

The Premier replied, "My dear friend, a revolution does not bother me. Students march across a bridge and sing bravely and foolishly. But when the security of my country is threatened, that is different. We can handle this revolution, and make it legitimate if we have to, and institute needed reforms. But these Germans coming across and mixing in and seizing the missile base, No. Never! I ask—will you seal off the frontier?"

Mr. Christiansen with an effort of will said firmly, "Mr. Radilov, in my country, we do not do things just like that. I will discuss this with my Cabinet and Congressional leaders, and if an agreement is reached, we will then close the border. But I do not want to be criticized for being dictatorial."

The Premier said, "We cannot wait. Will you promise not to interfere, then, if we bring troops in from East Germany to close the frontier, and we handle this affair in our own fashion."

Malcolm Christiansen wished fervently—he would have prayed if there was time and he knew exactly how—that this decision was not pointed at him. It was a bayonet, and it touched his heart so that he could hardly breathe.

He heard his voice say calmly, "We will not interfere." He was surprised and a little in awe of that voice.

# *Chapter* TWENTY-NINE

THE NEXT morning Secretary Lawrence brought a raw bit of news to the White House meeting. Mr. Christiansen, Silas King, Morgan the man from the National Security Council, Judge Herring and Mickie Moonan were present.

The President reflected on what he had heard and explored his teeth with his tongue. He located a tiny piece of breakfast sausage in an upper right molar and tried to work it loose. His labor, minute as it was, required concentration and helped to build a barrier against a rising tide of anxiety.

Mickie looked inquiringly at Morgan, on the President's left. He knew that Morgan had an uncommon sense of perspective in arranging facts—letting some fade into the background while others, more important, moved sharply into the foreground. Morgan seemed to Mickie a man who might have sat at the Greek council fires during the long siege of Troy. Not a warrior or a king, but useful to both.

"When these things break out," Morgan said sympathetically, "they don't stay in bounds. The human factor is unpredictable."

"Yes," Mickie agreed. "We stand on shifting sands. The geologists tell us the crust of the earth is always changing. It rises and falls. The oceans come and go. Once the Antarctic was green and may be again. You can't expect men to be stable."

"Just the same, I don't like it," Silas King said. "The Russians aren't playing ball."

Lawrence sat apologetically in a corner. He was, it seemed to

Mickie, almost too apologetic, as if he was hiding a vast glee that must be covered up in sober company. He stated in his precise, unemotional voice, "Our patrols in Fichte-Gebirge report that East German and Soviet units have penetrated to a depth of twenty miles into West Germany. Several West German border guards who attempted to halt them were shot or taken prisoner. The Eastern units claimed to be in pursuit of Germans who entered Czechoslovakia illegally and attacked the missile base. We estimate that the equivalent of an armored regiment took part in these actions of the Communist forces."

Silas King said simply, "God damn!"

Judge Herring asked, "What next?"

Morgan replied, "We can expect the German Chancellor to denounce what he will call an invasion. He will demand that NATO drive back the invaders, the United Nations pass a condemnatory resolution, and the World Court grant a billion dollars damages. He will make the most of it. He has to if he wants to stay in office."

"There will be much waving of the flag in Congress," the Judge reflected.

"What would we do, Mr. Secretary," Mickie asked Lawrence, "if Communists from Mexico attacked our missile base at Brownsville? Would we chase them back across the border?"

"That," the Secretary of Defense replied gravely, "is a question for the President and the Secretary of State."

This seemed to revive Silas King. With his old confidence he outlined a course of action. Follow a cautious path; stay out of the argument. The words went on. The President did not follow him carefully; he was interested mainly in the familiar, certain sound of Silas' voice. He was sure the storm would wear itself out. Hold tight. Don't worry.

An hour later, the President spoke quite cheerfully to a 4-H Congress, telling them, "I know a lot of pessimists come around and tell you that we've had our day, like Rome, and that we're going to pot and so is capitalism, and we'll probably be blown up in a war anyway. But don't you believe them. You kids have a great future, and let me tell you that Premier Radilov of Russia informed me there were lots of things about the United States he admired. The plumbing, he said, was excellent. Now, it is my thought and conviction that you young people will live a truly good life, not disturbed by the sound of bombs and relieved of the heavy taxes to keep up a gigantic military estalishment because of the danger of war. We are on the right track to peace. I am sure of that. Oh, yes, there will be minor outbreaks from time to time. But the thing you have to do is not let them pull you off the course, so to speak, and get you all excited. Because, if you've ever studied the causes of murder, it is the fellow who is excited who pulls the trigger most of the time. So keep cool and prepare to enjoy the good life!"

Shortly before noon, another scene took place on Capitol Hill. The law student who operated the public elevator in the Senate wing of the Capitol noted one of his passengers was a small, frail old woman whose remarkable red hair streamed out from under a shabby hat.

"Do you think there will be a good one, Mary?" he asked respectfully.

She whispered to him, "We are lost."

When he reached the street floor again, the operator whistled a policeman over to him and confided, "Little Mary is here." The knowledge spread rapidly to doorkeepers and pages and the senators themselves. For there was a legend that Mary O'Boyle, an odd but harmless pensioner, had a mysterious way of divining when the Senate would, without warning, erupt and spew forth the hot lava of angry oratory.

After the lunch hour, Senator Mahon entered the chamber. His good-looking Irish face, usually cheerful, was pale and resolved. The Chairman leaned over to Senator Fremont and remarked in a loud half-whisper, "He looks like his wife just ran off with a Baptist preacher."

When the minor business of the Senate was out of the way, Senator Mahon stood up and was recognized. He began speaking in the voice of controlled emotion, but his own words soon broke this reserve and his impassioned shouts were heard by reporters playing cards in the gallery. He was saying:

"The long road to futility and failure, upon which man has journeyed so much of his history, is marked by tombstones . . . the death of the Greek age of reason, the overthrow of Rome, the Russian Revolution, the Munich Conference, the Yalta Conference, the barbaric attack upon Budapest in 1956, and, perhaps, the Geneva Conference of this year. We must withhold our judgment until we learn what, if anything, this Administration is willing to do to save Czechoslovakia. The brave little nation has risen. Will it be slugged down again before our eyes?

"Greece did not die in a day. Rome did not fall in one battle. The Bolshevik revolution did not come overnight. Munich was the culmination of a whole series of less spectacular events which led to and foreordained those tragic happenings. The failure to oppose Nazi rearmament, the failure of courage, of sacrifice, of patriotism, the failure of the free nations to rearm themselves morally and militarily, the failure to stop Hitler's march into the Ruhr—these were all part of a sorrowful pattern. Munich was inevitable . . ."

The passion in his voice, the Irish tenor singing his lay, brought senators and their clerks out of the cloakrooms and onto the floor.

". . . Now in our time, we are repeating the same march of concessions to a tyranny which knows no end to its appetite. Our national policy lacks the positive, virile characteristics we need to win over the Communists, and bring freedom to the world. Day by day, the Communists have chipped away our strength and a new pattern of appeasement is beginning to unfold.

"Geneva! We held our President in such great honor that we felt he would meet the strength of communism with his own Christianity and moral courage. So we did not protest; we gave him our good wishes and our high hopes. And when he returned and offered us the treaty, most of us in the Senate felt a pang of apprehension. But again—we thought here is the one man who has shown he can rise and defeat communism. We stifled our fears.

"There has leaked out under the door information that is disquieting. Russia has not lived up to the letter of the law; it has haggled over the subsequent negotiations item by item until our agents are weary, and our military men are frightened by the prospect of disarmament which leaves us bare and naked. Now, we have the final treachery, the invasion of West German territory under a flimsy disguise.

"The day has arrived when we must show where we stand—with the free or the captive."

Senator Fremont sat with a questioning frown on his face. The Chairman buttoned and unbuttoned the top two buttons of his vest.

Mahon went on, "If we are to turn our backs on Czechoslovakia, it will confuse our own people, it will dishearten our allies, it will disillusion the hundred million captives in the Communist empire . . ."

The Chairman arose. His old man's bibulous nose, red and sharp, his scornful eyes gave him more than usual the look of the eagle. He called out, "Will the gentleman yield?"

Yes, he would.

"Let me ask you this?" the Chairman said, "Do you want to go to war over Czechoslovakia? These words are all very fine, and I have heard them before. But are you willing to pay the price? That is what I want to know."

Senator Mahon faltered, "There are means short of war."

"What are they? I want to know them," the relentless old man demanded. "Economic sanctions. Resolutions in the United Nations. Speeches. Who in tarnation cares about them? No sir, if you want us to intervene in Czechoslovakia and liberate these captive peoples, go ahead and have the nerve to introduce the one necessary step Congress can take, a declaration of war. Who will you find to back you then? I am a little tired of the Senate being used as a forum for futile protest. If you do not want to go to war, what do you want?"

Fremont said in an aside of encouragement, "Good work."

Mahon looked about the floor for allies. There had been so many outraged voices in the cloakrooms. Where were they now? He looked pointedly at Maze Bledsoe. Bledsoe returned the stare blandly.

Mahon replied grandly, "I say we cannot sit back without protest while Russia again rapes Czechoslovakia."

The Chairman said sarcastically, "Maybe there is a way, after all. I am told that in the medieval days kings and their nobles engaged their opposites in duels, instead of plunging their countries into war. Perhaps, the Senator from Massachusetts would care to challenge his opposite in the Soviet to a duel to the death with ballpoint pens?"

The sound of men's laughter moved across the Senate, Frank

Fremont relaxed. The little ball of fire in his chest went away. Mahon had lost his battle.

That night, before he retired, President Christiansen turned on the television set in his dressing room. He hoped for a good Western, but there was a news review. Film clips, he believed they called them. One was of Senator Mahon repeating portions of his speech. The Senator held before the camera the picture of the Czech official, the gaunt, hollow-eyed man, as he begged for assistance from the United States.

"Can any of you go to sleep tonight untroubled after seeing this face from hell?" the Senator asked passionately.

Oh damn it, the President told himself, that does it. He quickly turned off the set and went poking around in his top bureau drawer for the sleep-inducing pill. It was a green and red pill. His hidden cache was behind a stock of linen handkerchiefs. There would be a period now of half an hour before he would become drowsy, so he picked a Zane Grey novel off the table and undertook the chore of losing himself in the words. This was not easy. Mr. Christiansen read slowly and even then sometimes the words were like rows of fence posts, without meaning. When the comforting arms of drowsiness crept around him, Mr. Christiansen laid down the book and went to bed. He fell asleep almost at once.

Some hours later, he was drawn reluctantly from a sea of sleep. A burning feeling of anxiety partially awakened him. He felt it deep in his stomach, griping little pains; this must have been the trigger. And he experienced a vague, unknown and terrifying anxiety in his mind. He thought he was suffocating, and so opened his eyes and wildly looked about. A late-rising moon threw bands of light across the room. He listened for sounds of alarm. None. He sniffed for traces of fire. Nothing either. Yet the anxiety was so intense, he was perspiring. He felt the sweat on his forehead, under his arms and on the soles of his feet.

This was not a new sensation. He experienced it for the first time after he had stolen fifty cents from his mother's cupboard, in the old cream pitcher where he saw her hide it. He didn't want it, had no use for it, didn't spend it; just some queer kind of spite for her. He lost the money, out through a hole in his pants pocket. And he worried lest she discover the theft. He worried so much he became feverish and one night moaned in his sleep. His father heard and came up to the little room under the eaves, and the crying boy told him the story. It was all right, his father said, he was not a hardened criminal or he would not have felt so badly. Then it happened again after he left his father at the railroad station. He made so much noise in his sleep that fellow officers in the barracks complained. He had his affair then with the major's wife and forgot his father. One guilt erases another!

But why tonight? He lay in bed, his heart thumping so loudly it drowned out the quiet orderly whir of the bedside electric clock. His mind picked its way through the disorder of the day's events. Was it here? No. There? At last, he came to Senator Mahon and television. There was the damnable picture of the Czech staring at him, mutely entreating for his life. All right, I will address a note to Radilov. But you still look at me that way. You are accusing me of a crime. What crime? Betrayal?

The floodtide of grief broke through. Malcolm Christiansen felt he was drowning. He half rose in bed to get the weight of the water off his chest. He groaned and collapsed.

A Secret Service man came running in quickly and softly.

# *Chapter* THIRTY

THE DOCTORS gave their verdict gravely and sympathetically, as an undertaker does when submitting his bill. They must learn this in medical school, Mickie decided. Advanced Psychology, Chapters 10 through 20, "Handling the Patient and Family." How much better it would be if the doctor would clap the sick man heartily on the back and say cheerfully, "Congratulations old man, you have cancer. You can resign from your job. I know you didn't like it. Let the insurance company pay your bills. Do what you like. Write letters to the editor. Pinch waitresses. Join a nudist cult. Who is going to condemn a cancer patient? Antisocial."

The senior physician said, "I am happy to advise that the President did not suffer a heart attack. He had a nervous spasm stimulated by nervous exhaustion, acute anxiety and complicated by indigestion."

"Thank God," Silas King said, not so much with piety as with enthusiastic relief. "We need him to push the treaty through."

The physician cautioned, "Don't rush things, Mr. Secretary. These spasms, if they were to continue, could injure the heart or the brain or other vital organs. I would recommend a period of rest for six weeks. The President should be detached as far as practical from the cares of his office."

King energetically took over the job of organizing the vacation. Only, Moonan said, we won't call it a vacation. That has a bad connotation. The President off the job, not watching over his subjects like God. God never takes a vacation. We will call it a "refresher," that has a positive sound.

Mickie announced to the press that the President was "taking a refresher." He would carry the same load as usual, but he would work on a pine table and in his shirt sleeves. The Washington tabloid shouted, "Chris Takes Breather," and asked the man on the street for his reaction. Said Ross Scrimgeour, hardware salesman, "It's what every guy would like to do, and more power to Chris." Mae Donnell, Hot Shoppe cafeteria cashier, commented, "I think it's wonderful for Chris to get off like this. We don't want him to get sick or anything."

Ninety miles from Washington in the Blue Ridge mountains, a sanctuary was created for the President. Part of the Shenandoah National Park was fenced off, a jagged barbed wire running at the top level. The lodge with its huge fireplace where great logs always smoldered was turned over to the Presidential party. With binoculars slung around his neck and a gun or a fishing pole in his hand, Mr. Christiansen roamed the wooded paths and sunned himself on the big meadow. Czechoslovakia and even the Senate chamber grew more and more distant and unreal.

Silas King supplied companions to keep the President in good humor. They all had the breath and tone and stride of success and yet were good fellows—big, long-legged oil men who told stories at night as they stretched out in their chairs before the pine-wood fire roaring up the chimney, bankers in flannel shirts from Abercrombie & Fitch who joyfully proclaimed that Jack Daniels Tennessee whisky was the only poteen fit for a man; manufacturers of steel, chemicals, soft drinks, cigarettes; packers of meat and frozen food, all of the same pattern. They played cards with Mr. Christiansen, laughed heartily at his jokes, nodded in grave agreement to whatever he said ("A steak really isn't at its best unless it's served on a plate too hot to touch . . . a cup of old-fashioned cocoa with milk is relaxing before going to bed . . .") They explained to him earnestly that a lively fellow could make a million dollars in the old Horatio Alger style if the Government saw things the right way. Cut that perilous spending. Reduce the invidious taxes. Keep the unions in their place. Loosen the manacles on the hands of business.

Silas King himself came down two or three times a week. As

soon as he stepped out of the limousine, he shouted an Indian cry he had learned as a boy in upper Michigan, and, if he was within earshot, the President would shriek back. This so astonished the new German Ambassador who had come to present his credentials that he dropped his monocle and it shattered on the stone floor.

Silas always brought good news. Ten days after the Czechoslovakian revolution crisis, King arrived and, when the President appeared, took his arm and said, "Glad tidings, Chris. But first, let me take these damn shoes off." They went to the rooms set aside for him. King sank into a chair and kicked his shoes off and grunted. Mr. Christiansen sat on the bed grinning.

"Well, Mr. President, the Czech revolution is all cleaned up," the Secretary reported. "The Communists got out of West Germany; they didn't know they were over the line, or at least that's the story and we might as well buy it. They've a new government in Prague; the old boys were kicked out. Some reforms have been announced. Poets will get free lunches, and that kind of stuff. Do you remember that fellow who was on television asking for our help? They've made him director of the radio station. That's a pretty smart move. When I was in steel, we had a fellow who was always stirring up the union to strike or demand this or that. After about a year of that, I gave the fellow a job in the front office, Assistant to the Vice President in Charge of Production. No more problems."

King wriggled his toes with pleasure.

"And about the treaty," he added. "The Senate is cooled off, and we'll get the treaty through in a couple of weeks. Also, I've talked to the German Foreign Minister, and they've promised to behave and keep that Gottfried under control."

The President reached over and put his hand on the Secretary's shoulder.

"Si," he said warmly, "I don't know what in the hell I'd do without you."

That was the extent of their discussion. There was a benign conspiracy to keep from Mr. Christiansen anything that might disturb him. Silas King had put the question pragmatically to the Cabinet, "President Christiansen isn't any good to us or the country flat on his back or six feet under. If we want to get our pro-

gram through, we must realize that we can't drop one crisis after
another on Chris's head. We're going to have to take care of them
the best way we know how."

Judge Herring stayed at the White House and ran the shop by
telephone. Occasionally he sent visitors across the Potomac River
and out U.S. 29 to the mountain lodge. They arrived with dispatch cases, had a half hour with the President, and made the winding descent back to the flatland and on to Washington. Moonan
would telephone a report to the "refresher" press room in a
town at the base of the mountain. "The President and Secretary
of State had a vigorous and detailed discussion of the Czechoslovakian crisis, and the President gave the Secretary fresh instructions."

One morning Mickie came to the big center room of the lodge to
find out from the Secretary of Welfare what he had talked about
to the President. George Crowell had been in pharmaceuticals,
but many of his old business associates were wont to say, "George
takes this welfare business too seriously."

The Secretary seemed troubled. He asked, "Do you think the
President has any personal antagonism toward me?"

"No. What's happened?"

The earnest official said, "A few weeks ago, after the big fish
kill on the Shenandoah River from cellulose refuse, Mr. Christiansen asked me to prepare a report on stream pollution. We've
done a very thorough job both in the Department and in consultation with the finest authorities in the world. I gave the report to
the President this morning. He read halfway down the first page,
threw the report on the table, and told me that would be all. What
have I done; do you have any idea?"

"Let me see your report."

Crowell took a copy from his dispatch case. Mickie flipped
through it briefly: 200 pages long, and, at the end, five alternative
recommendations.

"Mr. Secretary," Moonan said mildly, "the President is not what
you would call partial to long reports. I would suggest you take
this back to Washington and boil it down to two pages double-
spaced and one recommendation."

He patted Mr. Crowell on the arm and walked out to the driveway with him.

Another incident took place which the press secretary knew nothing about. Judge Herring called to the lodge and said that the Attorney General wished to see the President on a personal matter. The Attorney General was not, truthfully, a good friend of Moonan's. Mickie had known him when he was a district attorney. At that time the lawyers had called him "a courtroom Napoleon," and to the reporters he was "buster." This was both an allusion and a comment. The Attorney General preferred the title of "racket-buster."

When "General" Rainey came early in the afternoon, he was closeted with the President in the small, pine-paneled room he used as an office. A smell of wood smoke came from a smoldering fire in the grate. The President was relaxed. He wore a faded khaki shirt open at the neck, and had on his walking boots.

Rainey said, "Mr. President, all of us are inspired by your crusade for peace. The world sleeps more soundly these nights because of your humane leadership."

The President felt pleasure mingled with curiosity. He asked himself, I wonder what he wants. This is the way they start out when they want something. He nodded for the Attorney General to proceed.

The lawyer, still supplicating, said, "It is unfortunate, Mr. President, most unfortunate that there are extremists who do not have faith in your crusade." He shook his head sadly. "They pursue, I am sorry to say, outrageous methods. They commit offenses against the statutes of the United States. They try to impede legitimate defense.

"One group of lost souls has been flourishing in the Midwest. They picket service recruiting offices. They pass out leaflets at defense-plant gates urging workers to cease producing munitions. But the most flagrant act is, in effect, to sabotage the construction of missile-launching sites. Mind you, they have been warned. We have pleaded with them, in person and by letter, to put their faith in your crusade for peace."

The Attorney General spoke rapidly, "There has been an episode recently in North Dakota, involving the missile center near Stady. It is quite appropriately named 'the Christiansen Citadel.' For the past four months, during construction, a group of these lost souls have tried to persuade the construction workers to leave their jobs."

He rushed on, a train which slows down, throws off the mail, and is off with renewed speed into the swift night.

"Their leader is a woman. She has trespassed on federal property. She was warned. The United States Marshal read her the law. She invited him to exercise his authority, claiming that she was responsible to a higher authority which stated, 'Thou shalt not kill.'

"The danger—and I have discussed this with the director of the FBI, who agrees with me—is that this insurrectionist attitude will spread to other installations if it is not stopped. We propose to prosecute this woman. I realize that prosecuting a woman may raise delicate questions. They do not greatly concern me. The national welfare is more important. But I felt obliged to report the matter to you."

Mr. Christiansen was mildly relieved that was all there was to it. He said, "Well, if you have a duty, and the law is violated, I guess you have to do your duty."

The Attorney General said, his eyes bright with meaning, "The woman is Mrs. Blake, Theandra Blake, a widow, aged sixty."

The President knew now why the Attorney General was there. How the past is like doors that suddenly open at the touch of a hand fumbling in the dark! Thea, Thea. She was the only woman who had ever given him solace. He could feel her comforting arms steady his sobbing child's body. She had heard his sobs and traced his path in the wet snow to a corner of the garage where he cowered waiting for the wrath of Jehovah. He could smell that corner now, grease and old papers and the dampness of the snow.

He was, what was it, eleven perhaps. She was the slim, large-eyed hired girl who came to their house once a week. He could not recall exactly the cause of his mother's anger, except that he had disobeyed her inflexible will, possibly by accident. She invoked on him the rage of Jehovah. "He will lay his hand in wrath upon you and strike you down." Fear is a cannibal; it eats its own kind when there is no other food. And so it was with the boy. Fear gorged upon fear. He could still remember the violent, ungovernable shaking that overwhelmed him. He lay quivering on the floor of the garage in a hysteria of fear. Thea reached down and pulled him up and held him close to her until his sobbing was tamed. He told her, "God is going to strike me down."

"No," she said gently, "God does not do that. He is kind and good. He is forgiving." She sounded so certain of her knowledge that he believed. His mother was never again able to terrorize him by threatening to call on Jehovah to punish him. He said nothing to her, but remembered the soothing words.

If Thea had learned pacifism, she learned it from his father. He was the spring that watered the dry land.

"General Rainey," the President said in a small voice, "I cannot believe this woman would break the law. I knew her many years ago. She worked for us."

"That is what I understand," the Attorney General said retiring into a neutral corner. "I can give you the FBI report elucidating the continued violation of the law and the spread of this sect. Time often plays cruel jests on those we once knew, Mr. President, and changes their whole character. This woman is endangering national defense, and the FBI is afraid her sect could become as perfidious as communism."

Mr. Christiansen did not answer. He knew the law was demanding, it must have its tithe, but why Thea? Why does its bruising touch have to come so close?

"Aren't there others you can prosecute first?" he asked. "If this is as widespread as you say, get some of the others—the men, and let them be an example."

General Rainey decided this was the moment to slam down his ace. He said, "Mr. President, we have considered all these alternatives, believe me. It is difficult for me to consider prosecuting a woman. I am a man of Christian charity. But the American Legion has been pressing us. Quite vigorously. It has threatened to accuse the Justice Department of failing to prosecute this woman because she was a friend of yours. One man has already been making statements to this effect, and has been quoted on a radio program by the commentator, Hamilton Green. I am very much afraid, Mr. President, that if this is taken up, it will become a very powerful weapon in the hands of your opposition and could hold up the treaty in the Senate. And, of course, the treaty and the peoples' faith in you are of supreme importance."

When it came time for the Attorney General to go, he walked

to his limousine with a little strut. Mickie found the President quite depressed, but he would not say what he had discussed with his Cabinet member. Two days later, a paragraph appeared on the AP wire noting that a woman "agitator" had been arrested and charged with obstructing national defense, and misspelled her first name.

And so the life went on up in the mountains where low clouds brushed against the pines and often covered the meadow so that nothing could be seen except the lodge. President Christiansen shot deer and fox and possum, and brought back trout in his creel. He seemed to have recovered his old sense of safety.

Moonan, though, was restless. He was too far up in the gallery; he had to be closer to the stage. So, occasionally at night, he slipped away and went down the mountain to the rambling, old-fashioned hotel where the reporters stayed. There he endured their insults and drank with them and picked up their gossip.

One night, midway in the "refresher," he ducked out on the President—they were showing a favorite movie of Mr. Christiansen's he had seen three times—and went down into the valley.

The long hotel porch with its row of wicker rocking chairs was empty except for an elderly couple engaged in subdued rocking. The only soul in the huge lobby was the clerk who cried out, "Good evening, Mr. Moonan."

"Where are the beasts?" he asked.

The clerk sighed with understanding. "In the bar, Mr. Moonan."

Mickie took the stairs to the nether regions. He stood in the doorway of the dark bar for a moment looking at a scene as familiar to him as his toothbrush, newsmen dumped down in a strange town and assembled in the nearest bar. Some were arguing, others consulting the bartender on local customs, still others around an upright piano and singing a lewd parody.

He was noticed. Someone shouted, "Cheese it, the law."

"Well, Uncle Michael Mewlin."

Moonan brought from under his coat a bottle of Irish whisky.

"Begorra, if it isn't St. Michael himself."

A shape untangled itself from a chair, stood up, made a low bow and said, "Welcome to our humble abode, your worship. Enjoy our fare and, if you wish, our youngest daughter."

Mickie's eyes became accustomed to the dark and he noticed a glossy news picture of the President over the bar. It was not a flattering pose—Mr. Christiansen at a press conference listening to a question, his head cocked to one side, his mouth agape. Over the photograph were spangled gold letters on a green background H. O. G. L.

"What the hell is this all about?" he asked.

The room was silent, except for the bartender stirring a drink. "Well."

"Your worship, we are poor people, and little we have but our faith. This is our ikon, and the mysterious letters signify 'Hail to Our Glorious Leader.' "

"That deserves a drink all around."

After the Irish whisky was poured out and drunk, Mickie was told, "Now, you must join our hymn. Bert, to the piano."

Bert played several bars of Mozart with feeling—the piano had not been tuned lately—and then swung into a familiar popular air. Voices sang loudly:

> "We're Chris' millionaires
> We're Wall Street bulls and bears
> Our bank accounts aren't amiss
> And that seems to be the kiss for Chris
> Oh, our pockets are full of dough, ray, me, fa, so!
>
> "We're triple A in Dun and Bradstreet
> We've got fleets of Cadillacs
> And we calculate we're overweight in income tax
> Chris is our cup of tea; he's our pal in luxury
> We've got oil and banking stocks
> We didn't buy them in odd lots
> Oh, our pockets are full of dough, ray, me, fa, so!
>
> "We make the stock exchange our hangout
> But when Chris wants us near
> Shine or rain—we hop a plane—and answer, 'Here.'
> Chris is our President
> Down to our last red cent
> Oh, our pockets are full of dough, ray, me, fa, so!"

Moonan, half angry, half amused, contented himself with saying, "You are a bunch of irreverent bastards."

"Nay, sir. We have thrown down the old gods, Jupiter, Odin,

Baal, Jehovah, and even Bacchus for the true faith, the worship of the true god of peace, Chris."

"Hail to Chris, hail, hail, hail!" The roomful of reporters bent over reverently, their fingers to their toes.

At midnight, when his driver came for him, Mickie was brought out and lifted into the car by his friends. He wore on his lapel a big green cardboard button with the initials "H. O. G. L." on it.

At the end of the six weeks "refresher," a mammoth "Welcome Back to Washington" celebration was arranged for the President. Government offices and schools were let out. Small flags were distributed, posters were produced, bands arrayed. As the small caravan crossed on the Memorial Bridge, a fireboat in the Potomac River spouted streams of water and a small cannon boomed a salute. The Marine Band waiting at the Lincoln Memorial played, "Hail to the Chief."

Huge crowds thronging the Memorial Circle raised a great cheer. It was taken up and echoed and re-echoed all along the route of the parade down Constitution Avenue. President Christiansen stood up in the touring car. He was transfigured, the evangelist greeting his howling hordes in the temple. His arms were outstretched, Father giving his love to all mankind. His face wore the rapture of beatitude.

In the last press car, a reporter casually waved a small green pennant with the gold letters on it "H. O. G. L."

## Chapter THIRTY-ONE

WITH THE dignity of an aristocratic old lady, a limousine with a curiously high build pulled into the cement arc in front of the State Department late in the summer afternoon. It was the British Embassy's Rolls-Royce. The Ambassador, Sir Stanley Drake, stepped down and under the green canvas marquee to the door and the precious coolness. He stopped in the gleaming marble lobby to dab a linen handkerchief against his perspiring forehead, and then took the elevator to the fifth floor.

The Ambassador paused to pay his invariable compliment to the Secretary's receptionist in a refined accent, "I never cease to wonder how you American girls contrive to always look lovely and desirable, even in the most terrible weather. We don't seem to have the hang of it in Europe. Our woman wilt in summer and freeze in winter. The male is left with only spring and autumn to pursue his mating instincts."

The receptionist replied saucily, "I wish, Sir Stanley, that you would give classes to American men on how to flatter women. They either don't know or they don't care."

The gentle laughter tinkled in the carpeted, well-lighted reception room.

Silas King greeted the Ambassador affectionately. Drake was a pretty good bird. The Secretary said, "I'm damned glad to see you, Stanley. I've spent most of the day at the White House hammering out the over-all budget. Some people just don't have any business sense." He sighed.

The Ambassador said, "The energy which you Americans devote to money fascinates me. I marvel at your dynamic force. You are like the early Christian martyrs, you are willing to give up anything for your faith. I don't know a single Communist who is as faithful to his dogma as you are to yours, Silas."

Secretary King was surprised, "I don't see anything strange about it. Money is power. Now this isn't a backwoods doctrine at all."

"You must admit it has a pioneer flavor to it," Sir Stanley said with a slight smile.

"Not at all. It is just being realistic. If I have money, I can buy brains to run my companies. Allies are attracted to me. Enemies are afraid to attack me, because they know I have the power to crush them."

"How would you explain then," the Ambassador asked, "the victory of the American colonists over Britain? We had the money on our side then, you know."

"Stanley, you've put me in a trap." Friendly laughter. "How about a drink?"

"A small one. Scotch, if you please. Silas, I am going to be an iconoclast, but I do not believe the dynamics of a nation depends on its wealth, its political or social structure, or its religion. Civilizations are like men; they are asleep in the womb, they are born, they reach a peak of vigor, and they fade or are bled to death, as the Greeks in the Peloponnesian War. They die and are reborn and the process begins all over again. Perhaps this may be true of mankind itself. But the point I want to make is that I do not consider the Bolshevik revolution was the cause or the starting point of Russia's modern power; it was merely a symptom. Russia was ready to free itself from the mother, and would have done so as communist, republic or monarchy. The United States would have become the greatest industrial nation, even if it had adopted the New Harmony experiment and was communist. Capitalism has nothing to do with your success. Oh, I will grant you that a number of basic assets are needed for dynamic growth —arable land and stout men. But look at the British Isles, mostly moors and rocky hillsides and marshes—no great supply of minerals or foods. Yet, we triumphed over poor Spain which had its rich empire long before we did."

He took a drink from the glass put before him.

"You know, Silas, I suspect this is why Radilov is so anxious to arrange a peace. He understands that Russia's day has come, and he does not want it prematurely shattered by a destructive war."

Secretary King grunted, "May be. But I know this is not your message for me."

Sir Stanley said regretfully, "You are so damnably direct, Silas. I never get to talk my full length. Well, frankly London is very much afraid the German situation has deteriorated badly. Our information is that the Chancellor is nothing more than a talkative old man, while the real power rests with Stuber, the Defense Minister, and his generals and Gottfried. These two forces which might be less dangerous if separate are now moving together. We have a record of five meetings between Gottfried and Stuber within the last two weeks. Hitler and the Reichswehr all over again. Gottfried is organizing a volunteer militia in small units, and the Army is helping him. Damned if I like it. And if we are nervous in England, imagine what the Russians are thinking."

King asked, "Why do the Russians get so upset every time a German curls his fist?"

The Ambassador said, "There is, of course, the obvious. We know how deeply wounded Russia has been in two wars by Germany. One tends to forget the agony of the past unless it is constantly kept alive. The Communists have kept it alive, and for a very pragmatic reason. Any state which demands not only the backs, but the minds and the spirits of its people is subject to periodic internal explosions. These fiery belches can be reduced by applying a present danger. For example, if the Kremlin says we must be united and work strenuously or the Germans will eat us up, this can be quite real and meaningful, and not just to Russians, but to Poles and Czechs and Hungarians. So the Communist propaganda machine has been doing its share in keeping the German menace alive. The Germans have not helped any by their arrogance. They hear voices in the mist telling them to rise and rule the world. A dangerous people!"

Sir Stanley said with sudden earnestness, "Silas, your people haven't been arming the Germans with some beastly secret weapon, have they?"

"Christ, no," King replied, startled. "Why do you ask that?"

"Our intelligence chaps have been picking up some odd bits. Someone is giving the Germans a nasty weapon. Is there anyone in Washington who might be doing this sort of thing without your knowledge? This is very important, Silas."

"That is a pretty ugly suspicion to raise, Stanley. You must have a reason."

"Unfortunately yes," the Ambassador replied, "the intelligence fellows, working on some knowledge they picked up, broke into a warehouse in Hamburg and stole a crate listed as containing automotive spare parts. They opened it up and found a thousand cartridges. Our chemists analyzed several cartridges. They contain nerve gas. Pretty little things." He put his hand in his waistcoat and drew out a cartridge and gave it to the Secretary.

King turned it around in his hand. Pretty little toy was right. On the bottom of the cartridge he noticed a small red dot. The Secretary was immediately conscious of feeling warm and of noticing how tightly his belt cut into his abdomen, as though his stomach had just this moment swollen. The cartridge was familiar. Jeff Lawrence had brought one just like this to the Security Council meeting last spring. He had explained in his sobersides manner how it might be used by a small force to effect a surprise attack.

How, in Christ's name, did this little cartridge get from Jeff Lawrence's soft, well-manicured hand to a German warehouse? Little threads of information and surmises wove together in Silas King's mind. A casual reference from a friend at Ajax Chemicals about a top-secret order, gas shells. The fraternization of American and German officers. Complaints, never nailed down, that high U.S. military personnel privately encouraged Gottfried. Lawrence's own occasional impassioned statements about Germany and Russia.

With no more evidence than this, Silas King knew, knew just as an animal feels the presence of an enemy, that Jeff Lawrence was involved in some damn fool conspiracy, and these shells were part of it.

Secretary King had an explosion of knowledge. Walls were shattered. Money was not the only corrupting force in life. He fingered the crisp new one-dollar bill in his pocket. There were times and circumstances when it would have no value, no power at all. Here was Jeff Lawrence, a prosperous, successful conservative American, gone wild, filled with a passion that resulted in this little cartridge. King did not understand—or care to understand—the process that had led to Lawrence's infatuation; it was enough to know that he was mad.

Sir Stanley observed his companion with shrewd intelligence. So his chaps had been right after all.

A half hour later, the Rolls-Royce made its decorous departure from the State Department. A heavy black sky hung glowering over Washington, and in a few moments broke into a lashing summer storm. The wind blew sheets of slanting rain in gusts across the street. Lightning flashed vividly and thunder rolled. People huddled in doorways. The trees lining the street bent in shivering terror.

## *Chapter* THIRTY-TWO

THE MOCKINGBIRD ended its evening rhapsody, and flew away from the antenna over the press room. Mickie could see him, a gray, gliding figure in the dusk. The mockingbird was one of the most successful of all God's chillun, he could imitate the joy and sorrow of his fellows without experiencing any of their pain. The mockingbird would inherit the earth.

Moonan returned to his typewriter. The words from these metal keys were supposed to soothe the savage German, sing him a song of peace. His fingers tapped over the keyboard in a spasm of energy and thought.

My friends, more than three hundred years ago, a wise man wrote words familiar but worth repeating now. "No man is an island, entire of itself; every man is a piece of the continent, a part of the main . . . any man's death diminishes me, because I am involved in mankind; and therefore never send to know for whom the bell tolls; it tolls for thee."

Thus it is that any act of violence, any harm to the dignity of man anywhere in the world, is the concern of all Americans. We are all living in a world so small, so subject to destruction by weapons of horror, that disagreements must not be allowed to remain anywhere. This is why tonight, I wish to speak to you and men everywhere of events in Germany . . .

That was it. Pull the American people in by the scruff of their fat necks and make them look at the world entire. A six-foot German with a saber-slash on his cheek can call off the country club dance. So can a nervous Russian or a hungry Chinese.

Secretary King had been in to see the President this morning, and asked him to put out the sputtering fuse by making a speech. He told Mr. Christiansen about the nerve-gas cartridges the Germans had obtained, probably from our people; of the chance that now the Chancellor would be overthrown by Gottfried and the military, and the West Germans would attack in the East to unify *das Vaterland*. But a few honest words by Chris, promising justice for all, would cool the fevered brows.

Mickie himself had no great trust in the fantasy of hope. He was not a fatalist, all this business about events having been written in a big book in Valhalla a million years ago. That was the Presbyterian for you. Catholics, being great historians, were more realistic. But there are tides and currents you cannot buck. He pounded the keys rapidly again.

There is in Germany today a normal desire to end the separation that has cut brother off from brother ever since the end of World War II. I mean by this the division of Germany into two distinct countries, one a part of the giant Communist system which extends from the Elbe River to the Pacific Ocean, the other a democratic Germany which considers itself—by its own choice—a member of the Western family of nations. The barrier which divides the two Germanys is artificial . . .

What barriers were real and justified? Man was man, wasn't he? Race, tongue, religion, geographical cohesion? If any of these were valid, the United States would not be. Every race under the sun, tongues not quite so, religion ditto. Two states way to hell and gone, Alaska and Hawaii. We are all living, Germans, Russians, Americans, Tibetans, on islands raised from the sea. The islands may sink back again. This unstable crust of land. What the hell, this wasn't writing the speech.

I respect and honor the German desire for unity. My great grandfather died in battle for the union of the United States. I pray and all men pray that the re-union of Germany can be achieved sensibly and without gunfire. For one shot in a world such as ours is likely to explode arsenals in many lands . . .

He wondered how it would feel to get a whiff of that nerve gas the Germans had. Nerves twitching, co-ordination all gone, gasping for breath, panic unchained like a man being dragged to the scaffold in the Dostoyevsky story. It was Dostoyevsky, wasn't it?

I ask our German friends not to resort to force. Any attempt to secure German unity in this manner would be, because of its consequences, a criminal act. It would be lynch law on a mass scale. The United States believes in law and justice and would feel obliged to react as any policeman to a criminal act . . .

There would be a hell of an argument with the State Department over this language. They never wanted to call a spade a spade; much preferred the more genteel word of "trowel." They didn't want to upset the digestion of any gentlemen, so avoid plain talk.

I can assure the German people that they have the support of the United States in their desire for unity. We will be their ally at the conference table . . .

Lot of hogwash, really. No one wanted a united German nation. Not the Russians. They were scared stiff of a powerful, united Germany. So was England. We had qualms, that is except for the generals and Secretary of Defense Jeff Lawrence. They saw Germany as the anti-Communist fortress holding off hordes of ferocious Russians, Chinese, Africans, Arabs, Jews. Well, you wouldn't want your sister to marry a Negro (Russian, Jew, Chinese, etc.), would you? What difference does the color of his pecker make—how's that for an answer. Finally, to make the point, the ruling Catholic Party of West Germany is not keen on union. The blessed would be outvoted by atheists, Lutherans, Methodists, Baptists *et al.* from the East.

Across the river, Jefferson Lawrence sat alone. He had been watching the twilight deepen and lose itself in night. The windows of Georgetown University were a hundred palettes where the artist mixed his paints. First in late afternoon, a shining brass. Then death and transfiguration of the day. Scarlet splashed grandly on the windows. Turned deeper and deeper as it is mixed with gray. Finally, lost in the depths of night. Gone like the hopes of youth. All the while the river changed subtly, a dark mirror of the sky. Now it had long, golden, wavering streams reflecting the lights on Key Bridge. The lower riverbank had turned into a jungle full of shadows and wonderment.

Around him, his house was quiet. It was the Renaissance castle so quaintly out of place among the opulent redwood ramblers cut into the high Virginia palisades. There were no footsteps, no sighs, no laughter but his tonight. Mrs. Lawrence was away. Another of the periodic, unexplained absences. This was the butler's night out. Lawrence might have stayed on at the Pentagon, and required his assistants to be about him, hearten him with their voices. But they had dinners and families waiting, and joy was short. This was a rare night when one wanted his love close to him, touching the flesh.

Jefferson Lawrence saw in the changing colors of night a substitute. The night was almost as fascinating as a woman, and not as cruel. Too, the night washed out the sharp angles of day. Man's crime against man became a little less real and vivid.

Yet the night could not muffle the doubts that sprang up like thieves from the shadows and assaulted him. Had he acted rightly and justly? Or? Was it true—"he had on his bosom a spike named Bitterness"? God, what vile things a man could do when under that torture. He could no longer bear to sit still. He walked restlessly up and down his library.

It was done. There was no calling back. Events had pressed him into action. He had no choice. "None will dare, when Fortune knocks, to bar the door proclaiming, 'Come thou here no more!' "

He summed up his arguments, as though pleading his case before a tribunal. Your Honor, Western civilization, that is free society with its richness of culture and its belief in the dignity of man, is under final attack. The enemy, like that of Greece and Rome, is the barbarian. The barbarian has no interest in art or justice or the individual human being. He was content to tear down the magnificent temples of Greece and neglect the aqueducts of Rome. He will destroy in our time the right, or the gift if you would call it that, your Honor, of independent thought. This will be his greatest crime, for the world may never recover. It is not the murder of men that I object to, may it please the court, for that is not a matter within the jurisdiction of this Court. A verdict will be rendered there by the Court of Public Opinion, a lesser Court. The crime I fear is the destruction of the human will. Man will be the servant of a soulless state, to decrees and judgments as barren as a sterile womb. The state will decide by a clanking movement of its mechanical brain what is good for man, whom he must love and hate, what he can say and write and think. I hold this is a world not worthy of containing the divine spark of life.

There is one chance to destroy the barbarian. I do not say it will succeed, but I appeal to your Honor that we cannot afford to let this chance slip by. For it is, I swear, the last chance. The barbarian is becoming too big, too powerful to be caged. The barbarian, like every man, lives with a fear, and we must make this fear consume him. His fear is of another man, one called a German. The German, I admit, is a strange man himself, part brute, part philosopher. But above all he is not afraid of blood. He is also strong and ingenious and industrious. The German might be likened, if the Court please, to the Biblical story of David and Goliath with one exception. Our David did not have five smooth stones and a sling until the defendant, Jefferson Lawrence, provided him with them. It is with these weapons that our David will slay the uncircumcised giant of the Philistines.

You ask whether or not this battle will not destroy all men. A good question, your Honor. I cannot give you an unequivocal answer. I want to be honest with the Court. First, let me suggest that man has no deed to immortality. He is a stage of evolution in one infinitely tiny part of the Universe. He exists on a surface which cracks and rises and falls. He is at the mercy of winds and tides, of sun and water. Any of these may cause him to perish by means more horrible than in such a battle as between David and Goliath. Second, I do not think the barbarian will allow the battle to spread beyond Germany. He has too much to lose, and he is eminently practical. He will come to terms with the German after the initial battling. These terms will put a fence around him, and save Western civilization for at least another twenty-five years. I rest my case, your Honor.

But he was a lawyer, and he knew as he paced back and forth in the library of the old castle that a lawyer's plea may be clever and even brilliant without being the truth. The cursed doubt beat at him. Would he have been so reckless with human life if it had not been for Claire, his wife? Did her lack of faith in him as a man turn him to violence? What cruel questions. He could hardly bear them. "I once hoped to pluck the fruits of life: but now, alas, they are all withered and dry . . ."

The house was so quiet. The night was so dark.

President Christiansen had returned from a ride down the Potomac River in his yacht. He felt the air warm and close now the boat idled at its mooring and was no longer flying over the water.

"I don't like this night," President Christiansen remarked with a grimace of distaste. "One of those trouble breeders. I could always spot them when I was O.D. at the base, and call out an extra detail of M.P.'s. Something gets in the blood. I don't know what it is."

His companion, a Southern textile manufacturer, agreed. "I know what you mean, Mr. President. When I was a boy, down south of Atlanta, there would come one of these still nights in the full moon, and you could hear the nigras howlin' and chantin', and afore the evenin' was over, there would be cuttin's and scrapin's."

Mr. Christiansen looked up. "There's a full moon beginning to rise."

Dr. Baker, the President's physician, said, "There have been some quite good technical studies on this. They indicate a full moon has a thus far mysterious effect on men and animals. Strange yearnings and frustrations. Just shows how little we sawbones really know about Homo sapiens."

President Christiansen shook his head and commented, "There are lots of things we'd better leave alone, and not want to know too much about."

All that night the message center in the bowels of the White House was busy. Berlin was six hours ahead of Washington, London five, Moscow eight, Peiping thirteen. Words of travail tapped out by unseen hands across the seas. At midnight, two men from the staff of the National Security Council were called in to digest and put together the messages. One of them after an hour asked, "Is the moon red tonight? Or do murder and rebellion always walk, but we only hear of them on nights like this when the senses are alert and the eyes see more?"

His companion replied, "Damned if I know, Joe."

Secretary King was called at his home at seven thirty the next morning, and told of an important message from the ambassador in Moscow. As he drove in from Georgetown, his chauffeur ran a red light. The air-conditioned limousine was almost struck by a bus which was forced to veer sharply. Horns honked. People glared.

"What's the matter with you?" King asked the driver irritably. "Didn't you see that light?"

"I am sorry, Mr. King. I had a bad night last night. Didn't get much sleep. Cats howling all night long."

In the office, his secretary sloshed some coffee bringing in the cup.

"I suppose you didn't get any sleep last night, either?" he demanded in exasperation. Yes, that was it.

The Ambassador's report was on his desk. "Premier Radilov is being pushed out on a ledge by events. He has gambled all on co-existence with the West and on guaranteeing Soviet security by peace. He has insisted that the United States could be trusted. From the very beginning, this position was aggressively disputed by the hard-core Marxists, like Andrevsky, and the Chinese comrades. It is their religion or dogma that capitalism never can be trusted. They believe it is innately evil and perfidious just as many Westerners regard communism in the same light. The marshals of the Red Army have been inclined to agree with Andrevsky, but they dislike and distrust him personally and like Radilov. In his last speech before the Central Committee, before he was exiled to Ulan Bator, Andrevsky warned that war would come with a secretly armed Germany rising up and striking the East. If this prophecy should come true, Radilov would be forced out of office by the Red Army. The marshals are grealy concerned by reports from Germany, and troops are being hurriedly summoned from Poland, Hungary and Czechoslovakia to guard East Germany. This in itself is a calculated risk, because if there is a successful uprising in East Germany, similar attempts would be made in other satellite nations. I urgently request that all possible be done to assure the Soviet Union publicly that the United States will not permit a seizure of power by the West Germans and a military adventure."

The words neatly typed on the white page were a dash of cold water on Silas King's face. He had not considered it likely that the Germans would start a war. The thought was too incredible. Thrifty, industrious builders. Giant steel mills, chemical plants, banks. They wouldn't possibly risk harm to these precious children by war. Or, would they? Would they? Would they? The question now echoed as though in a hollow hall.

Another cable was brought in. This one from the ambassador at Bonn, Bill Masters, once board chairman of Federal Steel. When he had retired, he had looked around for something to do. Just the right man for Germany. They respected men who could make steel. Masters had become devoted, in turn, to the Germans. So industrious. The wire read:

> The Chancellor assures me the present crisis would evaporate if the United States would tell Russia we mean business on the reunification of Germany, and I recommend same in strongest terms. There is no reason to keep Germany divided. Every delay in announcing this position strengthens the Chancellor's opposition.

This sounded just like Bill Masters. Tell the steelworkers to accept the company's terms and come back to work, or freeze in hell. The trouble was there was a gentleman's agreement between President Christiansen and Premier Radilov to keep the dragon severed. The dismembered parts could compete with one another in a little sweepstakes well refereed, and with no brass knucks. Together and whole, the dragon would be a trouble not just to Russia. It could produce steel, automobiles, electronics, oil, you name it, cheaper than America and as well made. This sounded very practical at the time. Secretary King thought now it was like two men agreeing to share the same woman.

At nine o'clock, Mickie Moonan was in the Secretary's office with his draft of the speech. King called in two assistants to offer advice. Waiting for them, he asked, "You don't think the Germans would really start shooting, do you? They can't win, and look at all they would lose. It's like a banker investing all his assets in a gold mine."

Moonan replied, "Silas, I was a police reporter once, and I can tell you there's a perverse and awful fascination in pulling the trigger. Probably a stray gene left over from our savage ancestors. I'll tell you a story. There's a quiet little town some fifty miles from Chicago, Alton or Alden, something like that, where a shocking murder took place. Two little girls, ten and eleven, were shot in the back as they walked through a grove. They were beautiful little kids, and as soon as we got the pictures, the city editor sent me up there. He knew there would be great public interest in the story. Beauty and the beast kind of thing.

"The town was flabbergasted. No clues. No motive. Nothing. Then a ballistics expert from the Chicago police force was called in. The shots, he said, were fired by an expert rifleman from a distance of a hundred yards, the mansion of the town's number one citizen, industrialist, philanthropist—he sent any number of bright kids from the town to college; church leader, played cello in the string quartet. A model citizen. Also, we found out, this bird was a crack shot. The town police chief refused to consider him or even talk to him about the crime. The Chicago officer told me what was up, so I went to see Mr. Burke. I asked him, 'Did you shoot the girls?' He looked at me queerly a moment, dropped his head, and said, 'Yes.' 'Why did you do it?' I asked. He dropped his hands, the most helpless gesture I've ever seen, and replied, 'I don't know. I just felt the urge. I was sitting there with the gun on my knee, and I saw the girls going through the woods, and the sunlight struck them, and I just drew up the rifle and shot. Two shots.'

"Man is a strange, contradictory, mixed-up beast, Silas. Never trust him."

The Secretary said sourly, "You must have had a bad night, too."

"The truth is a poor bedmate."

At nine fifteen, the President had an unexpected caller. The Soviet Ambassador, Yavolsky, requested an immediate interview. He had a personal message from his Premier.

Smiling, urbane, gallant "Andy" Yavolsky, as the society writers described him, was solemn and agitated. This was evident in the way his usually perfect English became mixed up with zees and vees. Yavolsky did not want to operate a hose factory in Irkutsk. Let us pluck a few more lovely flowers in this decadent garden first.

The Ambassador told Mr. Christiansen, "Zee Premier has asked me to perzonnally ovtain from you zee plans of your Government to prevent zee Zherman aggression."

The President looked up at him and smiled. Bright, innocent, good for the tired heart.

"Why yes, you can tell my good friend, Viktor Radilov, that I have a secret weapon. It is a speech to the German people. I am giving it tonight."

Yavolsky realized that he never truly understood the Americans. How did you know when they were laughing at you, telling a lie, or being frank? He gave up.

The Ambassador said in a tactful tone, with some small doubt showing through, "But do you believe the Germans will halt because of a speech? My Government does not find zhat easy to persuade."

The President smiled again and answered, "Well, I have pretty good reasons to believe they will be persuaded this time."

My dear President, this is not enough, not nearly enough for Viktor Radilov. He struggles for survival in a gloomier but more purposive world. My dear President, you are like a very attractive child, and we Russians love children. But, my child, the thunderheads are in the sky. You cannot lisp, 'Go away,' and away they will go. Yet, my grandmother at Kharkov told me many years ago—I was a child and responsive to strange ideas—that there are mysterious forces which play with the lives of men and nations. There is this thing called God, and at times one is tempted to fling oneself on the floor, and pray sobbing to this thing. For life can be trying, and the individual caught in a rising tide.

Ambassador Yavolsky asked, "Do you not have plans to mobilize zee troops if Zherman elements are not controllable? This would be very good news to my Government."

Mr. Christiansen felt sorry for the Ambassador. He was evidently under the influence of his emotions. Many things must happen inside that big stone Pullman mansion that no one on the outside could guess. Men and women rushing against each other accidentally in the dark hall. An embrace. Desperate clinging of one to the other. Discovered. Shouts, cries, screams. Not a tone heard outside where a chauffeur languidly polishes a car in the August sun.

The President said, "Why, certainly, if trouble did arise which

I do not anticipate we would get a good brush fire team out to fight the blaze. I will mention that to Silas King. Make a note of it here."

He picked up a gold pencil and wrote on a pad, "Troops, etc., if needed in Germany?"

Mr. Christiansen looked up and smiled again at the Ambassador. He offered his hand. "You can tell my friend, Viktor Radilov, not to worry. We'll take care of this matter."

Believe in me, believe in God!

# *Chapter* THIRTY-THREE

THE TALL grandfather's clock in the rear of the White House lobby noted the time, eleven forty-five, with a lingering, melancholy tone. The gray-haired usher sat as unperturbed, as indifferent to events, as Father Time. Time, that scalawag, would steal passion from the lover, his hoard from the miser, the purple robes from majesty, his applause from the favorite. So why strain the heart?

The usher looked at the typed Presidential appointment schedule (third carbon) on his desk. A last-minute notation in pencil, "See Lawrence."

Good man, that Lawrence. Not the usual blowhard they bring to Washington from a governor's mansion or political committee. He didn't make his way to fame strumming a banjo in the boondocks or raising the dough-ray-me for the candidate. He knows history. I've heard him, waiting for the Chief, recount the campaigns of Caesar, tell how Alexander the Great made the Persians his allies, describe the battle of Waterloo. Quiet, dedicated fellow. Remember that TV film of him at the Senate Committee hearing, and that boob of a Senator blustering at him. By the gods, Lawrence sat calmly, didn't blink an eyelash and told him what for. "Sir, I will do only what I think is best for the defense of the United States. That is my job." A man like that makes you feel more secure when you tie the string on your pajama cord and lie down for the night's forty winks.

At the far end of the lobby, the officer opened the door. Through a glimpse of the summer morning a figure entered.

Secretary Lawrence looked the part of Duty—severe, untiring. He wore a black lightweight suit, white shirt with buttoned-down collar, dark tie. Mouth tight, chin firm.

He bowed, a stiff, old-fashioned bow, to the usher. This way, Mr. Secretary. Through the appointment secretary's office, more stiff bows, then the President.

Mr. Christiansen was staring wistfully out the window, the child with his plaintive, yearning face pressed against the pane. He turned and said, "I'd sure like to get away for a little fishing tomorrow. You don't fish, do you, Jeff?"

"No, Mr. President."

"What do you do then for relaxation, you know, to get away from it all?"

"I enjoy reading."

Mr. Christiansen shook his head. "That isn't enough, Jeff. A man has to get out and exercise and work up a sweat. You're going to have to go out and walk with me in the mornings. I won't take no for an answer. I've pressed Mickie into the hikers' club, and I know he feels better for it, and he'll tell you so if you ask him, I think. . . . Well, what can I do for you?"

Lawrence pressed his lips tightly together. Two lines ran through his mind:

> Courage, brother! do not stumble,
> Though thy path be dark as night.

He said painfully, "Mr. President, I don't suppose you have any idea what it feels like to have committed a crime."

"No, I can't say that I do."

The magic lantern shows on the screen the bright, beautiful image—the clean, trustworthy, benevolent man, aura of good glowing about him. Next slide please, Professor. My God, what is this? There has been a horrible mistake. Turn on the lights. Everyone stay in his seat. Do not panic. This horrid figure on the screen. The same man, his eyes furtive with guilt, his hands stained and bloody, fleeing from the Avenging Angel.

The crimes, patricide and adultery. "Thou shalt not kill. Neither shalt thou commit adultery."

There is the smell of death in the small depot at Minot. Mixed with the odor of cheap cloth damp with heavy rain, disinfectant in the washrooms, and the agent's pipe. Darkness in the afternoon, a darkness of lost hope. The silent, uncomplaining man beside me. Father, Father, I cannot walk in your path! The lights flicker and dim. A sudden surge of power needed elsewhere. Don't you understand, Father, I must go my own way in my bright uniform? The smell of death, as deep as musk, is suffocating. I must get out of here, out into the wet air, under the dripping eaves. The desperate spring of energy to pick up the baggage, walk to the door, open it, and outside gasping for breath. My mouth is dry. Anything for a cool, fresh drink of water. He does not follow. He sits in desolation, water dripping slowly from his broad-brimmed hat on the bench. The faraway train sounds its ghostly note. I dare not look back. Yet each man kills the thing he loves, is that it, Father? You told me that. You read it from the dog-eared book you kept in the shop, "The World's Best Poems." And you told me, too, not angrily, but sadly, said with the weight of knowledge, "All they that take the sword shall perish with the sword." But I must be on my way in my bright new uniform. My heart is not in the dull business of peace. You do not answer. You are dying, not actually giving up the ghost then and there but six months later, while I am confounding crime with crime. Adultery.

She was the wife of the major. Old Crandall married too late. He didn't know how to handle a piece of toast that hot. He thought her problem was too much energy, and assigned young officers to ride horseback with her along the foaming sands at dusk. She was a wild thing, a mixture of Portuguese and French and cayenne pepper. He met her in Brasilia. Lieutenant Dave Hill said she was the kind of woman you could imagine one of Caesar's generals carting back to Rome, a defiant, hot-blooded, full-lipped Jewess or a spirited Trojan woman with the erotic incense of another civilization about her. Viole. They watched her with furtive, and therefore aroused, desire. She was too hot to touch. It would be like putting the palm of your hand against a hot iron. She belonged to The Major. Hands off, shavetails.

When he was assigned the duty, Lieutenant Christiansen met her at the stables. Not a word from her, how do you do, nice to see you. Just a quick, scathing glance from those wide dark eyes. She put a foot in the stirrup and pulled herself up lithe as a boy on her magnificent black creature. Even at this moment, there was a communion between them, wordless, as between two beasts. They rode through the soft sand, a jeep track, to the beach. She led the way, her horse's tail flicking back and forth as they cantered slowly. The tide was high. The rolling swells crashed close to shore, and sent a carpet of foam well up the sands. The sound, coupled with that of the screech of the terns and the horses' hoofs in the sand, created an illusion that they were in a separate world, where nature alone with her passions and caresses and hungers ruled. Strange, isn't it, the hypnotism of nature! The beach curved out of sight in the gathering grays of dusk. The evening star was out in a sky not yet turned to night, still touched by the purple clouds of sunset on the far horizon.

She looked back at him once. He did not know what she was saying, only that he grew hot in the cool evening breeze from the sea. He seemed, to himself, deprived of his everyday thoughts and reasons and emotions.

A mile down the beach, away from camp, was a shipwreck. It had broken on a reef and hung there for twenty years. Viole wanted to see it better. They tethered their horses on a log of driftwood and climbed a dune. His heart pounded unnaturally during the brief scaling of the dune, feet sinking in the shifting sand. She looked back. Was he coming? When they reached the top, she stumbled and fell among the high grasses. He reached his hand down to pull her up. She took his hand and he felt a slight tug, as though pulling him.

He fell to his knees beside her in the warm sand, and seized her fiercely. Like the clap of thunder, the brilliant flash of light and the summer storm, it was soon over. She looked at him with the still wild and enigmatic eyes of a cat. He was frightened then.

They rode back silently. No communications, each buried in his own thoughts. His, of the frightful danger he ran. What if, in a quarrel, she told the Major? He could be accused of rape. Things like that did happen. You read about it. What chance would a shavetail have?

Three days later, he was assigned to ride with her again. They rode down the long, deserted beach. She tethered at the same spot, ran up the dune, and laughed at him. Are you afraid? Again, the strange sense of unreality, caught in a hypnotic trance, desire breaking down every fear. All summer long this went on. His life teetered wildly back and forth between fear and desire. They were never lovers, in the romantic sense, or even friends. It ended when the Major left for a new assignment.

"I have known men to carry guilt in their hearts for years, without even knowing it was there, and then, without warning, it expanded so rapidly they could no longer stand it," Secretary Lawrence said.

The President was startled. He had forgotten the somber little man was there.

They have no relief until they confess it and do their penance. I have come to you to make a confession."

"What are you talking about?" the President asked. His apprehension rose quickly, as though it were a small stream in flood.

The Secretary's mouth worked and no words came out. For a time it seemed that he might break down altogether. Mr. Christiansen grew more agitated. "What is it?" he asked. "What's this all about now?"

Lawrence made an effort. He bit his lip. He said, "I joined your cause, Mr. President, because I was convinced of your high purpose and the affection you created among the people. You were a leader to regenerate a sagging nation. And I have always agreed with you that peace is the shining goal, too. But once we started out together, and now our paths are far apart. I stop and see with alarm where I have gone. You may say of me as Caesar did of Brutus." He lowered his head.

President Christiansen stared at him.

"Mr. President, I have violated your orders and your trust. I have conspired to turn over to the West German forces large quantities of nerve-gas cartridges." The President's mouth fell open. He dropped the pencil in his hand. It fell clattering to the floor. "I did this because I believed this was the only way to protect our country against an inevitable attack from the Communists. The Germans, I felt, were the only ones capable of holding back the flood and even extending the land. I, I no longer have faith in my own arguments. I have written my resignation."

He drew from his breast pocket a folded letter and laid it on the desk. His hand trembled. Mr. Christiansen made no move to touch the letter.

The Secretary's eyes were moist. He burst out, "My God, Mr. President, what putrid stews we make of our lives. Each man begins life with such promise, and before he is through he commits almost all the sins we are warned against. What vain hopes were Plato's, twenty-three hundred years ago! He thought man would grow wiser. But he still betrays his brother. He still plunges blindly toward death of his kind. He is fascinated by the holocaust. He loves his Armageddon . . ."

("And there were voices, and thunders and lightnings; and there was a great earthquake, such as was not since men were upon this earth, so mighty an earthquake, and so great.

"And the great city was divided into three parts, and the cities of the nations fell: and great Babylon came in remembrance before God, to give unto her the cup of the wine of the fierceness of His wrath.

"And every island fled away, and the mountains were not found.")

The President tried to picture what the end would be like. This was not hard. He thought of it often. A light breaking the darkness and so bright the eyes wept with pain. A noise rupturing the eardrum. The mind spinning in disordered panic. The scene afterward like the forward base in Korea where the munitions dump blew up, a direct hit. No whole man anywhere. Bits of guts. A leg torn off with the boot and sock still in place. Bloody rags strewn about in the mud. A severed head; it had a look of injured surprise. What did you do this to me for, God? What did I ever do to you? Not a damn thing. Buildings tumbled down and burning fiercely in the rain. Craters blasted into the side of the hill. Boulders scattered about. One hurled down on the privy and crushed three men, buried them in their own dung. The scrawny trees uprooted. After the great uproar of sound, silence.

Would this be observed by radio telescopes from other planets? Or do creatures blow themselves up as soon as they have the knowledge?

An anger beset him. It possessed him. He drove his tightly curled fist hard on his desk top.

"Damn it. Don't you know what you have done?" he cried.

"You have, you have . . ." He could not put the awful fact into words. "Get out. Get out."

The President swept his hand angrily across his desk. A plaster bust of Lincoln fell against a chair and chipped. Pencils, pens, letters dropped on the rug. A light pencil spun crazily across the room. Mr. Christiansen sat flushed and trembling. "All they that take the sword shall perish with the sword." His father's gentle voice. He could bear it no more. He was suffocating. His head dropped abruptly on his chest.

Secretary Lawrence, greatly agitated, opened the door into the appointment secretary's office, and called, "The President . . . I don't know what's happened to him."

In the ensuing excitement, Lawrence left. He walked rapidly through the milling throng of reporters in the lobby, not hearing their inquiries, not looking at them, but guiltily at the floor, walking as fast as his legs would take him, not knowing it but his lips forming syllables. Out into the hot August afternoon, not even noticing the change of temperature, the thermal shock.

Two Secret Service men helped the President, one limp arm around each shoulder, to a couch. Dr. Baker came quickly, made his tests swiftly and anxiously. It was probably another spasm. Take the President up to his quarters, call the specialist from Walter Reed Hospital.

While the more detailed examination took place, Silas King, Judge Herring and Mickie waited in the dressing room for the verdict. Ada Mae was visiting in Pender County, reconvening the imagined past.

Secretary King walked energetically back and forth, as though trying to defeat a treadmill. Judge Herring sat quietly, almost lifelessly, as he had trained himself to do during a score of filibusters. Moonan sprawled in a deep chair, cleaning his fingernails with a paper knife.

King flung out a question as he walked, "What in the hell do you suppose Jeff said to Chris that brought this on?"

Mickie said, "I'll guess. Confession. All your worst fears, Silas. He deliberately turned over the nerve-gas shells to the Germans."

Judge Herring said crossly, "What did he have to tell the President for?"

Moonan sighed. "He didn't want his sin to appear of no moment.

He wanted it to make the biggest bang. Every fanatic has a streak of drama in him; he doesn't wish to be ignored even in his guilt."

They could hear the doctors talking quietly in the next room. Just patterns of sound, nothing intelligible.

Mickie said, "We either produce the President on TV tonight, or pop goes the weasel, we have a revolution in Germany, and Gottfried."

King stopped and pointed his forefinger at Moonan, "Revolution? Nonsense. Can't have one unless there are four elements. Mass unrest from empty bellies. Nothing like that in Germany. The Germans are the most prosperous people in Europe. Two, the intellectuals must be brewing trouble as they did for a hundred years before the Russian Revolution. Not there. . . ."

"No intellectuals, period," Moonan said gloomily. "They are either making a million dollars or inventing devices to blow up the world."

"Number three, the military must be ready to swing behind the revolution and push it over the line. The chief of staff is a friend of ours. And four, the business community must be sufficiently dissatisfied to finance a revolution. That, I know, is not true. These are my personal friends."

The press secretary replied coarsely, "That's plain bull, and you know it. You let those people over in your Department sing you a lullaby, because it makes you feel better."

The Secretary stared at him angrily and resumed his pacing. The relentless voice followed him, "There are enough elements in Germany to blow us all to kingdom come. One hell-raising demagogue. A people dizzy with a mystic belief in their destiny. A government that is old and ineffectual. A young officer corps restless for promotion and a chance to run the show. Cautious bankers hedging their bets, just as they did with Hitler."

Secretary King paused to look curiously into the President's bedroom. He asked, of no one in particular, "What possessed us to promise to do away with war? Was it Jeebie's idea?"

"No," Mickie replied. "It was the Colonel's. This was the only way we could convince him to run for President."

Herring scratched his nose and said, "We won't get rid of war until the chemists find a pill to change man's nature. God created man at the end of a hard week. He had made the heaven and earth, light and dark, Earth and the seas, grasses and trees and herbs, the stars, birds and beasts. His imagination was worn pretty thin by that time. So here is man—bad-tempered, suspicious, easily led, too ingenious for his own good, and stubborn."

Moonan remarked, " 'What of the will to do?

It has vanished long ago . . .' "

Secretary King said, "We have to get Chris to the microphone tonight. It's the Russians I'm worried about . . . Radilov is in trouble. He may be on his way out. I haven't been able to get a telephone call through to the Soviet Foreign Minister or our Embassy in Moscow. Just before I came here we had a cable from the Ambassador. Radilov is fighting off the bears in a meeting of the Executive Committee of the Communist Party for more than twelve hours. The old guard and the Red Army are after him. They say he's led Russia into a trap in West Germany. At the same time, things aren't healthy to the East. Jap intelligence reports large troop movements in Manchuria northwest to Siberia. The idea is that if Russia is turned upside down, the Chinese will take back their old hunting grounds. So we have to have Chris on the screen tonight saying all is well."

Judge Herring asked quietly, "What makes you so sure they will believe him?"

The Secretary turned on the Judge and said in a rasping voice, "That is a hell of a question for you to ask."

Herring replied, "Merely a parliamentary inquiry."

The consulting physician came out and announced the President had suffered no serious injury. He strung out many fancy medical terms to show he was in the know. None of the three listeners knew exactly what had gone wrong except that Mr. Christiansen had blanked out. He was under sedation, another excellent medical term, and would be able to go on the air that evening. The three gave their expressions of joy, relief and delight, and returned to their tasks.

Moonan was still in his office at six o'clock waiting for the last page of the address to be typed in large type, and to proofread it, when the telephone rang. His secretary told him it was Fentriss, the Assistant Secretary of Defense for Public Information, in other words, the P.R. man there.

"What is it, Jim?" Mickie asked.

A voice scarcely under control, words slipping together, said, "Secretary Lawrence. Dead. Suicide."

"Did what?"

"Killed himself."

"All right, slow down. Give me the details."

"The Secretary came back from the White House, and his secretary, that is Mrs. Kingston—she's been with him a long time and knows him well—said he seemed depressed. He went in his office and asked not to be disturbed. No phone calls, buzzers or visitors. At the end of two hours calls were piling up from the Joint Chiefs of Staff and the Security Council. She thought she had better find out if he still wanted to be alone. She opened the door. He was slumped over the desk. She noticed a partly filled glass of water on the desk and a small pill case . . ."

"And?"

"She recognized the pill case. It had a small skull painted on it. The sort of case we give our secret agents. Four suicide pills. Knock you out in a few seconds. The Secretary was fascinated with it; he used to show it to visitors and give a little essay on the mortality of man."

"Did he leave any note?"

"Nothing. There was a small volume of Greek poetry on his desk lying open to a verse by Sophocles:

"What man is he that yearneth
For length unmeasured of days?
Folly mine eyes discerneth
Encompassing all his ways.
For years over-running the measure
Small change thee in evil wise:
Grief draweth nigh thee; and pleasure
Behold it is hid from thine eyes.
This to their wage have they
Which overlive their day . . .'"

Moonan said, "Listen to me. Put the book back in the shelf. Prepare an announcement. Say that Secretary Lawrence had been privately advised by his physician today of the presence of an inoperable brain tumor. If they ask you who the doctor is and that sort of guff, tell them the information is not available. Say that he came to the President today to impart this medical information and offer his resignation, and that the President would not accept the resignation. Then he returned to the Pentagon and took the suicide pills. I'll put out a statement from here on Mr. Christiansen's grief *et al.* O.K.?"

When the telephone was on the cradle, Moonan sat far back in his chair and thought about the poor bastard.

Give us this day our daily humiliation; that was Jeff Lawrence probably from the first day he was sent outdoors to play. He waited for it, expected it, let it undermine his life. Yet, withal, he had a dignity and integrity that, God knows, few of us have these days. Not I, the lark. What a great deal of darkness must fill your mind when you decide to get rid of your life. You throw away all chances for a rosy existence in the other place, if indeed there is such a place, in your damned impatience to get rid of this wretch who has so botched up his days. It is not suicide really; it is murder, anger at the creature who sits in your pants and wears your shoes. The antagonism and disgust is immense and personal. You cannot stand you. Begone, or I'll shoot you. Not begone, so pull the trigger. Loud noise, the end, soul flutters downward to be lectured by various priests on the way until it hits bottom and gets a hot welcome. Might not be such a bad place, if you could stand the climate; all kinds of delightful creatures, famous adulteresses, heretics, murderers, charming scoundrels, never a dull moment in that company. They accept you as one of the damned, no bigotry for race, creed, color or size of ears. Jeff Lawrence could move right in and for the first time be appreciated for his mind and wit, and perhaps become something of a social lion. After all, not many men have been so monstrously infamous as to start the last war. He would say modestly it wasn't his doing, really, but they would shout that down, and gradually he would accept the theory and be pointed out and bow to the newcomers.

Moonan's secretary brought in the sheets of the speech. He put his chair level, and began to read the copy.

At eight o'clock, a small deathwatch of reporters in the White House press room gathered around the television set. Bars ran across the screen in fluttering lines. Someone hit the set hard with the flat side of his hand, and the picture came into focus. Malcolm

Christiansen was at his desk, a look of solemn innocence on his face.

An announcer's voice, hushed and respectful, a different tone of voice altogether from the man announcing what wonderful relief Brighton Salve would give your piles, pronounced: "We bring you now the President of the United States speaking from his office in the White House."

Mr. Christiansen's voice, deep, meaningful, with a touch of the folksy in his twang, said, "Fellow members of the human race, there was a time when a fire lit on one side of the world was of no consequence to those who lived on the other . . ."

The little group made up of men who had no illusions about Malcolm Christiansen nonetheless was quieted and put into a thoughtful mood by this picture on the screen. One or two were made uncomfortable by his effect and had to light a cigarette or bang a drawer or look contemptuous to prove to whoever might be looking they weren't taken in by this fellow, yet of course they were.

"Flames, pestilence and war were stopped by the mighty oceans and the great mountains. This is no longer true. A missile equipped with bombs of absolute destruction can cross the world in fifteen minutes. This means that none of us can afford the angers and suspicions that breed war. We must live by the words of Abraham Lincoln, 'With malice toward none; with charity for all; with firmness in the right, as God gives us to see the right . . .'"

Someone growled, "All this make-believe you have to put on to get anything across to the public these days! A good man can't simply tell them what is wrong, and ask for their indulgence while the damage is repaired at a cost not too extravagant, if you value life at all. No, quote Jesus, George Washington, Abraham Lincoln, and say this won't hurt a bit."

The figure on the screen did not pause for this observance, but talked, gravely, precisely.

"Thus, the unhappiness of our German brethren fills us with alarm. We share with them the desire to bind up the wounds of war and remove the cause of pain. We recognize the anguish that must be caused when brothers and cousins and even fathers and sons look across an artificial border that divides them. This is a legitimate complaint, and I am sympathetic to it.

"But it would equally be wrong to correct this by force. Two wrongs do not make a right. The United States cannot condone, excuse or tolerate the use of force to unify Germany. No nation in the world would remain free of conflict if war should break out over this issue. Our homes on Main Street, U.S.A., would be just as much in danger as those in Magdeburg or Mühlhausen."

There was a pause. The eyes looked up solemnly from the typed page. For less than a second—a flash, really—the eyes revealed a terrible fright. Much like a person roused from sleep who sees a dark, unfriendly shape in the world. Then, the old discipline recovered. There was nothing there but the eyes looking deep into your own, half praying, half commanding your obedience for an act of honor.

The men around the set saw it. They stirred. One man started to say something and thought better of it. Nerves were jangled. Jesus, was it that bad? A clumsy hand pushed an ash tray on the floor and there was startled swearing. God damn! For Christ's sake! What the hell's going on?

The voice went on, "So, in the name of humanity, I appeal to the German people . . ."

## *Chapter* THIRTY-FOUR

"LADIES AND gentlemen, you have heard an address by the President of the United States. Mr. Christiansen spoke to you from his office in the White House."

The red lights of the cameras winked off. The floodlights were dimmed. An engineer let out a rattling cough he had been holding in for six minutes.

President Christiansen asked with an anxious frown, "Did it go all right?"

He knew something went wrong, what it was exactly he did not know. The slight moment of revelation was not conscious.

The announcer said, "Very good, Mr. President. Veeery good!"

Judge Herring nodded his head judiciously. Moonan smilingly made a circle with his thumb and forefinger, a sign of perfection. The President was relieved. He did have strange feelings or intuitions that amounted to nothing. Probably caused by gas on the stomach or a light head or even a dream. The doctors could talk for hours of these sudden changes of mood. It was all right; he didn't understand a word they said.

Mr. Christiansen felt an aching need to get out of this damned room. There was too much sorrow and crisis and anger accumulated in it. To go outside these walls would be better yet. He asked the Judge and Mickie to have a drink with him on the upstairs balcony.

The evening was hot and sultry. Lightning flashed in the distance, a light suddenly illuminating a far cloud beyond the Washington Monument and quickly dying out. No sound, because the phenomenon was too far away, say somewhere along the Virginia shore of the Potomac River near Quantico. A faint breeze blew spasmodically. They could see it lift up and flutter the flags at the base of the Monument. A butler brought them drinks.

The President had not yet been told of Jeff Lawrence. This was Mickie's chore. Judge Herring kept darting looks at him as if to say, "Come, come, on with your job." He finished his drink while Mr. Christiansen described a fishing lure made by an Indian. When the talk died out, Moonan said, "Colonel, Jeff Lawrence had a brain tumor. Incurable they told him. It was eating away at his brain. He killed himself this afternoon. *Ave atque vale*."

A more vivid flash of lightning broke the dark sky. It was followed by a distant rumble of thunder.

The Judge observed, "Looks like the storm is coming closer. We may have rain yet tonight."

As if in answer, a breeze with the smell of rain in it came out of the southeast. They heard it moving through the trees and then felt it on their faces.

Jeff Lawrence, the President told himself, he lit the fuse and ran. The world is a cage. A bomb ticks in the corner. No one knows how to stop it. He felt no sorrow or sympathy for Lawrence. Mickie's artfully contrived story of the tumor was a vain labor so far as the President was concerned. He was brooding over his own fate. Resenting it like hell.

Mr. Christiansen said, "You don't know what Lawrence told me."

"No."

"He gave the Germans nerve-gas shells in violation of our disarmament agreement. That was a, well, you might say, a traitorous act." He was indignant.

"Yes, we know about that," Judge Herring replied.

"The Germans have a gun in their hand. What if they decide to use it?"

Mickie tried to sound cheerful, "Your speech, Colonel, that should calm them down."

What if it doesn't, the President asked himself. What if it doesn't? Suppose you knew there were only fifteen days left, and you could have any wish, what would you do with the time?

A woman? No, too many long moments of bickering and emptiness between the clinging seconds of passion. A fishing camp on a
fresh mountain stream high in the Rockies? That would be pretty
good, but not good enough for the final hours left to you. No, a
journey back into childhood. Fifteen days with his father, the
comfort of his gentle voice, the joy of his knowledge of all wild
things, the shield of his strength. But this could never be here or
afterwards. He had failed his father. Not willfully or violently,
but because that was the way the river flowed. The President
sighed deeply.

Moonan chose at this point to tell a story about an Irishman
trapped in a sewer and his conversation with, to wit, a rabbi, a
Baptist minister, a prostitute, and a priest. They all laughed, but it
did not clear their minds entirely.

Judge Herring, who was patient, practical or cynical, depend-
ing on the way others looked at it, did not worry about the world
blowing up. That was beyond his sphere of competence. So was
the final resting place of his soul. He was wondering how long
they could keep Congress from erupting. If the Colonel really
pulled this thing off, did keep the Germans in their chairs and held
the Russians, if he made a miracle, Congress would be good. But
just let him falter once, and the hounds would be in baying. They
would tear him to pieces while Maze Bledsoe looked on vastly
amused. He could hear Maze telling him, "You should have taught
that Boy Scout he's got to play ball with a few of us old boys up
on the Hill. Hell, this wasn't my doing. He brought it on himself.
Damned shame, too—reflects on the good judgment of the Marine
Corps." And the friends of Father Werther would be crying that
this is what happens when one does business with the Russians.
They would scream this as the bombs fell, their minds closed even
in the minute of death. A man in public life couldn't afford to
keep his mind too open. That would be too confusing. But there
should be a legal limit on how far it could be narrowed. And once
failure of the Christiansen Crusade looked imminent, those who
had been for him in Congress because it would be good politics
would be making all kinds of excuses and damning him harder
than anyone. Just as though they were running hard for the next

election and not for the judgment of doomsday. Yes, a good deal depended on this speech.

Moonan could not get Jeff Lawrence out of his mind.

> Miniver Cheevy, child of scorn,
>   Grew lean while he assailed the seasons;
> He wept that he was ever born,
>   And he had reasons.
>
> Miniver loved the days of old
>   When swords were bright and steeds were prancing;
> The vision of a warrior bold
>   Would set him dancing.
> Miniver sighed for what was not . . .

That was Robinson, and no doubt Jeff read it, recognized himself with an amused scorn. But he would have liked better Santayana's:

> I would I might forget that I am I,
> And break the heavy chains that bind me fast,
> Whose links about myself my deeds have cast . . .

The secret of Jeff Lawrence, no doubt, was the fear that other men, and he himself, would take Jeff Lawrence for nothing more than a fool. He would read T. S. Eliot and smile bitterly at the lines

> No! I am not Prince Hamlet, nor was meant to be;
> Am an attendant lord, one that will do
> To swell a progress, start a scene or two,
> Advise the prince; no doubt, an easy tool,
> Deferential, glad to be of use,
> Polite, cautious and meticulous;
> Full of high sentence, but a bit obtuse;
> At times, indeed, almost ridiculous—
> Almost, at times, the Fool . . .

Mickie decided if they ever got out of this thing alive, he would stimulate action for a decent memorial to Jefferson Lawrence. Not a battleship or a missile-launching base. A poetry alcove in the Library of Congress. In this way, poetry lovers in the years to come would think of him vaguely and benignly as a scholar, a student of life. They would not know how he came to his end, or care. Here was a fellow who contributed for them, somehow, a quiet corner out of the traffic to read poetry.

The storm did come. They heard it first sweeping up from the south and east. The President did not want to go inside, so they drew their chairs back and let the awnings down. The rain pelted against the canvas. There were bright flashes nearby and noisy bursts of thunder.

"You can sit here on a stormy night and watch the lightning hit the Washington Monument," Mr. Christiansen said. "Sometimes the tip seems to be on fire. But it never seems to do much damage. I asked about it. A smell of sulphur, a streak of black on the stone."

The storm was soon over. With its end came Silas King, certain Silas, sure as sin, reeking with confidence. He read cables of congratulation from Buckingham Palace, the Indian Prime Minister, Negus of Ethiopia, President of Brazil, First Syndic of Andorra, Prime Minister of Canada, Emperor of Japan, King of Sweden, Sultan of Muscat.

"But the real prize, Chris," Secretary King said, "is from Bonn."

All had been waiting for this, and there was an involuntary relaxing, long breaths out through the nostrils, fingers unloosening, colon expanding.

"This is a public statement by the Chancellor of Germany. We had a hell of a time with the old cuss. He has a stubborn streak, and he'd be damned if he said anything. But we got it. Listen, 'We must put away our swords and resort to reason and persuasion, or we will become outlaws and forsaken by the nations of the world. President Christiansen's appeal to us comes from the hearts of all peoples, and we cannot ignore it. His word is a pledge to us that he will become our advocate. We could have no greater advocate.'"

The four men smiled at each other triumphantly. See, everything is going to come out all right! They had a drink on it.

"What about the Russians? What have you heard from them?" the President asked.

He did not want Radilov to be hurt. Sure, he was a queer bird. But they belonged to the same fraternity. PAX. That was Latin for peace, Mickie said. The President had not taken Latin. Spanish, it was much easier, everyone said, and thank God for that. The

Catholics, though, they went in for Latin in a big way, the priests murmured their benedictions in Latin. Few understood the words, but perhaps it was the tone of voice, or a striking figure in black talking in a mystic tongue. Like the magician saying abra cadabra, and lo! the rabbit comes out of the hat by his ears. But to get back to Radilov, he really believed in PAX. He had squinted his eyes at Mr. Christiansen and said in his fiercely pessimistic way, "We will keep the people of the world at peace, and be damned for it." Then, unexpectedly, he had put out his hand, and they shook on the bargain. PAX. Besides, if Radilov was lost, ground down in the unexplainable riddle of Communist politics, Malcolm Christiansen would lose his strongest ally. He would have to stand alone. The thought made him anxious. He preferred a good strong guard of men around him. Yet, none of his companions tonight belonged to PAX. They had other interests. Viktor Radilov had this feeling; it came as naturally from him as breathing.

Silas King seemed to have a compulsion to talk, to share his information, to get a collective O.K. to drive away his doubts. Mickie looked at him with some dismay. He wasn't sure how the President would take this.

The Secretary said, "Our Ambassador talked with Radilov privately. The Premier asked that the United States go on record publicly as stating it would use force to stop any German movement eastward. Otherwise, Radilov said, he would be compelled to mobilize the Red Army and move west to the German border, and put the missile stations on a ready alert. He said this would be necessary if he wanted to keep his job. He went on about the Russians' hatred of the Germans, and all that. I think he was bluffing."

King turned to Judge Herring, who sagaciously nodded his head.

"Well, Chris, I checked with the Chairman of the Foreign Relations Committee about a guarantee like this from you, and he said nothing doing. There are too many senators with large German populations in their states, or people who don't like the Russians and can't see us fighting their battles for them against the Germans, our good friends, and killing Christians. He said the roof of the Capitol would blow off. The Chairman—you know how he is—proposed we organize a volunteer corps of atheists, Jews and Arabs to police the Germans. . . . What the hell, we have what we wanted—the Chancellor's statement. That ought to satisfy the Russians. Don't you think so, Chris?"

"If you're satisfied, Silas, I am." I don't want that monkey on my back.

The Secretary of State told of an informal session that afternoon in his office with the military and Central Intelligence on what we might do if either the Germans or Russians attacked. But, of course, King pointed out, we were talking of a theoretical possibility and there is no cause to piss in your pants over theoretical possibilities.

President Christiansen interrupted King's recital. He said, "I think the storm is over. Pull up the awnings, Judge, so we can enjoy the evening."

Herring cranked the awning, and it was pleasant, indeed, on the balcony. The air was freshened by the storm, and the moon, almost full, stared at them over the Washington Monument.

Several times Secretary King tried to get back to the subject of what they might do if either the Russians or the Germans began firing. Each time Mr. Christiansen led the conversation away from it. King gave up. Mickie told a number of Irish stories. The group reluctantly broke up at about eleven o'clock.

President Christiansen went to bed shortly after midnight. He took a green sleeping pill. His last thoughts were of Jeff Lawrence.

Around three o'clock, an ambulance on its way to George Washington Hospital with the victim of a shooting scrape turned on its siren to hold back the traffic at Pennsylvania Avenue and 17th Street. The President heard the sound, but not as a siren. It was the cry of a frightened, abandoned baby. This child was all that was left alive, save for a few rats in the sewer, after the attack. It lay helpless amid the rubble. The siren grew fainter as the ambulance fled up Pennsylvania Avenue. So the baby's cries ceased, and other scenes came to his sleeping mind.

Premier Radilov and Jeff Lawrence were debating their respective positions before the Presidium of the Supreme Soviet. Lawrence wore the sober, apologetic look that did him so well in court or in the Cabinet. Radilov was stiff and alive like a bristling dog. The Russian made a telling point, and Lawrence fell to the floor and collapsed. All the air came out of him and he was nothing but a windless balloon. Then Red Army generals rushed in waving sabers fiercely with their medals rattling on their chests. They seized Radilov and began to drag him out. Silas King entered wearing a gas mask, and tried to fight off the generals. He shot a cap pistol and gas came from it. More and more people joined in the fray—Gottfried, the old German Chancellor, the Chinese leader in his gray sack uniform, his father. All were grappling with one another. Then the angry scene dissolved like an explosion under water. The President watched this phenomenon curiously and wondered where they had all gone. Is the universe filled with the wrecks of other planets? He fell wholly asleep again. The subject was too complicated for him.

# *Chapter* THIRTY-FIVE

THE WHITE-HAIRED usher went in for the President's appointment schedule. He complained to the secretary, "I think the cigarette companies manufacture these crises. There's so much smoke in the lobby, we'll never get it out. And I'm allergic to it. Swells up my sinuses. The reporters have no manners at all. They throw their cigarettes on the floor. They strew their papers on the chairs. They argue in loud voices. A few minutes ago some of them banged on Mr. Moonan's door with their fists and demanded he come out. The photographers took pictures, although I can't see any news in that. This might as well be a police station."

The secretary said all appointments were canceled.

"That bad, eh?" the usher said in subdued tones.

She shrugged her shoulders.

Across the little closed-off lane separating the White House and Executive Offices Building, Morgan, the National Security Council adviser, was emerging from the dark hole of the door. He limped a bit. The humid weather stirred up his arthritis. And being up half the night probably wasn't any good, either.

Morgan had in his dispatch case all the bad news, properly catalogued and evaluated. The President was to be briefed. Morgan did not relish the task and had crossly told his secretary, "He should have kept up with events all along. We wouldn't be in this predicament if he had. Louis XVI all over again."

The girl unaccountably began to cry.

The truth crashed through to Morgan. His head buried deeply

in the mire of world sickness, he had overlooked a simple fact. The people adored Chris, the Crusader. They were little children whose skinned elbows and bruised hearts were forgotten when he smiled. The warm, protective smile is our paregoric, opium, poteen, vodka, rauwolfia, serpentina, peyote, and snakeroot. We are addicted to it. Forbid us this day our daily truth. Look at the big man smile. And, no one can smile but fools and ignoramuses. Merrily, merrily, merrily, life is but a dream.

Morgan squinted his eyes as he came into the sun. Another hot day. Makes people more edgy. Creates a longing for the cool nights of autumn. If we can just get through the summer, then autumn will be here. And if winter comes, can spring be far behind.

Remembering what was in his dispatch case, Morgan returned to a theory he had been developing in odd moments, sitting on the toilet in the morning, lingering over coffee at noon, lying awake in bed at night. It was such an all-explaining theory, he was surprised some scholar had not published it, say in *Scientific American*. It was the application of the second law of thermodynamics to political systems. This law was, as he remembered it, and of course he could be mistaken, a system tends to a maximum entropy or disorganization the longer it continues. The world had now reached such maximum entropy that a sergeant scanning a radar screen, thinking of the wolf who made off with his girl, dreaming away, could destroy the earth. Formerly, it took a czar, a king, a sheik or at least a general to even get a good battle going. That was proper organization. Now it was out of control. Any boob with a cheap nuclear weapon and a moment's madness could do away with his sisters and his cousins and his aunts and all other inhabitants of Earth, a small planet in the Milky Way galaxy.

It would be interesting to know if God planned it this way, if it was an accident, or a laboratory test. God looked around in the universe and selected a choice planet. Several million more years of life. Good climate, fair water supply, arable land, minerals in abundance. And He dropped on this planet the spark of life, and He spoke to his assistant and said, "I have placed life in an excellent environment, almost perfect, and we shall see what happens to it as it acquires motion, senses and intelligence."

The assistant said, as Morgan imagined it walking across the lane in the warm sun, "I don't think we have that survival formula down pat, yet. The trouble is the drive needed to survive has bad side effects. It's too dynamic. The creatures have an urge to do away with their rivals, and the farther life progresses in intelligence the easier this is to do on a mass scale until, finally, boom!"

"Yes, I know," God replied sadly. "We haven't been very successful. But here on Earth we have ideal conditions. There is enough for all if it is wisely used. The survival drive can be turned to providing more sustenance for mind and body. At least, it is worth a try."

His assistant said, "I still think the formula is wrong."

"We'll see."

Morgan limped up to the White House. The Secret Service man at the side door told him there was such a crowd of reporters in the lobby, he should go through the first basement and up on the other side.

Morgan said, "I have observed the press rarely investigates the causes of trouble in the world. It waits and shows up with the fire engines and ambulances." He was a little put out at having to make the detour. His left knee pained him severely.

When he arrived in the President's office, Mr. Christiansen was at his desk, paler than usual. His eyes had the veiled look of fright of a boy pushed up to the high dive for the first time and told to jump. Not very pleasant to see in the President of the United States. A good thing no photographers were around. Judge Herring did not appear any different. Here was a man ready to accommodate to whatever changes occurred in the body politic. Secretary King was flushed and belligerent. Moonan was trying very hard to look cheerful, but not succeeding. The Chairman of the Joint Chiefs of Staff was the only impressive figure there. Rows of ribbons heaving with his broad chest. A sparkle in his eyes. Oh goody, we're going to be able to use live ammunition, and try out the gadgets.

The Judge said, "Mr. Morgan, you may proceed with your information."

He said, "Gentlemen, we might think of the present disturbance in terms of a storm." Corny, certainly, but that was the way Mr. Christiansen liked a presentation. "The center of the storm is West Germany. The Chancellor has resigned, under pressure of course, and Gottfried is his successor. Gottfried immediately went on television. His speech said nothing new. He pledged to unify the Fatherland but was careful not to say how or when. Of more significance, he has completely reorganized the German armed forces. The chief of staff, Marshal Von Blomberg, who, as you know, opposed an armed attack on the East, has been deposed. So have all his coterie. The new chief of staff is a General Strauss. He is a firebrand and has been associated with Gottfried in the organization of his armed volunteers. He is an expert at guerrilla warfare. All of this took place so swiftly and unexpectedly, the commander of U.S. forces in West Germany, General Kinder, has not been able to recover the nerve-gas cartridges. It is not considered likely that we will. General Strauss has ordered a mobilization of the armed forces according to Plan E. This is, to deploy troops along the eastern frontier, as though to meet an attack.

"The question is whether this action is intended as a form of blackmail of the Soviet Union, or is impelled by a real or imagined threat. Our best judgment is that Gottfried and Strauss have no specific plan at this time. They want their forces mobilized, so they may be quickly utilized.

"The British are quite concerned about the missile sites in West Germany and believe that a heavy guard should be placed around them, that the nuclear warheads should be removed, and Gottfried advised that any attempt to seize the missile bases or warheads would lead to immediate armed retaliation. This question has not been determined."

Morgan looked up to the Chairman of the Joint Chiefs. He nodded in confirmation.

President Christiansen appeared to have symptoms of shock— pale, clammy face; short breath, eyes dilated. He said dully, almost casually, "I want this done."

Judge Herring asked solicitously, "What done, Mr. President?"

Mr. Christiansen came suddenly alive and angry. He looked scornfully at the Judge, then addressed himself to the General, "I want those bases guarded and the warheads removed."

The Chairman of the Joint Chiefs opened his mouth to say something, felt better of it and merely replied, "Yes, sir."

"Give the order here. Use my phone."

Really rather magnificent, Morgan thought. The general was

taken by surprise, flanked, pounced upon. The military fellows were all for letting Germany fight Russia, hobble the blackguards, peel them down to size. No sense of the consequences of course. They must not teach history very thoroughly at the military academies. Just the battles, probably. The heroic stand at Valley Forge, and all's well that ends well.

The General rather sulkily gave the order for protection of the bases and warheads. He was an awkward figure leaning over the President's desk getting his uniform wrinkled. He was trying to appear dignified, obedient, yet uncommitted personally. Morgan wondered if anyone else in the room felt a tickling urge to belt the unguarded exposed rear of the officer. Nothing against the man. Purely impersonal. He caught Mickie's eye. The thought must have struck them both. They smiled, felt merrier.

Morgan continued, "Now, we shall consider the reactions to the storm center. President Radilov has sent a note to the Presidents of the United States and France and the Prime Minister of Britain. As you have all seen it, I believe, I will condense this to merely say he alleges the Germans are prepared to attack East Germany. He demands that the former Western occupation powers disarm the Germans according to agreement, and thus, in his view, avert the third World War. In a speech which Moscow Radio has broadcast throughout the world, Mr. Radilov is more brutal in his language, if I may so describe it."

"What does he say?" the President asked.

Morgan shuffled through the papers in his dispatch case, found what he wanted and read, "The brown gang in Bonn darkens the sky of Europe and intends to plunge Europe into a sea of blood in a fratricidal war. These gentry hope for a regionally limited blitzkrieg which will carry them forward to the Oder within twenty-four hours. We know all their plans. We are also prepared for them. Woe to them who want to saddle themselves with the crime for the third time in this century before the bar of history, before mankind. Gottfried speaks of the liberation of the eighteen million of the German Democratic Republic. Yes, there is a problem of liberation. The West German populace must liberate itself from its own executioners, from the Hitlerite generals and demagogues . . ."

Mr. Christiansen held up his hand. That was enough.

"Sounds like him," Secretary King grunted.

Moonan said, "I think he believes it. He is more romantic than you are, Si. You know that horns will grow on the most innocent brow. Even a teller with the best references. Theft and murder— the universal impulses. Only known cure is solitary confinement."

There were no smiles, no takers. Morgan went on, "We believe that Premier Radilov is no longer in command in the Kremlin. No faction would dare depose such a popular leader, but the military, under Marshal Povlitznov, and the conservatives identified with Karilov are able to exert enough pressure on him to force him to move to a more belligerent position. The Soviet and Poland, which can be expected to fight any German expansion, have moved four divisions to the border dividing the two Germanys. The East German Army, reliability unknown, is sandwiched in between Russian troops. Thus units which might wish to rebel could be shot from behind. A usual precaution. The missile bases in Czechoslovakia, Hungary and Poland have been placed on alert. This means that the forty-eight-hour preparation for firing has begun."

He glanced at the President. He was gray-faced with a look of suppressed agony, as though suffering from stomach cramps.

Mr. Christiansen was taking it hard, all right. But then the rest of them had an alibi. I wasn't behind the wheel, your Honor, when the accident occurred. It was the gentleman over there. No excuse for him to say he removed his hand from the rudder because it had gone to sleep. A pilot accepts extra responsibilities when he signs aboard. That is his price for the braid on the cap.

Relentless as time and death, Morgan continued, "The Chinese are massing forces in Mongolia and Sinkiang Province near the passes . . ."

There was a knock on the door. A secretary entered apologetically and said, "Additional material for Mr. Morgan."

He stepped forward to get the sheets. The arthritis stabbed him again. He read quickly and said, "The fighting has already begun. Patrols feeling each other out all along the border. Some riots in Berlin and Leipzig . . ."

Silas King stood up and walked impatiently a few steps. He said with burning bitterness, "Don't these fools know what they are doing?" He made an angry snort and sat down.

Morgan said, "It would appear that the Soviet has decided to take the initiative and attack the Germans first. The United States, as you know, has a non-aggression pact with both West Germany and the Soviet Union. We are also bound by an agreement to disarm Germany."

There was a long moment of silence. Judge Herring broke it by saying, "What are the alternative courses of action?"

He sounded to Morgan like a city clerk asking for bids on a street paving. What is the lowest price? Is the company reliable? We don't want any scandals. And has the Republican chairman approved?

Mickie said, "I'm willing to bet a bottle of hair oil, General, that you have war plans in your safes for bottling up the Russian fleet in the Baltic, bombing Turkestan or disrupting communications in Siberia, but not a solitary blueprint for halting an eastward movement of the West German army."

The Chairman of the Joint Chiefs replied, a little too jovially Morgan thought, "The military establishment is like any other business, Mr. Moonan. We do not waste manpower and brains on plans to destroy our friends and allies. We take our directions from the State Department." He bowed toward Silas King. "And they have always indicated to us that the enemy, the danger without, was Russia, not Germany. Germany was ranked as a valuable ally. The United States, at the request of the State Department and with the approval of Congress, has spent enormous sums in trying to cage the Communist giant. We have created bases around the world in areas most Americans before this generation never heard of. We have made defense our largest industry. All this was to contain Russia. A key part of this program was to rebuild one of the most remarkable and talented military machines in history, that of Germany. The Germans have a natural inclination for war, just as the Italians for making spaghetti. We in the armed services assumed the civilian departments were aware of the risks of this course; we were. We are prepared to prevent Communist Russia from entering Western Europe."

The General is getting his alibi in early, Morgan thought. Orders from headquarters were confused, never got through. He was in what was referred to as the second World War and remembered the whole platoon shot by our own mortars. Screams and fist-shakings. I saw it, too. A real shock, so unexpected to have your own friends put an end to you for no reason accept bad range. *Shalom chaverim! Le hit raot.* Farewell, good friends, farewell, good friends, till we meet again. They investigated that up and down and never did pin the responsibility. Finally some corporal or other got a bad mark on his record for taking a wrong reading.

Secretary King said, "Oh, no you don't, General. You don't put the monkey on my back. You have seen the Geneva Agreement. You have read the President's speeches, or at least I assume you have. All of us from myself down have been trying to follow the course set by Mr. Christiansen to reach peaceful agreements and reduce the heavy burden of armaments. This has been the President's strong point from the beginning."

O-ho, Morgan said to himself, Silas King is getting his alibi in early, too. He was merely following the leader. Just like my wife when the boy got into trouble. All my fault, she said, I hadn't given him a good example. Now, whatever happens, it's poor Chris's fault.

Moonan said, "Let me put in my votive offering. Let us find out what might happen if, *A*, the Germans do succeed in crashing through to the Oder, or *B*, Russia moves in and physically occupies West Germany. Mr. Morgan, do you have any guesses on that?"

"Yes, sir, there has been some work, but it is just an educated guess." Don't get out too far on that slender limb, Brother Morgan.

"Go ahead," Judge Herring ordered.

"If the Germans succeed in penetrating the Communist lines, and they could use the surprise weapon, Radilov would probably be thrown out in disgrace. His peace policy would be blamed. World communism would go through a violent change and reach anti-American policies. I can only imagine some of the possibilities—revolutions in Latin America, nationalization of oil in the Middle East, guerrilla forces striking at the Philippines, Greece, wherever the West is weak."

"What happens the other way around?"

"I think this would shift the whole balance of power. Nations which have been going along with us for a variety of reasons, none of them very profound, would feel the time had come to swing over cautiously to the Communists and make whatever peace they could with them. The United Arab Republic, Yugoslavia, Indonesia, hunks of South America. I have not pinpointed them. And, I suspect, there would be an enormous division of opinion in Congress, the press and the American public."

"Is there any chance for mediation, arbitration, or what-have-you?" King asked.

"It is too late and too early. Both sides have ignored an offer from the Secretary General of the United Nations and the Prime Minister of India to mediate. Perhaps, after both sides have drawn blood and been hurt, mediation might be tried."

The secretary did not knock this time. She came in and gave Morgan a new note.

He read it and thought with a sudden dropping of his spirits, a moment of near panic, this is the way Lee must have felt when he received the news on a misty April morning that Richmond had fallen; Job when he was asked, "Who hath loosed the bands of the wild ass?" My world is in flames and dying! And yet, as inevitable as sin. Why do we groan and make such scenes when the truth bursts in upon us? If we had kept our eyes open, we would have known.

"What is it?" Judge Herring asked.

"The German forces have seized our missile base in northern Bavaria. It has three ICBM's complete with warheads."

President Christiansen looked at Morgan with almost childlike wonder. What funny words the big man says, mamma. And look, he hasn't any hair on his head.

Secretary King shook his head and said, "I give up. The world has gone mad."

Mickie, sober as an old frog, the lines in his face all turned down, said, "It looks like there's only two courses open—we immediately bomb that base and put it out of action and serve an ultimatum on the Germans to lay down their arms or we attack, or we can sit tight and wait for the fire in the sky."

Morgan looked at Mickie admiringly. Who would have thought the vagabond, the minstrel, the jester would be the one man with the strength to look at the sun. All the others have turned away.

They have nothing left to protect them from the horrible brilliance of the truth.

No one spoke.

Moonan said, "Colonel, I'm afraid we can't sit here. We're like the unmarried lady who finds she's three months pregnant. We've got to do something damned soon."

The General laughed. That blew the cork out of the bottle. They all laughed explosively. The old maid three months gone. Ha, ha, ha! Mickie was a card, damned if he wasn't. Laughter at a wake, that was the Irish, and a good idea at that.

The General said almost cheerfully, "Well, Mr. President, what are your orders?"

Malcolm Christiansen stood up painfully. He shook his head like a football player jarred on a play.

"Give me a minute," he said. "A minute outdoors."

He went to the French doors, turned the knob and stepped into the August sunshine. They heard his steps on the gravel path.

Out into God's great out-of-doors, Crusader! Commune with nature. Capture the wisdom of the bees, the sagacity of the spider. Hear the advice of Him.

When the President had left, Judge Herring addressed the General. "What would happen if we tried to stop the Germans?"

"Heavy casualties for us, I'm afraid. We wouldn't have our hearts in it. Eventually, we would have to use the new weapon."

Morgan, sitting in a corner, his leg still paining him, thought of the fateful line of Emerson: "Things are in the saddle and ride mankind."

Mr. Christiansen stood a moment in the warm, humid summer afternoon. He stared blankly into the unaccustomed brightness. He felt as though he had been struck an unexpected, stunning blow. Dazed, bewildered, in pain.

He told himself numbly, "When you have done everything you can for peace—everything—and then this happens. God."

Yes, God, where do you stand on this? Those terrifying words from the cross: "My God, my God, why hast Thou forsaken me?" Roses withered by the first frost; the awful cries of a dying soldier, just a boy; a puppy struck by a car and blood on his muzzle. He shook his head in horror.

The shock passed, as the draining of the tide from the sands. He began to feel like the soldier moving into combat for the first time. The trip-hammer beating of fear. A confused sea of thoughts —prayers almost forgotten, minute and petty details floating aimlessly, the stubborn voice of authority crying out its harsh commands (Forward, on the double . . . ).

Malcolm Christiansen began to move slowly away from the White House. His shoes crunched on the pebbled walk.

He observed the gladioli on either side of the path. Stately creatures, very elegant, but he liked the phlox better. Especially the light blue ones that grew in the woods, their shade that of early morning. The President stooped down to examine the flowers. They had been watered and had a fresh smell. How lovely the petals were! You couldn't touch them for perfection. Not a woman anywhere had the style and shape and color of a flower.

You could blow up the whole confounded lot of mankind, and no great loss. But a flower, no. And not a mountain stream in a deep forest with its springy mat of rotted leaves and pine needles, with its scurrying little things, with the swiftly running clouds deepening the shadows or opening up patches of gloom to light.

He heard a mocking bird sing its bright, enameled aria from a chimney on the West Wing. Yes, and he would save the birds, too, the starlings excepted. Damn pests. Noisy and quarrelsome like men.

What would the world be like, he wondered, after men in their folly fired the missiles? What would be the desolation? Mr. Christiansen remembered a ride with his father through the still smoking area of a forest fire. Over all, the choking mist of smoke. It had brought on a spasm of coughing. The charred skeletons of trees. Some were crashed over on others and looked like doomed paupers clinging crazily to one another. The burned, blackened earth where the delicate ferns once grew. The sight of a small doe burned to death, stopped by the fire in its flight. Nothing ever shocked him so much as the sight of that deer.

His father had told him gently, "This is death, boy. Make the most of your life. Treat each day as a fresh opportunity."

And look what men had done with their lives! Right now, the sullen rumble of tanks moving through a frightened town . . .

sharp flashes of gunfire in the night . . . the missile rising ugly and cruel from its underground nest. What next? The mushroom cloud.

What did those old fellows know when they described Armageddon in The Revelation? Was it a true prophecy, handed down by Jesus Christ to his angel and then to John? Or was it something John dreamed up on an empty stomach after a rough day? We all dream of destruction. The end of me is the end of the world, surely. We're all condemned, sitting in the death cell, wondering what it's going to be like and not daring to think too much about it.

What a rotten trick to play on man!

The President left the path and walked on the grass. He liked the feel of it under his feet. That woman who wrote the prophecies for Mickie's paper had said grass would always grow where he walked.

He had to know—is history already written down, and are a few privileged people given a brief, tantalizing peek? Does this mean that all of us, Presidents and privates alike, are nothing but puppets in a show, and the end is written and can't be erased or changed? He had once sat on a trial board. A Marine sergeant was charged with the death of three men. Drowned in a swamp on a night training mission. The board listened to the evidence, sweating and puzzled, for three grimly hot days in July. Sitting there, reviewing the past, it was plain that no one was innocent, none guilty. Sergeant and privates alike were victims of the heavy tread of events. Every step came closer and closer to the swamp and the inevitable end.

Or, he wondered, are we just tumbleweeds broken loose from our roots, driven by the howling winter wind across the dreary plains, cruelly buffeted this way and that and finally disappearing over the flat horizon.

Or, is it possible that history is a path that men themselves, together and one by one, dig and chop out of the wilderness?

Walking down the lawn, Malcolm Christiansen was whipped and lashed by anger. What a damnable thing to do to me! All their sweet talk about peace. How easy it is, Colonel. You can do it, Colonel. Nothing to it, Colonel. All right, let them handle this mess. Take it, take it. You stop the Russians and the Germans. His mind was filled with curses and vile words. Then, quickly, they were gone, blown out with his rage. He was tired, and ashamed at the violence of his thoughts.

Perhaps it wasn't their fault. Even Jeff Lawrence. He thought of Silas King back there in the office looking like a cocky kid knocked down for the first time, and Mickie not able to laugh. They were all in the same boat, a ship without a rudder, tossed in the storm, and God only knows where they would end.

Mr. Christiansen groaned at the thought—a ship without a rudder. He knew with a sudden sense of despair his own guilt. It lay bright and clear before him. I am the captain of the rudderless ship. I alone. Not Silas or Mickie or the Judge, or all of them together. Just me. I deserted my command. I didn't check the winds and chart the course and hold the tiller strong when the gale blew up. No. I spoke the big talk of peace Mickie picked out for me on his typewriter, and I listened to the warm roar of the crowds. I didn't want to know anything else. I just wanted to be comfortable.

What was it Goodfellow told me way back there? "Colonel, if you really want to make peace in the world, you must feel it so deeply inside that it wakes you up at night, and won't let you go back to sleep. You must be willing to be hurt for it, to be knocked down, and pick yourself up again joyfully. This is what you must have in your soul, Colonel."

My God, my God, what have I done? He almost stumbled as the question struck him as if it were a club. What sin is there compared to this neglect? When you quarrel with your father or love another man's wife, the hurt is in small circles. But when you are the President of the United States and you tell the world you will lead it to peace, and millions count on you, and you turn your back and walk out on them—the hurt is too huge to fit into the narrow cell of the mind. It is gray and limitless and infinitely desolate.

An incoherent sound, deeply mournful, came from him. Oh God, if I could take back the wasted days. But the flames are lit, the winds are roaring, the forest will soon be full of flames.

He had let himself believe that if he said the word "peace," regularly and solemnly, it would come to pass. Peace was not like a pine seedling picked up by a brush of wind across a mountain slope and dropped in the valley, there to grow without any help, sturdy enough to survive alone. No, it must be cultivated and fertilized and encouraged and watered. A man must be willing to work in the hard glare of the summer sun, or the cold fall rains, or the long snowfalls of winter, to be burned and frosted and lonely. And in the depths he knew he hadn't been willing. He hadn't even tried. It probably was too late, and he, Malcolm Christiansen, had let it become so.

The glancing light of the sun on the white painted walls hurt his eyes. He heard clearly the nasty whine of an airplane coming in for a landing across the river and the shouts from a baseball game in Ellipse. He smelled the heavy fragrance of the rose bushes, deeply sweet. Suddenly he was overwhelmed by the desire to survive. He could taste it in his mouth, dry and acid.

Now at last there was no turning away. The world was still around him, not for long perhaps, but he and a few other men were the only ones who knew that. If he faced around and began to fight, could he mean it and stay with it? And if he did, could he expect the people to follow? Another crusade? In despair he knew that he was alone, that words weren't enough any more, and that he had gone too deep within himself to turn back, ever again.

For a moment he stood at the corner of the rose garden. Then he walked toward the White House.